A writer, a wife, and a mother of two, Sharon Page holds an industrial design degree and also manages a scientific research and development program in Ontario, Canada. She finds writing tales of sexy Regency rakes and seductive vampires is the perfect escape from her technical world.

She is the author of *The Club* and *Engaged in Sin,* also available from *Rouge*.

SHARON PAGE

THE
CLUB

R♥UGE
REGENCY

1 3 5 7 9 10 8 6 4 2

First published in the US in 2009 by Bantam Dell,
A Division of Random House, Inc.

Published in the UK in 2012 by *Rouge*, an imprint of Ebury Publishing
A Random House Group Company

The Random House Group Limited Reg. No. 954009

Addresses for companies within the Random House Group can be
found at: www.randomhouse.co.uk

A CIP catalogue record for this book is available from the British Library

The Random House Group Limited supports The Forest Stewardship
Council (FSC®), the leading international forest certification organisation.
Our books carrying the FSC label are printed on FSC® certified paper.
FSC is the only forest certification scheme endorsed by the
leading environmental organisations, including Greenpeace.
Our paper procurement policy can be found at:
www.randomhouse.co.uk/environment

MIX
Paper from
responsible sources
FSC® C016897

Printed and bound in Great Britain by Clays Ltd, St Ives PLC

ISBN 9780091949143

To buy books by your favourite authors and register for offers visit:
www.randomhouse.co.uk

Acknowledgments

Many, many thanks to my editor, Shauna Summers, for seeing the promise in this book and for being so enthusiastic as I developed the story into what it is here. Thank you, also, to her wonderful assistant, Jessica Sebor, for the many details she smoothed for mc. And, of course, thank you to the art department for the breathtaking cover on *The Club*.

Much gratitude as always to my agent, Jessica Faust, who said the right things at the right times and who astutely commented on the story as it evolved, and to my wonderful critique partners—Candice, Teresa, Vanessa, Connie, and Sandra—who looked at this book in its early stages.

Thank you to my husband for all his help and support, and to my children for giving me smiles that always make me smile, too.

Chapter One

*H*OW AM I GOING TO EXPLAIN to a man I've paid that I do not actually want him to make love to me?"

Jane St. Giles, Lady Sherringham, asked the question of her image in the cheval mirror, but her reflection could provide no answers, obviously, that she could not think of herself.

So speaking aloud to it was quite pointless.

Groaning, Jane stalked around the brothel's bed-chamber, biting her thumbnail, and dreading the knock that was soon to come.

She had come here searching for her best friend Delphina, Lady Treyworth. She had come for answers. She'd paid a veritable fortune for the services of one of the young men employed by Mrs. Brougham, the woman who ran this Georgian house on the fringe of Mayfair, known simply as the "The Club." But since it had been a ruse, she now had to convince the man to leave without touching her.

Would he be angry?

She shivered.

Would he come to her aroused? Fear coiled, tight and cold, around her heart. She knew—though she had never experienced it with her own late husband—a man could become belligerent when he was aroused and the woman refused to play.

With Sherringham, she'd never had the courage to refuse to play. She had always toed his line, terrified how brutal he would be if she pushed him too far. But he had now been dead for thirteen months, and she no longer had to endure the nights he came to her bedroom. She no longer had to fight to find the nerve to send him away, then despise herself when she couldn't.

Jane paced, hugging her chest.

Surely a large tip would soothe any ruffled ... well, whatever might be ruffled on a randy young man. The man she'd hired had intimate relations for money, so wasn't money the most important thing? And there were dozens of society ladies in attendance. Any reasonably attractive, healthy, and erect young man wouldn't be frustrated for long.

Oh, dear God, she thought, and she took hold of one of the bedposts for support.

The ostentatious bed almost filled the entire room. Shackles of iron—lined with velvet—hung from the carved gilt bedposts. Jane's stomach roiled as she stared at the relief crafted on the posts: entwined serpents and something that might be a sword, or could be the male privy part.

She remembered the afternoon two months ago when her two dearest friends had told her their husbands brought them to this club. Despite the sun pouring into her morning room and the cheery promise of the early spring day, a shiver of dread had rippled down her spine. "But ladies do not join a gentleman's club," she had said slowly.

"This one, they do," Charlotte had breathed. Her

eyes had been wide and in their cornflower blue depths, Jane had read surprising horror and shame.

"That is the novelty of this club," Del had explained, her voice as demure as if she were speaking of a successful rout. "The gentlemen bring their wives—in costume. Every Friday evening, the ladies are required to dress as nuns." Then her voice had lowered and her lashes had dropped. "I still have the marks on my derriere from the spankings with the crop."

Jane had felt her mouth form a soundless O of horror. She'd endured Sherringham's punishments with the flat of his hand, but he'd never dared touch her with a crop.

Now, she shuddered as she gazed around the bedchamber. *Del, is this horrible club the reason that you've disappeared?*

A sharp rap echoed on the door and Jane jolted so abruptly she stubbed her toe on the post. "Madam? May I enter?"

Her hired man possessed a seductive voice—low-timbered, not entirely cultured, but with a growling note that sent a shiver of fear...it must be fear...down her spine. What did it signify that he spoke so politely? Would the sort of prostitute who had an educated voice be easier to manage or more difficult?

"Y—yes," she answered shakily.

She had not even removed her cloak and she had chosen to wear her widow's weeds, with the veil lowered to shroud her face. But still, as the door opened, she turned her face so no one would see her, and waited with rigid shoulders for the door to click, the signal her male prostitute had shut it behind him.

While her husband had generally smelled of sweat, drink, and other women's perfume, this man was preceded by a combination of citrusy bergamot and sultry sandal-wood. She certainly couldn't smell his perspiration, and oddly, he didn't smell as though he had come to her from another woman.

But really, that didn't matter. All she had to do was get rid of him. There was no reason to feel so unnerved. She'd survived a whole half hour so far in this wretched club, after all.

But before she could force herself to face him, he asked, "Is—is there something wrong, love?"

Concern laced his gentle voice, and there was a surprising vulnerability in his hesitation. Obviously he wasn't accustomed to a woman who looked as though she wanted to hide from him.

Jane glanced to the cheval mirror to see what he looked like, but the glass only reflected part of his side. She saw a large hand clad in a black leather glove, and a long, long leg in well-tailored trousers. A lean line of hip that vanished into a tailcoat, a glimpse of a very broad shoulder, and that was all.

Big. He was big and male. Panic flared in her chest and she struggled to breathe. *He can't hurt you. Here you can scream. You can scream and bring help and he has no right to hurt you.*

She must search inside to find greater strength. She'd vowed to herself that this time—finally—she would take action. How many times had she made that promise before, then taken the easy path, and slipped back into being a coward? And because she had been a coward, Delphina had disappeared. Del was in trouble.

"Turn around, love."

Grasping for that courage, Jane did. "I am so sorry, but—"

Her words—her very thought—died abruptly. The man stood by the wall and leaned against it in a lazy, relaxed way, and though several feet separated them, she had the sudden sense of the room shrinking in on her.

Shoulders—he had shoulders that seemed as wide as her legs were long. His legs, crossed casually at the ankles, stretched endlessly in front of her, and when her gaze followed them upward from the tip of his gleaming boots, the moment lasted a lifetime.

A black leather mask left his eyes a mystery, but beneath she saw he had not shaved—dark stubble ringed his square jaw. A scar forked down beneath the mask, another cut deeply into his chin.

But his lips quirked up in a kindly, sympathetic smile and deep dimples showed in his cheeks. He held out his hand in a coaxing sort of way—as though offering food to a timid deer. "It's all right, love. I won't hurt you. I'm at your command, after all. Your slave, so to speak."

At her command. The exact words to remind her that, for once, she had power here.

But, faced with him, she didn't feel powerful.

"You are in mourning?" He took a slow, easy step away from the wall toward her.

"No, no!" she said hurriedly and she scrambled, back until her legs trapped her skirts against the bed. And as her heart pattered wildly, she saw the perfect escape.

"I—I mean, my mourning year has not quite passed." She fluttered her hands—it was no stretch to act like a nervous woman who had changed her mind. "And the truth is, I—I was . . . lonely. So I thought I could . . . but I can't. Not with you. Not now."

He was so near she could see his eyes in the oval holes of the mask. Indigo blue eyes surrounded by abundant black lashes. The bed pushed back on her as she tried to retreat.

Another slow step brought him terrifyingly closer. Her heart thundered. He had not understood.

"I can't . . . use you tonight. I—I've changed my mind. I'll pay you . . . extra, if you want. In case you are disappointed—"

His eyes lit up with understanding. "So that's why you did not give your name."

What on earth did he mean? She did give a name. A false one.

Goodness, the way he tilted his head, the thick black hair, the shape of his mouth, the straight, attractive nose—why was it all so suddenly familiar?

Ridiculous. When would she have ever encountered a male prostitute in her daily life?

But she couldn't tear her gaze away from his mouth—his sensual lips were wide and generous. His lower lip was much larger, much fuller than his upper. Again, she felt as though she had stared at this mouth before. His skin was the color of clover honey, a sign he had spent much time under a hot sun.

Surprising for a man who earned his living in a bedroom—though perhaps he hadn't been doing it for very long.

His lips smiled again, smugly. He knew she was staring and he must think it meant she desired him, this large man who stood between her and the door.

A dull roaring began in her ears. He wasn't going to take no for an answer.

"I hope I have not frightened you, madam."

"No, no, you've done nothing wrong. You've been . . ." What should she say here? "Lovely. Yes, you have been so very . . . wonderful, and I hope you are not upset. I *will* pay you. You won't have wasted your time—"

Then he was there—right in front of her, filling her vision with a black tailcoat and a white embroidered vest.

"Of course I'm not upset. But if you don't want me, I understand." He bowed over her hand and lifted it so slowly to his lips that she forgot to breathe and her legs swayed beneath her.

"No." She jerked her hand back from her prostitute's mouth.

"Do I not please you, Lady Sherringham?"

"Stop. Stop!" She dragged her hand away, aware of a louder rushing sound in her ears. She had not given her real name. Mere moments before he had even said that himself.

"How do you know who I am?" she cried.

His expression revealed him then. She knew exactly why he had looked familiar and she was so startled that she tumbled backward onto the soft, deep bed, grasping at air as she fell. Her skirts flew up, her legs parted as she tumbled back and she slammed her elbow against the bedpost in her fall.

Shooting pain and humiliation changed her shock to anger as she lay back on the bed in a tangled heap. "You aren't my hired man! I recognize you now. You are Delphina's brother. You are Lord Wickham."

Known, for very good reason, as *Lord Wicked*.

How could he be here, in this revolting club that had destroyed Del?

"I am surprised you recognize me, Lady Sherringham."

Jane scrambled up on her elbows. She saw it now— she saw the handsome young rake of twenty in the masked face of this older man. He had been Christian

Sutcliffe when she'd known him—his father had still been alive. Eight years had changed him. As well as the scars he now bore, his cheekbones were more prominent, his face more deeply lined. He was broader, tanned, and far more muscular.

"I suppose you would be surprised," she snapped, over the pounding of her heart. "After all, you've been away, on the Continent, in India, and the Far East. You have been everywhere but in England, where you could have helped your sister before she was forced to marry Lord Treyworth."

"And I remember you," he murmured, looking down on her. "The tartar."

Jane glared up at the dark blue eyes. But for the color, his eyes were just like Del's. "What are you doing here," she demanded, "in England *and* in this disgusting club?"

She dragged her legs closed as quicly as she could. Falling onto the bed. Of all the useless things for her to do.

She started as Wickham held out his black leather-clad hand to her. He didn't jump on her, as Sherringham would have done, and take advantage of the situation. He wore a bemused smile that barely reached his eyes as he helped her back on her feet. She had known Del's brother for three years before he'd left England and they'd never had a conversation that didn't include an argument.

A hundred questions raced through her mind, but oddly, she picked the most inconsequential to blurt out. "Where is the man I hired?"

Wickham's coal black eyebrows jerked up at that, above his mask. "Trussed up with his own selection of velvet ropes and stowed in a closet," he answered impatiently. "Now, Lady Sherringham, talk to me. What do you know of this club?"

His hand closed on hers, large, warm even through the supple leather.

"I'm not a member, if that's what you mean," she said. "And I asked you first—"

"Your husband did not bring you?" he continued, speaking over her indignation and cutting off her words.

"No, but I do know that Del's husband brought her. For over a year, Treyworth forced her to come here. She admitted to me that she was frightened of this place."

There—let him chew on that, the irresponsible wretch. He'd never once tried to help Del after he left England.

He lifted her with ease and Jane had to reach out and grasp his other arm to steady herself as he abruptly pulled her to her feet.

"If you believed Delphina was afraid of this place, Lady Sherringham, why did you come and hire a man for the night?"

"It wasn't for...for passion, if that's what you are thinking—which I am sure is all you've ever thought of." All her hopeless anger and fear was rushing to the surface now, making her tongue sharp and wicked. She jerked her hands from his and scurried around him, so she was the one closest to the door. "It was a ruse. I was stopped at the door and taken to Mrs. Brougham, so I told her I was a lonely and wealthy widow. She wouldn't let me enter unless I—I bought a man. Why did you tie him up in the closet?"

"To question you, Lady Sherringham."

"You were spying on me?"

"I'd gone to your house to talk to you about Del," he said. "You were leaving, obviously disguised, so I was intrigued enough to follow."

"Obviously disguised?"

"I know your husband has been dead for over a year. I heard he wasn't worth mourning."

"I assume, that if you were following me, you don't know where Del is?"

She saw the sharp flash of pain in his eyes, and he leaned heavily on the carved column of the bed. "No. Do you?"

"No!" Jane threw up her hands in exasperation. "That is why I am here. Her husband told me that she had gone to the Continent. But I know that is impossible. I was the one who talked about running away. Del and Charlotte didn't have the will—"

"Running away?"

In the end, she had not had the courage either to escape her husband. But she did not tell Wickham that. Instead a horrible thought began to take root. "Why are you in England?" she demanded. "Is it a coincidence?"

"Del wrote me to tell me she was afraid of her husband, that she had been debased by him, and she was afraid for her very life."

"So *finally*, you came home to help her."

Firelight glinted off his dark eyes. "Yes."

She felt the wild, foolish need to hurt him—to punish him. "Del *is* terrified of her husband, Treyworth. I know he beats her, but he does it in ways that do not leave marks."

"Christ," Lord Wickham muttered.

Jane jabbed her finger toward his broad chest. "She endured whippings at this club. She was forced to . . . to do things with multiple men at one time! She—"

He surged forward and clamped his hand over her mouth. She sucked in panic and the smell of fine leather. "Stop it," he growled. "This helps no one."

She couldn't breathe. Dizziness swamped her.

He bent close. "When you open your mouth, will it be to tell me something of use?"

Gritting her teeth, fighting fear, she nodded and his hand moved away. She pulled in a long breath. "What did Treyworth say?" she gasped out. "How did he explain Del's disappearance?"

"He told me, in a blind rage, that she had run off with a lover. Then he tried to force me out of his home at sword point—"

"Tried?"

"I got hold of his damned sword and snapped it in two." He raked his hand through his dark hair, leaving it in shiny black disarray.

He had snapped a sword in two? "I'm afraid he killed her." Jane was astonished she'd managed to get out the words without giving in to tears.

She should have tried harder. She should have forced Del to escape Treyworth. She should have had courage for once in her—

"So you think that." Wickham stalked away from her, over to the mantel, and braced his hands against it. His body gave a long shudder, then stilled. "I've found no evidence of it."

"Neither have I."

He turned in surprise, his face stark with anguish. It seemed . . . that he cared about Del, after all. But anger still boiled in her blood. Why could rakish Lord Wicked not have discovered that he possessed a heart a few months earlier? Or a few years earlier?

"And you came here, looking for her?"

Jane shook her head. "I did not think I would find her here. Because Charlotte still comes here, and Charlotte insisted that nothing had happened to Del here.

Charlotte—Lady Dartmore—is our other friend. She was very convincing, but I didn't believe her. You see, Charlotte has changed—I cannot define how, but I know she has. I cannot trust anything Charlotte says anymore, because she still loves her husband and always will."

Wickham was gaping at her, obviously lost somewhere in her rapid words.

"I came here looking for some . . . some sort of clue. Answers. I really do not know if this club has anything to do with Del's disappearance, but I know she was afraid of this place. And I know she was becoming more and more frightened."

"She told you that, too?"

"No, I know it because she began to refuse to talk to me. Only a woman who is very afraid would stop talking to her best friends."

"But she wrote to me," he muttered and he stared down at the flickering flames.

The mantel clock ticked away cheerfully and the fire crackled as it would in any drawing room, unaware that danger and sin lurked everywhere in this evil club.

"Obviously she felt you would help her," she said softly.

Could she really trust Del's brother? Had he finally accepted his responsibility, or was he here for a sinister reason? Could she tell if he was lying from his expression? She had always been able to tell when Sherringham had been lying, but she rather thought he made it deliberately easy for her. It was, for Sherringham, just another form of torture.

For two weeks, she had been writing desperate correspondence to Treyworth and making frantic visits to Charlotte in the hopes she would convince them that Del must be in danger. She hadn't expected Treyworth to agree with her—he was the most likely suspect, after all. But with Charlotte so adamantly certain that Del really had gone away, Jane had begun to think she was mad and delusional.

But if Del had written to her absent brother and begged him for help, she must have been truly afraid.

Which meant Jane had no time to waste. "You are perfect," she said to Wickham.

"I beg your pardon?" He jerked away from the fireplace to fully face her, so quickly that his thick dark hair flew across his brow.

"I have to search the club, but it is really for couples. Together we can get into rooms that I could not on my own, and—"

"No."

"What do you mean 'no'?"

"It's not a difficult concept, Jane Beau—Lady Sherringham," he corrected. He had almost used her maiden name. "You are going to leave this bedroom, and take your well-bred bottom out of this club. You are going to go home where you will be safe."

"I will not. And I'm not innocent—I might have a title, but I have never once been protected from the dark and dirty side of life, my lord."

A dark brow lifted. "Indeed. But you need me to partner you."

She felt her eyes narrow with suspicion. "I need a gentleman I can trust to help me get into the most secret parts of this club."

"But the problem is that you can't trust me."

Her stomach dropped away.

"Do you know what I originally planned to do, sweeting?"

The endearment raised the hair on the back of her neck. They were no longer speaking as equals with a common goal. He suddenly seemed larger, colder, and far more intimidating. Eight years ago they used to argue and spar whenever they met. Now he felt like a stranger to her.

"What did you plan to do?" Her words came slowly, hesitantly.

"I was intending to carry the ruse to its end, and ask you about Del while you were floating in the delicious aftermath of your many climaxes."

It took a moment for her wits to resume function after he had growled the word *climaxes*. "You were going to . . . to *sleep with me*?"

"Yes. For all I knew, you were involved in my sister's disappearance up to your pretty neck. I didn't plan to reveal that I knew you and that I was not your gigolo, until I realized you weren't going to invite me into bed."

"I would never hurt Del! You really are wicked. Wicked. Wicked. Wicked." She hated the childish sound of her words, but she couldn't think of any other to describe him.

"Which only proves, sweeting, that you don't belong here. You can't trust me, and if this place is what you say it is I doubt you could trust anyone else here. I believe Del is alive. I'm certain she's alive. And I'll find her. But you are going home."

"No, I—"

"I'm sure Mrs. Brougham already suspects your motives for coming here, since it appears this club is intended for gentlemen to bring their wives. She would have to wonder why you came alone, in widow's weeds, when your husband never brought you."

"She won't know who I am. I gave her a false name, asked her not to give it to you—I mean, to her employee."

"It doesn't matter who you are. She has to be wondering what it is that you really want."

Jane frowned. He could be right. Mrs. Brougham had insisted she hire one of the men, and she had played along to allay suspicion. What if Mrs. Brougham had been testing her and had hoped to use the prostitute to keep her busy and preoccupied?

But how could he think she could just go home? He had left Del. He had no understanding of what a person did for someone they cared for.

She could not waste anymore time with Lord *Wicked*. So she did what she would have done with Sherringham. She lowered her head obediently and mumbled. "All right. You must be right. I'll go home." She jerked up her head and met his blue eyes—it gave the convincing touch. "But you have to tell me what you find."

"Of course," he agreed, and she knew he was lying. "I will escort you to the front door."

"I am sure that you will," she muttered. But she knew from what Delphina had told her that there was a back door to the club. Brothels always had them—an escape route in case the law appeared.

She had prayed that Del had used that to escape the club, if she had met danger here. The problem was, she had no idea what Del might be running from, or where she would go. She wasn't anywhere where Jane had desperately hoped she would be—Del hadn't sought refuge with any friends or at any of Treyworth's country estates.

For Jane, tonight, that hidden door wouldn't be a way out of hell. It would be a way in.

Chapter Two

$\mathcal{T}$HE ENTIRE HOUSE SMELLED OF SEX. And at least a dozen well-bred ladies were wandering around in nothing more than corsets and stockings.

Christian Sutcliffe, Lord Wickham, clenched his fists as he prowled through the crowd that packed the salon of Mrs. Brougham's club. Had Treyworth paraded Del like this? His sister had been a pink-ribbons-and-ruffles sort of girl—sweet and docile. She would never have defied her husband. She would have done whatever he asked, and Christian wanted to tear Treyworth apart.

Guilt had ridden him on the long journey back from India, and it lanced him again like a knife in a fresh wound.

Just like Lady Jane Beaumont—Lady Sherringham now—he believed Del was alive. He had to. She was alive, but missing, and he would find her. He would bring her home safely. He would make up for everything he'd done wrong.

As for Lady Sheringham, she was now, thankfully,

ensconced in her unmarked carriage and heading for home. Perversely, Christian could not stop thinking of his bout with her. She'd always had a way of getting under his skin. She'd always liked to lash him with her sharp tongue, but not in the way he would have enjoyed.

Hell, the woman had once put pudding in his boot, when she'd been seventeen, and he'd said something risqué that had made her blush.

"I do not see why you refused that gentleman's offer to join us, dearest. It matters not to me whether he is better equipped than you."

Christian jerked in surprise at the irritated feminine voice, then stared at the couple who were standing at his side. The woman wore a filmy negligee but also held a bit between her teeth. Black leather reins dangled from the rings at the end of the bar. She'd been speaking to her escort. Dressed in evening attire, the man carried a whip, its tail coiled and held in his hand.

"You merely wished to spoil my fun," the woman went on in a plaintive tone.

"Hush up, woman," the man muttered.

Husband and wife, apparently. That was the point of this place. It was intended for couples. It seemed the *haute volée* had changed since he'd left England.

Applause from a corner of the overheated salon caught his attention and he headed that way, toward a large crowd. At the center of the group, a slender, pretty, dark-haired girl struck a series of poses.

She wore white in the way that only a young girl could—the soft muslin portrayed innocence and showcased her creamy skin, ripe red lips, and vivid dark eyes. But the brilliant light of the chandelier revealed her dress was almost transparent. She wore nothing beneath, and her small, pert nipples were rouged and pointed out behind her thin bodice. The slim lines of her thighs, the slender curve of her hip, even the dark thatch of hair between her legs were all enticingly revealed. Christian recognized several peers within her group of admirers, each man watching the girl with open lust.

In front of him, a masked lady remarked to her friend, "Exquisite, is she not? She's Pelcham's second bride and has just passed her eighteenth birthday."

He knew of Pelcham. A viscount trying for Byron's crown as England's romantic poet.

"So fresh and lovely," the other woman agreed. "My husband will spend the entire night in pursuit of her."

"Pelcham is seeking another couple tonight. He wishes to slowly indoctrinate his fresh and lovely wife."

"I shall have to acquire her, then. It will put my husband in deep debt to me, and I know what I shall ask in return—a young stallion with magnificent…endurance." This elicited wicked laughter from both ladies.

Christian watched Pelcham's young wife pirouette, obviously enthralled to be the center of attention. But her innocence made his heart ache. She looked like Del, the way he remembered his sister.

Then one gentleman shouted, "Lift your skirts, my dear, and let's have a look at your firm, young rump," and when she didn't immediately obey, a hand reached out for her ruffled hems.

The girl bit her lip and backed away.

Damnation, he didn't have time to rescue another woman, but he had no choice. As he shoved aside two aging rakes to reach her, Pelcham charged through from the opposite side. A dark-haired libertine of forty, Pelcham wrapped a protective arm around his bride.

"My dear, have you decided who you wish to join us in our bedchamber?"

Christ Jesus.

The girl nodded, black curls dancing, then shyly bent toward her husband. Suddenly her movements lost their innocence and uncertainty. She cupped her hand against her mouth in a fetching gesture and whispered in her husband's ear. Something glittered in her eyes—Christian recognized it with revulsion. Power. The girl foolishly believed she held power.

Treyworth must have forced Del to do this. Had she been scared or enthralled to have some of the most powerful men in England hanging on her word, her choice, her careless fancy?

Del, you deserved so very much more.

A hand clad in rose silk squeezed his arm and Christian looked down into a tigress's face. Startled, he almost reared back, then realized the small woman clad in pink wore a beautifully painted papier-mâché mask. "You appear fascinated, sirrah."

He forced a slow smile—the smile that made innocent girls catch their breath and jaded women eager for conquest. He lifted her hand to his lips. "I am looking for Lady Treyworth."

She gave no gesture of guilt. No sudden motion, no alarm that revealed itself in pursed lips and tightened grip. If anything, she looked dazzled by him. "Lady Treyworth? I have not seen her here for a week. Perhaps even longer than that."

"Do you remember the last night you saw her here?" He stroked the palm of her hand with his thumb. He had to play seducer, even while he was wound tight with tension.

"I don't. But the last night she was here, she performed in the theater with Salaberry."

"What kind of performance?"

The woman recoiled and he realized he'd shouted at her. To soothe her, he kissed her hand again, and suckled her index finger through the fine silk. "It was ... naughty," she said breathlessly. "Are you going to the theater? I shall look for you. But my husband summons me and I must attend him." She snatched her hand free of his.

"Wait—"

But she was already threading through the crowd.

A quarter of an hour later, Christian had found no one who had seen Salaberry, who was the Marquis of Salaberry. He didn't recognize the title.

Then one lady gave a lusty smile in answer to his question. "Lord Salaberry only arrives for the theater entertainment. He never comes before then." She tittered at her joke.

Abruptly, Christian left her and stalked out of the ballroom, aware of intrigued glances following him. Where was the theater? Upstairs. Somewhere.

He commanded directions from a bare-chested footman, then passed through the hallway.

He wanted to smash a fist through the plaster wall. He wanted to tear the brothel down with his bare hands. Damn Treyworth for what he'd forced Del to do. And he damned himself for not being here to stop it.

He threw his fury into mounting the stairs three steps at a time. Logic told him to slow down, to not appear so driven, so full of purpose and rage, but he couldn't translate his thought into action. What did it matter, anyway, when he knew Mrs. Brougham suspected his motives for being here?

What else would the cunning madam assume but that he held suspicions of her and her club? Short, voluptuous, and draped in diamonds, Mrs. Brougham had been sympathetic and gracious, but also on her guard when her servant had ushered him into her private parlor—after he had watched Lady Sherringham's carriage rumble down the street.

Mrs. Brougham's artfully made-up face had shown nothing more than concern when he'd asked about his sister, but her hands, which had been elegantly clasped together on her desk, had tightened. If he hadn't watched her so closely he would have missed it.

Christian reached the top of the stairs, fought his way through the couples milling there, then strode down the carpeted hallway. Erotic paintings adorned the walls and plaster statues depicted athletic carnal positions.

He'd been in a hundred brothels—some sensual and inviting, some dirty and rough, some elegant and expensive. This place didn't feel like any of them.

Maybe the tension he sensed was the result of married couples playing their sexual games together. In his experience, married couples embarked on affairs to escape each other. Or to hurt each other.

Or was Lady Sherringham correct and Del had found danger here?

Servants always knew everything.

At least Jane hoped so. Rain pattered her cloak as she tugged at the rear door of Mrs. Brougham's club. The garden gate had been unlocked and this door proved to be the same. It swung open smoothly and the savory scent of roasting meat rushed out to her.

It all smelled so impossibly ordinary that she had to clap her hand over her mouth to stifle the sob that threatened to well up.

"You must be in the wrong place, dearie."

Jane spun to meet the kindly blue eyes of a burly cook. The woman brushed back graying ringlets. "If yer looking for the dungeons, ye'd best go back up the servants' stairs and then go down one of the main staircases, for the door from 'ere to that part of the 'ouse is locked."

The woman spoke as though it was perfectly natural for a woman to be seeking out dungeons. And that was so completely wrong. Jane surged forward. "I'm not looking for that. I'm looking for a friend of mine and I desperately need help. I'll make it worth your while."

At the sink, two maids stopped scrubbing pots. Two dark heads swiveled around. "A friend of yours, mum?" asked one. Hope shone in her young face at the promise of money.

These women had no choice but to work here. Jane knew what it was like not to have a choice. "Lady Treyworth. I will reward you well if you can tell me anything about her."

But blank stares from both maids and the cook were her answer, and her hope of gleaning information faded away. She blinked back tears. "She's been missing now for two weeks."

The rolling pin landed hard on the table and Jane jumped at the sharp sudden sound. Even after being widowed a year, she would still leap at an unexpected noise. Sherringham had always exploded into her quiet by throwing something.

"You look white as a sheet. One of you—go and fetch a chair before the lady faints."

"I'm not going to faint." But Jane found herself pushed onto a rickety wooden chair. No, she wasn't going to faint now, not when she'd survived walking through a brothel and fighting with Lord Wickham in a bedroom, and listening to him wickedly warn her that he would have slept with her if he'd had to.

"You won't be finding your friend 'ere, mum," said the cook kindly. "The mistress runs a fine establishment, not the type of place that drags them in off the street or has girls stolen away from good families."

Sweat trickled down Jane's bodice. Fires blazed in the ovens and her head swam with the heat. "I can see that it is not like that. But it's still a sinful and dangerous place."

The maids looked at each other. "Oh, no," ventured one. "The mistress makes certain that we're not ever in danger from any of the gentlemen guests."

Heavens. Apparently, her idea of hell and a servant's version of it were quite a bit different.

The second maid came over and crouched beside her chair. "You said there was a reward?" she asked timidly.

How old could this girl be? She looked to be barely a teenager. "Yes," Jane said. "A very generous one." But as she spoke, she prayed she hadn't made a promise she couldn't keep. She knew of only one way to pay it—to borrow funds from Lord Wickham. Surely, since the reward was for Del, he wouldn't refuse. She'd beg for it if she had to.

Impetuously, she clasped the young maid's wet, callused hands. "I would be grateful for anything you could tell me."

"You said she was missing. There was an actress that was here—"

"You two don't know a thing," the cook snapped. "And ye'd best be advised to keep yer mouths shut."

But Jane pushed up to her feet and turned to the gray-haired cook. "Please—"

Blue eyes gazed guiltily down. The woman appeared to be fighting her conscience. Jane held her breath—it was torture to be on the brink, not knowing if she would hear something that would drain away all her hope.

"They're speaking of one o' the girls who worked 'ere and dreamed of treading the boards," the cook said. "And to be sure, she 'as nothing to do with Lady Treyworth, ma'am. Nothing, indeed. That one used to walk the streets and the mistress rescued her. But she slid back into her old ways, it seems." Sighing heavily, the cook set down the rolling pin. "Go fetch some more coal, girls, for we're running low."

As the girls bobbed curtsies and darted out, wiping their hands on their aprons, the cook whispered, "Those two chattering magpies will soon be back, and I can't spend time gossiping now, my lady. The mistress will be in a rage if the dinner isn't ready on time." She lowered her voice even further. "But I would like to 'elp."

Jane understood. What she needed to do was dangle the right bait. What would she want most if she had to toil in blazing heat in a cramped kitchen beneath a brothel?

Impulsively, she stepped to the cook's side. "I would very much like to help a woman who would like to better her situation. I would like to help you."

Jane saw a lifetime of thwarted hopes and dreams steal

the brightness from the woman's blue eyes. "Everyone deserves a chance to fulfill a dream," she added firmly.

"Well, yer a funny sort of lady for a place like this." The cook turned to lift a bowl from the counter behind her, but she paused, and Jane held her breath.

The cook's voice came soft and tentative. "A lodging house would be my dream. I'd rather like to be my own mistress for the end of my days."

"I can help you do that." Though she was racking up her debt to Wickham with every word—and she had no idea if he'd honor her promises. But what else could she do? She couldn't ask her Aunt Regina for the money, and Sherringham had so efficiently bankrupted the estate, she'd been left almost penniless.

"There was another girl that went missing too. Both over a year ago," the cook whispered hastily. "The mistress said they ran off with men. Lightskirts are always on the lookout for a protector to set them up in fine style. But there's things that go on in 'ere that scare me."

The cook pursed her lips and looked so deeply troubled, Jane had to swallow hard to tamp down swelling panic. "What sort of things?"

"I've heard of what 'appens in that theater."

"The theater?"

"I can't speak about it now. There isn't time."

With fumbling fingers, Jane fished a card from her reticule. "Here is my direction."

The eyes opened wide. "Lady Sherringham." Suddenly flustered, the cook bobbed a curtsy. "I'm Mrs. Small, milady. It's my afternoon off on Thursday. I could come then."

Two days. She couldn't wait that long. She wanted to

implore the cook to tell her more but the door flew open, and the maids burst back in the room.

A white and gold door beckoned at the end of the hallway. Christian jogged toward it. Mrs. Brougham had been quite clear on which areas were restricted to the unique games invented for the ton's husbands and wives. The theater. The bedchambers. The dungeons. The Oriental rooms. Only in the salons and ballrooms of the first floor was an unaccompanied gentleman or lady permitted.

Then, with a gleam in her eye, she had told him that a couple was welcome to invite a solitary patron to join them. So he had to find himself a partner or a couple looking for a third for their games, if he wanted to get access to the theater. Or he had to break in.

He reached the door, gambled he'd found the correct one, and twisted the knob. He expected to find it locked; instead, it swung open to quiet—though not dead silence. Two fires crackled in fireplaces that flanked the room. Curved in shape, filled with elevated rows of plush seats, and an intricate Turkish carpet on the floor, this had to be the theater.

Christian walked up to the low paneled wall that ringed the seating area. The stage below held a large bed mounded with pillows, along with a tall wardrobe.

His gut twisted. Had Del, his sweet, gentle sister done . . . things down here, while other men watched like a Drury Lane theater crowd?

Footsteps pounded down the hallway. Whoever approached was running fast. The doorknob rattled just as Christian retreated into the deepest shadows of the room, bumping against velvet drapery. The door swung open and Christian vanished behind the curtain—there was not even a ripple to give him away.

The person who entered wore a black cloak. Subtle feminine perfume wafted past him—rose and lavender. So did the scent of damp wool. Christian bit back a groan.

He stepped out. "Lady Sherringham."

Spinning toward him, she clapped a gloved hand over her mouth. At least she didn't scream. Her deep hood tipped back, snagging on her golden-red curls. She had lifted her veil.

"Lord Wickham." Her eyes were bitter-chocolate brown, almost black, and impossible to read in the dim light, but her voice slid over him, soft and frantic.

"Why in blazes did you come back?" He paced toward her. "I sent you home. Why did you disobey me?"

"Disobey *you*?"

She had always been the type of woman to rush in where she wasn't wanted and did not belong. His temper snapped. "Bloody hell, woman, can you not see how dangerous it is to be blundering around in this place? Do you want to cause my sister harm? Or did you damn well come back to sleep with me?"

She backed away from him, taking quick steps until she smacked against the low wall and she put out her hand to grasp it. "I—I would never invite you into my bed!"

The door opened. Christian blinked in the light that spilled in. Lady Sherringham's voice halted but her indignation still rang throughout the room.

If you do not obey these rules, I will have to ask you to leave the club and not return, Mrs. Brougham had said. He could get into this building whether the madam wanted it or not, but for now it would be easier if he played by her rules. In a second, though, he would be tossed out of the brothel for entering the theater in defiance of them.

Lady Sherringham's eyes went impossibly wider with surprise as he yanked her hard against his body.

"What are you—?"

"Come on darling, you've tempted me to play." He laughed as lustily as he could manage, clamped his hand on her bottom through her cloak, and pulled her into a kiss.

Her soft lips were stretched into a stunned O but his mouth covered hers in a forceful, intimate caress. Her shoe drove into his shin. He knew she intended to hurt but her foot glanced harmlessly off his boot. She was like a plank in his embrace, rigid and unyielding. She tasted like a clear English lake on a summer's day—cold but enticing. He kissed her harder, deeper and prayed her incoherent protests sounded like cries of passion.

Play along, he muttered in his head.

But she didn't. Her hands clamped on his biceps and she tried to pry his arms away.

Didn't she understand he was trying to make them look like a couple, like long-established lovers?

With the audience, he could not just give her a polite peck. He had to make it convincing. So he had to give Lady Sherringham the sort of kiss associated with raunchy foreplay, even as she wriggled and struggled in his arms.

He angled his head, forcing her to tip hers back and she instinctively wrapped her arms around his neck to stay upright. Her fingers bored into his flesh through his collar and cravat. Her mouth was hot and moist and clamped shut, but he teased her lips with his tongue, kissed her hard. He heard her slight gasp of shock. She stopped fighting.

Lavender and other lovely womanly scents surrounded him. His fingers bunched her cloak at her waist, his hand cupped a voluptuous bottom that spilled over his palm.

Though he was only pretending seduction, his cock could not differentiate. His erection strained in his trousers, and a rush of guilt accompanied the rush of blood. How could his body feel desire now, with Del in danger?

He remembered her harsh words. *I am sure passion is all you've ever thought of.*

Enough. He had to stop. And he let their lips part the same instant a throat cleared behind him.

"I beg your pardon," intoned an impassive servant.

Christian stared down into Lady Sherringham's eyes. It struck him as madness that in this club, anyone would beg a pardon. Then he heard the one sound that tore at his soul.

A woman's fearful, tortured breathing. Lady Sherringham was truly scared. Too scared to move or to fight his grip. Her gaze darted about as though she was a small, defenseless animal about to be snatched up in slavering jaws.

Behind them, a jovial baritone called out, "This is quite the show, but we're here for the planned entertainment."

Christian turned his head, still clamping Lady Sherringham to his body. Full breasts, lush thighs, rounded hips pressed tight to him. Out of the corner of his eye, he saw her head tip back, as though to put as much space as possible between their lips, and her ragged breathing rushed by his ear.

Behind them, six couples stood with a liveried footman who carried a candelabrum. He recognized only one gentleman—the man who had spoken. Lord Petersborough, a contemporary of his father's. A bluff earl with a barrel chest, broad shoulders, and a fleshy face.

"Carry on." Petersborough waved his hand. The woman at his side looked about half his age. A snug black silk corset cinched her waist; her breasts spilled out above it, covered by a wisp of black veiling. "It's always a pleasure to see foreplay intended to, shall we say, get the honey flowing."

Lady Sherringham looked as though she might swoon. Christian saw her throat move as she swallowed hard. But she suddenly arched up on tiptoe and whispered by his ear, "I—I have to stay. I have to."

A weakening, damning bolt of physical desire raced through his legs at the tickle of her breath on his earlobe.

"At your peril, angel," he muttered back. "You have to pretend to be my lover."

Chapter Three

IT WAS AS THOUGH SHE WERE racing in a curricle at top speed—caught in a crescendo of sheer terror heightened by the absolute fear that it would all end in a horrible crash.

Jane stared up into Wickham's blue eyes. His one hand was still clamped to her derriere, the other splayed across her back. She was pinned to his broad chest, and voices and laughter whirled around her like a maelstrom.

When his mouth had closed over hers, hot, wet, and demanding, she'd almost keeled over in shock. She'd expected him to force her mouth open, to brutally thrust in his tongue. She'd thought he would hurt her and she'd fought—kicked at him but hadn't even made a dent—

It had swept over her. The memory. So real and harsh and terrifying, it was as though she was living it all over again...

Cold, vicious eyes. A raised hand, a blow. Her shoulders driven down into her bed, her legs roughly flung apart.

Spittle on Sherringham's lips, wild excitement burning in his eyes. His mouth coming down hard upon hers—

"Would you care to take a seat, madam? And sir? The spectacle is about to begin."

Mrs. Brougham's servant could not have snapped her back to reality faster with a douse of cold water. She pushed memories back into dark recesses and focused on Wickham, who still held her close. She saw his eyes behind his mask, dark with suspicion, filled with surprise.

She couldn't think of a thing to say. His gaze held her, deep blue and fierce, demanding, without words, that she explain what was wrong with her. Then he reached out. She flinched, but he merely drew her veil down to cover her face.

"Spectacle indeed!" Petersborough's suggestive laugh exploded in the small room and Jane almost leapt out of her skin. He slapped his beefy hands on the backrest of one of the chairs and gave her a toothy leer. "Take this one, darling, and allow me the pleasure of sitting at your side."

The glare Wickham shot to the earl could shatter stone.

While Petersborough's wife's could set fire to ice. Jane blinked behind her shield of lace as the sharp-featured but attractive woman faced her like a dueling opponent. Good heavens, she could see his wife's nipples beneath that thin black veiling.

Elspeth, Lady Petersborough, did charity work for war widows. And Jane knew, from times she had taken tea with the woman, that Elspeth was the first to cast stones at a fallen woman.

"You are not sitting at his side." With his hand just

above the swell of her bottom, Wickham gave her a gentle push. "Go to the end of the first row. The *last* chair."

"But—"

"Go." It was a growl, low in his throat. And she was too shaky to fight.

Jane gathered her skirts and resolutely shuffled along the row. She understood Wickham's intention. This way only one man could sit at her side.

Wickham, who had passed along the row almost attached to her hip, claimed the seat beside her. She settled, and despite the soft velvet beneath her, sat rigidly and looked ahead. Out of the corner of her eyes, she saw Wickham lean close and she stiffened with apprehension.

Other men had their hands draped over their women—on their breasts, their thighs. What if Wickham intended to touch her that way?

She knew he did. She was supposed to pretend to be his lover.

Her heart began another thundering race.

She had to regain control. She hadn't thought a kiss, even a rough one, could do this to her.

Wickham's hand settled gently on top of hers. He gave a light, reassuring squeeze, but even that made her feel trapped. "I didn't mean to force the kiss, but it was essential," he murmured.

What a word to select! Essential. Was this also just essential—the slow path of his lips feathering her lobe? She supposed it was—she could see his gaze scanning the rest of the crowd even as he spoke to her.

His chiseled face showed no emotion, but she could almost smell his tension and anger. She glanced around the room too. Lord Pelcham, the dashing romantic poet, pulled his very young wife onto his knee and tickled her up under her skirts. The Duke of Fellingham, silver-haired war hero, was nuzzling his wife's breasts and making her giggle like a schoolgirl. One woman was bending to kiss her husband's lap . . .

Jane knew her cheeks were ablaze. But she had to look—to take note of the guests in the theater. Fellingham, Pelcham, Petersborough. The Earl of Coyne, who was a handsome, notorious gambler. The other two men were too well disguised. One wore a pirate's costume, complete with eye patch, kohl around the eyes, a beard, and curling mustache. The other man wore a black mask that covered his face from hairline to lips—

Wickham's lips suddenly brushed the rim of her ear and she bit back a startled cry.

"Why are you so frightened?" he asked.

What would Wickham do if she told him she'd confused him with her brutish late husband and had instinctively panicked? He'd never let her stay.

"I thought it was my kiss. But that doesn't make sense, angel," he continued, in a husky tone that made her shiver. "So it had to be something else. What are you hiding from me?"

Astonished, Jane understood. He thought she'd been lying to him. That she knew something about Del's disappearance she hadn't revealed. That she was maybe even *involved*. "H-how dare you," she sputtered. "I was the one here for Del." Indignation gave her a surprising amount of strength. "You should have let me speak to Petersborough. I need to question the members here."

His black brow shot up. "Absolutely not."

"You might remember I encounter all these people every day of my life. I will be careful."

He rolled dark eyes heavenward. "Give me strength. I can't risk you blundering about and causing trouble."

"I am not causing trouble," she protested. At Wickham's side, the Earl of Coyne was now sucking his partner's breasts through her bodice. Jane had no choice but to bend right to Wickham's ear so she would not be overhead. Her lips accidentally brushed his soft hair and a shock—a fierce, electric one—jolted through her. "I've already spoken to the cook—"

"Give me strength. You questioned the servants?"

"Yes," she hissed. "And do you wish to know what I learned? Two other women have gone missing from this place."

Both Wickham's brows went up and a look of fierce anguish twisted his handsome face.

He'd made her furious and nervous just like he always used to, and she'd blurted out the truth to hurt him. She should explain that it was not peers' wives who had disappeared, but applause rose around them and Jane knew she wouldn't be heard.

A bare-chested footman stood at the edge of the gallery, in front of the seats. A long, gold codpiece protruded from the front of his breeches, and he waved the appendage back and forth to the cheers of the ladies. The men were applauding a woman, equally bare above the waist, who was slowly walking up the aisle between the rows of seats.

What would it have been like to have been brought here by Sherringham? Jane had to swallow hard to keep down bile at the thought.

The woman turned to the audience, and clapped her hands to command attention. She was given it immediately—from dukes, earls, and highborn ladies. "The performance," she declared, "is about to begin."

Men stamped their boots to show their approval, and Jane knew it would be a while before she could speak to Wickham. She cast a sidelong glance at him. He looked as though he wanted to throttle her.

Her shoulders jerked. But Del's brother didn't have the rage in his eyes that used to smolder in her husband's. *Courtesans,* she mouthed.

His gaze bored into her. But had he understood?

The white-garbed woman continued in her sultry tones, "Women will appear in the room one after another. Each will display her charms and her skill for a gentleman who shall watch through peepholes in another adjoining room. The chosen woman will then join the gentleman. He will perform an act of discipline."

An act of discipline? Wickham leaned forward and now watched the stage with the intensity of a predator about to spring.

Jane looked. A woman stood on the stage below. An exotic Venetian-style mask, painted white and adorned with white plumes, hid the woman's face; she had long, dark hair. Clad in an ivory silk wrapper, the woman paused, staring at the bed.

As though she did not want to be there. As though she wanted to turn and run.

Dark hair. Del!

Jane almost jumped out of her chair, but Wickham's hand restrained her. What was he doing? They had to make haste!

He curtly shook his head.

What was wrong with the man? They had no time to—

The woman dropped her robe.

Not Del. Definitely not Del. Del did not possess—
The woman's breasts were enormous. Impossibly so.

Wickham pulled her back, forcing her to fall into her
seat. At the center of the stage, beneath the gleaming
candlelight, the woman pinched her exposed nipples,
drawing them to long, brown tips.

Jane's heart raced. Del had loved the theater. Their
husbands never took them—they took their mistresses.
But sometimes, she, Del, and Charlotte had gone alone
on the nights they knew one box would be empty. For a
few blessed hours, they'd been free—free to be giddy,
and giggly, and filled with joy.

As they'd been before they had wed. And since all
three of them had married young and married lecherous
men a quarter century their seniors, they'd shared many
troubled days together. They had all married in the same
Season, eight years before. But they'd each done so for a
different reason—Charlotte for love, Del for duty, and
Jane out of necessity. Her father had lost everything in
wild games of hazard and the Earl of Sherringham had
been willing to take her without a penny to her name.

Del had been there for her after the disaster that had
been her wedding night. And it was on Charlotte's
shoulder that Jane had cried, on the tragic day she'd lost
her second baby to another miscarriage. Her friends
were the two reasons she had survived in her marriage to
Sherringham without going mad or leaping out of an attic window.

It broke her heart to see one of Del's few pleasures
twisted into this perversion.

Wickham's hand settled on the nape of her neck. Her
spine stiffened until she felt as though a rod had been
shoved down her back.

Wickham was watching her, not the naked woman on stage—a new one who had blond hair and was licking an ivory rod from tip to base while the *gentlemen* hooted like excited owls.

"Tell me what the cook told you," he demanded, voice low. He moved close—so close she could see every detail of the scars that cut through his tanned face. His fingers still caressed her neck. "The women weren't society ladies?"

"L-lightskirts. Women who worked for Mrs. Brougham. The cook said they might have run off with men. She said things in this house, this theater, frighten her."

He let out a low breath. She smelled brandy, the smoke of a cheroot—all things she'd tasted in that fierce kiss. Sweat trickled down her bodice. She was still hot from being in the kitchens and her shift clung to her skin.

"Missing prostitutes from a year ago likely have nothing to do with Del," he said huskily. "They might have run away. They might have been dragged off to another brothel."

"B-but what if they do?" The thought made the blood rush from her head. "What if they were—were killed?"

Before Christian could answer, Lady Sherringham let out a startled gasp.

A blond man was on the stage alone, heading for the bed. "Who is he?" Christian growled.

"The Marquis of Salaberry. D-do you think he will remove that robe?"

"Yes. How well do you know Salaberry?"

"N-not very well," she stammered. "He was not in our circle—he revolved in a far, far higher orbit than Sherringham's."

"Was my sister in love with him?"

"Salaberry was Del's lov—?"

At that moment, the marquis dropped his robe.

On stage, Salaberry strutted about naked. The man possessed fair-haired, blue-eyed good looks, and a boyishly angelic face that gave no hint that he enjoyed this sort of sexual game. Christian placed Salaberry's age at a few years below his own. Possibly six-and-twenty. Closer to Del's age.

"I've learned that Salaberry had a performance with my sister in this theater on the last night she was seen in the club."

Lady Sherringham's chest rose with fast breaths. "Del *did* perform in here?"

"Yes." The thought made him want to strangle the naked marquis with a cravat. "Who are the other men my sister encountered here?"

Her eyes widened at him. "I don't know!" she cried in a fierce whisper. "She wouldn't tell me who they were. I think she was supposed to keep their identities a secret from people who weren't members. For some mad reason, she felt she had to do what she was told."

Lady Sherringham knew exactly how to slice into his heart. He had never met another woman who wielded honesty with such brutality.

"Del would have never dared take a lover," she said. "Treyworth is possessive, jealous, utterly mad. What he told you about Del running away with another man is a lie. He would accuse her of infidelities and rave at her until he reduced her to tears."

"But he brought her here?"

"It gave him a reason to punish her. He forced her to do these things and then he punished her for it."

What would drive a man to do that? Treyworth had to be insane. But what if Del did have a lover she truly cared about? That might have pushed Treyworth over the edge—

Abruptly he stopped thinking along those lines. He had to believe Del was alive. If she feared her husband and was forced to come to this club, it made sense that she would run. She had to be somewhere. He—or one of his investigators—would find her.

In his mind, he could only see Del the way she had been eight years ago. He had no idea even what she looked like now. No idea of the woman she had become. How she had changed. How her life with Treyworth had changed her.

The stage before his eyes blurred—he couldn't focus on it anymore. He was too afraid to ask Lady Sherringham how Del had changed. Too damned cowardly to learn what his absence had caused. To learn exactly how Del had suffered because he had abandoned her.

But Lady Sherringham would know. And he knew, without a doubt, she would tell him the truth.

"He cannot." Lady Sherringham gasped suddenly. "*That's wicked.*"

Christian blinked and refocused on the stage. An innocent-looking woman with long auburn hair had joined Salaberry. And she was obediently handing him a whip.

Perspiration trickled in down the back of Jane's dress. Even her thick veil could not hide the contents of the wardrobe. Whips and coils of rope and other strange devices hung within.

A cavalier wave of Salaberry's hand and the young woman took down a whip. The marquis rose from his chair and took slow, measured steps toward her. Although she trembled, the girl kissed the handle of the whip, then held it out to the man who would use it to hurt her.

Jane's hands tightened on the arms of her chair. She could not just look away.

The girl obediently bent over the bed. Salaberry swept up the hem of her robe and tossed it carelessly over her head. He twirled the whip in the air, then with a long, lazy stroke of his arm, he brought it down on the woman's bare bottom.

The girl's cry echoed in Jane's head.

And so did another. Her own.

Her cries, her sobs. All in vain, for he'd taken her then. Taken her in rage. Taken her until she'd shut her eyes and prayed she'd never open them again. And she'd vomited in the chamber pot afterward, then lain wretched and naked on the floor, and cried until she hoped that she would cry her life out of her body—

"No!" Jane began to rise, shakily.

The Marquis of Salaberry let his arm drop. With blazing sapphire blue eyes, he studied her and a leering grin turned his handsome face into a demon's countenance.

The hush of the crowd settled on her, stifling and heavy.

"Does this intrigue you?" Salaberry called in a mocking drawl. "I would very much like to teach you some discipline, my wicked widow—"

Out of the corner of her eye, Jane saw a footman approach. To drag her down there?

Suddenly an arm snaked around her waist. It was Wickham. "Leave her, Salaberry. She's new to this game." In a low voice, exclusively for her, he muttered, "You are coming with me. Now."

He dragged her along the row, and she had no choice but to stumble along beside him.

"Lord Wicked!" cried a feminine voice. "I did wish to ask if this rumor was true: Did you truly once keep Lady Beckworth tied up in your private dungeon?"

Chapter Four

"I WAS NOT *FRIGHTENED*."

But Wickham ignored her protest and draped her cloak around her shoulders. Any moment now, Jane realized, he'd propel her out the door and into the street.

In fact, she was certain that, had he not been unwilling to draw attention to himself, he would have flung her over his shoulder, clamped his hand on her buttocks, and transported her like a rolled-up carpet.

"You had no right to drag me down here," she argued, louder, but not loud enough that the doorman with the barrel chest and beefy neck would hear. A green velvet curtain separated them from him, the same sort of curtain that closed off this anteroom from the club. "I wasn't going to swoon. I was outraged."

But she was shaking—right down to the tips of her fingers—and she knew he could see it.

"Outraged. Indeed." Disbelief laced Wickham's growl, and he reached around from behind to fasten her cloak, imprisoning her with his arms. "What were you going to do? Charge in and spank Salaberry with his whip?"

"I—I thought to help that woman."

"You can't stop it. You saw the woman submit to him, a willing participant, caught up in the fantasy. This sort of thing goes on in every brothel in England."

She sputtered. It wasn't true. Acquiescence did *not* mean willingness.

"Some women like it, sweeting."

"They must be mad," she snapped.

"This is just like you, pest. Charging into trouble without thinking of the consequences. Exactly like the time you were almost run over trying to stop my carriage race."

Pest. He'd teased her with that name when they were young. That race had happened nine years ago. "One of the carriages overturned, *Wicked.*"

"Because the driver was trying to avoid you. I know you were scared in that theater, angel. If you couldn't bear to watch, why didn't you tell me?"

"I thought if Del and Charlotte could endure it, then I could too."

She heard his sharp hiss. It had been the truth, but she knew Wickham would feel she'd used Del's name like a weapon.

"Now every person in that theater is aware of you. Of us. And is wondering what in blazes we're doing here."

It was as though the solid, tiled floor had dropped away beneath her feet. Of course he was right. She'd made them conspicuous. She might have ruined their chances of learning anything here. All because she'd panicked.

"Well, this time, love," he murmured silkily, "I am

sending you home in my carriage. To ensure you go there and you do not come back. And I am tempted to go with you."

Her chest went tight, pressing out against the prison of her corset. Why would he want to be alone with her? Was it because he was so angry with her? Was it his intent to punish her?

"And if that doesn't work, I shall have to be more inventive in keeping you captive."

Her entire body went cold. She was trapped in the arms of a very angry man. One who had a real reason to be furious with her.

He snapped his fingers to summon the doorman. "We are leaving. Have my coach brought around."

"I—I am not going to get into a carriage with you—"

The curtain was flung aside with the loud rattle of hooks bouncing along the rod. "Wicked!"

At the shout of his nickname, Wickham abruptly turned. For one hopeful moment, Jane thought she could escape him, but his arm snaked out and wrapped around her waist. She squawked in shock. She drove her fingers into his rock-hard forearm to no avail. She couldn't pry his arm away.

The Earl of Petersborough stood in the doorway, mopping his brow with a white linen handkerchief. He looked like a bear Jane had seen at a menagerie—large and lumbering, with huge paws. His gray eyes fixed on Wickham and he barked, "Ah, it is Wicked. I did not recognize you with the mask. I want to know where your sister is. Treyworth has been spouting some rubbish that she's gone to the Continent to visit friends. Don't credit that myself."

"You don't think she is on the continent," Wickham said.

Petersborough hesitated for a moment. "No. No, I don't think she is. She would not have traveled without telling me. That jealous brute didn't like her popularity here. Gentlemen adored her. She was a delightful partner."

Wickham had pulled her against him—Jane suddenly realized she was caught in the crook of his arm and his forearm was pressed so tight around her, she could barely breathe. Del and "get the honey flowing" Petersborough? It couldn't be possible.

Wickham's jaw tightened. "You and Delphina were lovers."

"A beautiful and precious woman, Wickham. An angel. She bestowed her favors upon me here and I treasured every moment we spent together."

"Bloody hell, Petersborough. Are you telling me you were in love with Delphina?"

"Both of us were far too experienced to bother with sentiment." The earl's beefy hand gripped the curtain. "She did not write to you and tell you where she was really going? She did not tell you why she felt compelled to leave?"

"I've been away from England for eight years. My sister would have been more likely to confide in you, if she was your . . . lover."

Jane heard the rage simmering beneath Wickham's words. On the surface, he was controlled, but she knew how dangerous a man like that could be. Sherringham had always been coldest before his worst rages—

"She didn't," Petersborough barked. "I have no idea where she's gone or why."

The lumbering bear of an earl looked so genuinely worried, Jane felt her stomach clench with dread. *But what if this is an act*, a voice whispered in her mind. *What if he is trying to find out how much Wickham knows? Speak to him. It doesn't matter what Wickham wants.*

Suddenly Petersborough's large gray eyes trained on her. "You've not thrown on the leg shackles yet, Wicked, so who is your little minx?"

Her veil was made of tightly woven lace but Jane had the horrible feeling Petersborough could see through her disguise.

"She is my private treasure." Wickham gripped her bottom. She squeaked in surprise.

"In this place, no one's partner is a private treasure." Petersborough leered at her, licking fleshy lips. "The pleasure's in the sharing."

Dear heaven.

"Not tonight," Wickham answered in a jaded drawl.

Jane swallowed hard. She breathed in relief as Peterborough retreated to the doorway. But he paused. "If Delphina contacts you, you will tell me?"

"Only if my sister wishes it."

Petersborough's smile vanished. Shock registered in his eyes. Then anger. Wickham had implied that Del really did not want him, and those beefy hands fisted again.

They were going to fight. Jane flinched at the thought of Petersborough's fist slamming into Wickham's face. What could she do? How could she stop it?

Petersborough took a menacing step forward. The two men glared at each other in absolute silence. But, by some miracle, Petersborough backed down. Without a parting word, he turned and stalked out of the ante-room, and the green curtain fell back.

"Christ Jesus," Wickham muttered. "Petersborough. Salaberry."

"And Treyworth." Jane felt sick. "How did Del end up at the mercy of the most odious gentlemen in England?"

Before she could blink, she found her back pressed against the wall in a shadowed corner. Wickham's body loomed over her, blocking out light. His hand braced the wall by her head, his muscular arm a prison. He flicked back her veil so she could stare into his blazing dark blue eyes.

What was he doing? Preparing to take out his rage—?

"Not odious. Dangerous," he growled. "If one of these men *has* made courtesans disappear—if one of them has hurt Del—do you not think he'd do the same to you if he thought you a risk?"

Her corset was trying to squeeze her life out of her. Of course she knew the risk. She'd been terrified the very first time she'd spoken to Lord Treyworth and she'd seen the veins twitch in his forehead and she'd realized how very, very angry he was.

"A desperate man would be more than willing to slit your throat, Lady Sherringham. Or to wrap his arms around your neck and squeeze the life out of you. Do you think you could fight off a man like Petersborough, if he intended to see you dead?"

Her legs were dissolving beneath her, her hands felt oddly cold and numb. "No. Of course I couldn't." *She'd grabbed for her husband's wrists once and he'd looked down at her small hands wrapped around his forearms and he'd laughed—*

"My lord, your carriage."

Wickham's hand closed around her arm. Was he going to drag her to his carriage? Would she be trapped in that confined space with him?

No. Dear heaven, he was bending to her mouth—

She stared at his approaching lips until her eyes crossed. He wasn't going to haul her outside. He was going to kiss her. His lips would touch hers and—

And she would remember again. She would remember Sherringham's touches and she just couldn't bear it.

"No. Don't. Please don't! Don't touch me."

Surprised at her shrill cry, Wickham let her go. She backed away. "I'll go home. I'll go, I promise, and you don't need to come with me. I don't want to see what men do with whips and ropes. I want to go home and have a thorough bath in scalding water."

He was staring at her as though she was mad. Behind her, the carriage rumbled up to the steps. "I'll go home, just as you want, and I'll be safe. But there will be no comforting bath for Del, will there?"

Jane turned and raced out the door, then down the steps.

She heard no boots thudding on the stone in pursuit. The door of the carriage opened in welcome and she jumped in and flung herself onto the seat.

They took off. Breathing hard, she looked to the window. And saw Wickham standing on the front step of the club, staring as she clattered away—in his carriage.

She fell back against the velvet squabs.

She didn't even want to cry. Crying would be a release. She'd failed Del and because of that, she didn't deserve a release.

Chapter Five

JANE TROOPED THROUGH THE FRONT DOOR of her aunt's town house on Upper Brook Street and handed her cloak, gloves, and veil to the maid. A coachman's shouts and the rumble of wheels caught her attention. Her own carriage returned as Wickham's left.

At least she would not have to explain how she had come home without her vehicle. She rubbed her aching forehead with the heel of her hand. She was furious with herself. How could she have panicked again?

"Might I see you in the drawing room, my lady?"

Jane whirled to see her aunt's housekeeper, Mrs. Hodgkins, waiting patiently in the shadows. No, perhaps not patiently. Mrs. Hodgkin's brow was lined with obvious worry and her gray hair was in disarray, as though she had pulled off her cap and repeatedly run her fingers through it.

Jane really did not wish to speak to anyone but, ruefully aware she must be the cause of the distress, she relented and went in.

Mrs. Hodgkins twisted her hands. "You have not worn your black for a month, my lady."

Oh dear. "I needed it for tonight. For an event where I—I had to be discreet."

The housekeeper suddenly beamed at her. "Was it a clandestine appointment then?" Her kindly face lit up with . . . a surprisingly naughty and mischievous delight. "Do you the world of good, that sort of thing, my lady. But I don't put stock in foolish risk. I won't tell Lady Gardiner, I promise you, but next time, you must have accompaniment."

The world of good? After the not-so-clandestine activities she'd seen at the club, Jane could barely find her voice. "I am quite able to take care of myself."

"Now, that is simply not true, my lady. Every lady needs to ensure she is protected."

Sorrow and despair welled up. Yes, every lady did. Del did. Jane sank down into a chair, too tired to stand any longer.

Mrs. Hodgkins looked panic-stricken. "My lady!"

"Thank you, Hodgkins." Aunt Regina's firm tones came from the doorway. "I shall speak with my niece in private."

Aunt Regina was supposed to be at her daughter's house tonight. But here she stood, cane in hand, arms crossed over the front of her rose silk wrapper. Regina's cane lightly tapped the floor while Mrs. Hodgkins bustled out, then she firmly, quietly, shut the door. As soon as the latch clicked, she demanded, "Where did you go haring off to tonight, dear?"

Jane was caught. Like a fox in a hound's jaws.

*   *   *

"You will find the marquis in the cage room, my lord. The second floor—the first door before the theater."

Christian rubbed the back of his neck, beneath his collar, as he strode past the footman and wound his way through the crowd. He could easily imagine what this room contained.

A few minutes later he found his guess to be correct. A large gilded cage stood in the center of a generous room. Smaller ones of iron swung in the corners. Candles in fanciful lanterns cast patterns of golden light and shadow over the walls and the naked woman who stood by the open cage door and waited for Salaberry to instruct her to enter.

Carrying a whip, dressed in a gold robe, Salaberry paced around the voluptuous blonde, tapping her rump with the handle.

Christian fought the urge to grab the marquis by the throat, slam him to the floor, and throttle the truth out of him. Instead he walked into the room. "Salaberry."

"Ah, Wicked," drawled the marquis. "Where is your wicked widow?"

Unbidden, the image of Lady Sherringham rushed into his head. Her round brown eyes huge with fear and shock. She'd run from him as though he was going to chase her and attack.

"Awaiting my next command," he answered. He hoped. Why in blazes had he tried to kiss her? He'd looked at those trembling lips, had seen all her sorrow, and he'd bent to her, needing to touch and comfort her. He'd hated having to scare her.

But it had been necessary. She was Del's best friend and his best link to Del. Her fear had proven she couldn't be involved in Del's disappearance. Which meant he'd had no choice but to protect her. And that included frightening her away from this club.

"I wanted to run into you tonight, Wicked," Salaberry said congenially. He tweaked his lady's pink nipple. His blue eyes glowed with enthusiasm. "I believe you've learned a great deal about erotic play in the Far East. I'd hoped for a chance to discuss technique."

Christian was left speechless. *Del.* Had Del stood there in silence like a dutiful servant and allowed her bare...bosom to be groped?

Salaberry slapped the breast and made it jiggle. "Care to have a feel? She's got two. Tits fit for a duchess, aren't they?"

The duchess giggled. Scarlet marks crossed her rump. A riding crop lay discarded on the floor. Obediently, she stepped into the cage and Salaberry swung the door shut. The latch engaged with a clang.

A red glare seemed to seep in at the sides of Christian's gaze. His chest was squeezing his heart. The last time he'd seen everything tinged with red, he'd accepted the Earl of Harrington's challenge for a duel and had killed the man. "The hell with rope play. I'm here to talk about my sister."

The whip dropped from Salaberry's hand. "She's also Treyworth's wife," he said quickly. "The permission to enjoy her came from her husband. It doesn't matter if you approve or not."

Christian yearned to slam his fist into Salaberry's smug face. He had to clamp his left hand over his right to control it. "Unfortunately for you, it bloody well does. She has vanished."

"Vanished?" Salaberry recoiled. He paced away from the cage.

Christian followed. "Did your games with my sister ever get out of hand? Did you hurt her?"

Salaberry swung around. "I paddled your sister's bottom a time or two and tied her up. She enjoyed every minute of it, Wickham. Mewled like a kitten for me."

"As far as I can tell, you were the last gentleman seen with her here." Ice coated Christian's words, but his blood was on fire. He glanced at the whipped duchess. "And you're a sadist."

"A sadist. Now there's the pot calling the kettle black. You're accusing me of hurting a gently bred lady. Why don't we settle this like gentlemen?"

The chain of the swinging cage creaked into the silence. The duchess held tight to the bars. Her eyes were wide.

"Shall we say Chalk Farm at dawn?" Salaberry leaned forward. Fear, shock, and excitement warred in his eyes, making him look young. Stubborn, stupid, and young.

At twenty-eight, Christian suddenly felt old. "Christ, Salaberry. Killing you will not help me find my sister. I've already blown away one perfectly good gentleman to make a point."

The color leached from Salaberry's face—apparently he hadn't known about the old duel.

"Seemed a waste as soon as I'd done it," Christian continued, "and you've got more life ahead of you than he had."

"Y-you are backing down from the fight."

Noble English gentlemen didn't do that. Well, hell, he wasn't a noble gentleman. "If you insist, I'll kill you, but it's going to be a waste of my time. Once my sister is home safely, I'll happily shoot you for what you did to her. You're of more use to me alive at the moment."

"In what bloody way am I of use to you?"

"I've learned two other women went missing from here. Two of Brougham's lightskirts."

"I don't know what happened to them."

But Salaberry had admitted he knew exactly who Christian meant. "Were they ever your partners?"

"Of course. I've had every woman here."

"Their names?"

"No idea."

"Were you ever rough with them? Did you break a bone or leave a bruise?"

"My ropes left bruises all the time, but I always take care with my partners. I took special care with your *sister*."

Christian's fist broke free of his control and slammed into the marquis's gut. Salaberry doubled over and sank to his knees. It didn't ease his anger much but it had probably saved Salaberry's life. "Who else did Delphina—?"

Suddenly at a loss, Christian stopped. *What would be the word for it, when it involved your sister?*

Salaberry sputtered. "Treyworth . . . kept her on a tight leash. Pelcham—he and Treyworth swapped sometimes . . . some of the male prostitutes."

Christain ripped at the knot of his cravat. He understood Lady Sherringham's panic. It was hell to hear this and to look at this man and know he'd had Del. "What about the courtesans?"

Salaberry struggled to his feet. "Bedded every gentleman . . . and most of the women."

"What about protectors?"

Salaberry sneered, despite the fact he couldn't straighten up. "One of them was the special pet of Lord Sherringham, before she worked for the club. You think

I'm a sadist? I saw the results of his method of saying good-bye. He broke her nose with his fist."

"I was at Lady Dartmore's—" Jane began.

"You blush when you lie," her aunt broke in. "You were searching for your friend again tonight, weren't you?"

The drawing room fire crackled. Regina peered at her with a shrewd gaze. The intelligence behind that gaze had helped her aunt's late husband, banker Sir Richard Gardiner, rise to great wealth and stature. That had been seen as little better than *trade* in the eyes of Jane's mother, but Aunt Regina was the only member of Jane's family with whom she'd ever felt any kinship. She even preferred to be called informally "Aunt Regina" as opposed to "Aunt Gardiner." And she had been the only one to offer help when Jane had been left widowed and almost penniless.

For that Jane owed her so much. But she certainly couldn't give the whole truth.

Aunt Regina settled on the chair across and took Jane's hands. She gave a gentle squeeze. "You must stop worrying, dear. This fear is playing havoc with your appearance. You were finally regaining your pretty curves, but now you are beginning to look gaunt and tired again."

What did her appearance matter? She'd give up her curves forever to have Del back.

"I'm quite certain," Regina continued, "that Lady Treyworth is safe and sound."

That pricked her guilt like a saber blade. "I am *not* certain of that."

Her aunt's eyes held soft comfort. "I know you cannot

understand why she would leave and not tell you, but I can think of two perfectly plausible explanations."

"There is *no* plausible reason why she wouldn't have written to me."

"Listen to me, Jane. Either she has not written to you so that you would not be in the awkward position of keeping the secret from her husband, or she has gone off with a man."

"Del would not put herself in the power of another man. Del would have turned to *me*."

"Jane, you must think. Why would Lord Treyworth hurt his wife? Married life doesn't shackle him in any way. He can have all the freedom he wants."

"Then why did he ever hit her?" Jane cried. "Why is it acceptable that a husband will brutalize a defenseless wife?"

"Oh, dearest," said her aunt, her voice filled with sympathy. "You deserve to know happiness in marriage. You are only six-and-twenty. I had forty very wonderful years with my Richard. Jane, you must believe it is possible. I've seen you hold my Eleanore's little girl on your lap, and I've seen that wistful look in your eyes—"

"Aunt Regina, please." Tonight, she could not bear to listen to this usual refrain. "Del was frightened enough of Treyworth to write to her brother and ask for help."

"And how do you know that?"

"I—" She felt the heat of a telltale blush. "I encountered him tonight."

"Lord Wickham came back for his sister? I am surprised to hear that is the reason for his return. He'd washed his hands of his family. Anyone who has encountered him in the years since he left England paints him as the most coldhearted, incorrigible libertine who ever prowled from bed to bed. When he left this country, he reputedly vowed to heap as much scandal on his family name as he could. And given his behavior, he has certainly tried."

"What behavior exactly?" Jane knew mainly about his youth—from the three years she'd known him, from Del's stories about his very young years, and from his reputation.

But she remembered those parting words at the theater. *Did you truly keep Lady Beckworth tied up in your private dungeon?*

Regina's lined lips pursed. "Lord Wickham has destroyed countless marriages. He has seduced the wives of men who were reputedly his friends. He gambled fiercely with all the young bucks who went over to India for adventure, and he stripped most of them of their fortunes. It's said that when he ruined the young heir to the Earl of Langely in a game of cards, and the desperate boy asked for a pistol to end his life, Lord Wickham calmly handed over his."

"Good heavens. Did the young man shoot himself?"

"Well, no. But Lord Wickham could not have known for certain that the young man would back down."

Jane surged to her feet and paced. She'd thought it unforgivable that he left Del to the mercy of her family. He had been a wild, irrepressible rakehell. He had dueled over one married lady and killed the woman's husband—Lord Harrington.

That had been the reason he'd had to leave England. To avoid a trial.

But in her soul, she could not believe Wickham would have handed over the weapon if he'd thought the lad would use it.

Not after tonight. In the club, all he had done was try to protect her. She saw that now. Now that she was home, and safe, and she could think.

Even when he'd been angry with her, when she'd feared he'd want to punish her, he had actually protected her from Petersborough.

Regina suddenly looked stricken. She stamped her cane on the floor. "Jane, I want you to fall in love, but don't do so with Wickham. He's been known as Lord Wicked ever since the title fell into his hands. A nickname like that, on a man who was known to be an unmitigated rakehell in his youth, is a warning that you should heed. He would surely break your heart. He brought harem girls home with him to England."

"Harem girls?" she repeated, not certain she had heard Regina correctly.

"To return to their families, it is said. But they live with him, unchaperoned, in his house. He flaunts rules and conventions. He is not a cruel man, but he's known as a careless one. What you must do, Jane, is find a mild, generous, loving gentleman who will make you happy."

How could she? She hadn't escaped her memories. What if this mythical loving, generous man touched her on their wedding night and she could only think of Sherringham? Would she lie there, as tense as a board, waiting for loving caress to turn into brutal assault?

Aunt Regina meant well. But when the first handful of dirt had hit Sherringham's coffin, Jane had vowed never to put herself in a man's power once more. She'd had only one item of value—a small strand of her mother's pearls, which her mother must have hidden from her father's creditors, just as Jane hid them from Sherringham's. Using

Regina's knowledge of investments, she'd sold those pearls and leveraged the proceeds into a tiny nest egg.

When she found Del, she could buy them the freedom they'd both dreamed of.

Guiltily, Jane met Aunt Regina's gaze. Her aunt, who firmly believed in love, would be terribly disappointed. "What I must do is find Del and ensure she is safe. That is *all* I want."

Christian drew a lock pick from the sleeves of his coat.

The club was now closed, empty excerpt for servants and the madam. Mrs. Brougham had locks on almost every door. With heavy bolts on all the outside doors, he'd had to pry open a window, then play cat and mouse with the footmen guarding the house.

He eased the pick in and moved it gently, and the lock sprang open. Beyond the gilt-encrusted door, a long corridor led into gloom.

Earlier tonight, he'd been brought up here for his audience with Mrs. Brougham. Through a door in the madam's office, he'd glimpsed her ornate dressing room. The madam slept on the premises.

This would prove interesting, Christian thought, as he silently prowled down the hall.

So far his search had given him nothing. He'd scoured the bedrooms, the attic, the dungeons. Found all the obligatory things like manacles, whips, a few medieval torture devices. All things he'd used in his erotic play in the past. Things that Del should know nothing about.

He could barely focus. He kept picturing his sister here. Del looking just as fearful as Lady Sherringham.

Now he understood why Lady Sherringham had been

so terrified by his kiss. Why instead of being calmed by his gentle caresses in the theater, she had gone as rigid as a plank. And Treyworth had been, according to Lady Sherringham, as brutal with Del.

You have been everywhere but in England, where you could have helped your sister. He'd left the country to protect Del. He'd thought she would be protected from the stench of wickedness that his father claimed surrounded him. The first letter of Del's to reach him in India had told him of their mother's accidental death. He'd known he'd been responsible for that. The next letter had announced her marriage. *I want to do this,* she had written. *I am not in love, but I am happy. What I do is for the best.*

He'd clung to that word. Happy. Had she known the truth about him? He doubted it. He doubted either their father or mother had ever revealed to Del that her elder brother was actually a bastard. Living and breathing evidence of their mother's sin.

And he'd prayed that, if he left, his father would finally push aside his bitterness and begin to open his heart to Del. But he hadn't.

India had taught Christian about karma and about acceptance of fate, but it was in India he'd learned to fight his. He would fight for Del—down to the last drop of blood in his body.

He padded down the corridor, keeping his steps light.

But as he reached Mrs. Brougham's private rooms, the door was wrenched open. Beneath hennaed hair tousled from sleep, the madam glared at him.

She leveled a pistol at his heart.

Chapter Six

$\mathcal{M}$RS. BROUGHAM POURED BRANDY IN A snifter and held it over a candle. A silk robe was belted loosely around her waist. The strand of diamonds about her neck winked in the light. She handed Christian the warmed liquor, then settled into a chair opposite him.

He was amazed she would put down her pistol and give a drink to a housebreaker.

"Lord Wickham. I am surprised you would attempt to enter my home in such a clumsy manner." She leaned back, smiled, and let her wrapper slide lower on her shoulder, revealing a stretch of smooth ivory skin, the swell of a large breast. "What do you want, my lord? I suspect if you wanted to bed me, you would have done so earlier tonight."

Clumsy, true, because he couldn't focus. "I want the truth about my sister. I know she was a member here, and she's been missing from town for two weeks."

"I told you before I have no idea where she would be."

"Tell me who she encountered here, then. What she did, what her husband asked her to do."

The madam tilted her head, considering, making him wait. He'd expected this, but his impatience ratcheted up. As though to irritate him, she slowly unthreaded the belt at her waist. The wrapper fell slightly open. She toyed with the belt, looping it around her wrists. His hand tightened so hard on the brandy snifter he broke the delicate stem with a light *snap*.

If she heard, she didn't show it. "You know I cannot betray the confidences of my patrons," she purred. "Lord Treyworth would be very angry with me if I were to be indiscreet about his wife."

This banter was going to get him nowhere. He erupted out of his chair. "She may be in danger. Do you trust me not to wrap that belt around your neck and punish you for your loyalty to the wrong gentleman?"

Her eyes widened. He strolled to her, his boots sinking into her carpet. The rugs and the silk that draped the wall soaked up sound, but would not mask a truly desperate scream. A bell pull dangled within the reach of her hand. Would she call for a servant?

Christian hated acting the cruel brute. He'd watched his father do this to his mother—berate her, beat her down with his anger and accusations.

The madam's breasts rose with her breath and she flicked her tongue over her lips. He couldn't believe it. This woman was aroused—excited by the prospect of real fear.

"There is blood on my hands over women I cared much less about than I do my sister."

Her breath punctuated the stillness of the room. "I assure you, your sister came to no harm here, my lord. You do not understand the kind of club I run, which proves how remarkable and unique it is."

She titled her neck a fraction and the necklace moved. He saw it then. A fine scar across her throat. At some point, a blade had sliced into her neck. The cut had not been deep, but a wound like that would drive hard into a woman's soul.

He flicked the necklace higher along the pale column of her neck and deliberately traced his finger around the puckered scar.

"Do not touch me like that." She tossed her head like a tempestuous mare and he withdrew his hand.

"I did not mean it as a threat. You've climbed from great depths, Mrs. Brougham."

"Sapphire." Her blue eyes glittered. "You may call me Sapphire."

He doubted that was her real name. Her accents were refined, but a trace of London slum slipped in. "Are you going to tell me about my sister, Sapphire?"

She nodded. "Yes, but first you must understand this place. I have built the most talked-about club in England, because I understood that even gently bred women have fantasies of sexual domination. It allows them to escape their inner shame, to experience true passion with their husbands. So many women endure a husband's attentions and so very few acknowledge their own desires."

"So ladies are whipped for their own good. Ladies like my sister."

"Do not underestimate Lady Treyworth, simply because you have memories of her as a blushing innocent with her hair in braids. I know from your reputation that you enjoy such games, my lord Wicked. Why should your sister not also?"

It was like a knife to his heart. Naturally Del would have womanly desires. But he couldn't picture her doing things like...hell, the things he'd done with women. Had eight years in the control of an abusive libertine completely changed his sister?

No. In the letter Del had sent him, she'd revealed she was deeply unhappy and terribly afraid. This woman was using Del to manipulate him. "I want the names of my sister's lovers."

"Will you be discreet?"

"Of course," he snapped, with such venom the woman leapt back.

In a lower voice, letting his gaze rest on the scar, he added, "And you'll be hale and healthy, love." He'd never threatened a woman before in his life. But this woman was ruthless, and gentlemanly behavior counted for nothing against Del's safety.

Sapphire Brougham walked seductively to her desk. She drew out a sheet of paper.

As she scrawled out a list, he wondered—would she be honest or leave off some names?

She handed it over. He stared down at four names. And swallowed the rest of his brandy.

Jane set down her coffee and picked up Wickham's letter. She was alone—Aunt Regina had not yet risen, and she had the chance to read here, in the dining room, without being questioned.

Wickham's handwriting sprawled across the page.

For your protection, he had written, *I sought out Mrs. Small and gave my address instead. I made a search of the club last night. Mrs. Brougham caught me as I was about to break into her office—and held me at pistol point.*

I was able to talk my way out of disaster. The madam denies all knowledge of Del's disappearance, of course, but gave me a list of Del's lovers. From now on, you will leave this to me. You will not return to the club. You will not ask questions of the gentlemen you saw there.

As a side note, I learned that the cook expects to receive a lodging house. I will take the liberty of making good on your promise, crusading Lady Jane.

Jane put the page down beside her plate.

It was exactly the imperious sort of letter she would have expected from the man who had hauled her out of the theater and who had threatened to keep her captive. And the most startling one from the first gentleman in her life who had sought to protect her.

She could not understand Wickham. He had left England eight years ago and had not written. Yet he had come back to rescue Del and was willing to acquire a lodging house for a complete stranger because she had made an impetuous promise of information.

"Who is on that list?" she whispered aloud. How she wished she could see it. But she knew it would be painful to do so.

Could Del have loved Petersborough? Could demure, sweet Del really have loved any one of those sordid men?

Jane knew she could not leave this in Wickham's hands. How could she turn over Del's safety to a man she did not understand?

But she did not have to go back to the club and confront dangerous men. She could investigate in her world—the world of balls, routs, and the afternoon stroll in Hyde Park.

She would question the wives.

To begin, Jane knew exactly where to find Charlotte. For the last year, Charlotte had been obsessed with shopping. Each day she bought something new—gowns, jewels, carriages—and nothing she purchased engaged her interest for more than a few days.

As Jane pushed open the door of Mme. Laurier's salon, a bell tinkled softly. An assistant left a matron and her daughters and hurried forward.

"I must speak with Lady Dartmore," Jane announced.

From behind a curtain came a cry, followed by an accented feminine voice chastising, "My lady, if you move so suddenly I will stick you with a pin. You must stay still unless you wish a poke in your bosom."

"Oh, put your wretched pins down."

The fitting room curtain flew back to reveal Charlotte standing in a swath of ice blue silk. She clutched the unfinished bodice to her breasts. "Jane, what are you doing here?" Her blond curls danced around her face, but dark shadows rimmed her eyes and her normally rosy complexion was stark white.

Jane turned abruptly to the modiste. "I require a moment with Lady Dartmore."

The Frenchwoman's lips tightened around pins. She obviously did not like receiving orders in her own domain. She looked like the sort who enjoyed ordering quivering English ladies about.

But Jane grasped Charlotte's elbow and pushed her back into the fitting room. She drew the curtain shut with a fierce sweep of her hand. "Charlotte, you must tell me everything you know about the club. I discovered last night that two other women have gone missing."

"M-missing?" In the midst of reaching for tea from a silver tray, Charlotte knocked over the cup with shaking fingers. "That's impossible. No ladies have gone missing that I know of. The club is all fantasy, Jane. No one is ever really hurt."

"Whippings do not hurt? Two years ago, you warned me not to let my husband take me to the club. You told me feign illness rather than go, yet now you champion it. Is it because you are afraid to tell the truth?"

But Charlotte turned to the mirror, presenting her back. "I saw you at the club last night. I knew it was you—I recognized that dress and I caught a glimpse of your hair under the veil. You were with Lord Wicked, were you not?"

The nickname, which Jane herself had used on him, now made her flinch. "How did you know him when he has been away from England for so long?"

"He came to see me two days ago."

Wickham had not told her that. "What did you tell him?"

"That Del's husband believes she has left him." Charlotte spun around. Her cornflower blue eyes were large and imploring. "You are trying to help Wicked, but think, Jane! What if he *finds* Del? What would he be obliged to do? He will return her to her husband."

"He won't."

"Years ago, he left Del at the mercy of her father, knowing exactly what sort of tyrant that man was."

Jane stared at Charlotte. She had assumed Wickham's anger proved he felt exactly as she did. That he understood

Del would never go back to Treyworth. *I snapped his sword in two*, he had said. "It does not matter what Wickham wishes to do. I won't allow it."

"How could you stop them—Treyworth or Wickham? How can *you* fight them, Jane?"

How could she? Charlotte was reminding her of all the times she'd threatened to run away from Sherringham, but couldn't find the strength to do it. After all, she'd panicked last night.

"Perhaps I have finally learned that we women must try."

"I don't need to be rescued, Jane. There is nothing to save me from." But fear showed plain in Charlotte's eyes.

"Would you tell me who Del's lovers were, at the club?"

"I—I don't know." Charlotte hugged herself. "But I am sure Del is safe and happy. Why can you not believe that? I think you cannot accept that Del might be in love, that she found the happiness with a man that you can't."

Jane gaped at her friend.

Her face drawn and pale, Charlotte waved toward the curtain. "Go, Jane."

Oh, no. An insult was not going to frighten her away. "What about Dartmore?" A flush prickled Jane's cheeks. "Did he ever . . . bed Del?"

Charlotte did not answer, but the tremble of her lower lip, the dip of her brows told the truth.

"So he did."

A tear leaked down Charlotte's cheek. "No. He wanted to, but he didn't. Is that what you wanted to hear? That my husband yearned to make love to my best friend, even after he knew I was carrying his child?"

His child? Jane's gaze slide down to Charlotte's stomach, where her friend's hand cradled the silk gathered there. She could not believe Charlotte had not told her. And the news had been thrown out in anger—news that the three of them would have once shared with joy.

"I did not hate Del over it," Charlotte whispered. "It was not her fault. But I...I couldn't speak to her anymore. And Dartmore did not hurt Del. I know he did not." She flushed. "In truth, I...I enjoyed the club at first. It *was* like a fantasy to me. I pretended I had been stolen away for a harem and Dartmore was my master. I imagined that to survive as an odalisque, I must seduce him by making love in all the scandalous and exotic ways he demanded of me—" She broke off. "You look at me as though I've lost my mind. Dartmore was so excited by the things I did at the club, he treated me like a goddess—"

"As he did when you were first married," Jane observed sadly. Charlotte had been deeply in love with Dartmore, who had been dashing and charming despite silver hair and a rugged, well-weathered face. She'd always loved him hopelessly and painfully. Yet he had wanted Del...

And Charlotte had a reason to want Del gone. The traitorous thought leapt into Jane's head.

Charlotte was staring at her. Suddenly, she stalked to the fitting room curtain. "Madame," she called, "I am ready now."

"Charlotte, please." Jane was not entirely sure what to say. "I know you wanted a child so much. I am happy for—"

"No. You are not. You think I'd betray Del. I can see in your eyes that you don't trust me anymore. That you don't even like me." Charlotte yanked the curtain open. "I've lost both Del and you. Please, Jane, just leave me alone."

*　　*　　*

Christian found Treyworth at White's, reading in the lounge. Despite his years away, Christian was welcomed within the quiet corridors. His father had hated him for being another man's bastard, but he had swallowed bile and sponsored his son in England's venerable clubs.

Del's husband—his brother-in-law—sat in a club chair, newspaper open, a cup of coffee at his hand. The balding earl wore a tight coat of dark green over a striped waistcoat and neatly pressed trousers. An elaborate knot decorated his pristine cravat. He looked a bloody dandy.

With his wife missing.

Christian stared down at the beefy hands that had hurt Del. *I know he beats her*, Lady Sherringham had cried, *but he does it in ways that do not leave marks.*

When he left bruises on Treyworth—and he would—they would be seen.

Crossing his arms over his chest, Christian loomed over Treyworth. "I got your note."

The paper lowered with a sharp crackle. The face that met his was twisted with loathing. "You accused me of hurting my wife," Treyworth snapped. "When I know Delphina is alive and in the arms of another man."

"I don't know that. And there are other women missing from the club."

"What in blazes are you talking about? I know nothing about missing lightskirts. So you had better damn well call off your assassins, Wickham, before I shoot you."

His question about the missing women had startled Treyworth. This claim floored Christian. "Assassins?"

"A footpad attacked me last night as I was arriving at my home. Set upon me outside my front gate, the cocky bastard, and pointed a bloody pistol at my head."

"And obviously didn't fire."

Treyworth looked like a cobra preparing to spit. "Coachman ran him off. Almost put a ball through him. Did you send the footpad?"

Christian stared into the pale gray eyes. Treyworth had not asked him who the other women were but he had known they were courtesans, even though Brougham's club catered also to ladies. But if someone had tried to kill the brute, did that prove there was another man involved with Del? "If I shot you," he said, "you'd know it was me. Now, tell me exactly what happened."

She was here.

Christian gave gentle pressure of his thighs to Homer's flanks and the gelding obeyed, sidling around to give him a better view. Hooves clopped on the sand track of the Row, sending up a soft cloud of dust.

Roses of a dusky pink adorned a wide-brimmed bonnet, shading the oval face beneath it, but heat and awareness swept over his skin as he took in the curve of an ivory cheek, the vivid red curls, the glimpse of generous pink lips.

Lady Sherringham had decided to stroll in Hyde Park. And she was walking with Lady Coyne and the Duchess of Fellingham, wives who had been in the theater.

Just as last night, when he'd dragged Lady Sherringham into his arms and kissed her, his body responded physically. And against his will, it was happening again, forcing him to shift on the saddle of his horse.

Deep in the night, he'd even dreamed of her in her bath. She had told him she was going to cleanse herself in hot water and he'd envisioned it in his sleep. In his mind's eye he'd seen fiery red hair tied up in a topknot, tendrils curling along her ivory neck in the steam. Then smooth shoulders, and a mouthwatering swell of bosom teasingly hidden by the curve of her arm—

Christian shook his head. What in blazes was wrong with him? He was behaving exactly like the kind of wicked, incorrigible scoundrel his father had always accused him of being.

Del was all he should be thinking of. Not naked, bathing women.

He had to rein in Homer as three parasols twirled below him. Three ladies, along with their gentlemen companions, stepped in front of him and tried to impress with giggling charm.

He glanced back to Lady Sherringham but all he could see was the hat of dyed straw and the trailing ribbons that danced in the breeze. The Duchess of Fellingham gave a naughty smile in response to something she said.

He wanted to get to Lady Sherringham's side. To find out what she was asking the women.

"Wickham," a male voice hailed from behind him. "I hear you've established a harem of luscious Indian girls in your house."

The ladies all gasped—and Christian tore his gaze from Lady Sherringham.

Shocked glances made the rounds of every member of the ton within hearing. Matrons dragged their daughters away. Men threw him envious glances.

Bloody hell. "Hardly a harem, Axley." He glared down. "They are young ladies of English families who had been orphaned in the Far East, and who faced grave dangers. I brought them home to return them to a safe society."

"But they are living alone with you in your house!"

This exclamation of horror came from a matron, but he couldn't be certain which one.

Axley pressed onward. "I heard they'd served sultans as concubines."

Christian thought of the girls living in his care. Girls who had been kept prisoner, and then, when they'd escaped, had learned their families would not take them back.

"That's a lie," he snarled at Axley, though it wasn't. He'd refused to duel with Salaberry but his pent-up anger made him hunger to fight now. "Shall we say pistols at dawn?"

Axley paled. "D-dueling has become criminal."

Another man—some upright prig from Parliament, with auburn hair—leaned close, a horrified look on his face. One tempered by a glint of lasciviousness. "The girls must be lewd and wild, Wickham. There's no place for them here."

Bloody condemning society. Christian tightened his grip on his reins. "No matter what they had to do to survive, they are respectable English girls. Circumstance left them alone, without family, with no one to protect them."

But he saw no awakening of sympathy in the eyes of the privileged people surrounding him. Ruined, in their eyes, was ruined. No one could empathize with terrified young girls.

Ignoring good manners, Christian cantered away from the crowd, forcing gentlemen to jump out of his way. He was accustomed to the packed streets of Calcutta and Bombay, and he did not run down any members of the blasted ton as he guided Homer toward crusading Lady Sherringham.

A military man was conversing with her now—an

aging gentleman with a barrel chest, a glass eye, and a booming voice. With a start, Wickham recognized the man. And heard his name on her lips. "Lord Wickham," she said. "He has also recently returned from India."

"Indeed. He is over there, on the black gelding, my lady. Quite the madman."

Madman. It didn't surprise him Major Arbuthnot would use that word, but it surprised him that Lady Sherringham had been asking questions about him. Why? Curiosity? Suspicion? *Fascination,* whispered a voice deep inside.

Christian stared at Lady Sherringham for so long, she jerked her head up and looked at him. And unlike the women he'd known in his past who had been fascinated by him, her ladyship did not soften when she looked at him. She stiffened.

He saw exactly what she thought of him in the prim line of her mouth. She despised him. Just as she had done in the past. If it was because he'd forbidden her from investigating, it was the price he had to pay to keep her safe.

A chill slithered down Jane's spine. She jerked her gaze from Wickham to Arbuthnot. "What do you mean by the term *madman,* Major?"

"Daring would be the polite term, my lady," the major said. "Proved himself admirable in skirmishes and battles. But in the spring, when flooding comes to parts of India and the villages are rife with disease, Wickham went in to the most wretched areas to bring children out. Saved their lives no doubt. But risked getting sick himself. Risked his own death."

A picture came to Jane's head—of the poverty she had seen in London's East End when she did charity work, but in an exotic world she knew nothing about. And she saw Wickham in the midst of it, with a child cradled in his arms.

She forced out words through a tight throat. "Shouldn't *noble* be the term to use?"

"Not so noble in his dealings with ladies, I'm afraid—notorious would be more the word. And what I saw in Lord Wickham was a young gentleman who was seeking his own demise."

"That can't be," she protested. "By rescuing others?"

"His lordship didn't care if he caught sickness and died. During a flood, I almost lost three soldiers. The river we were crossing had swollen to a torrent in moments. Wickham was with me—he served the East India Company between the Marathas campaigns. Single-handedly, he rescued two of my men from the raging waters, then disappeared in the river himself. Fought his way to shore a mile downstream."

"He is a hero," Jane said. "Not a madman."

And the hero was coming closer.

Umbrellas tipped back as young ladies gazed up at Lord Wickham. He doffed his tall beaver hat absently, and even from so far away, Jane saw cheeks flush and ladies sparkle. But he was making his way to her, ignoring the debutantes. His dark blue eyes were riveted on her.

He must guess what she was doing. He must be angry.

She would not give in to panic again. Wickham had the list of Del's lovers. She had to get that list.

"Jane, I must introduce you to Mr. Flanders." Aunt Regina bustled to her side and bestowed a brilliant smile upon Arbuthnot. Faced with a matchmaking relative, the major beat a retreat.

Jane groaned, watching Wickham's approach. Mr. Flanders would be of no use to her—unless he'd been at the club, and she was certain the pale, mild-mannered man had not. "I don't wish to meet gentlemen. We have this conversation each time we come here. I'm virtually penniless and my husband died scandalously." And she must make Aunt Regina leave so she could speak to Wickham alone.

He held the reins tight in one hand as he guided his steed through the crowd. He did not stop watching her. *Don't quail. Don't back down.* She was in public. Surrounded and safe. She had every right to speak to women of her acquaintance.

Dimly she realized Aunt Regina was still talking. "You were the innocent party, and that scandal should not touch you now. Also, I see no reason why gentlemen should not be made aware that you have expectations—"

"I don't."

"You are my companion and niece. Of course you do."

"You have two daughters and two granddaughters. Do not dangle an imaginary inheritance as bait." *Please don't*, she added silently. *Don't try so hard to give me the marriage I don't want and can't have.*

Then Wickham was there. In front of her. Dismounting his horse with a lazy swing of his long leg. The drop to the ground did not even shake his tall beaver hat. He bowed to Aunt Regina and kissed her hand. With an uneven voice, Jane made the introductions.

"Lord Wickham, what a pleasure to see you here." Despite her disapproval, Aunt Regina sounded rather breathless.

Jane let him draw her fingers to his lips. Yesterday, she had snatched her hand away. Today, his mouth lightly grazed her fingers, barely touching her.

Suddenly, she realized he was backing her away from the crowd, Aunt Regina, and quite possibly a lurking Mr. Flanders. "I know what you are doing, you impossible woman," he muttered.

"I—I am speaking to women I know. That is what I am doing."

"Walk with me, Lady Sherringham."

It was a command, not a request, spoken in a rough growl that warned she should not refuse. Jane heard a squawk of protest from her aunt, but she said, "I would be delighted, Wickham."

She agreed, not because of fear, but because she had to talk to him. She used to back down from her angry husband. She was determined not to run away from Wickham again.

He offered his arm. Beneath his tailored coat, his arm was hard, the muscles bunched and tight.

"The list you mentioned in your letter," she said. "Who is on it?"

He caught her chin, making her gasp, and he forced her face up so she had to look at him. "Why in blazes won't you leave this to me, Lady Sherringham?"

"If I tell you, will you stop trying to keep me out of it?"

The dark brows rose in surprise. "Tell me first."

She should argue—she knew once she told him, he would not make any bargains. "All right. I was the lucky one of the three of us—myself and Del and Charlotte. I was given freedom from my husband. It didn't require any fortitude or any plan. Sherringham died in his mistress's bed when the woman's house burned to the ground."

He stopped, forcing strolling couples to flow around them. "You can't feel guilty because you're free, Jane Beaumont."

"Why not? I can't feel happy. Not until my friends are also free."

His magnetic blue eyes held her. "I want you to be *safe*."

"That has been all I've ever wanted," she said, hearing bitterness in her voice. "I cannot imagine what it would feel like." How could she, after a life with a rakish father who had gambled away his money and turned her mother into a brokenhearted madwoman? After eight years with a husband who made her flinch just by lifting his hand?

Could Wickham really believe that if he made her stay at home, she would feel safe?

"I am not searching for Del only because of *guilt*." She saw him wince. "I may not have much experience with gentlemen, but I have never known one to care enough about any woman—wife, daughter, or sister—to risk everything for her."

"You know one now."

Over his shoulder Jane spied a gleaming burgundy curricle, and a woman in a sky blue pelisse at the reins. "Lady Petersborough is approaching. I intend to speak to her."

He looped his horse's reins around the frame of a bench to secure the beautiful animal, "And I intend to stop you."

"Then try. I'm not afraid of you," she lied. "I've already spoken to Lady Coyne and Her Grace, the Duchess of Fellingham. Both were quite happy to discuss the club."

"Couldn't you have been more damned careful? Or do ladies normally discuss brothels in Hyde Park at the height of the fashionable hour?"

"You would be surprised," Lady Sherringham muttered. And Christian heard the sarcasm dripping from her words. That tone reminded him of the woman he'd known in the past.

He gripped Homer's tied reins, and rubbed the heel of his hand to his temple. "Tell me exactly what you asked—" he began, but the curricle drew up alongside them. George Fortescue, second son of a duke, sat at Lady Petersborough's side. Her thigh was pressed tight to Fortescue's leg. His hand could not be seen and Christian imagined his fingers were trapped beneath her ladyship's generous arse.

Lady Petersborough immediately turned to him. "Lord Wickham, how fares your sister? Is it true that she has gone to France? My husband is quite dejected."

Why would she ask about Del at once? Was she also searching for answers or testing how much he knew? Watching her closely, Christian answered, "No, Lady Petersborough. I do not believe my sister is on the Continent."

Her gaze shifted quickly to touch on Jane, then returned to him. "How could I have been so poorly informed? Pray tell me, do you know where she is?"

"I do not. She did not write to me to tell me where she intended to go. My sister seems to have disappeared without a trace."

Lady Sherringham took a step forward and before he could draw her back, she said earnestly, "But she must have shared her plans with you. I thought you and Delphina were such friends at the—the club."

He had to admit that Lady Sherrigham had recognized how to get Lady P.'s goat. "We were not. We merely shared my husband." At her side, Fortescue had the grace to flush red.

"Oh. But perhaps you remember when you last saw her there?" Lady Sherringham asked, and her cheeks were so pink, her freckles had disappeared.

Christian gritted his teeth. He would let her continue asking questions. For a while.

"A fortnight ago…yes, that was it," Lady P. answered. "I was with my husband for the entire night. I believe Treyworth had reserved one of Mrs. Brougham's men for the night's entertainment."

Lady Sherringham's jaw almost dropped to the gravel drive.

"Rory Douglas?" Christian asked. That name had been on Brougham's list, and he had already found the male prostitute's lodgings. The young man had remembered Del only as one of the many luscious married ladies he serviced at the club. As with the other men named on the list, Douglas had denied knowing where Del was.

Lady P. nodded. She abruptly turned to Lady Sherringham, with a sly, dangerous smile. "So I was correct, my dear. I did think that was you, in your black, at Mrs. Brougham's club."

"Yes."

"How delightful she allowed you entrance without a husband. If I were widowed, my dear, I should go there, too. Perhaps I shall see you there again."

With that and a flick of her whip, Lady P. moved her carriage onward.

Christian turned to Lady Sherringham. "Why, after wearing a veil and using a false name, have you given yourself away to all these women?"

He saw her swallow hard. "Because Del is worth the risk. My aunt may toss me out on the street if I cause a scandal, but I have to do whatever I can to find Del."

"Or you could leave it to me."

She ignored that. "Lady Petersborough does have a very good reason to have wanted to—to do Del harm."

"She can't be that jealous—she was groping Fortesque. Most well-bred women don't care who their husbands take to bed, as long as they can have affairs of their own."

Her brow lifted and Christian felt like a simpleton under her glare. "Some women do. And *she* definitely does."

Obviously she felt he had no understanding of women. But he could hear bitterness again, and knew Lady Sherringham was revealing something personal. Had she cared who her brutal late husband had taken to bed?

Why was it every time he looked into her chocolate brown eyes, he wanted to understand her? He'd never felt this way about a woman before. Even with Del, he didn't want to understand what had happened to her—he just wanted to erase the pain of her past.

"I want you to stop this," he growled.

"You haven't even bothered to ask me if I learned anything of importance. I've spoken to Lady Dartmore, Lady Coyne, and the Duchess of Fellingham. Perhaps I already hold the key to the mystery. For example, Lady Coyne was expected to marry Treyworth, but then he changed his mind, it was rumored, when he saw Del. Lady Coyne was, surprisingly, very much in love with him."

"You think she's waited eight years to get revenge on Del for stealing Treyworth? She should have owed Del a debt of gratitude." He took off his hat, raked his hand through his hair. "Fine. You have acquired information. Share it with me."

"I will, if you give me that list of names. Of Del's... lovers."

He almost tore out his hair. "Absolutely not."

"Then I will continue to talk to the wives."

But he saw the rapid rise of her bosom. She was trying to bravely bargain and it scared her. Which gave him another tack to take. The one he'd used with Sapphire Brougham. "I obtained that list from Brougham in a way that I'm not very proud of," he warned.

Lady Sherringham tipped up her chin. "You seduced her."

"I bullied her. I can be a very dangerous man when I want to be. Arbuthnot described me as a madman, didn't he?"

Her hand went to her throat and her eyes went wide.

He hated having to do it this way. But he had tried to explain the dangers. He had tried a nice letter. And none of those tactics had worked to keep Lady Sherringham out of this.

She backed away. "There is Lady Pelcham. I must talk to—"

"Stay here," he barked.

But the obstinate woman darted away into the crush of people.

Before he could push his way through and catch her,

he heard her startled cry. Through a gap in the crowd, he saw her arms flail. Lady Sherringham stumbled forward, snagging her feet in her skirts. She'd been knocked over. Or pushed. Christian elbowed gentlemen out of the way, but she fell and smacked hard to the gravel path.

A frantic whinnying rent the air, along with a feminine scream and the clatter of wheels. Lady Sherringham lay on the ground, several feet away from him. Two gray horses bore down on her, hooves swallowing the earth as they thundered onward. A blue curricle hurtled behind.

The woman at the reins drew back in panic—a panic that sent the horses rearing above Lady Sherringham.

Christ.

He launched forward through the frozen crowd, throwing his body beneath the pawing hooves. His knees skidded along the gravel and he scooped her into his arms.

The horses came down and he felt a crushing pain on his lower leg before he leaped to the side. He slammed onto his back. Lady Sherringham landed on top of him. Her breasts pressed against his face. Her legs spread wide over him. He clamped her to him, not caring how inappropriate the position was, not caring if he was scaring her by gripping her so tightly.

Inside his Hessian boot, his right calf throbbed. But it wasn't the kind of pain that made a man want to cast up his accounts. He must have missed the worst of the hooves.

The scent of roses wafted up from between Lady Sherringham's breasts to tease his nose. He shifted so they were both sitting up—which meant she was straddling his thighs. Blood rushed to his groin, giving him an erection to celebrate their survival. Groaning, he asked, "Are you all right?"

A mad question. Bits of gravel stuck to her face and blood welled in small cuts.

"Yes. Someone knocked me forward. Th-thank you. You saved my life."

"Indeed I did." He said it slowly. He caught hold of her wrist. Suddenly, he couldn't let her go. Had the push and her fall been an accident? Or deliberate?

Out of the corner of his eye, he saw two tall gentlemen take hold of the horses' bridles. The young female driver—whom he didn't know—was sobbing as men rushed forward to help her down.

"Good heavens, Jane!"

Lady Sherringham twisted her wrist but could not work free. "You must let me get up. To go to my aunt."

Gently, he brushed gravel from her cheek. A droplet of blood smeared across her pale skin. His gut clenched—at the sight of her wounds, at the fear of what might have been. But how could the woman who had fled the club in a panic not be almost swooning now? "You should be terrified. And you are not."

"I am. I truly am."

She hadn't flinched from his touch to her face. She was letting him stroke her cheek. She had even leaned into his hand. Any other woman would have been a screaming wreck.

Lady Sherringham mystified him. But he admired her. A good portion of his blood was now below his waist and, before he could think, the question in his head had fallen out of his mouth. "How could your husband not have looked in your eyes and seen what a treasure he had?"

She drew back then, and her face went stark white. "That was the problem. Before he hit me, he claimed he did."

This time, when she wrenched her wrist in his grip, he let her go. Several men thrust their hands forward to help her to her feet.

Gallant gentlemen crowded around her while Christian struggled to stand. Pain shot up his leg, but he could put his weight on it. Ladies flooded around him, praising and cooing, and he couldn't fight his way through them to get to Lady Sherringham. The curricle's driver was being fanned by an older woman who kept beseeching. "Lady Amelia, please do not swoon."

Lady Sherringham's aunt rushed in. "Good heavens!" Lady Gardiner thanked him, then firmly led her niece away. He watched Lady Sherringham walk—checking for a limp, any sign she might be injured. She moved slowly, but at least she appeared unhurt.

Brushing off his trousers, Christian overhead Lady Gardiner exclaim, "Lord Wicked was looking at you as though he'd never seen a woman before."

"He had just saved my life!"

"Well, that does not give him the right to devour you whole."

Chapter Seven

CHRISTIAN PROWLED THE LANE THAT RAN behind Mrs. Brougham's club. He grimaced as pain twinged in his leg—it still ached from the accident in Hyde Park, but had proved to be only bruised. The leftover damp in the air from last night's rain didn't help. This morning was gray and here, in the mews, tall stone walls cast deep shadows. The earthy stench of horse dung, urine, and smoke wafted to his nose, reminding him that England's cities smelled much like India's.

Younger stepped out of the gloom and tipped his cap. "Milord."

Christian nodded to the former Bow Street Runner and private investigator he'd hired to head up his search for Del. Younger had spent the wet night watching the rear gate of the club. "See anything of interest?"

"Aye. A gent went in through the back an hour ago. Tough-looking bloke, but respectably dressed. He talked to a woman with hennaed hair and the crown jewels sitting around her neck."

"That would be Mrs. Brougham, the madam. Did you hear their conversation?"

Younger grimaced. "I'm sorry, milord. Had to sneak in through the gate to do it, so I only caught their parting words. The bloke was peeved she didn't have any custom for him as late."

"What sort of custom?"

"Couldn't say, milord. I didn't recognize him from my days as a thief taker. He could be bringing her girls. A trade in innocents would be possible for a place like this."

Christian scrubbed his jaw. Mrs. Brougham had claimed her place was no sordid brothel, but an elegant club. But he sensed she was ruthless. And he knew the ton's gentlemen were willing to pay a fortune for innocence.

The ex-Runner looked nervous at the stretch of silence. "They did not speak of Lady Treyworth, milord. And I had young Bridges with me, so I sent him to—" Younger broke off, then grinned with a spark of white teeth in the gloom. "Here he is now, milord."

Christian swung around as a lanky boy ran up the lane. The youth panted and flopped back against the stone wall. "Followed 'im to a cemetery, Mr. Younger," the boy gasped. "The bloke's name is Tanner and he's got a gang of a grave robbers."

Yesterday, he had saved her life.

Today, would he even come down to speak to her?

Jane paced the carpet in Wickham's drawing room. Large and gloomy, the room had not changed one whit since the stern, heartless old earl had ruled here. Any of the early afternoon light that dared to venture in was soaked up by the dark paneling, the heavy furnishings, and the somber greens and browns.

"His lordship will be down at once," the butler had promised.

But it seemed an eternity since the elderly servant had retreated. Jane stared blankly out a window, and rubbed her sore cheek gently—the scratches had faded but still stung. Crushed in her left hand were two letters that had arrived this morning.

Letters from Lords Dartmore and Salaberry.

Suddenly, scampering feet sounded outside the closed door. Tittering feminine laughter floated through the paneled wood.

Jane remembered Aunt Regina's warning that Wickham kept harem girls unchaperoned in his house. She had not quite believed that. But as impossible as it sounded, it appeared it could be true. Inexplicably, her heart plummeted to her toes. She cupped her hand to her ear, frozen in the middle of the room, and, in the most unladylike way, strained to hear.

Hurried breathing came softly through the door—the women who had been running had obviously stopped.

"I saw him in his bath!" The voice belonged to a *young* woman.

"Mary, you should not have looked," replied a second feminine voice, quiet but frantic. "I'm sure there would have been the devil to pay if he'd caught you."

"I rather wish he had." Mary sounded petulant. "I am going to seduce him."

"You must stop this," cried the second. "What if he becomes angry and sends us all away?"

A stomp of a foot. "But I want him so. It's so dreadfully painful, wanting him this way and not having him."

Not having him. Jane blinked. If that were the case, obviously this wasn't his harem.

She measured the distance to the door with her eye. She sorely wanted to race over, fling open the door, and see the girls. But she couldn't. In her youth, would she have done? Strangely, she realized she didn't know. She couldn't quite remember who she had been.

"Mary." The other girl's voice held a desperate note. "He's coming."

"You go, Lucinda. I see no reason to run from him."

"He has a guest waiting upon him in the parlor. It's hardly proper for you to intrude, and he wants us to behave like proper ladies."

Quick footfalls told Jane one or both girls had fled.

"Good day, Mary. Have you been painting today?"

So the girl named Mary had stayed, and the languorous drawl belonged to Wickham, of course. The hairs on the nape of Jane's neck recognized the rich, sensuous sound of his voice and rose like hounds greeting a beloved master.

Since yesterday afternoon, when he had saved her life, she had not stopped thinking about him. She could not forget his astonishing words, when she had been sprawled all over his strong, hard body. *How could your husband not have looked in your eyes and seen what a treasure he had?*

She'd thought he would be furious with her. Instead, he called her a *treasure*. But then, as she'd told Wickham, so had Sherringham before they were married. Before he'd raised his fist to her. And he'd always implied she could be a treasure again, if she just learned how to make him happy.

"I was not painting," Mary answered, "but I did spy the most inspiring subject I have ever seen." Saucy innuendo danced through the words.

"Did you indeed?" There was a wretched pause. What was he doing?

"I saw you reflected in my mirror." Wickham's voice was cool and dismissive. "Don't spy on me again."

"But I believe two souls can be fated to unite. We are such souls, meant to be intimate—"

"Mary, enough. I am eight years your senior."

"But your sister married a much older man, did she not? I want an experienced man who is patient in giving pleasure—"

"Stop, Mary." His voice dropped from dangerous growl to bitter rasp. "Go and practice the pianoforte. Go to the music room and do not move from there."

"But, my lord," Mary purred, "what if I must use the necessary?"

Jane let her breath out in a hiss. The girl was certainly brazen.

"Go. This instant." Wickham sounded frazzled. "Go!" The door was abruptly flung open and, raking his hand harshly through his hair, he stalked inside. "Women," he muttered. "Good Christ, what was I thinking to surround myself with women?"

Suddenly words spilled out—words she would have said to him eight years ago, in the days when he had goaded her and she had been determined to spear him back. "Perhaps you were not thinking with your head."

His blue eyes captured rays of sunlight and shot sparks at her, but at the sight of her, his lips astonishingly quirked up in a wry smile. "You are absolutely correct. I was thinking with another part of my anatomy entirely. One that does not impress you."

"Another part—?" she broke off. A flush ran up from toes to hairline.

"My heart, Lady Sherringham. I was referring to my heart. Now, why are you here? Did something happen to you?"

"No." She thrust out the letters. "I came to show you these."

"You shouldn't have come here alone."

She lifted a brow. "As you well know, I wasn't alone. The man you sent to watch my aunt's house was going to follow me, but I invited him into my carriage instead. It seemed pointless to make the man jog along the sidewalk."

"It was necessary, Lady Sherringham. I had to make sure you were safe."

Wickham took the letters from her. He wore no gloves and for the first time she saw his bare hands. Scars crisscrossed the bronzed backs of them, a testament to hard work and battle and a rougher life. She looked at his hands and remembered them saving her life.

She'd been utterly astonished when Regina's footman had informed her the mysterious man watching her aunt's house claimed to be in Lord Wickham's employ. She had not known what to think. Now she saw she should appreciate the gesture. "I did not thank you properly for saving my life, and I apologize for my aunt. She all but insulted you."

He shrugged and unfolded one of the letters. "I assumed you were grateful."

"You don't believe it was an accident, do you? That's why you sent a man to watch me."

Suddenly he grasped her shoulders, steered her backward, the letter clasped in one hand, and lowered her to a chair. She hadn't intended to sit down. She couldn't. She was too anxious to have him read the letters.

But he'd decided she should sit, so sit she must.

Wickham crouched in front of her, bringing his eyes on level with hers. Did he do it deliberately, so he was not towering over her? "What happened, love? Your aunt whisked you away so quickly, I didn't have the chance to ask."

Because she was more afraid of you than of my accident. But she couldn't say that. And she knew Wickham did not want to devour her. He'd always disliked her for her sharp tongue and her disapproval of his rakish ways. He felt sorry for her now. That was all.

"I truly have no idea what happened," she said. "I was trying to walk away from you when I was pushed from behind. I didn't see who it was. My attention wasn't on the crowd around us. It was fixed on—"

"On Lady Pelcham," he supplied.

On you. But she could not admit that. She was ashamed that she kept thinking of him when she should be focusing on Del.

Wickham shook his head. "So much happened so quickly, so many people rushed in to the rescue, I had no idea who was there to begin with. Salaberry was in the crowd before you fell. As was Lord Pelcham. Lady Petersborough, I saw, had left her curricle."

She swallowed hard at the mention of Salaberry. Had someone pushed her in front of a carriage to stop her from searching for Del? "I did not see Lord Petersborough. Or Treyworth."

Charlotte had also been there. As her aunt had led her to their carriage, Jane had seen Charlotte's golden curls and royal purple riding habit. "I am certain Lady Amelia Wentworth, the young woman driving the curricle, had no reason to want to deliberately run me down. She appeared absolutely horror-struck."

"I'm not taking any chances with you," Wickham said.

He looked as he had when she had told him that Del's husband beat her. As though in pain. She had never had a man look worried over her before. *Don't let it go to your heart.*

"And you will *not* be taking any more chances," he added.

"Read the letters," she said. "Please . . . just look at them."

His brows jerked up as he read the first. " '*Come to the club tonight, for I was entranced to see you there. Dartmore.*' "

"Charlotte's husband. You went to see Charlotte— Lady Dartmore—and didn't tell me. Charlotte told me her husband wanted Del, but never . . . had her. And Charlotte is pregnant."

For a moment, Wickham looked as stunned as she had felt this morning when she'd opened the letters. Mrs. Hodgkins had brought them, trilling happily about letters from *gentlemen*. Not knowing these were sinister letters from repugnant men.

"The other is from Salaberry," she said, as emotionlessly as she could. Her voice still quivered. "He threatens to discipline me."

"Hades." This one Wickham didn't read aloud. But Jane would never forget a word of it.

Naughty ladies who desert my performances must be disciplined. Meet me tonight, my exquisite novice. Come and play with me.

"Do you think Lady Petersborough or one of the other ladies told Salaberry I was there? Charlotte knew—she saw me. And she must have told her husband. I can't believe Charlotte would do such a thing to me. How could she not see the danger?"

Wickham groaned. "I think Salaberry recognized you all along. I confirmed it for him."

"What?"

He rubbed the back of his neck, ruffling his hair. "Salaberry told me your late husband had been the protector of one of the missing courtesans, and that he broke the woman's nose."

It took a while for his words to sink in. *Her late husband. A woman's broken nose.* She might be sickened, but was not surprised. She knew Sherringham had bribed his mistresses to take his punishment.

She looked up. Wickham was pouring brandy into a large snifter.

"My husband was the protector of a woman who vanished?"

"Before she began working at Brougham's club."

A sick feeling settled in Jane's stomach. By then her husband had moved on to a woman named Fleur des Jardins. Miss des Jardins had not been an actress—she was the ambitious madam of a country brothel. That poor woman had perished in the fire with Sherringham.

"But you didn't tell Salaberry I was with you?" she asked.

"Of course not. But I understood, at that moment, why you were so frightened by the club—" Wickham broke off, and walked toward her. He held out the drink and she took it. She could never dare finish that much liquor, but she clasped the brandy balloon and took a sip.

To her astonishment, he perched on the arm of her chair. He rested his derriere on it, beside her hand.

The brandy caught in her throat. She sputtered, eyes watering.

"If Salaberry suspected you were the lady behind the veil," he murmured, "I imagine he read every thought going through my head. Because I thought of you being hurt and I know my face showed what I felt. I'm sorry, love."

Deep lines crossed his forehead and ringed his seductive mouth. Oh, yes, she could see how she could lose her heart to this man, this gentleman who appeared to care about her. Aunt Regina's warnings did not seem so unnecessary now.

Jane took another drink, the brandy heating her insides. "I have to go back to the club, Wickham. First I had the accident, and now two men who were involved with Del are trying to lure me back. I came to you as I have nowhere else to go. Nowhere else to turn. I need you to take me back to the club."

Wickham stared down at her as if she were mad. He must be remembering her panic, how she had drawn the attention of the entire theater to them.

His silence was more unnerving than a refusal.

"If I was deliberately pushed in front of a carriage, I

am in danger. Del is in danger. You are the only person I can trust, Wickham." She had one more card. And since he wasn't saying a word, she had to play it. "If you won't take me, I will have to go alone to meet both men."

"Hades, you will not." Christian erupted off the arm of her chair, and he swung around to brace his hands there instead.

"I will," Lady Sherringham insisted. "I would have to—for Del."

The door burst open. "My lord," a small female voice implored. Christian groaned. Now was not the time.

But he turned. Philomena ran in, wiping at her cheeks. Blast. The girl had been crying. "Please do not have this lady take us away, my lord. We shall not cause any more trouble."

Below him, Lady Sherringham lifted up, her hands braced on the chair. She leaned around him to look. "Why, she is only a child."

Jerking his hands off the arms of the chair, he left her to go to Philomena.

He swept the slim girl up into his arms. Philly was not a child; she was fifteen, but she was small for her age, and seemed to weigh little more than Del had done at twelve. She wrapped her thin arms around his neck and hugged him tight. He patted her back. "No one is taking any of you away, Philly. Lady Sherringham is a family friend."

"So this is where you are." The new, and now frightened, housekeeper—the second since he'd returned to England—stood in the doorway. She curtsied. "My apologies, my lord." The woman bustled in, her arms outstretched. Philly hugged him tighter.

Christian set her back on her feet. "Run along. You've nothing to worry about. I promise."

Hope shone through the tears. "Thank you," Philly whispered. In the seraglio, her small hands had worked diligently at embroidery. She had given up hope of rescue and had not spoken a word for six months before he'd found her.

The housekeeper snatched Philly's hand, gave him a dozen effusive, desperate apologies, then dragged the poor girl away.

Lady Sherringham leapt up from her chair the minute the door closed. She'd left a hairpin behind in the cushioned back and one auburn curl had fallen, spiraling like a flame over her neck.

"My aunt told me that you brought the girls back to return them to their families," she cried. "Is that the truth?"

"Yes. They are English girls left orphaned in India and the Far East. Philomena is the youngest at fifteen; the eldest is twenty. They were bought and sold like jewels. Three lived in Turkish seraglios, one in an Indian purdah."

Her brows drew together. "And you rescued them? How?"

"Not easily. The harems were within palace walls, heavily guarded by eunuchs and armed men."

Her eyes flashed indignantly. He remembered that expression on her face during their every conversation. "Why not send them home?"

"I made a mistake, Lady Sherringham. I thought their families would welcome them back. I had my secretary locate the girls' relatives. We returned to a stack of refusals. The girls aren't innocents. They know how to please men, and women, because that ensured their survival."

He was challenging her—waiting to see if she would

tip up her nose in haughty displeasure or cringe in shock.

"The poor girls!"

She sympathized with them. He was stunned. No one else did. "You don't blame them for their fall? Most gentlewomen do."

Her eyes blazed brighter. "Their fall is not their fault. Any woman who can't see that deserves to ... to have nothing but bread and water for the rest of her life."

In that moment, he understood Lady Sherringham's drive to find Del. The sex club scared her, but she was a tigress when defending someone she believed more defenseless than herself.

"But what are you going to do with them now?" she demanded.

"I'm going to settle generous dowries on them."

"You aren't going to bribe men to marry them, are you?" Her balled fists rested on her hips. "You can't sell them into marriages."

"I want them to make good marriages. Have the lives they deserve."

She smiled. And when she did, she sparkled. "You, the Earl of Wickham, notorious rake, plan on matchmaking." She instantly sobered. "Hopefully not the way your father did."

"I would never do anything the way my father did."

She frowned, and he didn't think she was entirely convinced.

"You are astonishing, Wickham." Her voice was soft—the strident tones gone. "First I learn that you saved lives in India. Then you saved my life. You came back for Del. And now this. I was so very wrong. You are a most heroic man—easily the most heroic I've ever known."

She had called him a hero to Major Arbuthnot. She was calling him one now.

But it wasn't true. Ruefully he said, "It's a poor rescuer who saves a life without due thought as to how that life will then be shaped."

Her brows drew together; her chin went up. She looked ready to argue. Their eyes met and held and Christian looked down to her expressive mouth and had never wanted to kiss a woman more—

And if he tried, she would run. She was far too vulnerable.

But Lady Sherringham stepped an inch closer. With her body rigid and her lips pursed, she rose on her toes and touched her mouth to his.

Chapter Eight

*V*ELVET AND SILK. ROSES AND VANILLA.

Christian's senses drank in Lady Sherringham as she pressed her mouth awkwardly to his. He was...paralyzed. Normally he'd sweep a woman into his kiss, entice her to play, and build up the heat until they both ignited.

With Lady Sherringham, that wouldn't work.

He stayed motionless, his lids half lowered, watching as she kissed him. Slowly, her lips softened against his. They parted a little. A soft moan whispered over his mouth.

He couldn't even take the risk of putting a hand to her slender back to hold her to him.

He let her do what she wanted. For the first time in his life, Christian stood awkwardly in a kiss, his back bent, his limbs held in rigid tension, stooping to present his mouth to her. Nothing but their lips touched.

She moved forward until her breasts grazed his chest. Awkwardly, her arms came up and her fists collided with his biceps. The kiss was so light he could speak to her while she moved her lips over his in an exploration as cautious as an uncertain general awaiting an ambush.

"Yes," he murmured. "Hold me."

He had to know she could. He had to know that a woman could endure what she had suffered and not be completely destroyed inside.

Her fists ran over his shoulders, then her arms linked around his neck. Her mouth opened against his, and as he instinctively took the signal as time to lure her into play, she pulled back.

Eyes wide. Astonished. "I did it," she whispered.

He bent and nuzzled her throat, touching his mouth to the fervent pulse beating at the base of her neck. He tasted the delectable sweetness of her skin. "You did it."

She pulled away. "It wasn't much of a kiss for you. I'm sorry."

It hadn't been a sexual kiss. It had been something entirely foreign to him. A sharing of fear, uncertainty—and the way she'd tentatively wrapped her arms around him had slammed him in the soul like no other kiss ever had.

Lady Sherringham hugged herself. "I can do it. Don't you see? I can go back to the club, as long as I have you at my side."

"That kiss was a test?"

She nodded, blushing. "I didn't think of my late husband. When I kissed you, you were all I thought of."

His chest was still tight, his heart hammering. "When I pulled you into that intense kiss in the theater, I reminded you of your husband? That's what frightened you?"

"Yes, but this time—"

A discreet rap at the door stopped her. Damnation.

He turned to see his father's butler on the threshold. Wilkins was an aging servant, so rigid and correct he creaked when he drew breath. "A Mrs. Small has arrived, my lord, claiming to have an audience with you."

"She does," he snapped.

"I installed her in the..." Wilkins cleared his throat. "The west parlor, despite its condition."

The room in which his father had provoked him until blind rage had consumed him, and he'd lost control of his temper. He had never wanted to walk again into the room in which he'd slammed his father up against the wall, his hands on the frail man's throat.

But Lady Sherringham hurried toward the door, her hems swishing around her ankles. Over her shoulder, she admonished, "Come, Wickham. We must speak to her."

She tied him in knots—one moment vulnerable, the next courageous. Had she come to his house for this reason all along? To question the cook, after he had tried to ensure she wouldn't.

Hell.

Mrs. Small dipped into a deep curtsy as Wickham strode into the parlor. Jane followed in his wake—she'd left the other room first but his long strides had outdistanced her in the corridor. Proof, at least, his leg had not been badly injured yesterday.

Jane suppressed a shudder as the atmosphere of the room engulfed her. If the drawing room was dismal, this one was even worse—it was crammed with oversized furniture, and Holland covers lay like lurking ghosts over the chairs.

Dressed in brown wool, with a crushed straw hat

perched on her gray curls, Mrs. Small's twitching shoulders revealed her nerves.

This room was enough to make anyone frightened.

Slipping around Wickham, Jane hurried forward and grasped Mrs. Small's hands. She felt his burning gaze like a hot poker prodding between her shoulder blades. She was infuriating him again.

But one look at the relieved smile on the elderly cook's lips and Jane knew she had been right to come with him, whether he wanted her or not.

"I am so glad you are here, my lady," Mrs. Small said. "Not much gets past the mistress and I feared she somehow knew where I was off to today."

How could she have backed down when this poor woman relied upon her?

Jane glanced back at Wickham's rigid jaw. "Of course I would be here. And you need not return to Mrs. Brougham's at all. Lord Wickham will ensure you are taken care of."

"Indeed," said Wickham coolly. "Lord Wickham will."

Jane's neck prickled. Of course he would hate her speaking for him, this man who believed he should dictate to her, but this was about Del.

A hand settled on the small of her back—Wickham's large hand. He gently nudged her to the side and strode past. "I believe a lodging house was promised," he drawled. He drew Mrs. Small to the settee—that and a monstrous wing chair were the only uncovered seats. "You'll get everything you were promised if you give me the truth, Mrs. Small. Will you do that?"

China blue eyes peered guilelessly at both her and Wickham. "I will and that's a fact, milord. I do so want my own establishment."

It warmed Jane's heart to see Mrs. Small glow. Jane sat on the other end of the large sofa, close enough to reassure the cook. Wickham settled in the enormous wing chair. "Let us get down to it then," he said. "Things are happening at Mrs. Brougham's club that concern you."

Mrs. Small leaned toward him. "I know that the Quality has its own way of going on. And I've always kept me eyes down and me mouth closed."

"You do not have to reassure me of your discretion." Wickham smiled at the cook. "I believe Mrs. Brougham would ensure her important staff were intelligent and mindful of their place."

Spots of color appeared on the cook's cheeks. She preened under his approval.

Wickham could dazzle any woman.

Jane felt her cheeks heat. She had not told him the truth. She had not kissed him as a test. When he'd looked at her after she'd blithered out something about him being a hero, impulse and need and an inexplicable madness had sent her lips careening into his.

Her kiss had been terrible. And he hadn't even responded—not like he had in the theater. He'd let her kiss him, but she'd felt his restraint like a wall between them.

She was so embarrassed that she'd kissed him at all.

It was best to forget it. Del was all that was important. "What," she began, "about the missing—"

"We are concerned about the women who disappeared, Mrs. Small," Wickham interrupted. "And about Lady Treyworth, my sister, who was, I believe, an unwilling member of the club. I must ask you what has frightened you there."

"There's naughty goings on, of course, but it was the men in the cloaks who made my spine quake. They come in through the rear of the house—through the kitchen door. There's four of them, at least I believe so."

"Men in cloaks?" Jane echoed.

Wickham glared at her. Obviously he expected her to be silent.

"Aye. They wear cloaks with hoods and are always masked."

"You've never seen their faces?" Wickham asked. "You don't know who they are?"

Mrs. Small shook her head. "Their names are never used—not even by the mistress. She describes them as the special gentlemen—and requests the best of the brandy for them."

"You've never seen their hair? Or their manner of dress?"

"They're gentlemen, that much I know. The cloaks are black wool, quite ordinary. Their black masks cover their faces, and with the hoods pulled low, I've never seen their eyes. And I'd never dare stare long enough to try to see." The cook shuddered.

"What of the height of these men?"

"Not as tall as you, milord. Two are short and broad and two are lean. Hard to judge with the flowing cloaks, but two seem big enough to almost fill the doorway, and two do not."

"Where do they go from the kitchens?"

"There's a door from the servants' area that leads to the dungerons. It's locked, but the men each have a key to get through."

"Do they come every night? Could you tell me how long they've been coming?"

"On Thursday and Fridays, milord, at midnight. For about a year and a half." Suddenly Mrs. Small looked nervous. "I forgot to tell ye—one of the men carries a walking stick. Once, one of the scullery girls locked the door from the kitchen to the rear yard. The gent had to rap on it. I was near in a panic as we were supposed to leave it open. I hurried to let him in and almost got beaned with his stick. 'E was going to hit the door with it again. I think he wanted to hit me, 'e was so angry."

Wickham shook his head in sympathy and Jane saw Mrs. Small look appreciative. "Can you describe the cane?" he asked.

"Silver, it was. A horse's head with a flowing mane. The eyes were like bloodred rubies."

Wickham leaned back in the chair, his legs stretched out, his arm hooked over the back. "Very distinctive for a gentleman concerned about disguising his identity."

Jane had been thinking that also. It seemed a brazen statement. But arrogant gentlemen thought themselves so clever, so untouchable, they carelessly revealed their sins.

Surely someone would recognize such an unusual piece. These men must be involved with the missing courtesans—why else wear such an elaborate disguise in a club where other members of the ton walked openly? But did they have anything to do with Del?

Twisting her hands in her lap, Mrs. Small gazed hopefully at Wickham. "I can't tell ye anymore, milord. Is it enough?"

Wickham's smile could melt butter. It melted Mrs. Small. "It is exceedingly helpful. Can you tell me more about the girls who went missing? Were they ever badly hurt at the club?"

The cook flushed under his praise. Wickham's gorgeous looks and practiced charm were definitely an advantage here, and he'd promised Mrs. Small a spectacular prize. What woman wouldn't be awestruck by her rescuer?

"The two who went missing are Molly Templeton and Kitty Wilson. Both wanted to be opera dancers and perform on the stage."

Wickham drew out details of the women's lives at the clubs. Molly had put on airs and was short-tempered with servants. She hungered to find a protector of merit, the cook said. She only blossomed when there was at least an earl in the room. Kitty was as slim as a prepubescent girl, delicate and well liked, but at heart she was a hardened whore, determined to survive.

The cook wagged her finger. "But no girls were ever allowed to be roughed up, and that's the truth. There were bruises, as the gentlemen do like their games of spanking and ropes, but nothing the girls couldn't handle. There were a few who'd been in rougher houses and they all thanked heaven they'd been taken in by the mistress."

Jane could not believe it. "They didn't mind being whipped?"

Mrs. Small turned to her with a wry chuckle. "I'm sure his lordship could tell you."

Jane frowned at Wickham, who glanced at her with an expression she could not decipher.

"It's the nature of an uprighter's life, my lady," continued Mrs. Small. "The gentlemen want to do things they can't do at home."

"Why should *gentlemen* get what they—"

"Mrs. Small," Wickham broke in. "A few more questions about the club . . ." For several minutes, he questioned her about the general workings of the place.

What happened in the evenings, whether she cooked for the courtesans, and where the girls slept in the house. He asked her about her culinary triumphs and lured her to reveal her secrets for making syllabub.

Jane tried to search for a reason for his questions. He looked genuinely interested in Mrs. Small's life, then he carefully coaxed her to talk about the guests.

So that was his game. Flatter the woman, then lure her into being completely free with her tongue. It occurred to Jane that Wickham knew women well. Of course he would—she knew he'd bedded hundreds, if not thousands, of them.

Mrs. Small admitted she rarely ventured upstairs and there was little she could tell them about the club's members. From maids' gossip, she could list some of the elite that came to the club, including two dukes, a dozen earls, and an impoverished Hapsburg prince.

"If there is anything more you can tell me, something you might be keeping back, I'll make it worth your while. Shall we say one thousand pounds?"

Mrs. Small's lips flapped helplessly.

Wickham gave his most engaging smile and the cook's reticence collapsed in the face of it. "I think the mistress brings in special girls for the masked men," she whispered, and she crushed her skirts between her fingers.

Jane slid to Mrs. Small's side, her heart in her throat. "What sort of special girls?"

The cook dabbed at the corner of her right eye. "Young girls. I saw one of them, when I was not supposed to. The poor child looked barely fourteen and frightened out of her wits. My mistress has been a good lady, but I fear that—for these men—she is kidnapping innocents."

Wickham stood and bowed. Mrs. Small goggled at him. "Thank you."

It was the most heartfelt thanks Jane had ever heard. He had a way of making himself sound completely in the woman's debt. Cheeks flushed, Mrs. Small turned to her. "Oh, thank you, milady, for bringing me to his lordship's attention."

Jane sighed. What could she have done alone? She certainly couldn't have produced a bribe of a thousand pounds and bought a boarding house.

"I will have my secretary make arrangements with you, Mrs. Small," Wickham said.

Mrs. Small heaved out of the seat and curtsied. "Thank you very kindly, milord."

Wickham bent to Jane's side. "My lady, if you will come with me?"

She did so, and as soon as he had sent a gray-haired, bespectacled gentleman into the parlor and closed the door, she rounded on him, determined to feel . . . useful. To take some action. "Do you know who that walking stick would belong to?"

"I've only been back for days, so no, I have no idea. But I will find out."

"Salaberry. Petersborough. Dartmore or Treyworth. Any of them could have been part of this group of masked men." Her voice rose. "What if Del knew Treyworth had been ruining innocent girls? It is Thursday today. We must go to the club."

Wickham put his finger to her lips. He ushered her away from the parlor. The secretary was escorting Mrs. Small out.

Against her ear, Wickham said, "I'm sending one of my servants to watch her."

"As you did for me. You fear for her life. You fear for *mine*."

"Yes, I do." He clasped her shoulders, as though preparing to shake sense into her. But he didn't. "You must go home, love. I'll send my servants to follow you, to watch your home again. I will keep you safe."

She shook her head. "Will you come for me tonight? To take me to the club." Before he could voice the "no" she knew was going to come, she pushed his hands away. "You know what I'll do. I'll go."

Once, when they were young and he'd teased her, she'd threatened to put pudding in his boot. The next morning, she'd heard the squish as his foot went in it. She'd carried through everything she'd threatened in anger. The pudding. Stinging ants in his trousers. Salt in his ale.

She hoped he thought that hadn't changed over eight years.

"You are a damnable woman."

She recoiled at that, but realized he had not said it in anger. "You would go alone if I don't take you, wouldn't you?" He raked his hair back. "I don't understand you. You were more frightened of the club than you were of that carriage accident."

He startled her. It was true.

"All right, I'll take you. But if you see anything that upsets you or frightens you or triggers your need to crusade, you have to warn me. I won't touch you any more than is necessary. And I won't let anyone else touch you."

I won't touch you. Something fractured inside her even as she said, "Thank you."

"Be dressed and waiting for me at nine."

She shook her head. Explaining Wickham to Aunt

Regina? Her aunt would never let her race off to the sordid club with Wickham, not even to find Del. And while as a widow she could do what she wanted, she did not want to repay Aunt Regina's kindness by upsetting her.

"No," she said, "I shall arrive on *your* doorstep at nine."

Chapter Nine

ALE DRIBBLED DOWN THE MAN'S CHIN and he wiped it away with a sweep of his ragged sleeve. From the corner of the taproom, Christian watched the heavy-set grave robber slam his empty tankard to the table, a signal he wanted another.

This man, Smith, worked for Tanner. He hauled the bodies out of the graves and took them to the medical schools who bought the corpses for dissection. And before he began his night's work, he usually visited this dockyard tavern, the Barrel and Anchor.

Christian got up. He had an hour and a half before he had to return to Wickham House, then take Lady Sherringham to the club and protect her from men who wanted to either do her harm or roger her until she couldn't walk.

He reached Smith's table as a new drink was placed in front of the slumped man. Christian stomped his boot on the bench to get the man's attention.

Bloodshot eyes peered at him. "What do yer want,

toff?" The stink of the stews—sour ale, stale sweat, rotting bodies—wafted up from the bulky body.

Christian drew out a gold sovereign and began to juggle it along his fingers. His greatcoat eased open to reveal the handle of his pistol in the waistband of his trousers. "Do you work with a man named Tanner?"

"What's it to you, nob? Who in Satan's stews are you?"

"Someone who has no interest in turning you over to the magistrates, but who has the power to see you hang." Christian flipped the sovereign to the grave robber and took out a small sack. Within, coins clinked lightly. "Yours. For information."

"Not much good to me if me throat's cut and I'm bobbing facedown in the Thames."

"There's enough there to buy a hell of a lot of protection. Have you done any services for Mrs. Brougham who runs a sex club on Bolton Street?"

Smith shook his head and fingered the black cloth bag. He lifted it, testing the weight. The coins jingled. At the sound, heads of other men rose in interest, and Smith carefully set the bag down on the bench by his leg. "Might have done."

"What were you doing for Mrs. Brougham?"

"Took some bodies away. The medical schools love the pretty young lasses."

Christian's throat tightened. "How young were they?"

For a moment, Smith looked misty-eyed. "Some were maybe fourteen."

In India, children in the fetid cities saw agonies before their ages reached double digits. So many died young. It was no different in London's East End. A twelve-year-old virgin girl was less likely to be found than a unicorn. "When did you take the bodies?"

"Now and again. Last one was a month ago."

Relief rushed through Christian. Too long ago to be Del. "From Mrs. Brougham's club?"

Smith took a sip of his ale. "I didn't pick up the bodies. Tanner took care of that. Then I'd take them to the schools. But he went to some house near Blackheath. Or it might have been Richmond. Tanner said 'e got the use of a carriage for the jobs."

Christian pulled out a miniature of Del. He had to make sure. "Did you take a woman who looked like this? She would be eight years older."

Smith squinted. "Pretty lady. The ones I took were tarts, not ladies—"

Christian heard the hesitation. He took out a five-pound note. "But you know something about a lady?"

The man's beady eyes flicked about the room. "Tanner's coming for me soon," he rasped. "But I might know something, milord. Me cousin got a job to guard a lady at one of the madam's houses. He's kept closed-mouthed about it, though he throws the blunt around."

"A lady? Who?"

"No idea. Mad, me cousin said. Has to be bound to the bed to keep her from hurting herself." He pointed at the miniature. "Could even be that one, milord, the one yer looking for."

Or it could be a tale spun to earn the five pounds. Christian didn't believe so. But he would cling to any story that promised Del was still alive.

Why was Brougham keeping Del a prisoner? Who was she doing it for?

With a wave of his hand, Christian summoned another tankard of ale and the man looked up at him gratefully.

Then he settled on the bench beside the grave robber. "I've got a proposition for you, Smith."

"Wot sort, milord?"

"I want your boss, Tanner. I'll pay you a king's ransom if you lead him to me. If you help, I'll ensure that you escape the noose."

Smith touched his throat beneath his dirty kerchief. "A king's ransom instead of swinging, milord? It's a bargain."

His home was in an uproar. Three steps down the corridor from his foyer, Christian found himself in the midst of a scene from Bedlam. The girls ran around, sobbing— and he seemed to count more than four of them in the house. Maids flurried about and the housekeeper ran from room to room like a decapitated chicken.

He grasped a maid by the arm. "What is going on? Is it news about Lady Treyworth?"

She goggled at him. "I—I don't know, milord. Truly, I don't." She stared at his black-gloved hand, where it clutched her arm—hard. He let her go and stalked into his study. His blood felt like ice water in his veins.

His gray-haired, stiff-rumped secretary, Jonathon Huntley, sat behind his desk, swiftly writing a letter. Huntley had been in this house longer than he, having served for thirty years. Christian reached the desk in long strides and dragged the paper out from beneath his secretary's pen. Gasping in shock, Huntley clapped his hand to his heart. "My lord, a bit of warning if you please. I don't wish to expire on your desk."

The page contained a description of Mary. Not Del.

"Did the flapping ladies not tell you?" Huntley

dabbed his pen into the inkwell. "We've had an elope-ment."

"*What?*"

"Miss Mary has run off with a footman."

Hell and the devil.

"You need not trouble yourself with this matter, my lord."

When he had first come home, Huntely had glared down his long nose and had warned that a house full of young ladies could bring nothing but trouble.

Christain grabbed a paperweight and hurled it. It burst through the plaster wall opposite. He had the small satisfaction of seeing Huntley spray ink across his blotter.

The problem was not with young ladies. This was his fault. His fault for bringing the girls back to England with the naïve belief there would be a home for them. And for impatiently rejecting Mary's advances without realizing there was a vulnerable girl behind them.

Lady Sherringham had called him a hero. Here was evidence that he was anything but.

He threw the letter down. "Let them go. Mary will contact me—because they'll be broke and desperate. When she does, let her have the dowry I promised. Until then, let them enjoy their excitement."

"Give her the dowry?" Huntley looked confused.

"She's done this out of wounded pride. I dragged them back to this world without considering whether it would accept them." And he, of all people, hated by his father for his bastard blood, should have known better. "Maybe she's found some ardent young man who is in love with her." After three years trapped in a seraglio,

Mary was starved for affection. Perhaps his generous dowry could buy her the love she deserved.

He saw from Huntley's expression that his secretary did not agree. "My lord, if I may take the liberty—"

He sighed. "Why even ask, Huntley?"

"The scandal will affect all the girls."

Christian threw up his hands. "The ton is already spinning black-hearted gossip about them. The only one who understands is Lady Sherringham."

"They cannot have made it far, my lord," Huntley argued calmly. "Most women elope at night, ensuring several hours pass before it is discovered they are gone. Mary left after tea."

"So you think Mary wants me to stop her in time?"

"Exactly."

Now he understood. "She did this to make me notice her." Mary had been hurt and, in a youthful, foolish way, she'd seen this as the way to make him care.

Did he save Mary or did he not?

He hadn't been here to save Del from a horrible marriage.

Would it ease his soul to help Mary? Would it help him to rescue a girl he barely knew, when he hadn't done so for Del? He couldn't just give Mary the money, wash his hands of her, and let her ruin her life. That was the sort of thing his father would have done—except his father wouldn't have handed over the blunt. "Pursue them," he snapped.

A graying brow arched. "Drag them back, my lord?"

He slumped into the wing-backed chair drawn up his desk. "Yes. Drag them back. Yes, I'll be the blackguard and take away her free will, because if she marries, she'll regret it afterward. She doesn't deserve to end up in another prison, even willingly."

To his surprise, Huntley nodded. "Very good."

Apparently the old codger had a soft spot for troublesome young ladies after all. Christian withdrew the pistol that was still lodged in the waistband of his trousers. He laid it on his desk.

"And your encounter with the resurrectionist, Smith? Was it satisfactory?" Huntley asked.

Only Huntley could put it that way. This was one of those times he was glad he'd kept the man. "Smith claims that a highborn lady is being held at another house belonging to Mrs. Brougham."

He looked up, surprised to see relief flooding Huntley's normally impassive face. "You believe it is Lady Treyworth? Thank God." Then his secretary hung his head, looking surprisingly ashamed of himself. "I'm sorry, my lord, but I haven't been able to find any other properties Mrs. Brougham owns. For her investments, she has covered her tracks well—"

Christian held up his hand. "You've handled the dozens of tasks I've thrown at you in the last few days. Apologies aren't needed. And I have a lead. A way to force the grave robber to take me right to that house. I'll need Younger and his men at the ready."

"Immediately, my lord. I have investigated the Marquis of Salaberry. As you suspected, he is in dun territory."

"Then tonight Salaberry is going to learn what it's like to be strung up by his ballocks."

"Very good, my lord," Huntley said.

*   *   *

The letter came by private messenger just before nine.

In his study, Christian sliced the seal and flicked open the letter. It couldn't be from Jane—his man would have told him if something had happened. Then he saw the handwriting, the salutation, and both hit him like a fist to his gut.

> *My dearest Christian,*
>
> *I saw you at the club two nights ago, but could not summon the pluck to approach you. Yet I have not slept or eaten since for thinking of you.*
>
> *I learned today that you are searching for your sister. She avoided me at all times at the club. She blamed me for the duel that forced you to leave, and so blamed me for losing you to your exotic travels. But I wish to help you, Christian. Treyworth brought your sister to the club to show how thoroughly he controlled her.*
>
> *I do not believe that Lady Treyworth would have dreamed of running away—it is such with prisoners. As for Treyworth, he wished to display his submissive wife before the appreciative audience he found. He gave exhibitions in the dungeons of the club. She gave no protest; she was forbidden to speak and she did not. But she spoke volumes with her eyes, with her posture, with the way she refused to moan or cry out, no matter what was done to her.*
>
> *If you have returned to find your sister, you may not, I fear, ever recover her soul.*
>
> *Your devoted servant,*
Georgiana, Lady Carlyle

Christian crumpled the letter. He tossed it, watching pristine white paper arc into the low fire. It wasn't a surprise that Georgiana, formerly the Countess of Harrington and formerly his lover, with her lusty appetite for inventive carnal games, was a member of Brougham's club.

She had been there and she had seen what had happened to Del.

You may not, I fear, ever recover her soul.

Christian pressed his forehead against the cold, hard marble of the mantelpiece. He had to believe he could save Del. Lady Sherringham did, and he had to have faith that she was right. Georgie had to be wrong.

"There is something I need to know, Lady Sherringham."

Jane cast a sidelong glance to Wickham. Bands of shadow lay along his mask. He looked dark, mysterious, and not at all like the charming but absolutely unrepentant rogue she remembered from eight years ago.

She swallowed hard. She had to trust this intimidating-looking man to be her protector when she met gentlemen who were far more frightening.

"What would that be, Lord Wickham?" She tried to appear completely in control. But his presence filled the carriage, formerly his father's—fitted with rigid, uncomfortable seats, the interior paneling stained funeral ebony. He might not be touching her, but perspiration and goosebumps alternately prickled her skin.

He ran his finger around his cravat. His Adam's apple bobbed nervously, and she stared in surprise. Wickham had never appeared ill at ease before.

"What was Del like?" he asked finally. "I've been too scared to ask you before. But I want the truth and I know you will give it to me."

Too scared. She could not believe he'd said that to her.

But Wickham, unlike her late husband, didn't seem to care about admitting weakness to her. It made her heart warm to him, but she could think of one reason he wanted to know, and she didn't like that reason very much.

"If you are searching for absolution, I can't give it to you."

"Just tell me, Jane Beaumont."

"I can't tell you that marriage to Treyworth didn't change her, because it did. Del was a gentle-hearted woman, one who went into her marriage hoping for the best. When a woman like that endures anger and violence, she is never the same again."

He waited in silence for her to go on, but his intense gaze never left her face. And that made her nervous. He wanted the truth, and she was so tense, she wanted to throw it at him.

"Del learned to retreat into herself. She would jump at loud noises and always listen for angry footfalls. She learned to try to be invisible."

Pain flashed in Wickham's midnight blue eyes.

Tears pricked at the corner of Jane's. "But she never lost her good heart and her gentle ways. She never once slapped a maid because she was hurt from Treyworth's abuse. She never turned her anger on someone weaker than she."

She rushed on, afraid the wobble in her voice would undo her. "Del once rescued a baby bird who had fallen from its nest. She took it into the house—hiding it from Treyworth—and she tried to feed it. But as soon as she saw she could not do that, she took it back outside and watched over it in hopes its mother would come."

"She was not . . . mad?"

Jane recoiled. She hadn't expected that. Her mother Margaret had gone mad—over love for her rogue of a husband, Anthony, and the unending fear she might find herself in a workhouse at any given moment. Margaret had let her life be ruled by him, until she had ended her days locked away in a private sanitarium. "No," Jane declared. "Del was most definitely not mad."

"I learned that Brougham was discussing business with a resurrectionist. A grave robber."

She knew what a resurrectionist was. A man who dug up corpses and sold them to medical schools.

"Don't faint, Lady Sherringham—" He vaulted over to her side of the carriage. His body pressed against hers and his arm came around her shoulders.

Two nights ago, it would have upset her to have him so close. Now, she found herself leaning into him, needing his warmth. Wanting his embrace. "I—I'm not going to faint."

Leather stroked her skin as Wickham caught hold of her chin. He tipped her face to look at him. The gesture was terse and quick, and one quiver of shock slithered down her spine. His mouth was a mere inch from hers. She could smell a light tang of alcohol and the rich, nose-tickling scent of a cheroot he must have smoked earlier.

"I found one of the men who works for the grave robber. He claims that Mrs. Brougham is keeping a lady a prisoner in one of her houses. I want to believe that woman is Del."

So did she. So very much. He eased back. There would be no kiss, she realized, because he'd promised.

"I need a name to call you in the club."

The abrupt change of his thoughts startled her. "Why? Everyone knows who I am now."

"I don't like calling you Lady Sherringham. I'd prefer to use a more intimate name with you." His gave a slow smile. "I remember once calling you 'pest.'"

He had. That was the day she'd tried to stop his neck-or-nothing carriage race.

"But that would hardly be appropriate in a sex club," he added.

He was teasing her. Why? Could he be trying to put her at ease, believing he'd frightened her witless with his talk of grave robbers? He was an astonishingly aware and considerate man.

"Jane. You can call me that. It is my given name." It had been given to curry favor with her mother's wealthy aunt, who'd left them a fortune her father had gambled away.

"How about Jewel?" he suggested.

She stared. The name that leapt to his mind for her was Jewel? Christian Sutcliffe could not possibly see her as a jewel. He must be speaking in jest. But he had also asked her why her husband had not seen she was a treasure.

"It's got the same letter," he mused. "And you sparkle like a jewel amongst that crowd. Hades, love, you sparkle here beside me."

Before she could speak—before she could even stumblingly accept his proposal of a new name—the carriage drew to a stop. Through the open curtain, Jane saw the flicker of street flare and couples wearing black cloaks scurrying up the front steps to the club. "Shouldn't we go in the back?"

"I have three men watching the back of the house.

We're going to enter through the front. If the masked men arrive, a signal will be given." He was confident and controlled again. There was no sign of his earlier vulnerability.

"At midnight." In the distance, a clock chimed the half hour. Half past nine.

"So we have time to meet your admirers and search Brougham's office."

Admirers. What a word to use. "Search her office?"

Wickham casually flicked his wrist and a long slim knife dropped from his sleeve into his hand. He reached inside the top of his boot and drew another blade from there. Then she spied the handle of a pistol tucked into the waistband of his trousers.

She had never seen a man so well armed. It made her remember the carriage accident and that one of the men—or women—she would meet tonight might have pushed her in front of flying hooves.

Wickham straightened from his boot. "You are to be lookout." His gaze grew serious. "And you will stay at my side. Like you are holding your mother's apron strings."

"I intend to," she muttered and tugged down her veil. Then Wickham jumped from the carriage and helped her down with gentlemanly aplomb. Which meant he clasped her hand firmly in his.

"Remember," he said, as they mounted the steps, "you are to obey me at all times."

A part of her rebelled but she had no choice except to nod. She did not doubt he would haul her back to the carriage if she refused. And at his side, she crossed the threshold of the club, stepping again into the world of public sin.

Chapter Ten

*W*HAT HAD HE BEEN THINKING TO have her walk in front of him? Christian cursed under his breath. Lady Sherringham's lush bottom collided with him each time they had to stop. And when she walked, her cheeks wriggled across his trousers—and the ridge of his unruly cock.

Couples were kissing, fondling, and copulating all around them. Moans and the slick sounds of slapping bodies filled his head. But none of that shook his focus, whereas Jane Beaumont did.

Two gentlemen had groped her rear the instant they'd walked into the crowded foyer. So he'd thought that putting her in front of him would be the gentlemanly thing to do.

More the fool he.

Before they had joined the crush, he had instructed a footman to tell Lords Salaberry and Dartmore Lady Sherringham had arrived. And he'd seen her face pale and her spine quake. The servant had informed him that

Salaberry never arrived before midnight, so he'd decided to head to Brougham's office.

Now, in front of him, his Jewel halted in her tracks. "W-what are those women doing?"

At her hesitant question, Christian groaned. And looked. He suspected that if he didn't explain it, she'd push ahead for a closer examination.

On a divan, encircled by a crowd of appreciative gentlemen, two bosomy ladies in chemises sprawled over each other. At this point, the women were only pressing kisses to the fabric bunched between each other's thighs, but one was already reaching for the other's hem.

"Oral sex," he whispered back. "Women pleasuring each other with their mouths."

At her long pause, he added, "You did ask, Jewel. Now, move on. No distractions."

"I am not distracted." She marched forward, only to almost collide with a half-naked brawny bloke in a kilt. In front of her eyes, Lady Butterfield—a horsy woman known for her love of Sapphic pleasures—jerked up the kilt, revealing a thatch of brown hair and a big erection that tilted to the right.

Jane—Christian realized it was easy to think of her as Jane—clapped her hand to her mouth.

The Scotsman's erection swayed toward Lady Butterfield. "Does it please you, lass?"

"Alas, my dear sir, your sword, while impressive, shall not breach my defenses." She leveled a look at Jane. "But perhaps a widow would care for a grope?"

Jane reared back and banged the top of her head against Christian's chin. He could tell her gaze dropped below the Scotsman's waist and frantically jerked up again. Her shoulders twitched like a rabbit's nose. "He is a complete stranger—"

"Not tonight," Christian coolly declined. And as he steered Jane onward, around the Scotsman, he spied a flood of pink through the lace veil. She had always been prickly and outraged about sexual matters. When he used to tease her about his rakish ways, she would turn red, then try to skewer him with a sharp-tongued comment.

But he now understood that her only experience with carnal activity had been with a man who'd hurt her. Put a cool, rigid woman with a bullying brute of a man, and Christian could imagine the hell she'd gone through. For Jane, coming to this club must be like walking through all the nightmares of her past. And his heart ached for her.

She abruptly stopped again, and his groin bumped against the voluptuous pillow of her rear. He ground his teeth.

"Shouldn't we ask Lady Butterfield about Del?" she whispered.

"I did. Yesterday. Like everyone else I've spoken to, she believes Del has run off. She also claimed she had never shared a bed with Del." That came out with a control that surprised him. It had stunned him to discover that Del had shared a bed with a female prostitute here—a cheery experienced woman of about thirty, named Sally Ryan.

Lady Sherringham swallowed hard. He saw the movement of her slender throat.

"Relax," he murmured. "I'm here as your protector. And remember, no outrage tonight."

"I won't. I promised." She sounded vulnerable. But at

least his awareness of her fear had brought his erection back under control.

Then, at their side, a woman cried out. One of those throaty moans that could give a man of eighty a cockstand.

Niches were set in the corridor walls. Jane stared in astonishment at the couple in the nearest one. Broad shoulders filled the space, and small hands in white gloves clutched the gentleman's neck. The man's arse was pumping for all he was worth. The statues beside them shook and rattled, the hidden woman made mewling sounds of pleasure each time she was slammed against the back wall. Jane stood transfixed, breathing quick and hard.

It was the sound of Jane's breathing that was setting his blood on fire and making it damned hard to think—

"Christian? Is that you behind the mask?"

The sultry feminine voice came from behind him. Christian hadn't heard that throaty purr for eight years but he knew it in an instant. It was the voice he'd once needed to hear cry out his name in ecstasy, the way he needed water and air to survive.

Drawing Jane back, he slowly turned. And stared down into green eyes framed by a mask encrusted with a fortune in diamonds.

"Georgiana." She had changed—her hair was more brown now than blond, her figure more full. Courtesy dictated he bend over her hand—fingers that carried the scent of a female who had once drove him mad. But his body didn't even respond now. He was only aware of Jane at his side, still gasping, and of how she smelled of roses and lavender, like a lush summer garden, while Georgie wore heavy, spicy perfume.

Georgiana had not even noticed Jane. Her luminous green eyes held on him. "I've heard that you lived like a maharajah in India," she purred, "consorting with the most skilled and exotic women. I heard you kept your own harem. Is that true?"

"True enough."

Her laugh rang out. "You kept dozens of women and satisfied them all?" Behind the mask, Georgie's eyes flashed with jealousy—real or feigned, he couldn't tell. Before she'd rejected him, he had believed her pouts and tantrums proved she loved him—because then, as now, he had no idea what love was.

"Did you ever fall in love again, Christian? Or was I the last woman you loved?" Georgie's eyes shone hopefully. Did she need to believe she'd broken his heart and ruined him for anyone else? That she'd been the most important woman in his life?

He didn't have the heart to destroy her illusion.

"Not a day has gone by that I haven't thought of you," she whispered. Her voice held the husky richness that had once mesmerized him. "Not one day that I haven't regretted what I said to you that . . . that morning."

"The morning I shot your husband." Christian said it bluntly. It was the truth—there was no denying it. "You made the right choice in rejecting me, Georgie. Never fear that."

"No, Christian," Georgiana exclaimed. "I don't think I did."

Jane caught her breath. The woman was the Marchioness of Carlyle, who had previously been married to Lord Harrington, the earl Wickham had shot in a duel. Her gossamer-thin gown clung to the largest breasts, the tiniest waist, and the most curvaceous hips Jane had ever seen.

Even though Jane stood right at Wickham's side, she was apparently invisible to them both.

Then Wickham lifted her hand. "Lady Carlyle, may I make you known to my partner, my very precious Jewel?" He turned to Jane, his eyes stark and hard behind the mask. "Dearest, may I present Lady Carlyle?"

She dipped into a curtsy and Lady Carlyle did the same. Obviously the woman wanted Christian, but Jane could not tell how he felt about Lady Carlyle. He seemed cold and angry.

"Jewel?" Behind the glittering mask, with her chin high, Lady Carlyle's gaze swept icily over Jane from head to toe. Her voice was no longer alluring. It was flat and brittle. "Come, you must tell me—who are you really?"

But Wickham caught the woman's hand. "I received your letter, Georgie. If you don't believe my sister ran away from Treyworth, where do you think she is?"

From the sidelines, avoiding the other couples walking past, Jane stared. What letter?

"I do not know. I just simply did not believe she had the mettle to leave him. But I fear that Treyworth pushed her too far."

"What do you mean?" Jane cried.

The diamond-covered mask turned to her. "She did not want to play the games here." Lady Carlyle delicately rested her hand on Wickham's forearm. She drew up her mask to reveal her beautiful face, and Jane felt as though she'd been punched in the chest.

"A fortnight ago," Lady Carlyle purred softly, "I found your sister in the ladies' retiring room, sobbing bitterly. I wished to comfort her, but she did not want me. She said she could not endure any more."

"What had happened to her?" Jane could not understand. She would have done anything to help Del, yet when Del had been in anguish, she'd kept it a secret. Why?

"What do you think Treyworth drove my sister to do, Georgiana?"

"I do not know. When I tried to help, she told me not to trouble myself and ran out."

"Do you know of any other places Mrs. Brougham runs?" Wickham asked.

Georgiana frowned, her mask dangling from her fingertips. "I have no idea. I suspect that she also owns common brothels and flashhouses. I am aware that she has a sordid side—as elegant as this place may be." The expressive lips pouted. Music swelled, forcing the woman to raise her voice. "I saw you two nights ago, Christian. I saw you walk through the club, condemning us all."

"My sister is missing. What difference does it make what I think of this place?"

"It matters to me what you think," Lady Carlyle said plaintively.

"I've been in worse places than this, sweetheart."

Sweetheart. He said it without thought to Lady Carlyle and Jane remembered—now embarrassed—how the name *Jewel* had made her heart patter.

"This place is not all sin and evil, Christian. Treyworth abused the principles of the club. Your sister was not the sort of sophisticated woman who belonged here."

Jane could not stay silent. "Sophisticated? You are condemning her for being decent."

A plucked brow arched and a condescending sneer distorted the beautiful mouth. "There are women here who enjoy the freedom we are allowed to pursue." Lady Carlyle turned to Christian. "You know what it is like to live a life entirely devoted to sexual pleasure. It is more addictive than opium. I spend each day preparing for sex, anticipating it, pursuing it. I could never go back to my life as it was. I need this constant awareness of senses, this endless excitement in my heart." She stroked Wickham. "It was once that way for us."

Wickham's face was expressionless. "You married the man you loved, Georgie. Now I—*we*—must go—"

"You used to live this way with me. Drowning in sex. Do you not miss those days? Do you not ache for what we once had? I do. Every moment of every day, I do. You need an open-minded, adventurous sort of woman. And I've realized I need you."

Jane had never heard a woman so openly profess her longing for a man. Even her mother had never put her yearnings into words—Margaret had just tried to cling to her husband.

She wished she knew what Wickham was thinking. What he felt behind the black leather mask and his cool, jaded expression.

"This isn't the time, Georgie, to rehash all this," he growled. "Right now all I can think about is Del. Finding her and bringing her home safely."

"What are you going to do, Christian? She is Treyworth's wife. Or do you plan to shoot him to free her?"

Jane recoiled in shock.

But Wickham looked down, his eyes dark with regret. "I'm sorry, Georgie. It doesn't change anything, but I'm sorry I took Harrington from you. I saw what he'd done to you, and I reacted in anger."

Jane's heart lurched at the vulnerability in his voice—in the harsh tones of self-recrimination. But Wickham had cuckolded the other man and dueling had been illegal. He *had* been in the wrong. He deserved to feel guilt.

Lady Carlyle caught both Wickham's wrists and held tight. "I'm not sorry. You saved me, Christian. I am only sorry that I pushed you away. I realized too late that I love you."

And he would say that he loved her, too. It made sense, didn't it? The woman he had loved, the one he had left England for, was forgiving him. But when Jane glanced at Wickham's face, his eyes locked on hers. He mouthed a word—*help*.

As she stared at him, he did it again. *Help*. He meant it.

Jane sashayed forward, trying to act the bold mistress, and tapped Lady Carlyle on the shoulder. "He is mine, dearie. And I don't like other women putting their paws on him. Now, come on, lover." She almost choked on the word. She'd never behaved like this in her *life*. Thrusting out her chest, she cuddled up to Christian and stroked his arm. "You promised me a wild night in the dungeons and I'm aching to get started."

Lady Carlyle drew back and gaped in astonishment. Jane caught a relieved, thankful wink from Wickham. He slid his arm around her waist—a touch she truly did not mind—and forced his way through the crowd. Away from the woman she'd thought was his former love.

Her thoughts churned. Had he actually not loved Georgiana, since he certainly didn't want to hear the words on the woman's lips now? But how . . . pointless to kill her husband then. Why kill a man over a woman he did not even want?

Pride? Stubbornness? The fact that a *gentleman* didn't back down?

Jane shook her head. It was long in the past, and there was no point in feeling so . . . inexplicably angry about it. But when they were headed once more down the corridor, she rounded on him. "Lady Carlyle sent you a letter and you did not tell me."

He frowned. "I told you what I'd learned in the carriage."

"You never mentioned Lady Carlyle. I showed you my letters—but you did not show me yours." Suddenly, she remembered one time, when he had been teasing her on a sultry August day, he had said almost those very words. *You show me yours and I'll show you mine.*

They had been picnicking with Del and others, but he'd spoken so only she could hear. She had been so entirely thrown off kilter, she'd spilled her lemonade on his trousers. "I thought . . . in coming here together, we were acting as partners."

At his startled look, she felt the heat of embarrassment creep up her neck.

"I brought you with me because I believed it was best to have you where I could see you." He gave a lopsided, entirely surprising, smile. "And you rescued me."

His lashes lowered, his mouth softened. "This isn't a necessary touch, but one I can't resist." He lifted her veil and slanted his lips over hers.

A clamor of emotions hit her at once. Humiliation burned into anger, which tumbled into astonishment, which kept her rooted on the spot as his mouth played over hers in an entirely new way. Gentle, so gentle, but not in the least innocent.

People surged around them as she returned his kiss awkwardly. Not as terribly as in his drawing room— she was not quite as much a waxwork—but she still felt like an unyielding board propped against him. What if he swept her off her feet into a forceful kiss again and that triggered her fears and memories?

But something worse happened. She began to feel like a puddle of melting butter.

She knew the feeling from before her marriage. The liquid sensation coursing through her. The wash of heat from her toes to the tip of her head. The first time she'd felt this, she had been spying on twenty-year-old Wickham bathing in the pond. He'd been nothing but a dark silhouette against brilliant sunlight, but she had been as hot as a dry leaf with a flame beneath it.

With Del in danger, she was feeling *desire*. How could she?

She pulled back and cried, "No."

Wickham let her go.

Jane stared down the empty corridor. Her duty was to keep watch while Wickham broke into Mrs. Brougham's office. Situated at the rear of the second floor, in the third town house overtaken by the club and a good distance from the other bedrooms, the madam's private sanctum was separated from the public area by a locked door.

Hunched over the doorknob, Wickham slid a metal strip from one sleeve.

"What is that?" Jane whispered.

"It's a lock pick, Jewel." He took one more glance down the quiet, shadowy hallway as though he didn't trust her to be a dedicated lookout, then set to work.

"You can open a lock with that? How?"

"In many ways, you have not changed at all, Lady Jane. Just warn me if anyone comes."

Jane had to admit Wickham's skill astonished her. The latch on the door did not slow him down for more than a moment. And she was too curious to stay quiet. "Where did you learn to do that?"

"When I was younger, I got a professional thief drunk and got him to teach me. Seemed a useful skill to have." He eased the door open.

"You consorted with thieves?"

He didn't respond, but it shouldn't surprise her— when he was in his late teens, he had consorted with anyone who was dangerous, scandalous, and would irritate his father. His hand closed around her wrist and he pulled her inside.

"What if Mrs. Brougham comes up here?" she whispered.

"I'll either throttle her until I've got the truth about Del, or tell her we fancied a threesome."

The preposterous alternative didn't shock her—it made her roll her eyes. "I mean, is there any way out of here?"

"If she comes up, we hide—you'll be quiet and do exactly as I tell you."

Firelight glinted on Wickham's hair and limned his profile in gold. He crouched to the fire, held a candle to the embers. The wick caught, flared, and he jammed the candle into its holder.

"Good heavens," Jane gasped. On her first night in

the club, she'd met Mrs. Brougham in a salon down-stairs. She had not seen *this*. The walls of the office were hung in silk the color of champagne. A Queen Anne desk of white and gilt stood before ivory drapes. Gilt gleamed on every surface, the walls painted in pastel beauty, covered with scrollwork in the Adams style.

"Sin pays well," Wickham muttered dryly. He set the candle on the desk and took out his lockpick as he bent to the drawers. Without looking at her, he instructed, "Go back to the door."

"What are you searching for?" She cracked it open. The hallway was empty.

"I want to find Brougham's other properties. She must keep deeds or lists of accounts." He brought a stack of papers out of the drawer and thudded them on the desk.

Another door led off from the office. Suddenly apprehensive, Jane left her post and glanced inside. But the room was silent and dark. In the faint light that spilled in from the office, she could distinguish an enormous bed. An oval one, with eight roman columns to hold a canopy that dripped silk.

"Go back to the door," Wickham said again.

But as she saw him scan through paper after paper, she ached to see them, too. To be a part of finding Del, of unraveling the mystery.

"I should look. In case you miss something."

His brow shot up. "I won't." He flicked open a ledger book, scanned it, then rifled through the other papers in the drawer—and did so in silence. He opened drawer after drawer while she peeked out the door, then peeked over at him, and the time seemed to rush by with un-nerving speed. Finally, he groaned. "There is no sign of leases or deeds to property here. No legal documents at all. No doubt the insufferable witch keeps them with her attorney."

Jane left the door. Papers lay in the drawer again, but no longer neatly stacked, with pages twisted haphazardly. "Won't she know someone has searched her desk?"

"She already knows what I want."

"Are you trying to push her—goad her into acting?"

His gaze met hers, filled with admiration. "Exactly. I'm trying to push the grave robbers. And push Mrs. Brougham. And push the members here. One will stumble—and lead us to Del."

Us. This time, he'd spoken of them as a team. And she was impressed by the plans he'd made, the thorough way he was searching for Del.

He closed the drawers. "I'm going to search the bedroom. The door, Jewel."

It was driving her mad to stay at her spot but she did it. She cocked her head toward the bedroom, straining to hear what he was doing. And when she looked out to the hallway again, she saw Mrs. Brougham hurrying down the corridor.

"She's here," she hissed. "Hide!"

Christian had just pulled a slim, leather-bound book from beneath the madam's mattress when he heard Jane's warning. The door to the office gave an ominous click. He reached the doorway to the bedroom to find his Jewel had vanished. Either she was the quickest woman alive, able to cross a room in a heartbeat, or—

"Lady Sherringham, what are you doing here?" Mrs. Brougham's voice came from the hallway. No sultry tones this time. It was edgy, nervous, and sharp with suspicion.

He had to echo the madam—what in blazes *was* she doing?

Sweat trickled down at his collar. How had Mrs. Brougham known who she was beneath the veil and the mourning gown? There was no answer from Jane. This revelation must have stunned her. Then softly, her voice reached him through the door. "You know me? You know who I really am?"

"I knew from the first moment you stepped into my club."

Through the door, he heard his Jewel's gasp. Damn, she was thrown by this. But then she stuttered, "I—I came here in search of you. I wished to speak to you but found the door locked."

"What did you wish to speak to me about, my lady?"

"Perhaps we could go downstairs and discuss it there."

His breath hissed through his teeth. She was trying to lead Brougham away. She was trying to rescue him.

"I assume this is a matter of some discretion. My office would be the most private place. Just let me unlock the door—"

The witch suspected. Christian jammed the lock pick in, used it to turn the lock. Then he sprinted for the bedroom.

He dove under the massive oval bed as the door opened and soft footsteps whispered across the carpet in the office. The counterpane hung to the floor, hiding him, and he lifted it a few inches to watch. He'd left the bedroom door open. He could just see Jane's skirts as she settled in a chair across the desk from Sapphire Brougham.

"Exactly how did you know who I was?" Jane spoke first and he silently applauded her.

There was a pause. "I did not think you would return. I was told you ran away in a panic, my lady, because the games of punishment horrified you. And, of course, I understand why. I can guess why you came back—how very noble to come in search of your friend. We should all have such devoted friends. But I assure you that I know nothing about Lady Treyworth."

Under the bed, Christian held his breath. Would Jane accuse the madam of hiding Del?

"I see," was all she said. "But I still wish to know how you knew who I am. And how you could *understand* why I despise games of punishment."

"I invited your late husband to my club once. I am an enterprising woman—I selected the gentlemen I felt would enjoy this venue and I pursued them. It did not take long before the men clamored to come here. Lord Sherringham came alone. He did not bring you, as I'd hoped."

Thank God for that, Christian thought.

"I allowed your husband to bend my rules and in return, he treated my girls like common street whores. He was not invited to return. So, my dear, I know exactly what sort of man your husband was. And I knew you— even with your disguise—because I had studied both you and your husband in the hopes of enticing you to join."

"I would like to return downstairs," Jane said. "I came here to ask you about my husband. To find out w-what kind of man he was with other women. And you have told me."

Was that a lie, or was it something Jane really had wanted to know?

"A bullying man is like that with most women," Brougham answered. "I doubt you provoked him."

"Thank you, then." Jane pushed back the chair. "Would you take me downstairs?"

"I watched you tonight with Lord Wickham."

Christian jerked up at that. He banged his head to the underside of the bed, but Jane had sputtered in shock, hiding the thud.

"Lord Wickham smolders when he looks at you, and you tremble when you are close to him. Do you tremble with desire, my dear, or fear?"

That was what Brougham had seen? His entirely inappropriate desire? Jane's tremble was fear. He could understand that. Her husband had made her afraid.

"That is—it is impertinent," Jane said.

"I could help you. Do you see this? I've suffered at a man's hand, just as you have."

He heard the gasp. Mrs. Brougham must have revealed her scar. With him, she had been ashamed of it. Why would she so willingly show it now?

"N-no thank you," Jane said. "I don't want help."

"The thing is, my dear, Lord Wicked is completely out of your ken."

Christ, it was hell to have to lay motionless and listen to the madam talk about him.

"Given Lord Wickham's interest in my establishment, I decided to return the favor and learn everything I could about him. His youthful sexual exploits were astounding, even to me. Perhaps you know he was expelled from university for being caught with two women in his bed? Or that he kept an apartment on St. James's that was equipped with a basket hanging over the bed in which his lovers would sit, suspended upon his cock?"

He saw Jane stiffen in shock at the crude word.

"It seems he sought darker and darker pleasures," Brougham continued. "Bondage and whipping. He even paid a brothel to build him a private dungeon, and he kept gently bred women as his willing prisoners. He got quite rough with his play. He broke Lady Matchell's arm. And left terrible bruises on the Countess of Durham."

"And he shot Lord Harrington, don't forget," Jane added in an odd, cold voice.

"I was told that the ton ladies feared he had become too dark and brutal before he left England. He was not a bully like your husband. He's a man driven to push pleasure into pain."

"He—" Jane broke off as the madam asked, "Would you wish to be imprisoned in a dungeon, Lady Sherringham?"

"Of course not," Jane cried, in the strident, appalled tone he knew well. "What woman of sense would? Those foolish women have no idea what it would truly be like to be frightened and hurt and abused. They would not like it one bit."

Everything Brougham had told Jane about his exploits was true. He'd done all those things, but years ago. Not because *he* believed pleasure should be pain, but because the women wanted him to, because they called him Wicked, and that damned nickname had made him angry. If they'd wanted him to be wicked, if they begged him for it, he'd give them what they wanted.

And once he'd gone to India, he'd had lovers, some very exotic and beautiful ones, but he'd never lifted a hand—or a lash—to a woman again.

Jane swept to her feet. "I will not hear any more of this. Would you take me downstairs?"

Christian held his breath. Then Brougham stood, too. "Of course, my lady."

The women left the office. Which meant Jane was being taken back to the club. Alone.

Damn Jane Beaumont for wanting to rescue him and throwing herself in danger as a result. He jammed Brougham's book in the inner pocket of his tailcoat and rushed out of the office.

Chapter Eleven

"WHERE ARE WE GOING?" JANE DEMANDED, as Mrs. Brougham led her down a corridor away from the main salons.

"I have a proposal to put to you, my lady. Would you not like the chance to explore pleasure? To do whatever you wish to a man, and have him entirely under your control?"

Mrs Brougham paused by a white door. She rapped, and it immediately opened.

Jane had no intention of following Mrs. Brougham into the room. "I do not know what you mean."

"All your married life you were in your husband's power. Would you not like to turn the tables for once? What if you could have a handsome gentleman—naked and entirely at your command? He would be bound to the bed. He could not hurt you in any way. He could not even touch you. You could explore him in whatever way you desired. You can ride him to oblivion or simply tease him mercilessly..."

Jane could not believe her ears. "Tied to a bed?"

"To give you ultimate power, my dear. It is possible for a woman to tease a gentleman until he begs for her. Until he howls."

"No!"

Within the small room, a maid held up a shimmering robe of gold silk. "Are you ready, my lady?"

Jane was certain her eyes could not grow any larger.

"You remember the theater, Lady Sherringham," Mrs. Brougham purred. "This room is attached to the stage. The seating gallery is above us. From here, you can view the performances unobserved. Tonight, I have arranged for the most skilled and attractive men to entertain the woman who watches from this chamber. That lady selects the partner who intrigues her the most."

Jane felt her lips move, but no sound came out.

"If you wish to be that lady, I can promise you an experience like no other. I could entice Lord Wickham to be one of the gentlemen. He would have to attempt to seduce you like all the others. You could, of course, choose more than one gentleman." Mrs. Brougham caught Jane's hand and patted it. "I only wish to help you."

Oh no, she was quite certain the woman did not. But the image rose unbidden of Wickham without any clothes on, with his arms and legs spread wide, and rope binding him to bedposts—

A forbidden, completely wrong image. But she grew hot again—even her toes went warm in her slippers. Her cheeks flushed with shame. She saw exactly what Mrs. Brougham intended to do. Frighten her away, because she had come here in search of Del.

She could call the woman's bluff and agree to play. It would ensure Wickham had the time to escape the office. But she sensed that Mrs. Brougham intended to take her beyond her limits, make her panic, and force her to run again.

And if she was pushed into something that involved a whipping, she might get hysterical again. Instead, she squared her shoulders and looked the overmade-up madam in the eye. "If you wish to help me, why did you not help Lady Treyworth?"

"Oh, but I did, Lady Sherringham. I ensured that your friend had my protection. I did take care of her. And I would be quite delighted to take care of you. And if you do not wish to play this game, perhaps you would like to see my famed dungeons?"

Christian grabbed the slender arm of a widow and whirled her around. She pulled up her veil. "Are you going to drag me to the dungeons, sirrah?" she cooed. She had blond curls. And wide, daft-looking blue eyes.

Not Jane. Abruptly he released her and threaded through the crowd. A footman suddenly barred his way. "Lord Wickham." The servant held out a note. "From Lord Dartmore."

Wickham took it and snapped it open.

Must decline the invitation. Lady Dartmore would not wish to play. I ask for your discretion, and I beg you both not to mention my note to Lady Sherringham to my lovely wife.

So Dartmore did not want his wife to know about his interest in Jane. Crumpling the page, Christian scanned the crowded ballroom. Dartmore wasn't in pursuit of her, but where was she?

Be brave, Jane thought. After she'd refused to play the theater game, and had been suitably shocked by the dungeons, Mrs. Brougham had led her down here to the ballroom, and had then abandoned her. At least it appeared that in here, in this large luxurious room draped in silk, there were only people making love. No whippings. No cruelty. No shackles, imprisonment, or cells with bizarre implements of torture.

She did not doubt Brougham thought she would be accosted and would flee for the door.

Jane backed against a fluted column. This way, no gentleman could get behind her and grope her bottom. She peered around the room for Wickham. Dozens of masked gentlemen prowled the room and at least half possessed dark hair. None looked determined to find *her.*

Wickham's midnight black hair, his determined gait, his *intensity,* would be impossible to miss. Even in the crowd, if she saw him she would know it at once.

The room was packed with members of the ton and Brougham's beautiful prostitutes—both male and female. Enormous chandeliers lit the elegantly decorated space. But there was no dancing on the parquet floor. Instead, chaises had been arranged in intimate groupings. In most, two sets of couples chatted amiably as though enjoying a polite dinner party, not partaking in a prelude to sex and infidelity.

Her brief time in the dungeons had left her confused. What she'd seen had been people in sexual bliss—

"Lady Sherringham?" A footman approached almost

fearfully. "The gentleman told me you were all in black, with strawberry blond hair."

"Yes," Jane answered, relief making her straighten away from the column. Wickham—he must have sent a servant to find her. He must have safely escaped Brougham's office. She pushed aside thoughts of the dungeon and focused on that. He must want to throttle her.

"The gentleman has inquired if you wish to join him in a game, my lady."

A game. Her stomach plummeted. "*Which* gentleman?"

"The Marquis of Salaberry, my lady."

It was not yet midnight. "Where is the marquis? I—I am waiting for my partner. Lord Wickham. If you would find him for me—then we will both join Lord Salaberry."

"The marquis requested that you come alone."

"Absolutely not." It was like having a burst of thunder sneak up on one. Wickham's threatening bark exploded from behind her. The young servant blanched.

Wickham's glower had the lad cowering. "Yes, my lord. As you wish."

Then Wickham moved to her side, not close enough to touch, but enough so she was aware of him even when she did not look at him. He made a sound in his throat like a snarling wolf.

Directed at the servant or at her?

He wrapped his arm around her waist. "This time I am not taking my hands off you."

She had not expected that. She had not anticipated he would be more determined to protect her. With Wickham's steely forearm pressed to her back, Jane followed the servant through the ballroom.

Sex surrounded her.

To the left, two women reclined on a chaise. Both wore masks framed with feathers; both their bodices were open. The young woman on top had clasped the massive breast of the older woman beneath her. She enthusiastically suckled a blushing nipple, while two gentlemen who lazed on chairs opposite laughed their approval—

Jane jerked her head quickly to the side and was confronted with a beautiful young man clad in nothing but open skintight breeches. He fell back into a brocade chair and pulled the giggling Countess of Pelcham onto his erection. Lady P. glowed. Her lover appeared to be her age.

On another settee of pale blue, two naked couples were entwined. Each man fondled both women. Jane could hardly tell which limbs belonged to which person.

It was scandalous. Yet the four laughed and moaned with pleasure, and all looked to be in utter ecstasy.

At her side Wickham pressed close. Her head swam with his spicy scents and the musk of his skin, all blended with the ripe smells of sex. She heard the low murmur he made in his throat, even heard the slippery, squishy sounds of the four lovers of the sofa.

None of the ladies in here looked frightened and abused. They were delighting in passion and excitement. Was that the allure of this place? A woman could have an affair sanctioned by her husband. There would be no duel such as Wickham had fought. How could either partner be jealous or possessive when each was blatantly doing the same thing?

Wouldn't a woman, perhaps one trapped in a loveless marriage, want this rather than no passion or pleasure at all?

Then Jane thought of Charlotte trying to capture the attention of a husband who didn't love her, and Del, who'd had lovers but not love. It was safer, better, to be alone. To be free—

Out of the corner of her eye, Jane saw movement overhead. A trapeze swung high above the crowd. On the bar, a nude woman performed. On one pass she spread her legs wide. On another, she hung from one knee. Her hair swung like a horse's tail and her breasts pointed toward the crowd below. A man shot a stream of champagne from his mouth and cheers resounded when the spray hit a nipple.

Jane shook her head. Was it the sex that drew the ton here or the chance to be childish?

"Jewel?"

She saw Wickham looking at her. Her steps had faltered and he looked worried. She waved her hand. "This doesn't shock me anymore. It is just the Hyde Park stroll with sex."

His brow lifted.

Her wry words had surprised him. She had stunned the experienced Lord Wicked. And she remembered three women—her aunt, Lady Carlyle, and Mrs. Brougham—had warned her away from him. Had he truly broken a woman's arm? And bruised another?

"This way, my lord, my lady," the footman urged. "We must go downstairs. Lord Salaberry is in the dungeons."

The walls of the corridor to the dungeons were of tooled stone, the flags on the floor well swept. Torches set in medieval brackets illuminated the hallway, and iron shackles hung off the wall. The heat of the flames along with the warm bodies of many people made the basement unbearably hot.

Wickham drew his hand across the wall. "Plaster made to look like stone," he said. "The shackles are real enough, but this is mainly play-acting, Jewel."

"I saw this earlier."

"What did you see?" he asked softly.

This was his world, according to Mrs. Brougham. "I saw one woman in a cage, being touched by two men. And a woman being spanked." She had seen one man present a whip to a lady, then drop to his knees and kiss the woman's polished leather boots.

"Were they frightened?"

"No," she said, more sharply than she'd intended. "They all looked absolutely delighted."

"My lord. My lady." The footman bowed beside the cell's entrance and retreated. Behind Wickham, Jane stepped inside.

Salaberry sat beside the fire in a large black leather chair. Behind him a mirror hung on the wall, an ornate oval rimmed with gilt leaves and cherubs. Against the spartan décor of the cell—a wooden bench and various shackles—both pieces looked oddly out of place. In Salaberry's hand was the handle and coiled lash of a bullwhip.

He rose and bowed. "My dear Lady Sherringham. Accompanied by Lord Wickham, yet I had intended for you to come alone. I see that part of my message was not relayed—"

"I got the message." Wickham stepped forward, his wide chest in front of her as though providing a shield.

"I have no intention of allowing Lady Sherringham to be alone with you."

The marquis dropped back into his chair. He arranged his hands—and the whip—gracefully on the overstuffed arms. He wanted, Jane could see, to look in control. "You were naughty to desert me, my dear," he drawled. "I've spent a day creating a delectable punishment for you."

"I've had enough of this game, Salaberry."

Firelight glinted off a length of silver held in Wickham's hand. He had his pistol trained on the marquis's heart.

From the way Salaberry's color drained from his face, Jane knew he was thinking of the duel, of the fact that Wickham had killed a man.

She was thinking of it, too, her blood moving like slush through her veins. As much as she despised the sadistic marquis, she couldn't bear to think of Wickham killing another man.

"Your note to Lady Sherringham frightened her."

"Outraged," she said.

Wickham lifted his weapon to point at the marquis's forehead. "Did you push her in front of a carriage in Hyde Park?"

"Christ, no! I saw the accident. I had nothing to do with it."

Wickham's rock-hard forearm did not waver. It was as though he had no emotion in him at all. Not even rage. She began to see why Major Arbuthnot would call him a madman.

With a quick motion of his left hand, Wickham yanked something from his pocket and tossed it at the marquis. A folded piece of paper landed on the floor at Salaberry's feet.

"Your vowels," Wickham said. "I've acquired them. The thirty thousand pounds you owe? You now owe it to me."

It was an astounding sum, yet Wickham spoke as though it was inconsequential.

Salaberry's elegant demeanor fled. He stared down at the paper as though he could not understand Wickham's words. "You purchased my vowels?"

"Give me what I want and you can consider them paid. You won't have to flee creditors. I won't destroy you." Wickham stepped forward. "Get on your feet."

Slowly, Salaberry complied, his gaze locked on the pistol.

"Tell me everything you know about my sister. Or I can shoot you where you stand. It makes no difference to me. I'm itching to kill someone over this, and you'd serve to give me a moment's satisfaction."

"You'd shoot me in cold blood, without honor?"

Jane's heart thundered erratically.

A tremble wracked the marquis's shoulders. The whip he clutched hung limply. "You said you wouldn't fight me. In the cage room, you backed down from a duel."

"I'm not fighting you," Wickham answered. "I'm talking about killing you because you're being uncooperative."

The marquis quaked. "I never hurt her. I swear to God I barely left a bruise on her."

Wickham's arm straightened, his eye sighting down the barrel of the weapon.

"Christ," Salaberry croaked.

"What happened to her? I think she's in one of

Brougham's houses. I want to know why." Wickham's cold voice froze Jane's blood. He sounded beyond mercy. "I don't give a damn about what you've done or what kind of games you've played with my sister. I want her home."

Beads of sweat dripped on the marquis's brow. Jane felt perspiration trickle down her back. But as Salaberry lifted his hand to wipe his forehead, Wickham barked, "Move and I shoot you right through your head."

Salaberry whimpered. He blinked furiously and Jane saw the sweat drip into his eye. "You wouldn't do it. It would be murder."

"True." Wickham launched forward, and his fist arced cleanly and smashed into Salaberry's jaw. At the sudden burst of violence, Jane froze.

Bent over, Salaberry put his hand gingerly to his face. "All right. Your sister tried to run away from Treyworth. She left him. After all Treyworth's blustering about how well trained she was, the fragile thing showed a spark of independence after all."

"Did you help her?"

Salaberry shook his head. "Treyworth caught her, of course. The man's like a hunting hound. He told me she was hysterical, out of her mind. So he stowed her in Sapphire's sanitarium where she could regain her wits."

Jane stared. Del—out of her wits? It could not be true.

Wickham's jaw became rigid. "Brougham has a sanitarium?"

"Yes. A manor house she rents in some idyllic country setting. She keeps mad gentlewomen in it—women who are a burden to their families. Her mother died a raving lunatic. Sapphire took in a former mistress of mine who had become so obsessive, she tried to shoot me outside the Drury Lane Theatre."

"Where is this place?"

Salaberry shrugged. "No idea. She collected Eloise for me and took her there."

Wickham doubled his fist.

"Damnation, don't hit me again. Not in the face. The house is in Blackheath, I believe. She crowed that she had rented a place close to Princess Caroline's house. But that's all I know."

Jane reached out for Wickham's arm, but stopped before her fingers touched him. She realized she'd wanted to grab his arm to ensure he didn't commit murder.

What was she thinking? He'd never let her drag him out. But Wickham's gaze flicked to her, then he relaxed his arm and moved his finger off the trigger. "Is my sister still alive?"

Salaberry shot him a look of pure hatred. "I've no idea. But given what Sapphire charged to board Eloise, I suspect she's raking in a fortune from Treyworth by keeping your sister hale and healthy."

"You bought his vowels."

Jane's skirts whirled around her legs as she tried to keep pace with Wickham. His long strides were taking them away from the main staircase, further into the dungeons.

"My secretary did," Wickham answered as they reached a narrow door at the end of the corridor. "I had him investigate Salaberry yesterday. Within hours he knew the extent of the man's debts. By this morning, he'd acquired them."

"Thirty thousand pounds!"

"It wasn't a great sum. Del is worth every penny I have. I'd cut out my heart for her."

Not a great sum. Even when she was married to Sherringham, such an amount would have staggered her. "Would you have shot him, if he wouldn't talk?"

Wickham shrugged. "Salaberry is a coward underneath."

It was all the answer he'd give, she realized. Her plan had been to find a little cottage for her and Del and live off her meager savings. That would not happen now. It would be unthinkable with Del's wealthy brother in charge. Wickham would take care of Del.

"W-where are we hurrying to?" As Wickham pulled open the door, Jane had a chance to catch her breath. "We don't know where the house in Blackheath is exactly."

"We are about to find out."

The door swung wide and a blast of hot air stuck her. Ahead, pots clanged. Knives thunked against wooden boards. She'd assumed they would have gone after Mrs. Brougham. Instead they were in the kitchens—or at least a shadowy hallway leading there.

"It's almost time," Wickam murmured, as he stealthily prowled ahead.

"Midnight?" Jane whispered, following. "It isn't midnight yet."

He turned, put his finger to her lips. They had reached a low doorway. With her back to them, a woman rolled pastry—a woman with dark curls beneath a white cap. A new cook.

"Mrs. Small has not returned," he said softly. "She has

gone on to her new, improved life. You look relieved, crusading Lady Jane."

"I am," she whispered.

"We're going to find Del soon," he promised. "I brought you this way so we could go out into the rear garden."

"Why?"

"To meet a grave robber."

The servants ignored them as Wickham opened the door to the rear yard—the same door Jane had entered through two nights ago.

A tall, swarthy man came forward as Wickham stepped outside, with her at his heels. The man was an ominous-looking sort with a patch over his right eye and a jagged scar that forked the length of the left side of his face. Wickham greeted him with a smile.

"Clever plan of yours, milord," the man said cheerfully. "We're got Tanner. He took the bait and came here believing the madam had a job for him."

"This was your plan?" Jane asked Wickham.

Younger answered, touching his cap. "Aye. To lure the lead man of the grave robbers."

"You did that as well as searching the office and planning blackmail."

"An attack on many fronts," Wickham said casually.

In that instant, Jane didn't care what wicked things Wickham had done to his lovers—she admired him to the depth of her soul.

"Younger carried out the orders." Younger was striding down toward the high stone wall at the rear of the yard. "He was in charge of the men I hired to search for Del."

"Who is he? He looks . . . terrifying."

"An ex-Bow Street Runner. Before I left England, he used to raid the brothels I frequented."

Yet now Younger worked for him. And both men obviously respected each other. Wickham took her hand and led her across the yard. They reached a door in the garden wall, and passed through to the lane behind, where Younger gave a low whistle.

Two large, black-haired men emerged out of the gloom, dragging a struggling gray-haired man between them. A third man held a pistol on the captive. Moonlight slanted between clouds and sprinkled through lilac bushes. In the bluish light, Jane could see the prisoner was heavy-set, with a flattened nose, fleshy lips, and black gaps in his mouth where his teeth should have been. A dirty coat strained to cover his bulky frame.

"Stay here," Wickham said to her. He handed his pistol to Younger, who stood at her side.

Pacing toward the resurrectionist, Wickham cracked his knuckles. "Punching the marquis barely dented my gloves. What I want to do, Tanner, is split my knuckles on a bastard's face."

Jane shivered. She was watching him transform from a protector into a dark, lethal predator who itched to kill. Wickham nodded toward Younger's men. "I assume you checked him for weapons."

"We found and took two blades."

"Then release him."

Jane gasped. "Milord—" one of the guards protested.

"I won't hit him when he can't defend himself."

Jane frowned. He had slammed his fist into *Salaberry's* face while holding a pistol. Yet with the grave robber, he was concerned about gentlemanly honor.

In the past, she'd never thought of him as an angry

man. He'd done wild things, but things that were dangerous only to him—leaping off cliffs into lakes, racing carriages, bedding married women. He had laughingly told her, when they were young, that he was a lover, not a fighter.

That was obviously not true.

Wickham pulled off his tailcoat and threw it toward her. She caught the sleeve and hefted it before it landed in the muck. She hugged the fine wool, breathing in bergamot and sandalwood and him.

The guards took their hands off Tanner and he stumbled forward. The man's face was black and blue, and there were companion blotches on the faces of the guards. Tanner hadn't been captured without a fight. Wickham paced around him. Tanner outweighed him by several stone—taller, bigger, with hulking arms and a thick neck.

"Are you certain about this, my lord?" Younger's voice rumbled from Jane's side.

"Certain I can beat a lout like this to a pulp if he doesn't give me what I want—?" Wickham broke off and moved like a blur through the shadows.

Jane blinked. One instant, he'd stood there, his fists raised. The next he seemed to fly over Tanner, as though he'd somersaulted over the man in midair.

"Christ Jesus," the grave robber gurgled.

Wickham was at Tanner's back, his arm braced hard against the man's chest, his gloved hand clamped on the man's chin. "One jerk of my arm and I break your neck. Where did you take the gently bred lady for Mrs. Brougham? The one being held prisoner. Was it Blackheath?"

"I'm dead if I tell you."

"You're dead if you don't. Talk and you might scurry away like the rat you are."

"Don't kill me, milord," Tanner begged. "I've got a family—Bess and four wee ones."

Clinging to Wickham's coat, Jane realized she was shaking. His dark, dangerous side was essential for this—*she* could never have intimidated a hardened criminal. But it scared her to see how savage and cold Wickham could be.

For Del, she reminded herself. He was doing this for Del.

"Talk," Wickham commanded, his voice icy and laced with threat. "You may find I pay better than the madam."

"It was 'er 'ouse in Blackheath. She keeps madwomen in there. Some of them are old or sick and they don't last long. There's some young ones—ones in the family way. She takes 'em in, makes 'em disappear while they 'ave the babes. But some don't survive the birth, their babies neither. The schools pay well to get them."

Wickham's grip tightened across Tanner's chest. "Good start. Do you take the dead infants?"

"She won't sell those. Has 'em buried. Sentimental old bitch, she is."

"Now, tell me where the house in Blackheath is."

Directions spilled out of Tanner's mouth so quickly, Jane could barely keep track. But Wickham nodded.

"There, I've 'elped, 'aven't I, milord? No need to be breaking me neck now, is there?"

"Unless you haven't told me the truth."

"It's the truth. Let God smite me down, if it's not."

"God won't smite you down. I will." Wickham abruptly pushed Tanner toward the other men. "You've helped me, Tanner. I won't kill you. But you are coming to Blackheath. And I'll rip your throat out if you've lied."

"I haven't, milord—"

At Jane's side, Younger sprang into action. He slapped irons on Tanner's hands. What would Wickham do to the resurrectionist afterward? Turn him over to the magistrates? But what would happen to Tanner's family—to a woman with four children and a husband in prison?

Her lips parted. Wickham caught her eye. His brows rose.

Abruptly, he turned to Tanner. "It does disturb me to leave your wife and children in financial straits. Give an address to Younger, and money will be provided to help them."

It was an act of kindness. But she was struck by more. Was it just the glimpse of her face that had prompted Wickham to do it? Had he taken one look at her and understood her thoughts?

"Thank you, milord," Tanner said. "A man 'as to support 'is family."

Jane saw the stark pain on Wickham's face. "He does, Tanner."

Chapter Twelve

Wᴵᴄᴋʜᴀᴍ ʟᴇᴀᴘᴛ ᴜᴘ ᴏɴ ᴛʜᴇ ʙᴏx of his carriage and grasped the reins. He took the streets of London at breakneck speed while Jane clung to the seat inside. Younger and one of his men shared the carriage with her—the other was outside with Tanner.

Gravel crunched as they charged up a driveway. Through the window, Jane saw the flares that fronted the stone pillars and then the glowing windows of Wickham House. The instant they stopped, Younger assisted her down, into the mad flurry on the drive.

Grooms trotted a curricle into a circle of lamplight, and Wickham stood there, within the glow. The moment he spied her, the grim resolution dropped from his face. He ran to her.

"We're close now, Jane. I'll have Del home in no time. Huntley will see to taking you home and—"

"No! I must go with you. I need to be there for Del."

"It's too dangerous—"

"She's been locked up. With madwomen. She will

need me. Wickham, she has not seen you for eight years. Del needs a best friend to be with her. A woman."

It was a truth he couldn't deny, the one weapon she had to make him agree.

She added, "I'm not afraid of the danger."

His brow cocked over a gaze of disbelief.

"All right, then," she said grudgingly. "I am. But I used to be afraid in my own home. I faced the club again—I will do this."

"You're a distraction to me, Jewel. I don't need to have to worry about you."

Suddenly that nickname grated on her. "Then *don't* worry about me. I am a grown woman. You are *not* responsible for me, Wickham."

He threw up his hands. "Come then. I'd rather lose this argument than waste time on it."

In a swift, fluid motion, Wickham half handed, half pushed her up into his high-sprung curricle. The grooms held the eager horses as he jumped up into the driver's seat and took up the ribbons. A snap of the reins and they were off. Jane grabbed for the handle on the side and gravel shot up around them.

"Hold tight," he warned.

Jane's heart lodged in her throat as Wickham tore down Park Lane. The way he'd driven the carriage to Wickham House from the club had been slow and cautious compared to his speed now. They charged around slower carriages, sliced through the narrowest of openings between two vehicles, and took cobbled streets so fast she feared the curricle would fly apart from the vibrations.

Her eyes jiggled and her bottom bounced on the seat.

Wind blasted her face, threw her hood back, and tossed her veil behind her.

"Blast," Wickham roared as they neared two ornate carriages that filled the road and moved at a leisurely pace. He didn't slow.

"Wickham—" She stopped. Now was not the time to distract him. He leaned ahead in his seat, his attention fixed on the two carriages. She wanted to scream but didn't dare.

He had won the carriage race. All those years ago, he had won the neck-or-nothing race she had tried to stop. He had driven like a madman, had taken a shortcut up a treacherous hill, had almost rolled his carriage, but he'd won.

A victory that he'd crowed about as she'd nursed her failure—her aim had been to make a bunch of irresponsible gentlemen see sense.

"There." He growled it and Jane saw the slimmest of space between the rattling wheels ahead. Shouldn't he slow down? If they went slower, the carriages would move farther apart and there would be room. But if anything, they were hurtling faster at that tiny opening.

Her stomach roiled as the curricle tipped onto two wheels. She slid—

Her body slammed into his. But he was strong enough to resist the force of the impact. He didn't move. She had to grab his thigh to gain her balance. *Hold tight,* he'd warned. She was doing it now, her hand clutching his leg, her fingers trying to drive into unyielding muscle.

She stole a glance at Wickham. His black hair streamed back from his face. He turned, flashed her a wild, almost feral, grin. He'd discarded his mask. Excitement glinted in his eyes.

There had been times in her younger years that she'd stolen glances like this at him—a glimpse of his cheek-bones, the strong sweep of his jaw, the dark beauty of his eyes. She'd always looked away just as quickly.

But she stared at him now as the carriage lurched beneath her. She'd always thought he looked like Del; now she saw all his differences. His face was harder, the bones more defined—obviously more masculine. Deep lines bracketed his mouth, and his large dark blue eyes could change from teasing to ruthless in a moment.

He must have felt her stare. He looked to her. The fire in his eyes extinguished. Concern replaced it. "Are you all right? You look green."

She refused to let him think that speeding in a carriage was sapping her courage. Not when she'd demanded he bring her.

They tore past the Palace of Westminister, raced across the bridge. Soon, they had left London behind, following the roads to the southeast, toward Greenwich Park and Blackheath. His horses' hooves tore up the dry surface of the road, throwing dust around them.

"Look out," she cried, pointing to an oncoming carriage.

With barely a glance, he guided his thundering horses to the side and they passed the other carriage with a whoosh. Fist raised, the driver shouted at them.

"We're getting closer. But I don't dare drive faster, in case we overturn. The road's rutted."

He could drive faster? "Just watch the road, Wickham," she shouted. The clatter of the wheels, the pounding of hooves, and the roar of the wind were deafening.

"Christian," he yelled. "If we're to be in a carriage wreck together, I think you should use my given name."

Jane knew, in that moment, she trusted him not to send them into a carriage wreck. He was the only man she would trust to drive like a maniac, yet get her to Blackheath alive.

Christian had to slow suddenly, to negotiate a series of deep ruts, which meant they weren't being buffeted by noise, and she could speak.

"Do you believe Salaberry?" she shouted. "Do you think this woman is really Del—that Treyworth sent her to Mrs. Brougham's madhouse? Brougham, the lying witch, told me she had tried to protect Del."

"We'll know soon." Christian looked to her and added, "I didn't see Treyworth in Hyde Park."

She nodded, understanding. "Neither did I. My accident must have been exactly that."

She fell into silence for a while. Clouds massed across the moon. A raindrop spattered on her hand.

"Blast," Christian muttered, and he drove his horses harder.

"You must have overheard Mrs. Brougham when she was speaking to me."

His head jerked up. She had to admit she was also rather amazed she was talking about it. But it was like a hairpin jabbing into her scalp. She had to know.

"Yes. I was under the bed."

"You didn't truly break Lady Matchell's arm, did you?"

He shrugged, his attention now fully on the road again. "She was tied up and fell off a swing in the middle of her climax."

"It was an accident."

"Yes, a sex-related accident."

Wicked teasing laced his careless tone. This was the way he had been with her in his youth.

"And the bruises on Lady Durham?"

"I did put them there. She liked her pleasures rough. Those things Brougham told you—about bondage, whipping, private dungeons, that was all true. I've whipped and been whipped."

"But why?" She felt more tossed about this than by his speeding carriage. She'd assumed he'd deny it all. "Why would you whip someone? Or tie them up? Why would you need to dominate a helpless person?"

"Mainly because they enjoyed it. But you're correct. It fed something in me."

"Do you . . . still do those things?" Jane asked.

Christian stared ahead at the road. There was no anger in Jane's voice—just bewilderment. And that lanced his heart like no furious, condemning words had ever done. She sounded disappointed, and for some mad reason, that bothered him. "Not since my last lover ended our affair."

"Your lover?"

What a complex voice she had. It could be so soft it made his heart race, so strident it made him grind his teeth, and so full of vulnerability it made him desperate to make her happy. Was he mad? "Wife of one of the few friends I had left in Bombay," he said.

"How could you betray a friend, Lord Wickham?"

"Don't, sweeting."

The endearment—or his tone—startled her.

"Do not embark on a crusade over me, Lady Jane Beaumont. Don't try to rescue me."

He flicked the reins to urge the horses to greater speed, and the clamor of the wheels on the road ensured Jane Beaumont could not ask him any more questions.

Ahead, Christian could see Greenwich Park. To the south, the spire of a church reached up to the cloud-strewn sky, and the heath stretched out, a flat, blue-black expanse in the dark. More rain splattered onto his face.

Why in Hades had he brought Jane? He could have thrust her into Huntley's arms and forced his staid old secretary to deal with her. Guiltily, he thought of how she'd rescued him from Georgie. To do it, she'd played the tart and touched him. He'd known how important the touch—which appeared light and casual—had been to her.

Strangely, he could remember, with astonishing clarity, their last argument before he'd left England. He could remember her precise last words, thrown at him when he'd told her he had bedded all the married beauties of the ton ...

"Don't smirk at me," she'd cried. "You're heartless. Isn't that a rather empty way to be?"

He had to slow the horses as they passed Greenwich Park. Princess Caroline's former home, Montague House, stood in a corner of the park. Brougham's place was near it. With his heart thundering, he scanned along the illuminated homes for a Georgian manor of stone with rows of eight windows, separated from Blackheath by the Greenwich Park wall.

"There!" Jane pointed. "There's the house, I think."

Christian drew the carriage up in front of the house. The jingle of the traces died away. His horses breathed hard. He'd driven them brutally and, worse, he had no shelter for them.

"What do we do?" Jane breathed. "Do we storm up and knock on the door?" She looked ready to pound until she woke the dead. But her hands trembled, too. Whenever he'd charged into danger, he hadn't cared whether he lived or died, which diluted the bravery of the act. Jane was truly brave.

"I don't think they will surrender my sister to my demand." He swung out of the vehicle, then handed her down, keeping watch around him. Brougham's house was dark and quiet. He could not see anyone guarding it, but that did not guarantee she didn't have servants on watch.

"Are you going to force your way in with your men?"

"I'd rather not put the servants on alert so quickly."

"You're going to break in to try to find her. You'll need me. We can search faster together."

"As if I would leave you alone out here. I've brought you, so I'm stuck with you." He spied her indignant, hurt look as he slid off his greatcoat—

"What are you doing?"

He flung the coat over one of his horses. Jane undid her cloak and held it out to him. He threw it over the other horse.

"We know the servants are being paid well to keep her here. We're going to meet opposition. So, Jewel—"

"Jane. Since we didn't die in a carriage accident, I want you to use my given name. No more nicknames. Just Jane."

Just Jane. He couldn't think there was anything "just" about her. "So, Jane—"

"I know." She discarded her veil, which had fallen back to cover her face. "You are going to demand that I stay at your side."

*   *   *

The house seemed to breathe around her, a live thing it-self, ready to crush her for invading it, ready to scream a warning to the servants within.

Jane shook off the fancy. But the house possessed an eerie stillness, even though it was not quiet. Distant cries and muffled screams floated through the air. Things clanged. Voices rose and fell.

She had followed Christian through a terrace door he had opened swiftly. Now they made their way tentatively down a pitch-dark corridor.

"I don't know anything about sanitariums," he muttered. "I assume servants sleep on the upper floors as they do in any house."

"I know a little," she whispered. Her throat tightened. Sherringham had insisted her mad mother be put away. Her late father's family had agreed when Margaret set fire to her bed and almost died—and almost destroyed the dower house. "There should be rooms for the matron or the physician who is in charge. And wards for the women, usually with a member of the staff on guard. In some places, wealthy guests can purchase the use of a private room. Those would be on the upper floor."

Jane remembered how Margaret had degraded in the madhouse. It had only been months before she died. And she'd forgotten she had a daughter long before that.

"Come." Christian growled the one imperious word. Hand in hand, they crept up the main staircase.

They had surveyed the house quickly from the outside. It was rectangular in shape, not large, with a passage off the right end that led to another building—a square tower that overlooked the Greenwich Park wall.

As they reached the gallery at the stop of the stair, Jane whispered, "She might be in a room at the rear of the house. With a—a garden view." Her voice broke on that. Her mother had a garden view, but had been a prisoner in her bed. "Or in the tower."

Obviously he thought the same way. With his hand on her wrist, he was already leading her down the hallway to the right. But instead of prowling directly to the tower, Christian paused by the first door. He quickly defeated the lock and eased it open. It creaked and lightly jostled a wooden chair. Through the small opening Jane saw a snoring woman slumped on the seat. The woman stirred.

Jane held her breath.

The woman grunted, then her hand fell limply. She'd dropped back into sleep. Beneath Christian's arm, Jane saw rows of cots. Someone suddenly moaned in her sleep and thrashed beneath the blankets.

Christian eased the door shut, his features set like stone. "A ward room. Ten beds packed in with a woman on guard. Christ."

"Bedlam is worse," she whispered. "And people visit it as though it is an entertainment."

"I know," he muttered.

They checked behind every door in the wing but each one opened to a room packed with simple beds. As they walked away from room after room, Jane saw Christian's face appear more strained, his eyes more grim. Her own jaw felt rigid, her heartbeat pounded in her head.

She pointed to a passage that led to the tower and he nodded.

A hallway sliced through the tall square structure,

leading to a window at the end. Faint gray light spilled in, and rain plunked against the glass.

The first room along the hall contained only one bed—a large four-poster one—along with elegant chairs and an escritoire. Jane's heart soared. This had to be the room of a wealthier woman. But there were no guards.

She slipped quietly inside before Wickham could stop her.

Though she had not made a sound, the bed's occupant sat bolt upright. Jane froze as she took in the elderly woman's white hair and lined face. Not Del.

"Is that you? Sapphire dear, have you come to see me?" The woman stared at her—at her hair—and held out her arms. "Oh, my love, you haven't been for so long. Please, dear. Come to your mother. Let me kiss you."

Out of the corner of her eye, Jane saw Christian shake his head. *Get back here,* he mouthed.

If she went closer, the woman would see she was not Sapphire Brougham. Salaberry had said Mrs. Brougham's mother was dead. But that could not be. This woman was the madam's mother.

"Sapphire, dear . . ."

"You must go to sleep now," Jane said softly. "I will see you in the morning. Please . . . Mother."

The woman tugged at the neckline of her nightdress, then nodded, and obediently lay back. "Would you sing for me? It makes the shadows retreat . . . makes the voices stop . . . when I hear you sing . . ."

Jane bit her lip. She had sung for her mother once, when her mother had been locked away in the sanitarium. Margaret had stared at her blankly and did not even seem to hear her. She had no idea if she would sound convincingly like the madam. She stumbled through a gentle lullaby, and retreated as she sang, taking cautious steps backward. The woman settled in her bed, began to breathe softly and steadily. When Jane reached the doorway, Christian wrapped his arm around her waist and hauled her out.

"Do not do that again."

"I don't intend to," Jane whispered as he eased open the next door.

A high-pitched scream rang out, and Christian launched into the room.

He had no choice but to clamp his hand over the young woman's mouth. The slender, panic-stricken girl sank her teeth in, but he kept his palm clamped firmly in place. In his peripheral vision, he saw Jane close the door, then she hastened over.

Jane dropped to the girl's right foot and tugged at the strip of fabric that bound the prisoner to the bed.

"Stop," he warned. "She could be violent."

"It is unthinkable that she should be tied up," Jane protested, sotto voce, and she continued to tear fiercely at the bonds.

Christian bent to the prisoner, who looked no older than sixteen. "We're here to help you, not hurt you. Promise not to scream, and I'll move my hand."

He might be trying to bargain with a madwoman, but the girl nodded her head jerkily and her greasy blond waves flew around her face. He eased his hand from her lips. Wide violet eyes peered at him. With her oval face and delicate nose, the lass would be pretty if cleaned up.

"Are you one of them?" she whispered.

Her choked sob lanced his heart. "One of who, love? What is your name?"

"It's—" She stopped and looked stricken. "It's Anne. Anne Fielding."

"Christian, she is obviously gently bred." To the girl, Jane said, "Where are you from, Anne?" She began to untie the girl's right hand.

"I can't say. I'll be beaten for telling you my name."

"No one will beat you," Christian vowed. "You will be going home."

Anne trembled. "They won't let me go. Not until I please the men who come here. They want me next. They told me so. I thought you must be one of them, without your mask, without your cloak. You aren't, are you?"

"Shh," he soothed.

Tears tracked down the girl's face. He dragged out his handkerchief and gently wiped her cheeks. She was so very young.

Jane clasped the girl's hand and massaged the vicious red marks that ringed the child's wrist. "Do they wear black masks and cloaks?"

Anne nodded. "They never take them off."

"What have they done to you, Anne? Do you know who these men are?"

The girl shrank back.

"I am so sorry." Jane's voice dropped to a soft, soothing tone he'd never heard her use. "You must be very frightened. But we will help you."

Anne fiercely shook her head. "I'll be punished. I'll be chained up like the others and whipped. They hung one in a cage and left her there for days—"

Christian put his arm around her and drew her to his chest. She was as thin as Philly, frail and fragile. "No one will hurt you anymore. I promise you that." Once Anne stopped heaving with sobs, he released her. "But you must be brave. We have to go, but—"

"Oh, no." Anne clutched at his sleeve. "Don't leave."

"There will be others coming, soon, who will help you. But you must be quiet. You can't sound the alarm."

Eyes wide, she nodded. "I'm so afraid. I've been sick and they think I've got a babe now, and I think they want to kill me. I'm no good to them if I'm all large with a babe."

Jane made a strangled sound. She stroked Anne's hair. Quietly she asked about Del—if Anne knew about a gentlewoman who had been brought to the house.

Anne shook her head. "I don't know. I am always blindfolded when I leave the room, but I heard the maids complain of a titled lady on the top floor of the tower and how they had to do so much work for her."

Christian eased Anne back, so she was lying in her bed, and Jane drew her covers up. "You have to lie down and stay quiet. You cannot tell anyone you saw us. It won't be long and you'll be free." He prayed the girl would listen. He knew she wanted to run and that her instincts would be screaming for escape.

He got to his feet and crooked his finger. Jane followed him to the door. Her eyes were huge and dark against her pale face. "Mrs. Brougham is keeping innocents here," she cried. "Forcing them to service those men. And this girl is enceinte. It's . . . it's evil."

"And it's over now," he said grimly.

"Guards," Jane whispered. She knew Christian had seen them, but her nerves were strung so tightly, the word popped out before she could stop it.

The window at the end of this hallway let in moonlight—the clouds must have rolled onward—and silvery rays fell upon two men who slumbered on chairs about twenty feet from where she stood with Christian, pressed tight against the wall, swathed in shadow.

"Should we wait for your men?"

"I can dispatch those two," he answered. "But I want you to take this. Can you shoot?"

Shoot? Something hard and cool pressed to her palm. She stared down at the gleaming metal of a pistol barrel and her fingers closed around the handle.

"For your protection," he murmured.

"But what about yours?"

He held his finger to his lips. Then he left her. He crossed the floorboards so silently it was as though his feet didn't touch them at all. The two bulky guards slept on blissfully.

Jane clasped the pistol with both hands. It was surprisingly heavy. If the time came, she prayed she could aim true.

She expected Christian to sneak past the men. Instead, he stopped, grabbed the first guard by the scruff of his neck and dragged the man's head up to meet the arc of his fist.

The pistol wobbled in her hand.

Blood and spittle sprayed from the guard's mouth and there was a horrible gurgling, then the man's head lolled to the side. One blow had knocked him out and Christian let him slump over.

The other guard jerked awake at the soft thud of his partner landing on the floor. It took only seconds for the man to be aware of imminent danger and he jerked out a knife as Christian's fist swung again.

Christian danced back to avoid the swipe of the blade so his blow missed the guard's face. Unsteadily, Jane followed the guard's movement with the pistol barrel.

Christian punched the guard in the stomach and the large body doubled over. But the beefy man straightened almost instantly and drove his knife forward again. It caught the side of Christian's waistcoat and sliced.

Christian sent a flurry of blows to the man's gut. The guard reeled, and he flailed with the knife. The blade sliced Christian's cheek. As blood spurted, Jane's legs went weak.

Should she just shoot the man?

What if she hit Christian instead?

The guard landed a punch to Christian's cheek. Her heart leapt to her throat as his head snapped with it and blood sprayed, but he returned with two blows, one beneath the man's chin, the other to his nose. For heart-stopping minutes, both men pounded each other mercilessly.

Jane's hand tightened on the pistol's grip and her finger cramped near the trigger. She was trying not to accidentally pull it. But should she fire at the guard? How much of this punishment could Christian take?

Footsteps pounded behind her and she swung around. More servants! Eight men. Three carried knives, the others held bats or fireplace pokers. Jane's heart stuttered in her chest but she held the pistol trained on the leader of the group. "Stop or I shoot!"

The servants lurched to a stop. Eyes wide, the men stared at the muzzle of the weapon, then at her in horror. She felt a spurt of confidence.

She could not believe she had run from the club in panic, but now held a loaded pistol on a group of men. It was Christian—it was as though he had brought her back to life.

She would not let him be hurt now.

"Damned hell," Christian yelled behind her.

Still holding the weapon on the servants, she tried to turn, without putting her back to them. She saw Christian grab the wrist of the guard and snap it. A scream echoed down the hall and the knife fell to the ground. But a scarlet blotch was soaking into Christian's shirt on his right side.

"There's one shot, you fools," shouted the guard as Christian shoved him to the floor and slammed his booted foot onto the man's back.

"I'm not the one taking it," cried one of the servants.

"Get him, you louts!" the guard bellowed.

Shots exploded below, shrieks rang out, and the house seemed to shudder with thundering footsteps. Christian's men had arrived.

The armed servants in front of her began to back up. Slowly at first; then, when they realized she wouldn't shoot, they turned and bolted.

Jane looked to Christian. "What do I do? They're escaping."

"They won't get far." Christian held out his hand and she surrendered the weapon. Sweating, breathing hard, he bent down to the captive guard. A quick blow to the back of the man's neck and the guard joined his partner in quiet unconsciousness.

Jane filled his vision, hesitantly reaching toward the bloody patch on his shirt. "It's all right, love," he assured. "It was a glancing blow, not deep."

She frowned and stood on tiptoe, peering at the stinging

slice in his cheek. "You are a mess. You're cut to pieces. Why didn't you hold the *pistol* on them?"

He shrugged, unwinding his cravat. "Two men. One shot. I couldn't be certain they wouldn't try to rush us, and I knew I could knock them out."

"You wanted to fight, I think."

He made his cravat into a pad and stuffed it beneath his waistcoat. "Perhaps I did. Perhaps you know me too well, Jane." Something dripped in his eye. He wiped blood from his forehead so he could see clearly enough to spring the lock on the door.

Inside the room, a woman lay in large canopied bed. Long dark waves framed her face and poured over her pale nightdress. Like young Anne, she was bound. His heart lurched, and for one moment he was frozen, staring at the woman he should have been responsible for.

Jane pushed past him. "Del!"

But his sister did not even recognize him.

As Christian ripped apart the cords that bound Del to the bed, she pulled away from him, and the fear mounting in her eyes was the worst condemnation he'd ever known.

Then Jane wrapped her arms around Del and his sister's eyes lit up. "Jane? Oh, dear heaven, it can't truly be you. It can't—"

"It is." Jane hugged her tightly and he saw tears leak to Jane's freckled cheeks. "And this is your brother. It's Christian. He's come for you and he's going to take you home."

"Christian? Oh, Christian, you did come." But a wild look of panic leapt to Del's eyes. "Home?"

"Mine, Del," he promised.

"But my husband will be so angry. I can't—"

He fought to keep his voice gentle, to tamp down his rage. "What Treyworth wants doesn't matter. I intend to protect you, Del."

"But, Jane..." Del swung around, rubbing her bruised wrists. "My husband will be furious that you've found me. Please, Jane, he might try to hurt you."

Jane looked shaken but before Christian could insist he would protect them both, she firmly said, "He cannot hurt me. And he will no longer hurt you." She began to pull clothes from the wardrobe.

Jane sounded confident, but Christian was staring helplessly down at Del. It had been far easier to give orders to Younger and his other men, to race here at breakneck speed, and to fight a knife-wielding guard than to face his sister and realize he had no idea how to help a woman who'd been through hell.

Jane draped Del's pelisse around her shoulders and he gathered Del in his arms. She rested there stiffly for a moment, then relaxed a bit and let her head press against his chest.

He bent and kissed the top of her head.

Then he kissed Jane on the bridge of her nose. She blinked in surprise. "I need you, Jane. Will you help me bring Del to my house? Will you come home with me?"

Chapter Thirteen

"HE WILL COME FOR ME, JANE. He will come here to take me home." Perched on the edge of the bed, Del shivered.

Jane quickly pulled the flannel night rail over Del's head and dragged it down as hurriedly as she could to cover her best friend's trembling body. Impulsively, she wrapped her arms around the thin shoulders. As though to convince herself Del was truly here, at Christian's house and safe.

When she'd helped Del bathe, the sight of the thin body, the remnants of old scars, the shadowed exhaustion in the large pale blue eyes had speared Jane to her soul. Obviously Del had not been eating for much longer than the fortnight she'd been missing.

"You will never have to go back to him," Jane said firmly. With that, she guided Del to the vanity. A plate of sugar biscuits sat there along with a pot of steaming tea.

A maid had laid out a set of silver brushes. Gently pressing on Del's shoulders, Jane compelled her to sit in front of the plate. She picked up a brush. Del was frightened and tired, but she was not hysterical. Del was *not* mad.

"He'll be furious." Del lifted a biscuit with shaky fingers. "I ran away. I humiliated him."

Jane paused, the brush poised over the crown of black hair. For all she'd insisted it wasn't possible, Del had in fact run away. "Why did you not come to me?"

"I couldn't. You have no one to protect you, Jane."

Sadly, Jane realized Del meant she had no *man* to protect her. Aunt Regina had been correct. Del had avoided coming to her in order to keep her safe.

Del buried her face in her hands. "Does he know you were searching for me?"

"Yes, of course. I confronted Treyworth, and he lied to me. He told me you had gone off to the Continent with a lover."

"Jane, why didn't you leave it at that? Why did you provoke him?"

Jane coaxed the brush through Del's hair. "I am not the least concerned that Treyworth is provoked." She spoke confidently, though there was an annoying ripple of unease in her stomach. "And I was not going to let you suffer at his hands."

"He was so very kind when he found me," Del said softly. "So apologetic and so loving and gentle. I think he took me to Mrs. Brougham's to . . . to help me. I know, if I speak to him, I—"

"No!" Jane cried. Her blood felt like ice. The wretch had lied to Del, had convinced her to return to him willingly, and had managed to make her believe that locking her up was helping her. "You are not going to speak to him. I am not going to let him anywhere near you."

"It isn't your decision to make!" Del's fierce tone was startling.

Jane met Del's gaze in the mirror. "If you speak to Treyworth, he will tell you lies again. He will apologize and beg and plead. I don't think you are strong enough yet to face him. Your brother and I will take care of you."

"My brother won't. He can't."

Jane dropped to one knee and took Del's hand. "He will. He came back for you. He was frantic with worry when I first encountered him at the club."

"You went to the club?" Del's eyes opened wide with horror.

"Yes. That was how we found you. The Marquis of Salaberry admitted that Treyworth had sent you to Mrs. Brougham's sanitarium—after your brother spent thirty thousand pounds to purchase his vowels and threatened the little ferret at pistol point."

Tea sloshed over the rim of the cup Del held in her trembling hand. "He did that for me? But don't you see, Jane? Christian shouldn't have come back. I shouldn't have written to him. He shot a man in a duel. There still could be a trial. I've dragged him back to face that—"

"Don't think about this now," Jane soothed. But she had not thought of that at all. If a man was killed in a duel, there was supposed to be a trial. For a peer, it would be held in the House of Lords. Christian hadn't been the first gentleman to run to avoid one.

"They say the other man—the earl—shot first," Del whispered. "He cheated. But then Christian coldly shot him right through the heart. Father said he didn't even try to miss. M-men do that . . . to spare a life . . ."

And Christian hadn't. Jane thought of the dark streak she'd seen in him tonight and how he'd itched to find someone to hit. But he hadn't shot anyone, even with ample opportunity to do it.

What would happen if he were found guilty? Could he be hanged?

"You need to eat something," Jane urged. If Christian were sentenced to hang—if he were taken away—she would protect Del. Just as she'd planned from the beginning. But she could picture Christian being led to the gallows. In her mind's eye, she could see hands place a noose around his strong, tanned neck, and her stomach lurched . . .

Del shook her head. "I'm not hungry. They brought me food. I'm just . . . tired. So very tired." She slowly got to her feet. Jane steered her to the bed and tucked her in.

In only a moment, Del's eyes drifted shut.

Jane glanced around at the somber brown and green décor, the yellowed wallpaper, the heavy draperies and hangings. Ugh. This had always been Del's room and it had always been miserable. The late Earl of Wickham had been cold and distant to both his children—he had spent all his time in his library. He had espoused the obligation of a gentleman to constantly expand his mind.

He should have spared a moment or two for his heart.

"Jane, love? Are you both . . . all right?"

Christian's voice startled Jane out of her thoughts and she spun around.

She picked up the candle by the bedside and held it aloft. It threw light on the doorway—on him, Christian, standing there. His shirt, a clean, white one, lay open at his throat. His cravat was undone and threatened to slip off his shoulders. His hair was damp; it looked as though he'd simply shaken his head to dry.

Bruises blossomed on his eye, nose, chin, and right

cheek. But they only made him far more dangerously handsome. With a shudder, Jane realized someone had sewn in a few stitches to knit together the cut along the ridge of his cheekbone.

"She is sleeping." She did not want to tell him that Del wanted to speak to Treyworth when he came to find her. They had never talked about what would happen after they found Del. *Finding* her had been the most important thing.

A lock of her hair fell before her eyes and she brushed it back. How miserable did she look? Her hair hung around her, matted and disheveled from the wind. Splatters of mud from the road marred her dismal black gown.

"It's your turn now, love. Why don't you bathe and I'll take you to bed?"

She froze at Christian's words. Behind him, she could see maids hurrying past with buckets of steaming water.

"I've had the bedroom beside Del's prepared," he continued. "I thought you'd want to bathe, eat, then stay here tonight. But if you want to go home—" He stopped, and raked his free hand through his wet hair.

He didn't mean *take her to bed* in the way it happened at the club. What was she thinking?

"I'd like you to stay," he continued softly. "I want to know you are safe. And Hades, I'll admit it—" he looked intensely awkward "—I need you here to help me with Del. You are her friend. You know her. It's been so long and . . . and she looks at me as though she's afraid of me. I guess I deserve that for leaving her to this fate."

"She's not afraid of you. I think she's afraid for you. Afraid that she's brought you back into trouble over the duel."

"That." His broad shoulders gave an elegant shrug. Beneath his shirt, his muscles rippled. "She has no need to worry. I doubt there's much danger there."

Suddenly, looking up into his battered but beautiful face, Jane remembered Major Arbuthnot's words. *A young gentleman who was seeking his own demise.* "But couldn't there be a trial?"

He didn't answer. "I've sent a message to Bow Street," he said instead. "About the sanitarium and Brougham's trade in innocents."

She wanted to speak of his life, but guessed he would not. To send a note to Bow Street meant he had brought the magistrates' attention to him, and the duel would be remembered. For those women and girls in the madhouse, who probably had no one to champion them, he was risking his freedom and possibly his life.

What sort of punishment did the House of Lords hand down to one of its own for a duel? She couldn't remember any cases. Most of the peers involved in such scandals did what he had done—leave the country.

She cast a sidelong glance at him. He had killed a man when he could have deloped—when he could have fired in the air, retaining his honor but sparing a life. And he'd done it for Georgiana, whom he had warned against falling in love with him.

He would be a rescuer one moment, then remind her he was wicked the next.

Steam billowed out of an open door. They'd reached the bathing room.

Christian's husky voice broke their silence. "I would not have shot Salaberry. You asked earlier and I didn't give you a direct answer. It was a bluff. That's why I had to hit him. And I'm sorry you had to see that."

Astonished, she realized he was explaining himself to her. "Oh," she said. "Well, I might have shot the servants at the house. If I'd had to."

"Lady Jane Beaumont, you astound me at every turn."

His skin had dampened his shirt and it was sticking to him. She could see the planes of muscle on his chest where the linen clung. Even his brown nipples. The fresh, citrus scent of bergamot drifted from his skin to tease her nose. Christian leaned one arm against the wall and lowered his lips toward hers—

"My lord." An elderly, bespectacled man hurried down the hallway toward them.

"Huntley," Christian muttered. "My secretary."

Huntley looked like a correct servant who'd been thrown into a maelstrom—his gray hair stuck out, his glasses were askew, and he sighed as though bearing the weight of the world. "We've found Mary and brought both her and that ignoble footman home *before* they wed. The girl is too distraught to realize she has been rescued and won't speak to anyone but you."

Christian slapped his hand to his forehead. "I'd forgotten Mary." He turned to her. "One of the girls fled off to Gretna with a footman."

Mary, the brazen girl who had flirted with him outside his drawing room. "I should bathe," Jane said. "Why don't you go to Mary?"

"Thank you, sweeting," he murmured and she saw Huntley's gray brows shoot up in disapproval at the endearment.

They arched even higher as Christian lifted her hand and pressed his lips to her bare palm—she'd long since discarded her crumpled black gloves. Fire seemed to ignite where his lips touched her skin. He lazily trailed his mouth to her wrist. He suckled—

Sensation roared through her. She gasped. Swayed. Let out an unladylike whimper and had to put her hand against the wall.

Christian's blue eyes met hers as he rose. His eyes had darkened to the rich color of a night sky in that heartbeat before twilight vanished. "Enjoy your bath. You deserve it."

She could not leave Del, and, dangerous though it may be, she could not leave him. "I'll stay," she whispered.

A wide grin lit up his handsome face. Then he was gone, off with his secretary.

And that one kiss to her wrist seemed to have knocked her legs out from beneath her.

Steam swirled out of the bathing room—rose-scented steam. It smelled heavenly. Jane went in, lured by the warmth and the comforting smell.

Maids helped her strip off her horrible mourning gown, her corset and shift. Christian had thought of everything. Towels ringed one side of the tub and a mat was laid to spare her the discomfort of wet feet on a chilled floor. Then she thought sensibly. It wasn't Christian who had arranged this. It would be servants accustomed to serving a countess.

Candless flickered, the fire roared. A few rose petals of innocent pink floated on the water.

That had to be Christian.

As Jane sank into the warm water, she closed her eyes, and let her mind go back over the night. After they had safely loaded Del in the carriage, Christian had shaken the matron awake. Confused, then toadying, then blubbering about her innocence, the woman had denied knowing anything about masked men or Lady Treyworth. She was obviously lying. To protect the women, Christian had left his armed men on guard.

But those women needed to go home. Jane feared some of them had no home to go to. For a moment, the weight of it settled on her shoulders.

She set to scrubbing with the rose-scented soap, and she washed out her hair as quickly as she could. Maids brought fresh hot water for her to rinse, then she stepped out into a warmed towel held at the ready.

"Here is a robe for you, my lady." One of the maids held out a creation of heavy pink silk.

"Thank you." She wrapped it around her. Slippers were produced and the maid promised that a night rail had been laid out on her bed. As she dried out her hair by the fire, the maid said, "His lordship asked me to tell you that a note has been sent to your aunt."

Aunt Regina! Heavens, she'd almost forgotten.

How kind of Christian to remember. How astonishing that he would be thinking of her right now, for that must be why he would do such a thing.

When she left the bathing chamber, Jane went to Del's room. She had to reassure herself Del was really there. And she was—asleep in the bed, her black hair spilling over the covers. Then Jane saw Christian.

He sat in a chair by the fireplace, one leg crossed over the other, his chin propped on his hand. He was watching Del, and Jane had never seen such softness in his eyes.

He must want to be alone. She retreated...but

Christian soundlessly leapt up from the chair and caught her before she reached the door.

"You must want to go to bed," he whispered hoarsely. "But first I wanted to do this—"

His lips came down on hers and warmth rushed through her. His mouth commanded hers while his fingers threaded in her loose hair. His body pressed so close she felt his heart pound against her breast. Against her own thundering heart.

This was nothing like the hard, demanding kiss he'd pushed on her in the theater. Nor was it like the awkward one he'd let her give him in his drawing room. Or even the melting one in the club.

This was like plunging into a fire—and doing it willingly. There was no fear, no hesitation, no frightening memories. Nothing but the need to kiss him back as wildly as he was kissing her.

Impulsively, she clutched his cheeks with both her hands. Stubble tickled her fingertips. His skin was miraculous—scratchy yet soft and smooth. She traced his jaw, his nose, then his sculpted cheekbones, savoring the planes of his handsome face, until her right hand encountered puckered skin. His wound.

Awkwardly, she pulled her hands away.

Christian didn't seem to care. He slipped his tongue between her lips, plunged it in and out, teasing her mouth in ways she hadn't imagined possible. Ways that made her breasts swell against his chest and the place between her thighs burn and ache. To keep from slithering to the ground in a puddle of melted limbs, she wrapped her arms around his strong neck. And touched velvet skin, hard muscle, silken hair.

Her lips smoldered from his kiss, the way tendrils of

smoke poured from an extinguished candle. The rest of her body boiled like an overheated kettle.

He eased back lightly from her lips and before she could surge forward and claim him again, he whispered, "Thank you for being at my side, Jane."

She gazed up into his eyes—into irises the dark violet-blue of the night sky. She was twenty-six years of age. She had just had her first truly wonderful kiss.

The eight years of her marriage dropped away. Instead she was remembering how she had once watched Christian drink his wine at his family's dinner table. She had fumbled with her cutlery, staring at his beautiful mouth... She'd imagined kissing him.

But she'd never dreamed of how hot his kiss would be. Or the way it would make her feel as though she was soaring. She'd played out a kiss with Christian Sutcliffe a dozen more times in her youthful dreams. The reality was so much more.

He seemed to be waiting for her. Waiting for her to say something.

"Th-thank you for being at my side," she stuttered. The words were inadequate. Without him, she couldn't have rescued Del. The truth was she had needed him.

He scooped her up into his arms, with the same tenderness with which he had carried Del, whom she now knew he loved very dearly. His hand splayed on her low back and cupped her bottom. She'd never been carried like this before. It was exhilarating to know he was so strong, but a little frightening too. Then Jane realized what he was doing and her heart raced like a careening carriage.

He was carrying her to bed.

Chapter Fourteen

"MARY," JANE SAID DESPERATELY, AS HE shut the door of her bedchamber with a kick of his foot, then set her gently on her feet in the middle of the room, beside the enormous bed. "What happened to Mary?"

He stared at her in surprise. "Mary?"

"After you saved her from marrying the footman. What did you do to her?" She backed against the bed-post at the foot of the bed.

Anything to give her time to think. Her body burned for him still, and her mouth ached to be touching his, but she was scared. She could kiss him, but did she dare let him go further?

What if the memories came back? She didn't think she could bear it, to be thrown back into that horrible past. Her kiss with Christian had been lovely—a memory to cherish. She would love a thousand such melting, perfect kisses. She would be blissfully happy with that. Did she dare risk trying more?

And what would he do? She didn't want to be hurt in a . . . a sex accident.

Dark brows drawn together, he watched her. "I didn't have the heart to chastise Mary. In the end, I told her I'd found my sister. She apologized, burst into tears, and rushed off to her bedroom. She'd slept with the lad, but she wasn't an innocent before that. It doesn't make sense to force a marriage with a rogue of a servant who lusts as much for her dowry as for her."

"No, it doesn't," Jane echoed.

Christian leaned back against the bedpost at the headboard, so tall his head brushed the underside of the hideous green canopy. "But the story will get out. One more black mark against the poor girls. And I've got to do something. They were all in tears, the lot of them. God, when women cry—" He shook his head.

"It bothers you? You must have made many women cry."

Her words made him wince and she suddenly regretted doing that.

"I made both Del and our mother cry when I left," he said. "The way Del looked has haunted me to this day. And the duel broke our mother's heart. I think it's the reason she died so soon after I left." He glanced down. "Yes, I have made women cry. But I never enjoyed it."

The erotically charged moment had passed. The fiery light in his eyes had gone out. Jane felt a sense of loss. Why? For she'd been the one to extinguish it. And by doing so, she'd caused him pain. "Your mother's death was an accident, Christian. She fell—"

"I know," he broke in. "Del wrote to tell me—the letter reached me months later. My mother was walking on a path along the ridge that flanked the country house.

But why else would she have gone walking on a wet, stormy day? What would make her so inattentive that she would lose her footing on a path she knew so well? The fault lies with me."

He leaned back against the post. He looked so troubled, so racked with guilt. Just as she had felt when her mother had died in the private madhouse—utterly alone, for she couldn't remember by then who anyone was.

"Del told me your parents had fought just before your mother went walking," she said. "If anyone is to blame, I suspect it was your father."

Christian tilted his head and his coal black hair drifted over his eyes. "I never thought you would come to my defense, Jane."

She wanted to stroke his face, trace the grim line of his full lips. She wanted to touch him tenderly. "I was angry with you for leaving Del, but I am not going to condemn you for things that are not your fault. Not when you have rescued my best friend. And when you have saved my life."

He cradled her face and simply held her. She was accustomed to his touch now. Then his thick black lashes lowered, and she fell into that breathless moment before he kissed her.

But he moved past her lips and lowered to her neck. A flick of his tongue and Jane felt as she had when playing ring-around-the-rosy with Del in the fields of his country home. Exhilarated. Disoriented.

"Oh!" she gasped because it tickled. Then sizzled.

He nibbled the base of her throat and her legs became as insubstantial as steam. Only his hands at her waist kept her from sinking to the bed. The convenient bed. The tempting bed...

No. She wasn't sure she was ready.

He blew along the back of her neck and just the brush of his hot breath wreaked havoc through her entire body.

"Touch me," he urged.

Yes, she wanted to. She knew her caresses would be awkward and clumsy, but she wanted to explore him . . .

She planted her hands on his chest. Her fingers curled against the broad expanse and the solid muscle beneath his shirt. As with his kiss, the feel of his chest was like nothing she could have ever imagined. This was how strength felt, firm yet soft, as solid as marble, as warm as a flame. She splayed her fingers wide, trying to span the hard mounds of his pectoral muscles.

His ragged groan stilled her hands. The men in the club had groaned like that. She might have averted her eyes from the couples, but she hadn't clamped her hands over her ears. She'd made Christian moan with need.

He cupped her breasts through the thick, brocaded silk of her robe. Her bosom swelled and heated as his hands gently massaged.

"Tit for tat," he whispered, and the wicked smile of his youth curved his mouth. "My hands aren't quite big enough to encompass all of you, either."

She could barely think with his hands stroking. "It's the robe," she whispered. "It's thick."

"Always scrupulously honest." He brushed a kiss to her forehead.

"I'm not."

"Mmm, I like that." His languorous, contented murmur startled her and she looked down. Her fingers had closed around his right nipple—she had it lightly pinched between her thumb and finger. He had released her breasts and was reaching for his shirt.

"This is in the way." The hem rushed up, revealing planes of muscle, all burnished to bronze by the sun. A white bandage was wrapped around his waist, just above the hard line of his hip, and strangely, confronted with so much sheer masculine beauty, his wound was the place she wanted to touch—as though she could gently rub it and make it better.

His shirt flew over his shoulder. He drew her hand to his chest and coaxed her to brush her fingers across his skin so her nails trailed over his flesh.

"Ooh," she whispered. She'd never dared say a word to Sherringham in their bed, not after the very first time...but here, now, she felt Christian would let her say anything she wished.

He smiled—and his brilliant grin took her back to the very first time she'd seen him, on the terrace of his country home.

She had been fifteen, with her hair up and her bodice lowered. He'd seen her and it had been as though the sun had suddenly touched his face. His eyes had lit up and he'd smiled.

A smile so dazzling to a young, awkward girl that she had stopped in her tracks, turned in gauche panic, and raced away...

But now she let her fingers brush through the dark curls on his chest, slowly centering on his nipple. She heard him catch his breath. Hesitantly, she traced the smooth brown disc, amazed to find it puckering more beneath her fingers. She squeezed it again, harder than she had before.

"God," he moaned.

She snatched her hand back.

"It didn't hurt. I like your rough play, love."

Love. It spoke of the intimacy of this. She replaced her hand. "I don't want to be rough—"

"In India, there are texts about making love, about erotic arts." Beneath her palm, his chest rumbled as he spoke. "Nail marks on a woman's body are an ornament, as precious as jewelry, adding to her beauty as proof of the deep affection of her lover."

"That can't be true."

"It shows the power of her lover's desire for her." His eyes twinkled. "I would be honored to wear your scratches on my skin."

"Christian," she admonished. She felt lost and confused. To scratch him—wouldn't that mean she was fighting him? She wasn't ready to discover what he'd learned in India.

He raked his nails—his blunt, short nails—lightly across the top of her chest, where her robe gaped open. A tremor rushed from her skin to the place between her thighs.

"But right now," Christian murmured hoarsely, "I want to open your robe and lift your breasts to my greedy mouth and feast."

The bed bumped against the back of her legs. He'd moved her away from the bedpost and she hadn't even noticed. His hands closed on the lapels of her robe, and she froze—expecting him to yank it open. She expected him to grasp her breasts and roughly knead—

"You're tense." He stroked her cheek instead of tearing off her robe. "I can feel it. Relax."

He took her mouth again in a kiss as breathtaking as his first smile on the terrace had been. He eased her back; she clung to his strong neck, and he swept her off her feet. Literally. She was in his arms, his mouth plundering hers. As the green brocade canopy came into view, and softness pressed against her back, reality jolted through her.

She was lying on a bed. With Christian. And just as she'd feared, she went rigid.

"Talk to me. I won't hurt you, love."

She stared up into his eyes—eyes filled with concern, gleaming with desire. He'd rolled up on his side, his powerful body stretched out beside hers. He was so big—his shoulders unbelievably wide, his body a sculpture of muscle. Even his neck was corded with it. His biceps were hard and massive and the veins on his forearms bulged as though they could find no space under his skin when his muscles tensed.

She shivered. "I—it's just that you—you've done all those things. The things we saw at the club. I—I don't know what will happen to me, if you do those things to me."

"Bruise you, you mean? I'd never do that. I swear it."

"Not that. I used to lie beneath my husband and try to send my mind somewhere else—"

"Shh." Christian put his finger to Jane's mouth. "I'm not him."

"But I know nothing of . . . of making love."

Christian stroked the just-kissed plumpness of Jane's lower lip, feeling her turn to stone beneath him—unable to move, just rigidly enduring. Obviously violence had followed her and Sherringham into the bedroom, and he had turned lovemaking into something that terrified her.

He had let his sister marry a monster. Jane had also married one. For both women, the scars were deep. Christian intended to heal them both. Del he would protect from harm from now on.

Jane he would tempt into surrendering to pleasure and discovering what she was made to have. But how did he start? How did he stop her from being a statue?

Take it slowly, an inner voice urged. "We don't have to make love, but I'd like to hold you."

"Hold me?"

The tentative whisper gripped his heart. "I'll lie at your side and cradle you close," Christian promised. "I'd like to do that." He toyed with a golden-red curl.

"Y-yes."

His blood thundered in his head. His cock was as rigid as an iron poker. God, he wanted her. But he couldn't unleash that need. Not now.

He wrapped his arm gently around her waist. She smelled of roses and sandalwood soap. The soft scent of rose petals reminded him of the night he'd first seen her. When he'd been seventeen, smoking a forbidden cheroot, and standing on the terrace. She had stepped out from the drawing room, all fiery red-gold hair and large brown eyes.

She'd run from him back then. He didn't want her to run from him now.

He kissed Jane again, kissed her until they were both breathing raggedly and his back was coated in sweat from their heat. "You like that, don't you?"

"Yes." She blinked up at him. "I want you to find pleasure. You must need it—"

She was offering her body for his sexual release and it broke his heart.

"I should have known kissing you would be as hot as it is," he murmured. "After all those heated arguments we had, I knew we would be explosive together."

She stared at him, frowning. "Is that why you used to say all those rude things? To *make* me grow hot?"

He'd meant to tease her, and saw, in her indignation, her fire was coming back. "You mean, Jane, you were hot when you were angry at me?"

"You always spoke of the most inappropriate things."

"Did I? I don't remember that."

"I was a maiden! You would say things—things to which there was no possible response."

"You always seemed to think of one." He traced the slope of her shoulder, where the neckline of her robe revealed her ivory skin.

"Well, your words would not leave me. I would think of them for days. They popped into my head at the most awkward times. At breakfast, when I was handing the ham platter to my father. Or when the vicar dined at our house. I—"

"What scandalous things did I say?" He tried to sound as sincerely indignant as her. "I can't think of one."

Amber flashed in her brown eyes. "You told me women's nipples grow erect with pleasure. You said those very words one night on the terrace while your family hosted a dinner party."

"I might remember that night . . . the air was cool and crisp, and I remember your sweet little nipples were tight with the chill."

She glared. "You told me that some men kiss women . . . down there. You described exactly what a man did and what it tasted like." Her cheeks went scarlet. "That's what I remembered in front of the vicar."

He laughed, suddenly understanding. "You weren't annoyed, sweeting, you were aroused."

Conversations with Lady Jane Beaumont had been

like falling into a bramble bush—prickles from unexpected directions. But instead of trying to fight free, he used to prickle back. Oddly, he'd liked getting spiked—and apparently she had, too. "You naughty thing."

Her delightful flush swept down her chest. "I—I am not."

"Deep down inside you, I think you are." He winked at her, just like he would have done in the past. "Now that you've revealed you used to think about sex when you thought about me, I want to search for naughty Jane."

She'd said too much. She had told the truth, but Christian had seen far more in it than she ever had. She hadn't realized that she, who had known better, who had seen her mother shrivel up over hopeless love for a rake, had lusted for Christian Sutcliffe so much.

"Is she in here?" Christian pulled her robe wide.

Her nipples, suddenly exposed to the cool air and his hot gaze, leapt up at once.

"No nightdress," he observed.

"I—It's on the bed," she stuttered. "Underneath us."

"The best place for it."

He looked wicked, grinning like that. Her heart made an abrupt somersault in her chest. He lowered to her breasts. With his hands curled around the lapels of her robe, he explored with just his mouth. Soft tongue, the rasp of stubble, the brush of his thick hair. It was too much—almost too much.

He sucked her left nipple deeply into his hot mouth. She stiffened beneath him, waiting for a jolt of pain, the harsh scrape of his teeth. But he swirled his tongue lovingly, and she'd never known it could be like this—

He stopped to look up. With a naughty smile on his face, he looked so proud of himself. "You have beautiful breasts. I wish I'd known that when I was a randy seventeen and you were a blossoming lady." He blew across her bosom and the blend of hot and cold was astonishingly good. He took her right nipple between his lips and his tongue flicked.

She arched off the bed. "You wouldn't have seduced me out of my bodice." If he wanted to tease, she could do the same—it was enthralling to feel free enough to clash words while surrendering to pleasure. "You were probably more interested in some matron's huge breasts."

"But yours are incomparable. I might not have seduced you out of your bodice, but it would have been fun to try."

Memories rushed over her. Running down the field to stop his carriage race. Dumping pudding in his boot because *she'd* run out of biting things to say and he never did. "No," she whispered. "They would have been false words of love and I'm so very glad you never said those to me."

"Jane—"

Her robe was open. With a tug, he'd released the belt and laid her bare. As he licked her nipple, his hand skimmed down her belly, then gently stroked between her nether lips. Her thighs tightened and she felt her body resist.

Christian lifted from her breast. "It will be good, Jane. Let it be good."

Her thighs were tensed and she gripped his arm. "I don't know."

"I'll stop if it's not. I promise you that."

She forced her body to relax, her legs to open wider, and she clung to his shoulder.

"There, Jane. One finger inside your creamy heat."

His words, his blunt direct words, shocked her, but she loved the sound of them in his husky voice. His finger slid in and out. She was lifting to take him inside deeper. *Yes. She did want this. It was good. Yes.* She took deep breaths and moved with his finger.

Two fingers slid inside. He splayed them, teasing her hot, tight walls, and he kissed her.

Jane moaned into his mouth, and Christian had never heard a sweeter, more perfect erotic sound. He loved a woman's moans, and Jane's were precious. She'd probably never moaned for any man but him.

His rigid cock was throbbing, trapped in his trousers, between their bellies, and it was hell to yank his mind back from her heat and her delectable smell of welcome. *He had to stay in control.*

But she was wet for him now. Drenched for him.

She clung to his shoulders as he plunged his fingers into her snug, hot passage and stroked with his thumb. Her nails bit into his shoulders and he knew he'd brushed her clit.

"*Nadikshobhana*," he whispered teasingly, stroking the small nub. "Not only do your nipples grow erect to my touch. So does your sensitive clitoris."

Her eyes almost rolled back in her head. "Christian!"

He rubbed in gentle circles, watching her face. When her eyes went wide, he changed his rhythm, his speed, his pressure. When he made her moan and whimper, he kept doing exactly what he was doing right.

She began to rock against his hand, seeking pleasure.

Yes, Jane. He whispered it aloud, "Yes, Jane, sweeting."

"Christian—" She gasped. "Something is happening. Stop!"

He didn't stop. She was afraid and couldn't understand the responses of her own body. He could see she'd never known physical pleasure. His body was on fire and he'd never wanted anything more than to see Jane come.

"Stop now! It's so intense." She was trying to crawl back up the bed to escape.

He'd promised to stop. But if he did now, she'd never know what her body could feel. "Trust me," he growled.

"No! Stop! There's something wrong. It's strange. Stop!"

He didn't. He couldn't.

"It's—oh, oh, oh. Oh!"

She rocked on the bed, her hand tearing into his shoulders. "Oh! Oh heavens, it's good."

He was watching her first orgasm. He had given her very first experience with pleasure—and for the first time in his life, he felt something other than triumph and masculine victory. His chest felt tight, his heart large, and he wanted to make love to Jane Beaumont with a yearning that was so much more than lust, he refused to think about it.

Lust was a safer place to be.

He yanked open the placket of his trousers, but gently rolled on top of her. She was still coming—too wrapped up in gasping and quivering to protest. Bracing his weight, he spread her legs apart to settle his hips in between. Her slick quim pressed against his shaft. Her inner thighs were a sweet grip of satin against his legs.

"Christian," she whispered.

He eased inside her . . . gently . . . as gently as he could. God, she was hot, and as silky as fresh cream. Taking a slow, calming breath, he pushed in one exquisite inch. Still fluttering from her climax, her tight passage clutched at him, drawing his cock inside.

Her eyes were shut. She tensed.

"Trust me," he murmured.

She bit her lip and nodded, her lashes glued together, and she looked so adorable, so sweet, so trusting, he knew why he'd never once tried to seduce a virgin. But Jane wasn't a virgin—she was a lady sorely in need of a lesson in the delights of making love—

He slid inside her easily, but being inside her wasn't easy at all. It hit him like a charging elephant—took his breath from his chest, his sense from his head, and shattered his control. He fondled her breasts, squeezed, ravaged, delighted in them, rained kisses to her closed lids and parted lips, and thrust into her. Thrust in one long, powerful stroke that took him in to the hilt.

Her eyes flared open. "Heavens."

"Is it good?" he asked. Or something like that, something barely coherent.

She didn't answer. She lifted up to him. And it was all he needed. They pumped together, their rhythms wrong, awkward, like dancers listening to two different tunes. He couldn't even pause long enough to figure out what she wanted, to give her the speed, the depth, the strokes she needed. He wanted her too much.

Her inarticulate cries surrounded him. Their combined scent drugged him.

He drove deeper and deeper, wanting to bring his name to her lips again. But her teeth bit into her lower lip and her eyes were shut tight.

"Oh!"

The desperate sound signaled the sudden clench of her quim around his shaft. Her fingernails drove into his back, not in practiced art, but in pure ecstasy.

She scratched him as her hips pumped up to him and her cries rang out.

Christian couldn't hold back. His body tensed like a stretched spring. His cock swelled, then finally, mercifully, exploded. A blinding white bolt of pleasure seared his brain. His muscles turned to jelly, his mind shattered.

"Jane—" Her name came out on the harsh rush of his wits racing out of his body. He jerked on top of her, his body beyond his control, his seed pumping into her. She clawed at his shoulders and the stinging pain sent one last rush of semen from his body. He had nothing left. Then it was over, leaving him spent, exhausted, barely able to hold his body up.

He collapsed beside her, his cock still buried deep.

She gave a little squeak of protest and he tilted his hips. His softening member slid out on the flood of his juices and hers, and he wrapped his arm over her damp chest. Days without sleep had sapped his strength and he didn't have enough left to move.

You're lying half naked on her bed. On top of her night-gown. In the early morning.

The warnings drummed in his head, but he couldn't heed them

Christian let his eyes drift shut.

*   *   *

She felt lips on hers, a wet mouth claiming her roughly in a kiss. She wrapped her arms around a strong neck—

"I never guessed you could feel such passion."

The cold, sneering voice wasn't Christian's. She opened her eyes. And stared into the face of her husband—his looks destroyed by fat and drink. She tried to pull her arms back but he grabbed her wrists.

"You never kissed me like that. You never acted the whore for me before—"

Jane jerked awake. She couldn't catch her breath. Her heart hammered frantically.

She blinked at the hideous green canopy above her. It had just been a dream. Her skin felt crusty with sweat and she was pinned to the bed. Panic roared through her. She shoved at the weight holding her down—

Christian. His arm lay over her waist, over the silken robe bundled around her, and he was cuddled up to her side, breathing in the relaxed rhythm of sleep. She closed her fingers around his strong forearm, and felt his velvet skin and silky hairs. She smelled a rich, ripe scent on her body, and remembered...

They'd made love last night.

She had tensed beneath him, just as she'd feared. But Christian hadn't behaved like the devil incarnate. He'd been so gentle. So patient. And the pleasure he'd shown her—

She had soared. Shattered. Surrendered to something so exquisite she could find no words to describe it. She'd had no idea it was possible to feel so good. And he had done it to her twice.

It was as though she'd opened a door and stepped through it into the past—the past before her marriage.

As though she were fifteen again, seeing Christian for the very first time, standing beneath blush pink roses, smoking a cheroot, and she had her future ahead of her all over again—

But she wasn't fifteen anymore. She hadn't had a nightmare about Sherringham for two months. But tonight it had come back. Proof she hadn't put her marriage behind her.

And Christian had spoken of texts in India about erotic arts, of fingernail scratches, and he'd known exactly how to give her pleasure. It reminded her how different they were. *Lord Wicked is completely out of your ken,* Mrs. B. had said. The madam may have wanted to frighten her, but perhaps the words were simply the truth.

With an aching heart, Jane wriggled out from beneath him. He grunted and his arm flopped to the bed, but he settled back into sleep. The hem of her nightgown stuck out from beneath his legs. His trousers were pulled down past his hips, leaving most of his taut, firm bottom bare.

For a moment, she could do nothing but stare at those cheeks—at the shadowed indent of his haunches and tight rounded shape of his rump.

Then, she spied a box bench at the foot of the bed. In moments, armed with a dreary brown blanket dug from the box, she had Christian covered. He would be warm this way.

"Thank you," she said softly. "For showing me so much more."

She tied the sash of her robe tightly. Then she left the room to check on Del.

*   *   *

Christian woke to find daylight slanting in through a small gap in the drapes. Beside him the counterpane stretched out, crumpled, empty. Jane had left him.

He glanced at the mantel clock. A quarter of eight. As he levered up, a blanket fell away, taking its warmth with it. He must have fallen asleep on top of the bed. And Jane had arranged a blanket over him.

Swiftly he did up his trousers and pulled on his shirt. He went to Del's room. His sister still slept, snuggled beneath a heavy counterpane. On the chair pulled up beside the bed, with her head flopped to the side, Jane snoozed.

Should he move her? He'd wake her if he tried. Instead, he fetched the blanket she'd used on him and draped it over her.

"Returning the favor," he murmured. He kissed the top of her auburn hair, and gave the tangled curls a taming stroke with his hand. He couldn't forget how beautiful she'd looked, climaxing beneath him, and gasping his name—

The reality of what he'd done hit him hard.

He dragged his hand from her hair, raked it through his. What in blazes had he been thinking? He'd made love to her without protection. Never once had he made such a mistake. Even now she could be quickening with their baby.

And there was nothing he could do to stop it.

Two breakfast trays sat on the bedside tables and a maid was tiptoeing out of the room. Jane rubbed her eyes, gave the young servant a smile, and pushed off the blanket. As it plopped to the floor, she stared at it, puzzled.

She must have gone to sleep while watching Del. But where had the blanket come from—?

Jane leapt off the chair. Was Christian still asleep on her bed? She rushed to the door and had her hand on the knob before her thoughts clicked into place.

The brown blanket that had slid off her looked exactly like the one she'd laid over him. To make sure, she stepped out into the hallway. The maid emerged from her room, humming, and she had the crumpled nightgown over her arm. Had she guessed it had not been worn, and that two people had slept on the disordered counterpane?

Jane retreated, closing the door. There would be gossip below stairs, if the girl had, she feared. But she was a widow, not an innocent miss. Gossip only mattered when a widow wanted to wed.

As she crept to one of the trays and poured herself tea, a maid's voice floated in from the hall. "What do ye think 'as 'appened to the master's sister? Do ye think she's mad?"

Jane paused, teapot in hand.

Another woman answered. "Her husband had her stowed away in a convalescent house and you know what that means. She seemed as normal as you and me, but her husband's a brute. That's the tale below stairs. He beat her. The master came back to save her."

The first gave a long sigh. "The poor master. And now 'e's got Miss Mary to deal with. Do ye think she's ruined?"

"She was ruined before he ever found her. I hope he takes care. The girl's infatuated with him. She hoped he would run after her. That girl is trouble, mark my words."

"I 'eard Lord Wickham took Mary in 'is arms and let 'er cry against 'is chest."

Jane's hand tightened on the teapot—she burned her knuckles against the side.

The second maid made a disapproving sound. "His lordship should know better than that."

"Well, 'e is called Lord Wicked, and I do think 'e would be wonderfully wicked in a girl's bed. Do ye know what else I 'eard? From 'is lordship's own lips, when 'e was speaking to Mr. 'Untley. 'E is going to free 'is sister from 'er 'orrible marriage."

"A divorce? It will be a scandal—"

"No!" the first maid breathed, her voice high-pitched. " 'E's gone after the 'usband. Said 'e would meet the gentleman and blow the bloke's 'eart out of 'is chest."

Jane jerked. The half-filled teacup tumbled off the tray to the floor.

Chapter Fifteen

*P*ORCELAIN SHATTERED.

For the first time in her life, Jane prayed a man had hurled something against the wall in anger, for it meant Christian was alive. *Alive*. Walking. Breathing. Throwing porcelain.

Thank heaven.

She hurried down the hall toward his study. The last two hours had been a nightmare, since the moment she'd learned from the highly disapproving Mr. Huntley that Christian had gone to Treyworth House. As soon as she'd spied a carriage on the drive, she'd raced down to find him.

Now, as she approached his study, she slowed her steps.

Three young women lurked outside the door. Each had hair of a different color, each wore a dainty white muslin dress—they reminded Jane of how Charlotte, Del, and she had once looked. But these were Christian's rescued girls. Taken as prisoners in a foreign land, held in seraglios, these girls had been even more trapped than she'd been.

She cleared her throat. The girls spun around guiltily.

One, a sturdy brunette with large brown eyes, curtsied to her. "I know we shouldn't be here, my lady." She had a crisp, firm voice. "But we saw his lordship storm into his study."

"To get his pistols," added the girl with brilliant red curls, waving her hands expressively.

The blond girl sniffed—she was the one who had rushed into Wickham's parlor. The redhead cast a withering glance. "Stop whimpering, Philly. It's annoying." She turned to Jane. "We know he's found his sister. We thought that would make him happy. Why has it not?"

What was she meant to say? It was impertinent to ask about Christian's private matters, but the girl looked distressed. Each of the three did.

They obviously cared very deeply about their rescuer. And she couldn't simply shoo them away without trying to reassure them. "His lordship is very happy to have his sister home," she said, though her legs shook a little at the thought of Christian's pistols.

"But what is wrong?" their leader asked bluntly.

"I think it is because of Mary," the redheaded declared. "He's angry that she took off with the footman and didn't get wed."

The brunette spun around impatiently. "Mary didn't get wed because *he* stopped it."

"Is it us?" asked the frightened blond, Philly. "His sister might not want us here."

"I promise you have nothing to worry about. His lordship and his sister are very kind." Jane didn't think Del would object, but what if she did?

She would take them. Then a logical voice cried in her head—*How do you think to do that? You have practically nothing to your name. Not enough to support four young women.*

"I-is she very ill?" Philly asked.

"She is recovering," Jane said. And that was true.

"We're to be quiet and not giggle and not be too boisterous on the pianoforte." The redhead thrust out her lip in a pout. "That's what Mr. Huntley said."

"We know how to be quiet," Philly declared. "I know how to be almost invisible."

Jane's heart lurched. "While Lord Wickham's sister heals," she said firmly, "you are to be quiet and respectful, but you are also allowed to be normal girls."

They stared at her, uncertain.

"You can trust me." She wondered if she had gone in direct opposition to a command from Christian. But it was too late. The girls giggled nervously, then scurried off down the hallway.

Jane pushed open the study door without knocking—something she would never have done with her husband.

Sunlight spilled in through the windows. Christian sat behind the desk. Light fell on the ridges of his cheekbones, the knuckles of his bare hands, and on the silver barrel of a pistol.

"Dueling is illegal." The instant the words came out, she regretted them. If anyone knew that, he did, of course.

He did not look up. He wiped a cloth with deliberate care along the gleaming metal of the weapon. "I saw the bruises on my sister's body. But there is no court in England that would give Treyworth the punishment he deserves."

She wanted Del free, but all she could picture was a misty field at dawn, and Christian holding a pistol while Treyworth aimed one at him. "Del could divorce him and become free."

"We'd have to prove he was violent to her. What would we gain to make public everything that happened at the club, when Treyworth would argue Del did it willingly?"

Jane winced. Del would be the subject of lewd cartoons in the print shops and vicious rumors in the ballrooms. Del would bear the brunt of society's punishment for immoral behavior, when she was the victim. "There has to be a way."

"There is. This, sweeting, is retribution. Retribution for every blow he ever laid on her. This is what a gentleman should do to protect his family."

"Protection and retribution are entirely different things."

He stared at her. The easy intimacy of last night had vanished. She felt as though she looked at him across a huge gulf.

It seemed so nonsensical. Her goal for years had simply been survival. But in the gentleman's world of honor, life was so quickly gambled away.

She took a step back. Something sharp poked the sole of her foot. "Ouch!" Littered around her feet were shards of pottery of a bilious green.

"Careful where you step, love." He put down the pistol, and took two long strides to her side. Just like last night, he swept her up into his arms. He deposited her on a heavy-framed chaise. "It was one of my father's favorites. I'd wanted to smash it for years."

"B-but why did you?"

"Frustration. When I went to Treyworth's house, I found that he's not at home. He rode out to Newmarket to enjoy the races. So I left a note." Christian perched on the curved backrest of the chaise and gave a sour laugh. "I went there to make him pay and ended up writing a note. I also went back to the club, but it was locked up and Mrs. Brougham was gone."

"She ran?"

"Like a rat. I assume she's trying to flee England, so I've had Huntley hire men to comb the docks for her." Suddenly Christian focused on her, his brilliant blue eyes making a slow passage from her curls to her hems. "I've just noticed you are wearing a different dress."

"You could be killed and you are commenting on my *dress*?"

He shrugged. "Every gentleman notices a flattering gown. You look remarkably lovely. The one good thing I did was to remember to have your clothes sent."

In the midst of planning to duel, Christian had thought of her clothing. He kept doing this to her— showing she was in his thoughts. "I don't trust Treyworth," she said. "Why would he follow rules with his life at stake? He's hardly honorable. He could shoot first."

Again, his shoulders rose in a sensual, casual motion. "I faced that eventuality and survived."

She remembered that shrug. He'd used it in his rakish youth. It had infuriated her that he would use a shrug in place of a defense. Now, she wondered if it was a shield. "Which is all the more reason not to tempt fate."

"I'm not allowing Del to return to him, and she did it once already. You didn't tell me that, Jane."

He had overheard her conversation. "I couldn't," she

cried. "I feared it might make you do exactly what you are doing—talk of throwing your life away!"

"If she were to decide to go back, I couldn't stop her." He leapt off the back of the chaise and ran his hand over his jaw. "Hades, what a mess I've made."

"W-what do you mean?"

"Do you remember last night, Jane. When we made love?"

She swallowed hard at the note of self-recrimination in his voice. Did he now regret it?

"I was so carried away with you I didn't use a sheath." He lowered his voice. "I've always taken care to prevent conception of illegitimate children. But last night with you, planning, preparation, my wits—all three went out the window."

A child. She had not thought of that at all. Her hand strayed to her stomach.

He lifted her hand and raised it to his lips. "If you quicken with my child, I will do the honorable thing. I will marry you. I promise you I won't get myself killed, Jane, because I may need to stand at the altar with you."

The *honorable* thing. A duty marriage, but only if she proved to be pregnant. He sounded more resolved to a horrible fate than when he spoke of dueling. "No," she said.

At his look of surprise, she rushed on. "I married one man who was not in love with me and I will not do it again. I won't trap you into marriage." She clenched her hands into fists. Why had she not thought last night? What would she do if there were a child? Would she have to hide in the country to bear Christian's bastard? Aunt Regina, who had been so very good to her during the scandal after Sherringham's death, who only wanted her to find happiness, would have to endure more vicious talk and pointing fingers. After losing two babies, she couldn't bear to think of giving one away. But what else could she do?

She took a deep breath. She *had* lost the two babies in the first months of pregnancy, during her marriage. Even if she were enceinte, she might lose this one too. And it would be for the best.

Christian caught her chin and tipped up her face. "I would never treat you the way Sherringham did."

She pulled back. "I don't fear that you'd beat me. That has nothing to do with it." But she couldn't bear to live with him, knowing he could grow to resent her. And what would she do when he took mistresses—a man who married for duty would certainly do that. "I vowed never to marry again. I will never let a man control me again."

"I won't control you. I'm not one of those gentlemen who insists on dictating to his wife."

No, she couldn't envision Christian telling her what gown to wear, what social event she could attend, how much pin money she could spend. She couldn't imagine him finding fault with everything she did.

But he would control her life. She would spend each day wondering if he would come home, if he would come to her bed, if she should try to please him or simply retreat into her own life.

She couldn't marry him when she was still having nightmares about Sherringham.

As the silence stretched, he ducked his head to meet her gaze. "I wanted to teach you about pleasure, Jane. You deserve to know what lovemaking could be like. But

I made an error, and I won't leave you to suffer the consequences alone."

Shock stole her voice. Had all his teasing words been part of *lessons*? He hadn't been swept away by passion. He had been rescuing her. No roguish thing he'd ever said to her had toppled her like this. "Thank you, then, for our lovely night. But you have no responsibility to me. I will not marry you." She scrambled off the chaise and began to walk to the door.

"Jane, stop."

She did. She turned to find he had gone back to the desk.

"I want to go back to the sanitarium—to question the matron, oversee the removal of the patients," he said. "Will you stay, Jane? Even if you despise *me*, would you stay for Del?"

"Of course I will stay for Del. I am going to her room."

He picked up the pistol and rag once more.

Embarrassed as she was, she could not just walk away. She had to try one last time to talk sense into him. "But Del needs *you*, Christian. The girls you rescued need you. You can't duel."

He did not look up. She knew her words had touched him, but the reaction was not what she intended. He wasn't going to listen to her.

Instead, he set the pistol back in its wood box and picked up its twin.

He'd made a promise of marriage but had rammed his boot in his mouth while doing it.

Christian drove his vehicle up the drive to Mrs.

Brougham's sanitarium, leapt down, and tossed the reins to one of his men.

Last night, he'd been here with Jane. He never let anyone close to him—not mistresses, not friends. But now, he found that he expected Jane to be at his side. He actually missed looking down to see her eyes glowing with crusading fire. Anyway, he doubted he'd see her eyes light up with passion for him again.

But what was he going to do if she was pregnant with his child?

He'd vowed never to marry, never to have children. He couldn't. Marriage meant revealing the truth about his bloodlines to his wife. As for children...children would be too great a risk—

Yet, with Jane, he'd thrown those rules aside...hell, he hadn't even thought about them.

The scent of smoke whisked past his nose. *Fire.*

Christian scanned the windows, which glinted with reflected sunlight. Then he saw it. The brilliant flare behind a window on the ground floor. In an instant, he was racing across to the front steps, shouting to his men as the cry came from inside.

"Fire!"

In the house, panic reigned. Screams came from above, and men dashed about in confusion. Younger yelled at everyone, trying to gain control.

Christian grabbed two men and shoved them toward the stairs. "Get the women out," he commanded. He sent another two to follow. Then he ran toward the room where he'd seen the flames. He'd been through fire before—it had blazed through many an Indian village after a lightning storm, greedily devouring dry grass and simple homes—

The door was closed. He pressed his hand to the wood. Cool still. He shoved open the door, jumped back against the wall. There was no burst of flame. Steeling himself, he raced inside.

He was in a sitting room. Flames ate at the cushions of a sofa and licked at the drapes hanging behind. Out of the corner of his eye, he saw Younger at his heels. He pointed to the curtains, then he yanked out cushions, threw them to the carpet, and stomped them with his boots. Smoke coiled around him, filling his lungs. His eyes watered. Younger pulled down the drapes and kicked out the flames that raced along them.

Behind him, Christian heard women's cries, thudding footsteps. Then a surprisingly calm, "My lord."

He swung around.

A tall, blond man stood in the doorway, holding the struggling matron, Mrs. Dow. "You looked to have the fire under control, my lord, so I went after this one as she tried to make a break for it. I am Hadrian Radcliffe, an officer of Bow Street."

Radcliffe, the Bow Street Runner, hauled the matron to a second sitting room across the hall and shoved her into a chair. "You set that fire, didn't you? Did you set any more?"

Mrs. Dow shook, her hands clasped to her breast. "N-no. No, I swear I did not."

But Christian read the truth in the desperate flicks of her gaze to the door and the fury he sensed beneath her fear.

He had stayed at the door. He turned and shouted orders to his men for them to check the other rooms, to open windows and clear out the smoke. Then he strode to the thin, black-haired matron, who sat shivering on the edge of the chair. "You did," he said simply, cold authority in his voice.

She recognized him from the night before and she pulled back into the chair. Her eyes went fearfully from him to Radcliffe. "I didn't intend anyone to be hurt. I wanted a distraction to make my escape. I thought with so many men in the house, the patients wouldn't come to harm."

Her piteous tone grated. Christian glowered down at her. "You won't escape now. There's only one way left for you to save yourself."

Save yourself. Her beady black eyes lit up at those words, even as she trembled. He knew he had to be wary of everything she said.

At his shoulder, Radcliffe cleared his throat. Christian motioned for the Runner to follow. They stepped away from the woman, but Christian watched her. "I want to propose that she is looked on more kindly by the magistrates in return for helping us with information," he told Radcliffe. It was not a question. He expected agreement.

Radcliffe ran his hand around the rim of his hat. "My lord, it's my duty to question the woman, not yours, if I may be so bold to say. This is unorthodox and I don't like it. Lady Treyworth is safe. What is it you want, my lord?"

Christian had to admit, in any other circumstance, he would have liked the man's directness. He crossed his arms over his chest, looking every inch a peer. "I left my men to protect the women here—it was my duty to return. As for what I want—to find Brougham and make her pay for what she's done to my sister." There was

Jane's carriage accident and the footpad who had attacked Treyworth. Could Brougham have been behind those?

He rubbed his neck. He hadn't come here because he was running from Jane. He was *not* running from his botched proposal and his mistake.

"Unless you're bold enough to try to have me hauled out bodily, Radcliffe," he continued, "I am talking to this woman." He returned to Mrs. Dow, who wiped at tears. She was afraid for herself. Good. "I am an earl, madam. I can ask for clemency for you if you help me. Do you wish to swing for Mrs. Brougham?"

Thin shoulders jerked. "No."

"Then help me. Where has Sapphire Brougham gone?"

She looked at him beseechingly. "I don't know. I had to do what I was told. I kept my nose out—at least I tried. Then the men began to come."

"Men in black masks and cloaks." Out of the corner of his eye, Christian saw Radcliffe's brows lift.

"You know about them," Radcliffe said.

"Yes, we do. Tell me what they did here, madam."

He waited, watching her inner war flash over her sharp features. "Those men would come into the house," she said softly, "then go to a locked room at the rear of the first floor. New girls, brought here by the mistress, would be taken down to them. I knew those girls were prostitutes, not patients. I realized what the intent of this house had been—a blind, a cover for her true business of whoring. But I stayed in this house because I do have truly ill women to care for, and that is what I have always done. Perhaps I should have left, but you must understand, my lord—once the men came here, I believed I would not leave this place alive."

Christian remembered Brougham defending her club as a place to find sexual freedom. Blasted witch. And he remembered Jane speculating—*What if Del knew Treyworth had been ruining innocent girls?* "Do you know the identities of the men?"

"I could tell they were gentlemen. There were six. They called themselves the Demons Club, and would joke that they were demons sent to teach angels about sin."

"They spoke so freely in front of you?" Christian asked.

Two spots of color dotted her cheeks. "To protect myself, I thought it wise to gather information on the sly."

"What sort of information?" Radcliffe, like a hound on a scent, surged forward.

She shrank back and Christian took the seat at her side. He cast an autocratic, quelling look that made the Runner bristle. "You can speak in front of him," he assured Mrs. Dow. "I am here as witness that you are co-operating with us."

"I saw the men, my lord. I would watch those six demons through the keyhole—a great risk, but as I said, I feared I could never escape this house alive any other way. That door led to a small anteroom. The men would gather in there, then go into another room to visit the girls. When they finished, they would drink brandy in the anteroom, and they would tip up their masks to do it."

She took a deep breath. With a nod, Christian urged her to continue.

"One was bald, and he had a large, beaked nose. One had fair hair and a handsome face. The third had thinning brown hair laced with gray. I did not see his features. And two had dark hair—as black as yours, my lord."

Christian tensed. The description of the third man was vague, but it could be Treyworth. The fair-haired man could be Salaberry.

"The sixth?" he prompted.

"He was the largest of them—a handsome man with thick, silver hair. He was always laughing and he looked like the devil himself. I learned his name because I once heard one of the others address him as Sherringham."

Christian almost reeled back. Sherringham. "It must have been a long time ago that you saw him."

Mrs. Dow nodded. "They have been coming for over a year. The sixth man only came a few times. There was an accident, you see—" She broke off.

"What kind of accident?"

Though it pained him to do it, he softened his eyes and bit back his rage. "Please tell me."

She played with the neckline of her bodice. "Not long after the men had started coming, a woman arrived one night with the mistress. She was different from the usual, certainly no innocent. Instead she was a bold, showy sort of woman wearing a fancy crimson gown. She put on airs, and was rude and condescending, but she was obviously a tart."

Christian had to bite his tongue as Mrs. Dow sneered. This heartless woman had bound innocent girls to their beds.

"I did not go downstairs that night. I stayed in my room, but I heard a commotion so I went to look. I didn't intend to be seen, but the mistress was coming out of a room and she caught me in the hallway. She motioned to me to come to her—my heart was pounding—"

"Go on," he urged, though he'd guessed what he would hear.

"Over her shoulder I saw the woman in the crimson dress lying on the bed. The mistress said she'd had a fit and had died. But I didn't think it was that. The girl was lying there with her head at a strange angle. And Sherringham was the man in the room with her."

Radcliffe paced the carpet. "You believe Sherringham murdered this woman."

"What else would I be saying? You wanted the truth from me. That woman's death was the first one. Other young women died too. Strangled, they were. And Sherringham was the only one of the Demons Club who came on those nights."

Christian turned to Radcliffe as he took up the reins of his curricle hours later. "The Earl of Sherringham died in a house fire just over a year ago."

The Runner gave a shrewd glance. "And the others? Your sister's husband, Lord Treyworth, knew of this place."

Christian inclined his head. "Yes. And Treyworth has brown hair laced with gray. However, so do any number of other men."

"At Bow Street, we have to tread lightly around the peers we unearth at brothels." Radcliffe sneered in distaste. "I don't believe a man should ever be above the law, no matter what his station. But I'm a sufficient realist to know that's often the case. It means an officer has to be a damn sight more cunning to get that man to put himself in the noose."

Radcliffe laid his gloved hand on the side of the curricle. "What of the others? Would you have any ideas, my lord, who they are?"

"From vague descriptions, I can't tell you. There's nothing I can prove, Radcliffe. Not yet."

"Not yet," Radcliffe repeated. "I ask you to keep out of my investigation, my lord."

Christian laughed. "Not likely, Radcliffe." He thought of Jane, who must have inwardly said the same thing when he made the same demand.

With crop in hand, he leaned down. "Lady Sherringham is not to endure scandal, when there is no justice that can be found now." He held up his hand to quell Radcliffe. "I know that you need to find the truth, but I want to protect Lady Sherringham, who is my sister's dearest friend."

Radcliffe glowered. "That may not be possible, my lord."

"It will be," Christian barked, his temper breaking free. He flicked the reins, setting his blacks off at a swift trot, and the horses were soon devouring the stretch of road.

He was going to have to tell Jane about her husband. It wasn't as if she had loved Sherringham or didn't know the man's character. He remembered her reaction to learning that her husband had been the actress's protector. Had she already suspected?

His blood went cold. Further questioning of Mrs. Dow revealed Sherringham had killed not only the woman in the crimson gown—who sounded like Molly Templeton—but also another flashily dressed woman named Kitty, very likely Kitty Wilson, and four other young women in the sanitarium. If Sherringham was capable of murder, what exactly had Jane endured with him?

And his thoughts went to Del. If Treyworth had been part of the Demons Club, and he could prove it, it would be leverage to free Del. But none of the other women in the sanitarium had seen the men with their masks off. Brougham was his only chance. She could give him names. He had to find her.

The problem was, he'd likely have to face Treyworth over pistols before he found Brougham. *Which is all the more reason not to tempt fate,* Jane had said. Another duel might be one too many. This time he might be the one on his back, growing cold as his blood pumped out of him.

She could not walk into Del's room looking fearful.

Jane tried to push aside her fears for Christian and his duel, along with the worry she might be pregnant, and she pasted on the smile Del deserved to see when she walked in.

Del was lying in the bed, her hands clasped on sheets pulled up to her nose.

Jane rushed to her side. "What's wrong?"

Del sat up, panic on her pale face. "The maids told me my brother is going to shoot Treyworth. He must be stopped!"

The pain of the scene in Christian's study rushed up. She couldn't give Del any reassurance. Christian had been itching to fight all along, she realized. She had no idea how to stop an angry man who hungered for violence.

Jane picked up the bowl from the tray on the bedside table. The aroma of beef tea swirled into the air. "You must eat some food. Please, Del."

"I didn't really think he would come back for me. And now he's going to be killed."

"He's dueled before," Jane said slowly, hating to bring up the past incident that had upset Del last night. "He won. He will survive."

Del lifted her face, to reveal scrunched red eyes and tears running down her cheeks. "Treyworth will never go away. He won't face my brother honorably. He'll cheat."

Jane saw how afraid of Treyworth Del was. She feared he was invincible and unstoppable. So why had she defended him before?

Del's expression became resolute. *Dear God*—in that instant, Jane understood what she intended to do. "You are not going to return to Treyworth."

"What if Christian is killed? I can't live with that, Jane. I can't!"

Chapter Sixteen

*J*ANE LEFT DEL'S BEDROOM AN HOUR later, once Del had finally calmed. Subdued steps murmured behind her, and she turned to find Mr. Huntley approaching.

"His lordship had not given any instructions on meals and, as Lady Treyworth is indisposed, I thought I should consult with you, my lady."

Meals. Del was in anguish because Christian had challenged her husband to a duel, a state Mr. Huntley had just described delicately as *indisposed*. The madness of it all made Jane sway.

"My lady?" Huntley was stepping forward as though he feared he might have to catch her.

It seemed so ludicrous to worry about meals. But of course Christian's girls would need to be fed. "I think we should try to adhere to the usual routine, Mr. Huntley."

With so much shock and turmoil, it would be best for the girls and Del to keep to a schedule, steeped in as much normalcy as possible. That was something she could strive to do. It would keep her mind from dwelling on Christian. It would keep her hand from straying to her belly.

"I shall have a meal served in the dining room within the half hour," Huntley intoned.

"Lady Treyworth is not ready to come down. I would like to have a tray sent up to her."

"Of course, my lady."

She tried to sound calm and collected, but her heart was pounding. Still, she squared her shoulders. She had been given a glimpse of what she would be doing if Christian was killed in a duel. She would be trying to protect Del and look after Christian's girls alone. She couldn't desert them.

But what, whispered a fearful voice in her head, *if there is a child?*

"It was a secret club!"

Jane heard the girl's strident tones before she reached the dining room. She recognized the voice. Mary, the girl who was in love with Christian.

Gossip, it appeared, had spread quickly.

"I heard," the girl continued, as Jane opened the door, "that he went to the club to rescue his sister. A scandalous club where—"

"Mary, hush!" The girl with brunette curls rolled her serious brown eyes and cocked her head toward the door.

Jane forced a calm smile to her lips, and four heads turned to watch as she glided to her place at the foot of the table. "Good afternoon, girls," she said, as she let the footman slide her seat in beneath her.

Her voice wanted to shake, but Jane knew she couldn't let it. Sherringham's anger and disapproval had chipped away at her confidence when she'd been his wife. It had been hard to give orders to servants who knew how her husband hit her.

But these young women needed someone to take charge. It was as straightforward as that.

Jane cleared her throat quietly. "I do not think we shall discuss such things at lunch."

She laid her napkin in her lap and took up her spoon, and each young woman followed suit. All eyes diverted to the plates. Even Mary's. And even with a sullen glare on her face, Mary, with her deep honey gold curls and almond-shaped green eyes, was a beauty.

Tension sat heavily in the air, in the subdued expressions on the girls' faces. Jane glanced at each one as they sipped their soup. They expected her to disapprove of them—simply because they had been kidnapped and forced to live in harems.

Jane frowned. "After lunch," she declared, "we will practice music."

"I should like that." The soft murmur came from Philly, the shy blonde.

Scowling, Mary stirred her soup. "But where did Lord—?"

"Mary!" the redhead snapped sharply. "Do you want trouble so very badly?"

"Let us finish our food," Jane said.

Spoons clinked rhythmically. The girls exchanged glances, and only spoke to ask for platters of meat, vegetables, and roast potatoes.

Routine did seem to be a controlling thing. But Jane felt as though, if she relaxed and took a deep breath, the ceiling would collapse on them all. And was this strained

calm really good for the girls? Or would it be better—
though more treacherous—to let everyone be honest?

After the meal, Jane hustled the girls to the music
room. Philly went to the pianoforte and looked long-
ingly at it. She turned to Jane. "Do you play? Would you
play something for us?"

"I play very ill," Jane admitted.

"How could you?" Mary looked aghast. "You are a
lady."

Mary's expression of horror made Jane think of her
mother, who had been so unhappy and exasperated that
she did not excel in music, for that was what accomplished young ladies did. Her mother's sharp, bitter
voice rushed through her head...

*You cannot sing or dance creditably, you cannot play,
and in your manner of speaking with gentlemen, you are
never agreeable. You have to try harder, you wretched girl.
How else will you make a good match? Or do you want to
die in a workhouse?*

But Sherringham had offered for her, claiming he desired her for who she was, which hadn't been the truth
at all—

Jane abruptly pushed those thoughts away. "I loved
the look of music," she said, "The bars and the notes.
But when I laid these hands on the keys—" She held
them up and wiggled them. "They are too small to span
an octave."

It felt strangely freeing to be honest about her failure.
No excuses. No promises to try harder, to do better. Just
the truth.

Jane saw Philly look down at her hands and she
smiled for the girl alone. "And once I felt I could not
play as well as I should, I was too afraid to play again."

Philly ducked her head. "I'm afraid to project my sour notes and be laughed at."

Jane slipped her arm around the girl's shoulders and gave her a sympathetic squeeze. "But we should not care who laughs, and in fact, no one should laugh at us for trying to improve."

How she wished it were as easy as believing those words. She'd found the temerity to have a sharp tongue with Christian in her past, even to put pudding in his boot—how *that* must have enraged him—but not the nerve to try to stumble over a piece of music in public.

"I do not know all your names yet," she said.

"We know who you are," Mary said. "You are Lord Wickham's mistress."

Gasps came out all around and Philly clapped her hands to her mouth and cried a muffled, "Mary!"

For a moment, Jane was too astonished to speak. It was true and not true at the same time.

Mary thrust her lower lip forward. "We know she is his lover, so it is hardly scandalous to ask her to voice the truth."

"She's a lady," whispered Philly from behind her small, gloved hand. "You do not speak so to a lady. What if his lordship is angry and throws us out? What will we do then?"

"Find protectors," Mary declared, glowering.

"I don't want a protector," exclaimed the redhead. "I want a husband. I want children and a house of my own."

"It is well known," Mary said airily, "that a mistress has a better situation than a wife."

Jane felt a sad smile tug at her lips. Any mistress who had put up with the worst of her late husband's behavior had ensured she was well paid for her trouble—but was that better? Those years with Sherringham let her understand the emotion vibrating behind Mary's bold words. She calmly walked over and stared the girl in the eye. "I understand that you are angry—that you must be frightened and hurt, and that you must be furious with fate. That does not give you the right to abuse others, to be rude, or to hurt those trying to help you."

Mary blinked in surprise, dark lashes sweeping over brilliant green irises. "You know nothing about what happened to me!"

"Then I wish to be told," Jane said simply.

But Mary broke free of her grip and threw herself dramatically into the wing chair that sat kitty-corner to the settee. She folded her legs up and hugged them.

Jane realized shouting wouldn't gain her command, so she turned to the blonde who stood with her hands clasped in her skirts. "I know your name is Philly. What is your full name?"

"Ph-Philomena Melford," the girl stuttered.

"And you?" she asked the redhead.

The girl abruptly curtsied. "My name is Arabella, but everyone calls me Bella."

The sturdy-looking young woman who had been the leader in the hallway curtsied also. "I am Lucinda."

"My family name is Thomas," Bella declared. "But that hardly matters, does it?"

"You are part of your families, whether you have foolish relatives or not." But Jane saw the girls looked unconvinced. Despite being a group of four, they all looked lonely.

Idly plucking one of the harp strings, Bella glanced to the pianoforte. "I do play, and I play very well."

Jane was pleased to see the glow of confidence on the girl's face.

"You do not play well," muttered Mary. "And please don't sing!"

"You may play, Bella." Jane touched the girl's shoulders and guided her to sit at the bench. "And why don't you have a turn afterward, Philomena?"

The girl looked stricken, and Mary laughed. "There is no point in teaching us to play like ladies, for we are not ladies and can never be considered respectable or allowed into society."

"Of course you could be." But Jane saw at once that her firm tones had only angered Mary.

"I thought you knew what we are," she snapped, green eyes flashing.

"I know what happened to you. That is not 'what you are.'"

Lucinda spoke then, with a solemn air. "But it is, surely. We were raised as proper ladies and do know the consequence for the transgressions we committed."

"But you committed no transgressions. You were victims."

Mary snorted with derision. "I was locked up in a seraglio, kept with many women. To survive, I had to learn to become the sultan's prized possession. It was either that or be discarded—and that meant being tied up in a bag and thrown in the river. No *respectable* English man would ever marry me."

"There is more," Jane said decisively, "to a woman's life than marriage."

"Yes." Mary tilted her head to the side in a coquettish way, a way that would certainly tempt a man to madness.

"A woman can be a gentleman's mistress. And I shall be the companion of dukes."

"You were going to marry a footman," Bella pointed out.

Mary tipped her nose in the air. "I knew Lord Wickham would never allow that to happen. And just as I expected, he pursued."

"He stopped you to keep you from making an idiotic mistake," Bella argued, wrinkling her freckled nose.

"And he might not have stopped you," Mary retorted.

As Bella opened her mouth, Jane realized the girls would soon say cruel things that could never be retracted. She hurried Bella to the pianoforte's bench.

As Bella painstakingly played a sonata, Jane sat on the settee beside Lucinda. Philomena stood hesitantly by her and she held out her arm to invite the girl to sit on her right.

Christian, Jane realized, had meant well, but he was out of his depth. For heaven's sake, she was out of hers. She'd said that they could have futures that did not include marriage. But what could they do? If their pasts were known, they could not become governesses. They could not even take up a trade.

The girls were correct. But Jane was fed up. It was time the victims stopped paying for crimes they had not committed.

Mary gave a soft sigh. "Lord Wickham rescued me from my prison in the most daring and romantic way." Her starry-eyed hero worship made the girl look so vulnerable. "He came to my window and carried me down to a waiting horse. We were pursued and almost captured. I must admit that I fell madly in love with his lordship that night."

"Yes, we all know how violently you love him," Bella shouted as her fingers hit a sour note.

The other girls cried out in feigned pain but Bella shrugged. Mary leaned forward on the wing chair, glaring at Jane as though she was the enemy. "Do you *love* Lord Wickham? Do you think he is in love with *you?*"

Jane let her finger hover over the pianoforte's keyboard. She gently brought it down to touch the smooth ivory. But she could not bring herself to press down the key. She could not bring herself to make a noise.

It wasn't because she feared disturbing the girls or Del. They were all in their bedrooms—even Mary, who had provoked her a little too far.

Mary's brash question had been a line Jane had not wanted to cross, but once confronted with it, she'd known she had to. She'd calmly explained to Mary that Lord Wickham wanted the girls to behave like ladies, that he wanted good futures for them, and that he wanted them to heal.

You've been through a tragic experience, Mary, but you can claim your future, she'd insisted.

And then, whether it had been wise or not, she'd sent Mary up to her room. She had not discussed whether she loved Christian or whether she thought, or hoped—or didn't—that he loved her.

She knew Christian didn't love her. He saw her as he saw the girls—someone to rescue.

"You are a fraud, Jane," she said aloud, but so softly that it was only in a whisper. "It's so easy to tell those girls what to do. What to hope for. And so very hard to listen to your own advice."

"Do you wish to play?"

The deep, beautiful baritone made her jump and she knocked the music sheets to the floor. They floated back and forth through the air, twisting, flashing alternately bars of complex notes and a plane of smooth white as she turned to face Christian.

The bruises on his face had dulled to blotches of blue and purple. Even slightly swollen, his full lips looked seductive. "I would love to hear you play."

"I wish to, but I cannot. You see, I am terrible player. I've always been too afraid to make a sound—"

One last step brought him in front of her, and she forgot her words. A deep breath lost her in his scent. Her chest tightened, her breasts plumped against her bodice, and treacherous heat uncoiled in her belly.

She forced her voice to stay level. "What did you learn at Blackheath?"

"The matron and the other poor girls verified what we'd discovered. Mrs. Brougham used the house to provide innocents for the group of cloaked men, called the Demons Club, and the men also used the women there."

She was so angry she could manage only a squawk of indignant outrage.

"Those young women will be safe now," he said. "I've already sent them home under the care of my men. Huntley is finding places for the women who are ill. I'd rather use my wealth to save them, than throw it away at cards."

Unbidden, Aunt Regina's story came into her head—the tale of him handing over his pistol after a card game. One look at the man before her, with his troubled eyes that spoke of a caring soul, and she knew she would never believe that story.

Dear heaven. She wasn't at *risk* of falling in love with him. She already had. "W-what of Mrs. Brougham's mother?" she asked shakily.

"She's been sent to Bedlam, love."

"Bedlam! Oh no, she can't go there. It's a deplorable place. She doesn't deserve to suffer so." There, by worrying about Mrs. Brougham's mother, she could push aside thoughts of love. "There must be something that can be done, some way to raise funds to have her in a private place, a better—"

"I will rescue her, too, then, Jane. I promise you."

Two fingers clasped her chin and she moved with his hand to tip up her lips to his. Feather-soft, he brushed them over hers. The slightest contact and it set her mouth aflame.

She was astonished he would kiss her again after the angry way she had dismissed his proposal.

He eased back. "After this I want to take Del to India. I want her to put this behind her and have a fresh start."

The floor under Jane's feet roiled like the deck of a ship. "You want to take Del away?"

"Only if you aren't with child."

But it didn't matter if she was with child. She would not ask him to stay.

Christian raked his hand through his hair. "I have to. Even if Treyworth dies, Del will still suffer under scandal. I have to protect her."

Along her neck, his fingers stroked, sending tremors to the tips of her fingers, to the ends of her toes. With the simplest touch, he could give her sensations she'd never dreamed her body could feel.

"B-but is Del willing to go?"

"I hope to convince her. I think it would help her to

heal." He kissed her harder, his hands splayed on her lower back.

He was going to leave England again. Soon, he would sail away and she would lose both Christian and her very best friend.

She hooked her leg up around him, her soft calf pressed to the steely back of his thigh. To lock him to her, to keep him her prisoner, so she could kiss him like this forever.

Shame. She felt it suddenly. She didn't want a prisoner.

She wanted him to want to be with her. And not because of a child. Simply for her.

Her mother had loved her father hopelessly until she went mad. She had to fall out of love with Christian. He did not love her. He would leave her. And all she would have left would be pain.

His hands slid up and settled gently on the flare of her hips. Beneath his large, masculine fingers, her waist seemed tiny. She placed her hands on top of his, determined to move them away.

But he kissed her more deeply. His fingers slid out from under hers, teasingly crept down her back, and shivers radiated from the gentle caress. Shivers that seemed to ignite sparks all over her skin like tiny fireflies landing upon her. He cupped her bottom. Lifted her—

Too late she realized he was lowering her. Her rump landed squarely on the pianoforte keys. Dozens of them struck and an ear-splitting cacophony exploded out around her.

The vibrations rushed up her spine. She gasped in shock and clutched the silky fabric of his waistcoat.

"There, my jewel, you've made sound and the world

hasn't ended, has it?" On a chuckle, he shifted her, her bottom moved and a bizarre melody rang out in the room.

"You must get me off here. What if someone comes to investigate these odd...odd sounds? They might think—" What? A cat was in the house and running on the keys? Surely they would not think it could only be a woman's derriere on the piano—

Christian lifted his head, and discarded his coat. Hunger burned in his eyes. "I locked the door," he promised. His hands caught between her thighs and spread her legs wide.

"No—" she gasped. The lace at her hems skimmed her skin as all her skirts rode up. Her heels rested on the bench, and his hands held her legs open as he dropped to his knees. The bench skidded on the floor—his waist had shoved it back, beneath the piano keys. Now her heels were in the air, and he held up her legs.

"There are many places on you I'd like to kiss, Jane. I suspect you don't know what delight they can give you."

She gazed down at him through her spread thighs. Her cheeks felt like burning coals. She didn't want him to speak of this. "I saw mouths on the most scandalous places at the club, so I believe I know all—"

A wicked grin winked dimples at her. "I'll wager you don't. Can you name me one that isn't quite so scandalous but would make you melt?"

"Put me down, Christian. I want to stop—"

"The backs of your knees," he whispered, making a mundane place sound enticingly naughty. "The insides of your wrists. The warm curves beneath your breasts. The base of your spine just above your delectable bottom. The soles of your feet—"

"What?"

He languorously drew circles behind her knees with his fingers, and suddenly, she could barely think at all.

"I—I felt that everywhere," she stammered. He teased with his fingernails. "Goodness, the backs of my knees can level me like this?"

"Imagine then the power of the very scandalous places." He pushed her skirts up to her hips, revealing her nether curls and her private place. "Rest your feet on my shoulders," he urged, even as he arranged her in the position himself.

He was going to pleasure her with his mouth.

She couldn't do this. She couldn't. It was too shocking. She was so ... exposed. And if she made love with him, she would never ensure she protected her heart.

Retreat, her instincts warned. *Retreat inside and protect yourself.* Unable to draw a breath, she watched his head near her inner thighs.

He groaned, hoarsely. "So hot, juicy, and sweetly pink."

"Oh, don't," she whispered. She could even smell her ripe scent and her shoulders curled in protectively.

"But it is, and it is just as lovely as the rest of you."

His lips touched the sensitive skin of her right thigh, only inches below her wet, aching nether area. At once, she became as rigid, straight, and unyielding as the piano leg.

His tongue skated over her flesh. He suckled gently. And then she felt like a candle held to a fire—all her tension melted in the heat.

He kissed her damp nether curls and her hip shifted on the piano—a dissonant chord reverberated through the room.

His tongue slicked over her curls and she had to throw out her hand for support. Tinkling high notes serenaded them.

Lips parted, he planted a kiss right on her sticky folds and she slapped her hand on the lowest keys. The entire pianoforte seemed to shake beneath her, and the vibrations washed through her as his tongue touched her most sensitive place . . . her clitoris.

Her hands landed on the keys, and low notes and high notes screamed together.

Relentless, masterfully, he teased and suckled, and her bottom played a wild and merry tune beneath her. Over the notes, she heard him groan in pleasure, heard him moan as though she were the one pleasuring him. His beautiful blue eyes locked on hers.

He was doing this to teach her about pleasure, to rescue her from her fears. But she was too dizzy and heady with delight—too hungry for release—to stop him now.

The piano rocked beneath her, its feet jittering on the polished floor.

She gasped in shock but her hand struck three keys at once and drowned out the sound.

He stopped long enough to groan, "Trust me, Jane."

"I do," Jane breathed. "Right now I am trusting you to keep me safely on this piano. I trust you as I have trusted no one before."

Christian's low laugh in answer came straight from his heart.

He knew nothing of music, nothing but whether he liked the rhythm and sound, and how the melody spoke to his heart or stirred his desire. But he knew the urgency of the music they were making. The ringing notes came faster as he devoured her cunny and her body rocked more violently on the keys.

He loved her taste, loved the earthy sweetness of it. Loved the way she gasped when he slicked his tongue over her. He teased the very tip of her clit, tenderly, but the caress was so new to her she screamed out and banged hard on the piano.

It must be hurting her now to be on the keys.

He had to move her.

He shifted.

"No," she gasped. "Don't—don't move."

He gave a few languorous licks and then he suckled her again, finding the rhythm that made her hips arch, and her breaths come so fiercely she began to sob. Her moans rang out in the room as loud and frantic as the tune they were smashing out on the keyboard. Her heels rocked on his shoulders, she gripped her fingers around the keys to hold tight, and she surged to him in the way she needed.

She was not holding back. She wasn't fearful. She was giving him trust that he didn't deserve.

His cock strained against the placket of his trousers, yearning to join in the fun. But he wouldn't do that— not after he'd placed her at risk of pregnancy by being careless. Tonight, sexual frustration was his cross to bear.

Then the most amazing sound of all hit him. She cried out—a shocked, thrilled, agonized cry of ecstasy.

Once he'd loved to make Lady Jane Beaumont blush. Now he loved making her come.

She tumbled forward and he quickly let her feet go so he could catch her as she went boneless in pleasure. He kissed her moaning lips.

She jerked back, her lids half-closed, her lashes a fringe of gold. "You taste of..."

"Of you, Jane. You taste delicious." He kissed her again.

A blush rose on her skin. He held her close and lifted her off the piano. Her trembling legs wrapped around his waist and her slick quim pressed against the ridge of his trapped erection. The jolt of lust and desire staggered him and he had to grab the piano to keep from toppling.

She put her hand to her mouth and mumbled around her fingers. "It was far more... more devastating than I thought it would be."

That devastated *him,* and it brought guilt slamming into him like a black wave.

What was he going to do? He'd realized that taking Del away from England would protect her from scandal. But what about Jane? If Sherringham were proved a murderer of young innocents, the scandal would crush her. She'd told him she intended to never marry, but would she be willing to travel with him to the other side of the world to find escape?

And if there was no child—if he hadn't trapped her with his mistake—did he have any right to ask her?

A rap came fiercely at the door.

Catching up his discarded tailcoat, Christian went to the door and drew it open. A footman stood there, his eyes wide. "Lord Treyworth has arrived, my lord. And Lady T-Treyworth—" The footman broke off.

The servant twisted his hands. "Her ladyship has insisted she must return home with him."

Chapter Seventeen

OUTSIDE DEL'S BEDCHAMBER, JANE FACED CHRISTIAN, standing between him and the door. "You cannot go in. You are too angry. Issuing commands will not help Del."

He pounded his fist against the wall. "I have to make her see she can't go back to him."

With Sherringham, she would have retreated. But this time Jane moved forward even as her mind screamed at her to keep back. "You can't frighten her into staying with you. That's what Treyworth has done to her—he's forced her to bend to his will."

His deep blue eyes went forebodingly dark and cold. "You are saying I'm like him?"

"I am saying that you can't be as controlling as Treyworth, even if your motives are good."

He lifted his hand and she flinched. Had she pushed him too far?

But he rubbed his palm over his jaw, and Jane sucked in a deep breath of relief. Then he slammed his fist harder against the wall, and she almost leapt out of her slippers. But at the *bang,* something inside her snapped. She grasped his elbow, to stop him before he struck again, before he drove a hole in the plaster. She had never done such a thing—she had never before tried to stop a man's blow.

It astonished her to try.

Beneath her hands, Christian's muscles flexed, as though he intended to drag his arm from her grasp to pummel the wall again. Or push his way past her into Del's room.

"Breaking your knuckles—or this wall—won't help." Her heart raced but she stood firm. "Let me try to talk to her."

And strangely, standing up to him seemed to shatter his anger. He stared at her as though he had only just seen her, and he lowered his arm. "She's not going back to him. He'll be in his grave tomorrow."

"This is what Del is afraid of. I believe this is why she is saying she will return to him. She is trying to stop you being killed."

"God—" he rasped. He shoved his hair back. "You're saying she is doing this for me?"

She nodded.

Then he did the most extraordinary thing. Despite the anger driving him, Christian gently cradled her cheek. The change from angered male to gentle lover left her breathless. She'd never seen a man grapple control of his emotions so quickly. "Please try to make her see sense. I don't know if I can make her understand. I believe *you* can. You are the only person I trust, Jane."

Before she could say a word, he added. "But I'm not letting her into his clutches again, even if I have to shoot him in my drawing room."

He spoke so coolly about killing a man, it unnerved her. It reminded her of how dark and deadly he had been when he had threatened the Marquis of Salaberry and the grave robber.

Without another word, Christian turned and strode down the hallway, leaving Jane with damp palms and a thundering heart. She might not be afraid of his anger—but she was terrified of what it might do to him.

She understood why Aunt Regina had urged her to find a docile man. But she knew, dangerous to her heart though it might be, she could not turn away from Christian. She could not simply stand back and let him risk his life.

Startled, she realized she was far more worried about his survival than her own.

Del had her dress pulled over her head and was struggling to fasten it. "I can't do this," she gasped. "Will you help me or will I have to go with the back open?"

Jane closed the door firmly. "You aren't going downstairs. Christian will not let you sacrifice yourself for him." Guiltily, she realized she had only been in the room a moment before issuing *her* commands, after condemning him. "Del, you must stay here, with people who love and care about you."

At her words, Del stopped glaring at her as though she was an opponent. "I want to, I want to so much, but I can't. Treyworth will never let me be free. He can't let me go and I have to protect Christian—tell me, Jane, what else am I to do?"

In truth, she didn't know. "You will stay here, where it is safe, and I will go and speak to your husband."

"You mustn't!"

Jane had never seen such stark fear in Del's light blue eyes. And Del's hands clenched so hard on the bodice of her gown, she tore the lace. "Treyworth could—he would—" She broke off, and quickly looked away. Her shoulders shook, and all her initial bravado had fled.

Suddenly, Jane thought of Georgiana's story. "Something changed to make you run away. Something happened to make you more afraid of Treyworth, didn't it? That is why you were sobbing in the retiring room of the club. And it is why you wouldn't speak to me anymore. It is why you ran away without coming to me."

Del didn't answer, but Jane had known Del too long not to see she had hit the truth. She gently turned her friend to look at her. "I know about the Demons Club. Is that what you learned? That Treyworth belonged to that horrible club?"

Taken aback, Del nodded. Her shoulders sagged in relief. "I've been such a coward, Jane. What Treyworth did at Mrs. Brougham's club was nothing to his true perversions."

Jane sank to the bed, onto the dreadful mud brown and green counterpane, at Del's side. "How did you find out?"

"Lord Petersborough had warned me that my husband went to brothels where the girls were very young. I didn't understand what he meant. Oh Jane, I had no idea at all! After all, I was young when I got married. I knew it was why he'd wanted me—"

Del stopped and took a deep, shaky breath. "I found the truth because my husband kept a journal. It was usually locked in his desk, but one time he left the drawer open and I looked. It was madness to take the risk, but he had been behaving so oddly. He lost his temper all the time. There used to be days—weeks even—where he would be happy and loving, but over the last year, he had changed. I dared not even let out a breath without infuriating him. I thought I might find a clue in his journal. I suspected he might have been told he was dying. He *had* gone to some physicians in Harley Street—"

Del must have been very afraid to take such a risk. For all her talk about outwitting their husbands, Jane knew she would have never have dared rifle Sherringham's drawers. "What did you find in it?" she coaxed softly.

Del put her hand to her mouth and whispered around it. "He'd recorded his . . . his conquests. Some were barely more than children. Some were . . . they were not willing and he forced himself on them. Even just reading it made me nauseous. I couldn't stand it."

The mattress creaked beneath Jane as she shifted. "He found out you knew, didn't he?"

"When I put it back, I was so shocked and distraught, I put it back the wrong way. He confronted me and . . . you know I'm a terrible dissembler, Jane. I gave myself away. He was completely drunk, and he admitted to everything he'd done. He cried while he did. He held my hand and poured out these unthinkably wicked stories. Then he told me it was my duty to keep his secrets. The next day I ran away, but he found me . . ." Del clutched the torn bodice, her knuckles white. "He ruined children. Oh, Jane, it was so awful. And I could have stopped him."

"You couldn't, Del."

The candle light turned Del's eyes into large, shadowed circles of despair. "I could have poisoned his food. I could have shot him."

Jane stared at Del in horror. "You could not have done that. You would have hanged."

"Wasn't it my responsibility to stop a monster?" Del hung her head. "But I didn't do it. I was too afraid."

"It was not your responsibility," Jane cried. "Christian and I have stopped Mrs. Brougham's trade in children. Going back to Treyworth is not the solution."

"He threatened to kill me if I revealed his secrets. I knew if he could hurt innocents so callously, he could kill me. He threatened to kill anyone who helped me. That was why I couldn't turn to you, Jane." With both hands, Del wiped tears. The crumpled bodice dropped. "But you came for me anyway."

"Of course I did. You are my best friend." Jane rubbed the heel of her hand against her forehead. Was there a way to protect Del that didn't put Christian at risk? Then hope glimmered. "What of the journal? If we could find it, we could use it as evidence for a divorce. We could use it to stop the duel."

Del's shoulders sagged. "He burnt it. He threw it in the fire in front of my eyes. I think the fact I had found it made him fear someone else would."

Jane racked her brain. "Bow Street. We could go to the magistrates at once and have Treyworth charged for his pursuit of innocents."

"The magistrates will turn a blind eye. He's a peer."

"It might force Treyworth to flee England."

"But what proof can we give, Jane?"

Blast. There was nothing but Del's evidence, and Del could not give testimony against Treyworth. The members of the Demons Club had been masked. Without Mrs. Brougham, they could not prove Treyworth had ruined those girls. And Christian would know that. He would know that the law could not pursue Treyworth. He would go ahead and fight—

Jane leapt up from the bed. "I've thought of a way."

"What? *What?*"

"We have no evidence, but Treyworth does not know that. We could bluff him, make him believe we have proof. See if we can make him run." Del would still be married to him, but he would be gone. Then Christian could take Del to India, as he'd vowed to do, and keep her safe.

Jane rushed to the door.

"Stop, Jane! Where are you going?"

"I must get to Christian before the challenge is made."

Was she too late?

Treyworth's bellowing voice reached Jane through the closed doors of the drawing room. "You are accusing me of beating my wife, Wickham? What gentleman has not struck an unruly woman? It is my right to govern my wife as I see fit!"

Panic and fury exploded in her. Two footmen flanked the entrance, and one moved smartly in front of the entry to stop her. "You must not go inside, my lady."

"I have to. Unless you want to be responsible for your master's death!"

Astonished, the footman actually jumped aside. Jane pushed open the door, determined to drag Christian out so she could speak to him, but as she burst into the room, she stopped dead.

In the center, on a worn carpet, the two men were pacing around each other, like predators preparing to spring. Though a fire burned, the room felt ice-cold—as though it had been neglected for years.

"I want my wife." Treyworth snarled. "Legally, she is under my power. You have no right to keep her here." Given they moved in a circle, it was hard to tell, but Treyworth appeared to be retreating from Christian. Still, Del's husband was a formidable looking man. Short, square, muscular, he had the build of a sporting Corinthian and a love of pugilism and rough sport.

Jane shuddered. His hands were clenched into meaty fists—fists that had landed blows on Del's defenseless body.

She felt Christian's gaze settle on her. "Lady Sherringham, please turn around and leave. This is no place for a woman."

At Christian's frosty words, Treyworth stopped and glared at her with sheer loathing. And with the smugness of a man who believed he could make her crumble with just a sneer.

And damn him, he made her step back. "D-Del is not going anywhere with you," she said shakily.

Out of the corner of her eye, she saw Christian walking toward her, irritation with her plain on his face. At the same time he growled to Treyworth, "Delphina is recovering from what you did to her. I'm not letting you near her."

The room was dimly lit, but she saw the apprehension in Treyworth's eyes. She saw the tremble of his jaw. And realized he was afraid—he must be afraid that Christian had learned about the Demons Club from Del. "Delphina was ill and needed care," Treyworth threw out. He stood near the fireplace, the light hellishly red on his face. "She was going mad. She was imagining things and was becoming hysterical. I sent her to a private sanitarium for her own good. I did not wish my wife to be the subject of gossip."

Christian stopped, and he swung back to confront Treyworth. "You told me she ran away with a lover."

Christian's attention was focused entirely on Treyworth now. Jane wanted to shout the truth. *Treyworth had Del locked up because she knew he was debauching innocents.* But she hesitated. She wanted to talk to Christian before she spoke, and he would not look her way.

Treyworth banged his walking stick on the floor, striking the wood boards beyond the carpet fringe. Jane suspected that a lethal blade was hidden in the carved shaft—she knew Sherringham had carried such a weapon.

"That, Wickham, was the truth. I caught her at a dockyard inn where she waited for a man, a common paramour. I told my beloved wife how much I adored her. Delphina had been abandoned there. She was frightened, and the realization of how brutally she'd been used finally pushed her over the brink of madness."

"Give me the name of the man you say she went to meet," Christian snapped. Anger seemed to crackle around him like lightning in a dark, humid sky.

"But it's not true," Jane cried, stepping closer to the angry men. "None of it. You locked her up because of the club."

Slowly, Treyworth turned at the mantel, to glare down at her as though she were an insect. Something he could crush. "I don't know his name," he said. "She was too ashamed to tell me. Then she began to deny it had ever happened. She was deeply sorrowful and humiliated. You see her as she is now, after being under watchful eyes in Mrs. Brougham's house. You did not see her two weeks ago when I found her."

Jane felt her jaw drop open in horror. Now she understood why Christian was asking for details. Treyworth had concocted a story that would easily be believed. If Del denied it, proof could be provided that she'd been taken to the madhouse to convalesce under the care of Mrs. Brougham, who could claim to be Del's friend. With his wealth and power, Treyworth could even bribe a physician to invent proof Del had been "mad."

Jane hurried to Christian's side. Her slippers whispered over the rug. She reached for his arm. "I must speak to you."

"Not now. Stay back," he warned. He had discarded his coat. A glint of silver caught her eye. She gasped as she saw the pistol, held in the waistband of his trousers, tucked against his low back.

"I never hurt my wife." Spittle flecked at Treyworth's mouth. "I want her *now*."

"Christian—"

He held up a quelling hand. But she had to stop this—even if she grabbed Christian's pistol and fired it into the ceiling to do it. Goosebumps rushed over her arms and her chest, and prickled their way up her back.

In a low, deadly voice, Christian said, "We can solve this three ways, Treyworth. Bow Street is investigating Mrs. Brougham's madhouse where we found Del. Some of her 'patients' were innocent young women, held there to be debauched."

The fire hissed into the silence. Treyworth faced them with a hollow, deadened gaze. He knew they'd discovered the truth.

"If you were involved in that," Christian continued,

"you would face prosecution. Or you could be wise and leave England and Del while you still have the chance."

"We have proof," Jane cried, for she had to carry through with the bluff. "Proof that you were involved in that horrible trade."

With a guttural bellow of rage, Treyworth lunged toward her and his arm swung back. Jane winced, eyes shut, prepared to be knocked off her feet.

The blow never came. Slowly, she lifted her lids to see Christian with his hand clamped on Treyworth's arm. The marquis jerked free and wiped his hand over his lined brow, sweeping away droplets of sweat. "I don't know what in hell you are talking about. These are dangerous insinuations. You've attacked my honor."

"And you almost struck a defenseless woman."

Jane gaped. By bluffing, she had hurtled everything toward the end she'd wanted to avoid.

"Shall we say pistols?" Treyworth bellowed. "Chalk Farm. Dawn."

"No," Jane shouted, even as she heard Christian's cool response. "Agreed."

Jane found him in the gallery. Christian had set a candelabra on the floor and he stood beside the circle of light, his arms crossed. He stared up at two enormous portraits amongst the sea of frames that lined the white-painted wall.

His parents, she realized, as she ventured close enough to see the towering canvases. She stopped in the shadows. She had come in search of him; now she feared she would intrude on a private moment. She turned to retreat, but under her slipper, a floorboard creaked.

"Jane." Christian scooped up the candle and padded over to her. He was still dressed. His cravat dangled around his neck. Beneath his waistcoat, his shirt, open at his throat, hung loosely around his hips. "You should be in bed."

"I knew I wouldn't sleep." Due to fear, guilt over her botched plan, and a restlessness that throbbed low in her belly as she gazed at him. "I looked in your bedchamber, but you weren't there. So I came searching for you. But of course, you must want time to...to prepare...or whatever it is you must do." She moved to leave, to disappear again into the gloom of the long gallery.

"Stay. Please."

She stopped.

"I came down here to heartily curse my father for pushing Del into that marriage."

He held the candle aloft, throwing light where he had stood. Jane looked back at the painting of the austere former earl with his fair hair, beaked nose, and bulging eyes. He wore his most condescending expression, his gaze fixed down the length of his prominent nose. "He deserves it."

Christian's arm slid around her waist. It felt so natural now to have him touch her.

"Why did she agree to it?" he asked. "She was beautiful—she could have had anyone. My father must have forced her into it, but what did he gain from it?"

"Your father wanted Del to marry Treyworth because he is a marquis."

Christian halted at her side. "He wanted the *title*." He pulled his hand from her waist.

"Yes. He pushed her into it by insisting it would alleviate the scandal of the duel. Del had just ended her mourning for her mother—she was vulnerable, and she agreed."

He hung his head. "No wonder you condemned me. My hotheadedness ruined Del's life—"

"The fault lies with your father," she broke in. "What father would push his young daughter into a marriage with a man a quarter century her senior? Only a heartless and selfish one."

"It isn't as straightforward as that, Jane."

"You are not the man I thought you once were," she said impulsively. "I thought you nothing more than a rake and a scoundrel, interested only in your own pleasure. Obviously that wasn't true. You've—you've changed so much."

His soft laugh was harsh and unforgiving.

"Once she is free of Treyworth, Del can have a happy life. I believe that." Jane tentatively touched his arm, running her fingers along the tensed bulge of his biceps through his shirt.

She realized he condemned himself for his past far more than she had done. *Do not embark on a crusade over me, Lady Jane Beaumont,* he'd warned. But she had to.

She was defending him and he did not deserve it.

The flash of amber in Jane's eyes was as strong when she argued in his support as when she argued against him. He had never had anyone come to his defense before.

Christian took a deep breath as Jane sweetly clasped his hand and threaded her fingers between his. She was only defending him because she didn't know the truth. He was the reason for his father's bitterness. He was living proof of his mother's sin, and the reason his father had used Del to secure a better title.

Jane believed Sutcliffe blood ran in his veins. She didn't know he was really a bastard child. A cuckoo accepted into the nest because his father, Henry Sutcliffe, the Earl of Wickham had desperately needed his pregnant mother Eliza's dowry. His father was willing to take Eliza for the money, even though she had slept with another man while promised to him. But Henry Sutcliffe had never stopped punishing her for it.

Not even Del knew the truth. Only his father and mother had done, conspirators and enemies to the bitter end.

Christian let Jane lead him along the length of the gallery. Past portraits of generations of the noble Sutcliffe family, former Earls of Wickham. Past men who had served the courts of Henry the Eighth, Charles the Second, George the First. Men whose blood he did not claim.

Jane's familiar scent wrapped around him. When he drank it in, he could almost forget his shadows—something sex with many, many women hadn't done for him.

She was making him forget the stark memory of his last conversation with his father. He kept hearing, in his mind, the last words Henry Sutcliffe had said before Christian had wrapped his hands in rage around the man's throat...

"You have no idea what you really are," his father had spat.

For once his father had not been cold and controlled. The educated gentlemanly veneer dropped away and vicious hatred had burned in the earl's eyes, which were normally as cold as hoarfrost. "Tainted blood runs through your veins. You were born in wickedness—"

"I know," Christian had thrown back, in pain and pride. "I'm a bastard."

"You are much worse than that. I wanted to spare you the knowledge of your father's identity. But you don't deserve that, you murderer. I'll tell you who your father was—"

"Christian?"

Jane's gentle voice pulled him back to the present.

"Does Del know about the duel?" he asked softly, forcing the demons of the past back into the recesses of his mind.

She nodded. "I did not tell her. I couldn't admit to her that my plan to bluff Treyworth had failed. And I thought there was no point in frightening her. But she'd already learned the truth from a maid. I convinced her to take some laudanum, and eventually she fell asleep."

"I looked on her, and she was sleeping then." He had stroked Del's hair, apologized wordlessly, then crept out of the room. "Your plan was a good one, Jane."

Ruefully, she whispered, "I thought it was the perfect solution. But it all went wrong. I ended up pushing you two into a duel."

"It's not your fault. We were determined to shoot at each other from the start."

She frowned at him. "How can you be so . . . so light-hearted about a duel?"

He didn't answer. Instead, he said, "You are the bravest, most resourceful woman I have ever met."

Wavering, the candle's flame touched her with gold.

She looked frankly astonished. "I'm hardly brave. You've seen that yourself."

"You faced Treyworth, and he's an intimidating hulk. You endured a marriage with a brutal man, but you've had the strength to prevail. I am in awe of your courage, Jane Beaumont."

If he did die at dawn, he wanted her to know how much he admired her. "I've never forgotten the afternoon you tried to stop my carriage race." It was the truth. He'd held on to so many memories of Jane because, for all she'd infuriated him, she'd also made him laugh. When he used to arrive at the country estate and learn she was visiting, he went in search of her at once. He'd needed to see her, and spar with her, before he had to face his father's hateful words.

Gently, he squeezed her hand. The intimacy of walking handfasted speared him. It spoke of friendship as much as desire, and friendship was a precious thing he'd always avoided. A friend might see too closely into his soul. "I can still see you, gripping your bonnet to keep that straw thing clamped to your head as you skidded down the grassy hill. Your chin was jutting out and your eyes were ablaze with determination."

"How could you have seen all that? You were at the reins of a speeding curricle."

"Why did you come searching for me, Jane Beaumont?"

The pink wash to her cheeks gave him his answer.

"Naughty Jane," he teased.

Her pink flush went scarlet. "But I wasn't *thinking*, you see. Surely you shouldn't do that before you duel. Won't it . . . wear you out? Exhaust you?"

"Come with me." He lengthened his strides, and she began to jog, then run, and he had to lope along to keep up as they raced toward the gallery door. They reached it, laughing softly, and Jane sparkled up at him, all apprehension and anticipation.

"I want this night with you," he said.

And he intended to make it spectacular for her.

Chapter Eighteen

SHE HAD NEVER BEEN IN A man's bedroom before.

From the first night of their marriage, Sherringham had always come to her room. Jane could not imagine having gone to his of her own volition.

But here she stood, in Christian's bedchamber, drinking in every detail, fascinated to discover unique traces of him. They stood out against the dark austerity of the heavy furniture and the faded burgundy drapes. Loose trousers of gold silk lay across a chair. A tall Indian pipe sat upon a dresser. A simple shaving kit rested beside the ewer and basin.

Christian sat on the edge of the bed, his legs splayed apart—a pose that tugged creases into his trousers and made her aware again of how long-limbed he was. How beautifully made. Wearing a heart-melting smile, he crooked his finger. "Undress me, Jane."

She had not expected that. He kept introducing things she had never imagined doing. Things that made her body tense and her heart thunder even as they enticed her. "I couldn't."

"There's nothing to fear, love."

She approached as far as the column of the bed canopy and stopped. "I can't do it. I'd struggle with your clothes. I'd be awkward and clumsy."

Beneath straight brows, his eyes were earnest. "I'd never think that of you."

"But I don't want you to make love to me because you think you have to heal me."

"Damnation, Jane." Christian bit off a laugh. "I'm not that noble. I want to make love to you because you are beautiful, tempting, and luscious, and that taste of you I had in the music room has left me hungering for more."

Slowly, he drew off his neckcloth, let it drop to the floor. Heat unfurled low in her belly. Even just that casual action—with his gaze locked on her—was unbearably erotic.

She had wanted to protect her heart, but now, at this moment, she couldn't walk away. It was all she could do to stand on her two feet and watch Christian undress.

The sight stole her breath. The play of his neck muscles as he concentrated on flicking free his waistcoat buttons. The way the throat of his shirt pulled open as he moved, to give a glimpse of straight collarbones and the ridge of his beautiful shoulder.

Then his shirt was gone and all that remained was his trousers. He undid the placket, then pushed them down with one abrupt motion. He caught the band of his linens with his thumbs and they swiftly followed.

She had seen him completely undressed only once before—when she'd spied on him swimming as a young man. But that had been a glimpse of a man half sub-merged in a sparkling pond. Now, he stood before her, entirely naked, and she had to clasp both arms around the post.

She'd felt his erection on their first night together, felt the hardness against her belly, felt it deep inside her. But to see it was another thing altogether. The thick length jutted from his body amidst a thicket of black curls and it seemed to stretch out forever, straight and rigid.

"I'd like you to touch me, Jane."

She jerked her gaze up—past cobbled abdomen, broad chest, square chin, to deep blue eyes.

With his head tilted, he grinned. He braced his arm against the post that was her support. There was nothing to fear, but her hand shook a little as she reached out. And before her eyes, his member lifted upwards, as though stretching to her.

"How did you do that?" she asked.

"Alas, love, I don't control it that much. It's preening under your attention."

She gave an uncertain giggle. He stood only inches away but her fingers took a lifetime to reach the velvety skin at his navel. Crisp hair tickled. She stroked down, toward the taut head of his erection. She delicately touched the plum-shaped head, making it bob.

Christian sucked in a sharp breath. He was accus-tomed to the deliberate caresses of an experienced woman's hands. But Jane's touches—awkward bumps against his skin, tugs of his hairs, feather-light stroking he could barely feel—were more intense, more meaning-ful than any manipulations intended to entice. "You can grip me tighter and stroke me hard. I won't break."

"Oh, I couldn't—"

"Yes, you could."

Her fingers skimmed up to the swollen head. Biting her lip, she closed her hand around his knob and squeezed gently. Blood surged, making his shaft leap again. His ballocks tightened. She swirled her palm over him, spreading his fluid.

"Very sticky," she murmured. "And adorable. It looks as though it is wearing a bonnet."

A chuckle rumbled up. "Not quite what a gentleman expects to hear."

"No?" Her lips lifted in a teasing smile. "Then it is like a lance. Powerful. Is that better?"

Never had he known this combination of laughter and pleasure. Her hand jerked along his shaft and his groan of desire wracked him. He'd never seen a woman look so fascinated with exploring him. She stroked him, rubbed his juices into him, then trailed her fingers down and delicately cradled his balls.

It was exquisite.

But he eased her hand away and prowled around until he stood behind her. "My turn to undress you." He clasped her slim arms, led her to the large cheval mirror in the corner of the room. Each step made his cock slap her silk-clad bottom. An exquisite torture, one that intensely sensitized the taut, throbbing head.

"In front of the mirror?" she gasped. "I can't."

"Why not?" He undid her gown. "You are lovely." Before she could protest again, he drew the dress off her arms and eased it past her hips. It fell into a puddle of pale green silk around her. He helped her step free. "A nymph rising from the sea."

She shook her head. "My breasts are small and so are my hips. It was why . . . why I could not bear a child. I lost two babies, and my husband believed it was because my body is flawed." Guiltily she met his gaze in the mirror. "I should have told you. Even if I were enceinte—"

"You are exquisite and he didn't deserve you." His heart ached for her. She'd lost babies and Sherringham had made it her fault.

And then he had told her he would marry her if she were pregnant. Could he have jammed his boot any further into his mouth?

He slanted his mouth over Jane's lush lips. Soft and pliant, her mouth accepted his. But she didn't just take his kiss, she arched into it. Her tongue thrust into his mouth, playing with his. And with surprisingly unwieldy fingers, he fumbled with her corset ties, all the while letting Jane plunder his mouth.

A stab of guilt hit him. He hadn't yet told Jane about the matron's evidence and that a Runner was investigating her late husband. But if he told her now he'd drain away her passion.

It was selfish. But he needed her. He needed this night with her.

Corset down, shift up. In moments her slim, curvaceous figure was bared to him. Almost. Her white stockings clung to her shapely calves, ruched garters holding them in place.

"Now, sweeting." Christian dropped to one knee. "Watch in the mirror."

Jane gasped as warmth and wet swirled over her bare bottom. The mirror revealed Christian's mouth pressed to the cheeks of her derriere. She twisted to see. But even then she could not quite believe the sight unfolding behind her. Christian's coal black hair drifted over her rump but, far more shockingly, his tongue licked her naked cheeks.

She should be scandalized. This—*this* was far beyond her limits.

But it felt so good, she couldn't protest. She didn't want to stop him—and was certain she couldn't. If he wanted to do this to her, he would. But with him, that thought didn't scare her.

Dark and smoldering, his gaze never left her face. Even as he delved his tongue into the vee at the very base of her tailbone and her bottom arched up, like a kitten hungering for a pat.

His tongue slid down *between* her cheeks.

She almost leapt forward into the mirror. This had to be an exotic skill he'd learned in India, for she'd never heard of such a shocking act. But then, what did she know of making love?

Apparently not a blessed thing.

His tongue touched the puckered entrance of her derriere. "Christian!" she cried. And froze as his wet, warm tongue probed that unthinkable place.

Never could she have imagined he would kiss her there—or that it would feel so wonderful. Once again, he made her body melt. His tongue plunged in and out, and her toes curled. She swayed and found Christian's hands there, ready to support her.

"Good, was it?" he asked, as he rose to his feet behind her.

"D-did you learn that in India?" Not that it mattered, but she could not think of anything else to say. After such an intimate moment, she wanted to withdraw. She forced herself not to.

The mirror reflected his wicked grin. "No, sweeting. I

learned it before I left England." His laugh sent heat over the nape of her neck. "There is no shame in pleasure, Jane. This is sharing—intimacy. This is what making love is supposed to be about."

Making love. With him, it felt so dangerously like love.

The mirror reflected them together, his golden-brown arms entwined around her pale, naked curves. "You have generous, lovely hips. Have you ever seen a picture of a dancer in India?"

He began to move her hips in a gentle sway, back and forth. Jane tried to let her body follow his command and rock as his hands guided her.

"Even the gestures of the dancer's hands tell a story," he murmured. "I can imagine you dancing for me, silks swirling around your limbs. You would be rubbed with perfumed oils, leaving your skin smooth and fragrant. Imagine a fountain bubbling behind you and sensual music that envelops us both."

Jane caught her breath. With her hips undulating before the mirror, she could envision her body draped in jewel-toned silk. She could imagine music—she loved music even if she couldn't play it. And she could not resist the fantasy he evoked . . .

Soft, exotic breezes. Fragrant blooms rippling on a terrace. The merry splash of a fountain. He would lie on cushions and watch her with hot, aroused eyes while she gracefully wove him a story.

"What story would you tell me?" he whispered, as though he'd read her thoughts.

"I—I don't know."

"We could invent a language of our own to share with your hands. You could tell me what you wished me to do to you. You could be commanding me to be prepared to run my tongue over your lush derriere. Or you could be urging me to taste the sweet juices of your quim—"

She jerked her hips so abruptly she almost tripped.

"Would you dance for me?" Tugging out her pins, he unraveled her coiled hair and it tumbled down her back. Then he backed away from her, leaving her to her own devices. At once she stilled, uncertain now that his hands were gone.

"Just let your body sway." A low chuckle set her senses tingling. "I am a very lucky man—from here I can watch the jiggle of your sweet derriere and plump breasts."

She felt a warm blush wash over her bottom, bosom, and face. She saw him in the mirror. He was seated on the edge of the bed, his muscular legs spread wide. His hand wrapped around the long shaft of his erection, and he gave an audacious wink. "Come here then, Jane, and dance on top of me."

She could not sashay naked across his bedchamber. Instead, she used her long hair as a shield as she crossed to him, with her hands over her breasts. "How?"

"Plant your bottom in my hands and let me guide you."

He caught her hips and she let him lower her, watching the bounce of her breasts. In the mirror, she saw her dark red nether curls approach the long curve of his remarkable erection.

He cupped between her thighs, and his finger gently teased her aching clitoris. That made her strength evaporate like steam, and she sank down. But he stopped her as just an inch pushed up inside her. A dizzying, delightful inch.

"Take me as *you* want, Jane. You are in control."

He nuzzled her neck, cradled her breast, and held his

erection upright, letting her slowly lower onto him. The mirror threw the image of a wanton woman back at her. Wild coppery curls danced around the face of this woman, a face with heavy-lidded, sultry eyes, and a slack, kiss-plumped mouth. Her breasts swayed freely, reddened nipples pointing straight out.

The mirror revealed the astonishing, arousing sight of his thick, veined column disappearing within her. He filled her and lifted his hips with each thrust, teasing the tight walls inside her.

She bit her lip. Gave whimpering sobs of delight. And she pumped on him. She could not believe she was this naked woman who was not cowering beneath a sheet, but was bouncing on Christian—and watching every thrilling, exotic moment.

A playful slap landed—a light one that set her bottom jiggling. She twisted to see his eyes and, in a trick of the light, she saw flames flickering in their blue-black depths. The sight drained her strength completely. She plopped down hard on to him. His erection invaded her to the hilt.

All she could do was sit on him and let him take control. He turned her slightly and bent to her left breast. He ravished her nipple—suckled it, nibbled it, and pulled at it with his lips until she was crying his name. She clung to his forearms, her nails tugging his skin as he lifted her in the air with each fierce thrust.

Oh, he was an expert. Suckling her nipple, teasing her clitoris with his broad, strong fingers, and thrusting, thrusting, thrusting, until she burst.

She shouted. Screamed out his name. She gripped him and rode on him as wave after wave of sheer delight consumed her.

Then she slumped on him, exhausted, disheveled, and once again fiercely shy.

The wicked woman in the mirror faced her.

Christian laughed. Laughed! He pumped up again into her sated body, and she felt the twinge of pleasure through her womb. "I love your look of surprise when you come, Jane. And after, you look like a smug little kitten who has been given cream, a ball of yarn, and a mouse."

She had to giggle. And that moved her muscles down there, pulsed her around him, and made her *feel*.

"I can feel you fluttering around me when you come. Your cunny holds me and tries to pull me deep inside."

She couldn't think of a thing to say. But she loved to hear him tell her what he felt. It fascinated her to know.

"But you didn't . . . come," she whispered. He must be intensely frustrated.

"I can't—this time, I am trying to be responsible."

"But I want you to. The choice is mine, Christian. I want you—"

"The choice should be ours," he argued. "But I can, if you'll let me wear a sheath."

Confused, she nodded. "Of course. Why would I not?"

It took only a moment to unseat her, but she stood awkwardly while he withdrew a sheath from a drawer and slid it over his rigid member. Then his hand wrapped around her waist; she squealed, and found herself on top of him again. It felt so very right to take him inside.

He nibbled her earlobe. Suckled it and drove up into her. She couldn't think—

Sweat gleamed on his arms, her breasts and belly as he arched up into her and she slammed down on him. He was buried in her deeply, and her legs lay over his thighs. Lower and lower his fingers went, through her sticky curls to reach her nether lips. They felt like molten silk to her—what did they feel like to him?

She was hot, sweaty, and messy, and it was so good. She bounced on him but, with her legs dangling over his, she was clumsy. She could not find his rhythm; she danced ineptly, but he groaned, "Come for me, Jane."

His skillful fingers circled her throbbing clitoris. He caught her nipple between his lips once more. Pleasure roared in from everywhere—her breasts, her quim, deep inside her body. *Too much.* But she wasn't afraid. Not afraid to be greedy and want too much.

"Christian!" She was coming again.

He kept pounding into her. Each stroke made her climax go on and on. She panted because she couldn't breathe anymore and her mind might simply shatter if this didn't stop, but she didn't care, and she could do nothing but surrender—to heat and delight and heaven.

Incoherent cries flooded her ears. Her screams of release. She clung to him, riding him as stars exploded behind her eyelids and she soared in ecstasy.

"I'm going to come, Jane," he rasped. He drove in deep and pushed hard against her womb. His head dropped forward, his body suddenly bucked. "Yes," he cried out. "Yes, my love, yes."

She held him, loving his orgasm, loving the way it racked his body, loving the look of agony on his face, and knowing the pleasure he was feeling.

With a low groan, one that made her toes tingle, Christian fell back on the bed, pulling her with him. He kissed the top of her head and laughed. She giggled again in return. Their shared laughter made her feel bonded to him. It helped her push aside fears of what dawn would bring.

His arm snaked around her. He pinned her to him, with her hot, damp back pressed tight to his hard, sweaty front. "You dance beautifully, Jane. Your every movement mesmerized me. Did you enjoy it, love?"

"What you taught me tonight enthralled me." She had to swallow hard. "You enthrall me, Christian." That sounded perilously close to an admission of love. If she were trying to fight that hopeless emotion, she'd best not put it into words.

But love was not something one could avoid. It was not an emotion one turned off. She, who had learned to subdue all emotion before her late husband, could not will herself not to love Christian.

It was not that easy. "I should go to my bed," she whispered.

He blew a warm kiss at her ear and gave a sigh of contentment—a sound she'd never heard a man make before. "Stay with me tonight, Jane. You are where you belong."

His breathing came in an even rhythm. Jane listened so intently, her heart began to beat in the same pattern. She longed to close her eyes, to join him in sleep.

But she couldn't. At dawn, he would duel with Treyworth. She had only two hours left.

She gently coaxed his arm to open and wriggled away from his chest. The mattress creaked and shifted beneath her as she sat up.

She should watch his face for a flicker of his lids—a signal he'd noticed she wasn't curled up against him anymore. But her heart felt soft and molten as she gazed down on him. Long black lashes lay on his cheeks. His features were relaxed, giving him the look of boyish innocence men were supposed to wear in their sleep but that she'd never seen for herself.

His lids moved just a bit, but then he sighed softly. He'd said her name. In his sleep, he'd asked for her.

She had to do what she planned while she still had resolve.

Holding her breath, Jane made the final leap to the floor. He didn't stir, so she crossed the floor to his wardrobe.

For a gentleman he had few clothes, but perhaps he had not brought many things with him. He had rushed back for Del. He must have always intended to return to India.

Jane touched a shirt. Even washing could not take away the rich, delectable smell of him.

A row of drawers lined one side. She opened one. There were cufflinks of gold within, along with a pocket watch. The next drawer contained cravats. She laid four over her arm. These would work for what she wished to do. For what she *had* to do. She shivered as she thought of that moment at the club, when Sapphire Brougham had told her she could tie a man to the bed.

"Hurrr?" Christian muttered. He shifted, tried to roll, and couldn't. "What the—" He pulled with his arms. He really couldn't move them.

Something was holding him down. Ropes. Or a burly servant's arms. His father would cane him now—to beat the wickedness out of him.

He thrashed wildly. Sheets slid off his naked body. The bed lifted and slammed to the floor as he struggled to break free. "Christ Jesus," he shouted, fighting the fear that had always made him take his father's punishment in silence. "No. Let me go——"

"Christian, Christian! Stop. Please stop!"

Jane's voice cut in through his confused thoughts like a sharp blade. His eyes shot open and he realized he'd been shouting at the top of his lungs.

"Jane?" He craned his head up. "What in blazes are you doing? I thought—I don't even know what the hell I thought."

"This way you cannot go and get killed," Jane said defiantly, but she bit her lip.

He looked down at his feet. Bindings bit into his ankles, and wrapped around his wrists. She had him spread-eagle on the bed, tied to the four bedposts. Hell and the devil, what was she thinking? He knew she would have never dared do this to Sherringham.

Well, that had to be good, didn't it? She was not afraid of him.

His heart still pounded from the fear that had haunted him when he'd woken up.

She paced at the foot of the bed. "We can defeat Treyworth with the law, not with risky pistol shots on a foggy field."

He sighed. "You can't do that to Pomersby, love."

"To *who?*"

"Reginald Smithwick, Viscount Pomersby. He's to be my second—just as he was eight years ago. Though this time, I didn't give the poor bloke much warning about the duty." He tugged again at the cravats, but her knots were too strong. "I sent a note a few hours ago to let him know he should be ready at dawn, to reassure him there'd be no chance he'd have to fight in my place, and to advise him not to waste any time attempting to negotiate a reconciliation."

The color drained from her face. "I'd forgotten about your second entirely."

"If I do not show up, he has to fight for me."

She looked so demoralized it made his heart clench. "Then there's no way I can stop this blasted duel from taking place. No way to ensure you're safe, unless..." She hesitated. "Could you not...shoot first?"

"I won't cheat, Jane."

"No." She sighed. "You wouldn't, would you? You are entirely too noble for that."

"What was your plan, Jane? To keep me bound to the bed for how long? Forever?"

"I needed to keep you...in one place. Long enough to talk sense into you."

"You know, Jane," he rasped, "in this position, I am entirely at your command."

Her brow arched. "I was told that, but I fear not."

"It's the truth. You are the one in charge." She'd left a sheet over his groin and he could see it lift as blood rushed down from his head. "You can do anything to me you wish."

"How can you be thinking of that!" She paused, then firmly shook her head. "That would be inflicting things on you against your will. I could not do that."

But she could, with a clear conscience, tie him up. He winked at her. "Not even if I assured you I am very willing?"

"How can you smile in that way when I—I have you tied to the bed?"

"In what way?" he asked, all innocence.

"That devilish way, as though you are about to do something very wicked to me."

"What I want, love, is for you to do wicked things to me."

"I should untie you."

"Not until you climb on top and ride me to oblivion, sweeting. I'd like you to do it while I'm bound."

She gaped at him. He expected her to chastise him for the blunt request. Instead she cocked her head, frowned, nibbled her lip, then finally said, "All right."

All right? Before he could even smile at his good fortune, she was climbing onto the bed, pulling back the sheet. Delicately, she held back her hair. She ran her tongue over her lips in a slow, enticing sweep, and his heartbeat ratcheted up until it was a roar in his ears. Suddenly she bent forward and pressed her mouth to the head of his cock.

He jerked against the ropes, stunned and aroused. She looked so dashed dainty as she bestowed a loving kiss to his rigid prick. The shaft listed toward her, the head straining to meet her mouth. He saw his fluid shimmer on her lips.

God, yes, sweeting.

He almost lost control and exploded at the considering expression Jane wore as she licked her lips and tasted his juices. It was infinitely more erotic than any calculated gesture.

"It's so . . . intriguing," she mused.

"A good taste?"

"Delicious." With a wicked smile, she enveloped the head of his cock in her heavenly mouth once more.

The head on his shoulders almost shattered. Her

cheeks hollowed, her pink lips stretched wide around him. She sucked him forcefully, bobbing up and down. His heart hammered as she took him deeper and deeper. He gripped the cravats, leaning up as far as he could to watch.

The naughty angel took him to the hilt, then pulled back, let him spring out, and spluttered.

"Sweeting—"

But she took him back in. She suckled him hard, then soft, playing, exploring, so sweetly curious, he thought his heart would burst.

He'd never climaxed into a woman's mouth. He's always hung onto his control. But Jane's tongue slid into his slit. At the same moment her hand caressed his balls. Like an untutored schoolboy, he let go. The orgasm slammed into him. He shouted up at the bed canopy. And he felt her mouth move around him as she swallowed his seed. *Jane*—

He slumped back, his heart beating a fervent tattoo, his brain swamped with pleasure.

"I liked that," she whispered. "I liked pleasing you."

He chuckled. "You are a treasure. I should be thanking you for taking me to heaven."

She sat back on her haunches, and a shadow came to her face. Her hand strayed to her stomach and the truth of her sadness speared him. She must be thinking of the child who might be growing in her womb. Of course she would, when she feared he could be killed and she would be left on her own. "I'm so sorry, Jane," he muttered. He had done exactly what his natural father had done to his mother—condemned her to disaster. "You deserve to marry a man who adores you, to—"

"Stop. I vowed not to marry again. Even if I am

pregnant, I won't marry. It is as simple as that." But the catch in her voice told him it was anything but simple.

She leaned over to untie him, her breasts dangling in front of his face. He couldn't stand leaving her unhappy. He leaned up and captured a nipple in his mouth.

"Christian!" But she let him suckle.

He teased her, but his thoughts ran deeper than sexual play. He had never met such a complicated woman. Tonight she'd tied him in knots, literally. Who was she really? The shy girl who had run from him on the terrace? The crusader who had tried to stop his carriage race? The stubborn rescuer who had faced her fears at a sex club to save her friend?

Jane was all those—a complex brew of femininity, strength, and vulnerability. And he'd discovered another side to her—a sensual woman who wanted to love, who denied herself dreams of happiness, marriage, and children to protect her heart.

But she deserved them.

A powerful desire welled up. The desire to be the man who could offer them to her. But he wasn't. He never could be. If she was already carrying his child, she needed to know the truth about him. But he didn't want to tell her.

Chapter Nineteen

*H*E WAS BEYOND RAGE.

He dragged her to face him. "I know there is someone else. I can see it in your eyes. Were you thinking of him when you said your vows to me? Has he had you first?"

He shoved her and she fell back on the bed. The skirt of her new peignoir flew up to bare her legs. This morning she had said her vows to this man. This was her wedding night.

"I—" She did not know what to do. She was too stunned to speak. What had happened? Should she protest her virginity? But she didn't love him, and he had known—he had seen it. He'd told her he knew they weren't marrying for love. But he was angry, so terrifying and angry—

Jane jerked awake, her heart pounding. Damp with sweat, the sheets clung to her bare skin and tangled like rope around her legs.

It had been just a dream. Another nightmare. Rubbing her eyes, she rolled over—

She was in Christian's bed, and he was not. He must have left for Chalk Farm.

Sunlight crept around the heavy velvet drapes and she bolted up, peering desperately at the mantel clock, but too bleary-eyed to see it. It was obviously long past dawn, and she could do nothing to change what had happened to him.

Shaking, she shoved back the linen sheets and the heavy counterpane, then leapt off the bed. Her robe lay across a chair. Before leaving for the duel, Christian had brought it for her?

A white square on the bedside table. He had also considerately left her a note.

I will return soon, sweetheart. This I promise, it read.

"Oh, Christian, you cannot promise that."

But the message was so very like the Christian she remembered from their youth—confident and arrogant. Now she'd seen aspects to him she'd never have guessed existed. Self-doubt. Uncertainty. Regret.

Dragging on her robe, Jane peeked out the door, then stepped into the hall, preparing to race across to her own room, where she would summon a maid. She stopped in her tracks.

Two brawny footmen flanked the door to Del's bed-chamber.

"Where is he? A maid told me he hasn't returned yet. That could only mean—"

"No," Jane broke in.

Del's normally soft, light voice was as cold as her clammy hand. Jane squeezed that hand, sat at Del's side on the bed, and tried to soothe her with a hug across her shoulders. "He might not have come back yet, but I believe he soon will. We mustn't worry."

She voiced hope, as though speaking it aloud would make it real.

But Del shook her head. Her lips were bloodless and her eyes hollow. "He should have returned by now." She got up from the bed, and went to the window, but this room looked out over the rear garden. "If he's not yet back—"

"It doesn't mean anything until we know. I've never seen a duel, but it must take quite a time for it to happen. And the men...they must talk afterward, of things." *A physician may have had to attend to a wounded man.* Her stomach clenched. *Or an undertaker had to be fetched.*

"For three hours?"

While Jane searched for a plausible, hopeful answer, Del said, "I am being kept a prisoner in my room."

Jane thought of the footmen, but lied, "I don't believe that's so."

Del turned slowly from the window, and the panes cast patterned shadow across her pale oval face. She looked not hurt, not angry, but perplexed. "It is. I tried to leave and the footmen refused to let me. On my brother's orders. And a maid stayed in my room."

"He's doing it for your protection. To keep you safe, because he loves you." And because, she realized, he feared Del might try again to return to Treyworth.

Guiltily, Jane remembered warning Christian he was behaving like Treyworth. It had hurt him then, and she wondered if it had hurt him to instruct his servants to keep Del in her room.

But she understood why Christian had put his footmen on guard. She would have been willing to do it herself. She, who believed a woman should be independent and free, would have been very willing to lock Del up to keep her from going back to her monster of a husband.

"I know he does, but I—" Del broke off and blushed.

Jane eyed Del with suspicion. "Why did you try to leave your room?"

Del averted her eyes. She fiddled with her hair. "I just wanted to talk to my brother. I wasn't going to race home to Treyworth. I promise."

But Del kept twirling her hair with her finger and staring at the window—keeping her head tilted so Jane could not look directly into her eyes. Things she would do while lying. Jane's heart sank—Del *had* planned to escape and go back to Treyworth. And would not tell her the truth.

Jane glanced at the mantel clock. A gold hand ticked away another minute. It was almost nine. Suddenly she realized what that meant. "Christian must be alive."

Del jerked around to face her. "What do you mean? How can you be sure?"

"He must be. If Christian had been killed, Treyworth would have come here at once to fetch you, Del. That brute would not have let three hours go by."

Hope shone in Del's eyes, and Jane felt such relief. But she sobered instantly. Treyworth must be dead, but why was Christian not back?

What if he'd been arrested? Or worse—wounded?

Some instinct sent her spine tingling. She found herself rising to her feet. She hurried to the doorway and leaned out. Below she heard a slam and muffled shouts. Something was happening downstairs. The two footmen were still on guard—she could safely leave Del.

Jane hauled up her skirts and ran.

*   *   *

At the bottom of the stairs, Jane collided with Mr. Huntley. He immediately leapt away, and shoved his spectacles back up his nose. After a bow of apology, he let his brows jerk up as he took in her state—her loose hair falling in a disheveled mess, her belted robe. The bottom of it parted to reveal her bare calf.

She didn't care.

Huntley cleared his throat. "His lordship had asked for you, my lady. He is in his study."

He spoke as though Christian had merely risen late this morning. How could he be so calm?

Jane hared to the study like a hoyden, but stopped at the doorway, suddenly hesitant. This was just like the morning on which he'd proposed, his study the place where she had rejected that offer of marriage. Obviously it hadn't broken his heart, if he wanted to see her here.

She pushed open the door, realizing Christian had asked for her as soon as he'd returned. He had not gone to Del first. What did that mean?

He stood at the sideboard, limned by sunlight, and he held a glass of brandy. He looked so normal, she clutched the doorknob and fought the need to laugh or cry or do both at once.

Christian looked up. His midnight black hair was in disarray over his brow, his eyes bleary and tired. She did not think this was his first glass of liquor.

She stepped into the study and pushed the door shut behind her. "You killed him."

It had spilled out before she could stop it. And she winced. Her stark words sounded like an accusation.

"He's dead, sweetheart. But not in the duel."

His glass landed hard on the table. Droplets flew. Suddenly he strode to her and caught her around the waist and lifted her. Flooded with relief, she reached out and cradled his face. She savored his warm skin against her hands. She deeply drank in his scent—sandalwood, leather, witchhazel. She'd never treasured anything so much.

He was alive, he'd come back, and it meant Del was free and safe. . . .

She kissed him, hungrily taking his mouth. All she could think was that she might never have been able to kiss him again. She might have been bestowing one last kiss on a cold forehead—

"Stop, Jane." He pulled back, set her down on her feet. Then his words sank in. "What do you mean 'not in the duel'?"

"I waited at the field but he did not show up, so I went to his house and found him."

"You shot him in his home?" But that was murder. Just as he had threatened last night when she'd stopped him from going into Del's room. And even a peer would hang for that. A flash of pain in his eyes made her hesitate. Slowly, she asked, "Were you the one to kill him?"

Christian wasn't surprised at the direct question. He'd already killed one man in a duel and had threatened to shoot Treyworth. Of course, Jane thought him capable of murder.

His heart still pounded from that moment when she'd burst into the room. She had looked at him and she'd glowed. Warmth and light seemed to radiate from her.

For him.

Now she frowned at him. "What happened, Christian? Please tell me."

He could tell her the truth, but would she believe he was innocent? "As I said, Treyworth did not show at Chalk Field. I dueled with his second, who was your friend Charlotte's husband, Dartmore."

"Dartmore?" she cried, suddenly indignant. "He agreed to fight—with Charlotte enceinte?"

Christian had to shake his head. Her reaction was so typically Jane. "Don't worry, love. Killing him was of no use to me, so I shot an innocent tree instead. Before we measured our paces, I told him I intended to do that and, surprisingly, he did the same. Then I headed to Treyworth's house."

He couldn't put into words the icy fear that had coursed through his veins as the mist had cleared off the field and he'd realized Treyworth wasn't coming. He'd thought the rogue had double-crossed him. Faced with two choices—go to Treyworth House or race home—he'd chosen the first. And even as he'd driven there like a madman, he'd been terrified he was making a mistake. He'd feared Treyworth had gone after Del.

"And you confronted him?"

"He had already been found, lying dead on the floor of his study, stabbed in the back."

Color faded from Jane's face, but she shook her head as he came toward her. "I can listen. Don't stop."

"Radcliffe, the officer from Bow Street, was already there, summoned by Treyworth's butler."

She did not say anything. She held the back of a chair, and seemed to be waiting. For what? Him to plead his innocence? Everyone who had been in Treyworth's home—the butler, Radcliffe, even insignificant footmen—had looked on him with more than suspicion in their eyes. They had looked at him with certainty. They believed, without a doubt, that he had decided to stab Treyworth before facing the bugger in a duel.

Christian picked up his brandy and drained it.

"Tell me what happened."

Strangely, the soft tone of Jane's voice acted like a command. It made him want to talk. "Two witnesses saw a dark-haired gentleman cross the grounds of Treyworth House just before dawn. One of the witnesses, a footman in service for twenty years, insisted the man he saw was me. He had even overhead a man speaking with his master about four o'clock in the morning. He heard this visitor speak of recently returning to England by sea.

"The Bow Street investigator believes I'm guilty, given the eyewitnesses' evidence, my wicked reputation, and the fact I killed Lord Harrington in a previous duel. He vowed that if he can prove me guilty, he intends to see me hang."

"Hang!" This time Jane swayed on her feet, but she grasped the sideboard for support.

"He will be coming here—to question Del, if she's able to talk. And to question you, Jane, about me."

Jane stepped forward, just as she'd done when he'd been about to storm into Del's room, when she'd bravely planted her slim body between his anger and his goal. She laid her hand on his wrist. "You haven't said whether you did it or not. You've told me that others think you did. But I don't believe you could have."

She amazed him. His father had believed he was destined to be evil, wicked, and warped due to his parentage. Everyone at Treyworth's home had assumed his guilt. Jane, who knew he had killed before, was coming to his defense.

"Sweeting, no, I didn't do it. That is the truth, though I doubt anyone will believe it. Now I have to go and tell my sister that her husband is dead."

But Jane moved between him and the door. "Someone killed Treyworth. He could not have taken his own life with a knife to his back, could he?"

Grimly, Christian shook his head. Warning bells rang in his brain.

"Who could have done it? Who else could have wanted him dead?"

"It couldn't have been Del," he said. "I posted two footmen on guard outside her door and a maid to watch over her in her room."

"Of course not! I would never have thought Del would do such a thing." But she averted her eyes—there was something she was not telling him. Before he could ask, she began to pace in front of him, muttering, "Who? Who else?" Her brows drew together in a firm line, and she rubbed her chin.

"I've been considering that since I found him and learned I'm the odds-on favorite for the gallows," he said.

His attempt at black humor did not stop her stride up and down his floor. "A gentleman from the club . . ." she mused. "One of Del's lovers, perhaps, to protect her. Or free her." She whirled on him. "You had the list of names of those men. A man who loved Del would surely hate Treyworth." She frowned, thinking. "Treyworth ruined innocent girls. It could have been a father or a brother of one of those young women."

The need to stop Jane's determined march, to hold her to him and capture her mouth again in a deep, heated kiss hit him so hard it stunned him, and he tamped down the yearning. *She was the only one to believe in him.* Instead he propped his elbow on the back of a wing chair, and reminded her, "There are other possibilities beyond the club. It could have been an irate husband. It could have been over a debt. A servant, caught stealing, might have done it." In other words, Radcliffe might hound him to the gallows rather than search endlessly for the truth.

Her hands fisted at her sides. "We *have* to find the killer. Before you are arrested for something you did not do! To start, you must tell me the names on that list." She pensively bit her lip and glanced to the door. "Or I could try to ask Del—"

"*You* are not going to search for a murderer to protect me. I will not allow it."

Her eyes snapped, and in them he saw the blazing determination of the loyal friend who had plunged herself into danger for Del.

Only this time, all her fire and passion was for him.

"Intriguingly enough, Christian," she declared, "you don't control me."

"Am I a terrible person, Jane? I should want to cry. I should feel grief. But I don't. All I feel is relief."

Jane felt her heart lurch as Del blinked at her, a dry handkerchief balled in her tight fist. She faced Del's reflection in the vanity mirror. "Of course you feel relief. And Treyworth, monster that he was, doesn't deserve your tears."

Del looked doubtful. "Do you know what I did after Christian told me? When he had left the room? No, of course, you couldn't—I was alone then." She squeezed the lace-trimmed linen in her grip. "I looked up to the heavens and said, 'Thank you.' Then I smiled. I should have cried, but I stood there and smiled and thanked heaven. Perhaps I am mad, after—"

"No, you are not," Jane broke in. "I did the same thing when I learned Sherringham was dead. I walked out onto the terrace and I drank in the spring air, and I felt free at last. It is not wrong, Del."

She helped Del stand. For the first time since her rescue, Del wore a gown and had her hair neatly arranged in a sleek coil pinned to the back of her head. Jane smiled. "You look...strong and brave, Del. For that's what you are."

It lifted her heart to see Del's slight smile in return. When Sherringham had died, she'd needed Aunt Regina's support to see her through those first few days, weeks, months. She would do that for Del.

And for Christian, she would help discover who had killed Treyworth. Did he think she would sit idly by and hope that the true killer was caught? The stubborn man was determined not to involve her. He'd refused to reveal the names on the list of Del's lovers, while warning her not to speak to Del of it. But she said softly, "Petersborough said he was in love with you, Del."

Del shook her head. "He said he was—I think he merely liked to be my 'protector' at the club." Her eyes went wide. "You could not be thinking he killed Treyworth for me. He would not have done. Even if he did care for me, he would not have...have murdered my husband."

"I'm sorry. I shouldn't have spoken of it."

"I am—I'm glad you did. For these will be the sort of

questions I will be asked." Del sighed heavily. "I think I am ready to go downstairs, Jane."

"Are you certain you wish to speak to the Bow Street Runner?"

Del took a long breath, nodded, then reached behind to check her hair—such a normal gesture, Jane's lips wobbled. "To help protect Christian, yes. I am as determined to do that as you, Jane, and I can face this with you at my side."

"Lady Sherringham. Lady Treyworth, my condolences on your loss."

Jane shivered as she looked up into the chiseled face and narrowed eyes of Hadrian Radcliffe, the Bow Street Runner. He did not wear a scarlet waistcoat like the Bow Street men who were on foot or horse patrol. Instead, he dressed as any gentleman. He had fair hair like Salaberry's, but his eyes were coal black, rimmed by black lashes, and possessed an intensity that made Jane step back.

This was the man who believed Christian a murderer.

She settled at Del's side on the sofa in the west parlor—the grim room in which she and Christian had interviewed Mrs. Small. Radcliffe took a chair opposite but Christian remained standing. The Runner began with Del, who sat rigidly still, her hands clasped on her lap. Even in shock, Del was beautiful and Radcliffe's eyes softened as he gazed at her. "Might I ask, Lady Treyworth, if you knew of any enemies of your husband?"

"I—I don't know." But her glance went to Christian and Jane's heart sank. Did Del believe Christian guilty?

She hadn't thought to ask. She'd assumed Del believed in him as she did.

"I spoke to the two footmen who stood guard," Radcliffe said gently to Del. "Both men claim they remained awake and alert for the night. Both claim you did not leave the room. However, these servants are in your brother's employ and are loyal to him."

Jane saw Christian surge forward, ready to speak. But Radcliffe rounded on him. "If you please, my lord—otherwise I will have to speak to Lady Treyworth alone."

If Christian had been a wolf, his hackles would have been raised, his fur on end. Low in his throat, he growled like one, but paced back.

Del took a deep breath and Jane gave her an encouraging smile.

"That is true, but their word spares me, not my brother. I assure you they are not lying, Mr. Radcliffe."

Touché, Mr. Radcliffe, Jane thought.

"May I be so bold as to ask why Lord Wickham placed you under guard? Was this to protect you from your husband?"

"P-perhaps. I did not ask him." Del glanced down at her lap. "I woke to discover the men were there. Yes, it did make me feel more . . . safe."

"Was it also because his lordship feared that you wished to return to your husband?"

Del stayed silent.

"I have spoken to your maid, Alice. Alice claimed that you were insisting you must return to your husband. You were determined to go down to him when he came here to collect you."

"I—"

"Did you love your husband and wish to return to him?"

Jane's heart leapt to her throat. Again, Christian stepped forward, his stance intimidating, but Del looked to him. "I wish Mr. Radcliffe to know the truth about my husband."

Christian inclined his head to Del. It was like watching a dove command a panther.

"My husband was a terrible man, Mr. Radcliffe. He was no gentleman, and—" Del faltered. "No, I did not love him."

Jane met Del's pale blue eyes and whispered, "You don't have to," but Del gave a resolute nod. She shakily told the Runner everything she knew—about the innocents, Treyworth's journal, his drunken admission to her, and finally his imprisonment of her.

Radcliffe's expression became grim, regretful. "I understand, Lady Treyworth, and I will not plague you with questions any longer today. You have my apologies. I humbly give you both my admiration and my sympathy— but it is my duty to see justice done. And I see your brother was prepared to protect you at any cost."

Del blanched. Jane clasped her hand and whirled around to Radcliffe. "I suggested to Lord Wickham that he cheat at the duel to ensure that he was not killed and Del would be safe. But he refused to do it, because he is a gentleman and too honorable. He would hardly kill Treyworth in cold blood—"

"He wouldn't cheat in front of witnesses, my lady." Radcliffe cast a long, appraising look at Christian. "Is it true, my lord, that eight years ago you dueled and killed a man over your mistress, who happened to be that gentleman's wife?"

"That's true."

Jane made a strangled sound. She wanted to shout

about all the noble things he had done. How he had rescued girls from harems. Saved men in India. Rescued Del. Saved her life—

"I've heard that you did not delope, even after Lord Harrington fired at you and missed."

Christian raked his hand through his hair, a jab of black glove through gleaming black silk. "He missed my heart, but hit my shoulder. And like an arrogant fool, I thought I could spare him by hitting his shoulder in return. But the wound threw off my aim and, as I fired, Harrington tried to leap out of the way. He jumped into the path of my shot. It wasn't my intention to kill him, but I wanted to put the fear of God into him. Yes, I was having an affair with his wife, but he took out his rage on her. He'd battered her black and blue and I wanted to warn him never to hurt her again. My intention wasn't murder, but I had no right to take that shot—no right to take that risk."

Jane saw the pain etched in Christian's eyes. The regret.

Del broke the silence. "My God! After what Father said—what I said to you . . . And you never meant to kill him." A tear rolled down her cheek. Jane squeezed her hand gently.

Radcliffe gave Christian a curt nod, then bowed to Del. "My apologies again, my lady."

Jane released Del's hand and erupted from the settee. "But you do see that Lord Wickham did not deliberately murder Lord Harrington. That was an accident."

"On Lord Wickham's word alone."

"Did you speak to the seconds, Radcliffe?" Christian asked coolly. "Viscount Pomersby was mine. Lord Carlyle, ironically, was Harrington's. They'll tell you that

Harrington jumped. But the result, whether my act was intentional or not, was the earl's death."

He hadn't forgiven himself for the duel. After all these years, he was angry with himself for causing Harrington's death. Now she saw why he had dueled. It had not been male pride, or stubbornness, or the desire to have Georgiana. He had done it because he believed he should protect a woman from her abusive husband.

Oh no, she would never be able to stop loving Christian. And she had to help him now.

She believed Christian was innocent. Believed it with all her heart. But she had to ensure they had time to prove it.

"He could not have been the murderer," Jane said. "For he spent last night in his bedchamber with *me*."

She'd lied for him.

Rocked back on his heels, Christian knew he could not let Jane do that. But before he could deny it, Radcliffe leapt on the flaw like a hunting hound. "Were you awake with his lordship for the entire night, my lady? Apologies for the impertinent question—"

"Don't apologize," Jane responded, her face pale.

In that instant, Christian knew she would lie again. He stepped forward. "She did sleep, Radcliffe. Let us cut to the chase. There is at least one hour in which neither Lady Sherringham nor any of my staff can account for my whereabouts. I was in my study, but can offer no witness."

"Christian—"

But Radcliffe smiled. "I admire a gentleman who doesn't tell desperate lies."

Christian said nothing. He looked still and cool, waiting while Radcliffe tapped his jaw, and Jane feared her heart would burst in its frantic pounding.

"At first, my lord," Radcliffe stated, "I have to admit you appeared to have the strongest motive. Apart from Lady Treyworth—again, my apologies, my lady. But I searched Lord Treyworth's desk late this morning, under the watchful eye of his butler." His voice took on a dry, sarcastic edge. "I think he suspected I'd abscond with the silver during my investigation."

Jane opened her mouth to reply, but Del spoke up. "That was inappropriate of Worthington. I shall ask him not to hinder your investigation."

Jane saw Christian give Del the same shocked look she did. At the look of surprise on the Runner's face, Jane sent up a silent cheer for Del.

Radcliffe looked abashed. "I am sorry to put you through this, my lady. The fact is, I found a stack of letters fixed to the underside of one of the desk drawers."

"On the bottom?" The terse question came from Christian.

"No stone unturned, my lord. It appears Lord Treyworth was blackmailing Lord Sherringham shortly before his death."

Jane stared, perplexed, at Radcliffe. "How could that be? They were close friends."

"Lord Treyworth had kept Sherringham's letters—full of vitriol and rage, but Sherringham had paid up. To the tune of twenty thousand pounds before his death."

Jane could hear the words, but could not seem to process them. The estate had been bankrupt on Sherringham's death. He had been giving Treyworth money?

Del covered her mouth. "Oh, goodness. He had been spending lavishly. I thought he'd won money at cards."

Del's words snapped Jane out of her shock. "But what hold did he have over my husband?"

Christian. His large frame loomed at her side. A warning to Radcliffe? But she must know the truth. She must have the strength to hear the truth about her husband.

Radcliffe glanced to Christian. "His lordship asked me to keep quiet about this until it was necessary to tell you. A witness has accused Lord Sherringham of murder—the murders of two actresses and of other young women at Mrs. Brougham's house on Blackheath."

"Accused only," Christian growled. "The matron wasn't a witness to the murder, Radcliffe. I heard what the woman said. She could not say for certain that Lord Sherringham was a killer."

Two actresses. The two women missing from the club. And Christian had known. He'd learned this about Sherringham and had not told her. And Mrs. Brougham had lied.

Arms folded over his chest, face impassive, Radcliffe was studying her. Assessing her reaction. Well, it was shock. What was that telling him? Then, through the dull roaring in her ears, Jane saw hope and grasped at it. "If Treyworth was blackmailing someone else, that person could be his killer. Not Christian."

She heard Christian's surprised intake of breath.

"That's true, my lady. Problem is, I've found no other letters. No sign he was blackmailing anyone else."

"But he could have been," Del cried. "A month ago, he bought several horses for his stable. He acquired a hunting box previously owned by one of the royal dukes. He was racking up bills. He must have been blackmailing someone!"

Chapter Twenty

H E FOUND HER IN THE GARDEN after dinner. Del had retired early to her bedchamber, so Christian had come in search of Jane.

She leaned against a rose bower, her arms crossed over her chest. White blossoms framed her red-gold hair and the breeze sent a shower of sweetly scented petals fluttering around her. She hugged a shawl around her shoulders.

Acrid guilt wrapped around Christian's heart. He should have told Jane about Sherringham's purported crimes. It should have come from him—he would have done it gently and carefully. She should not have learned about her husband's brutality from a Bow Street Runner. And that had happened only because of his selfish sexual need for her.

Jane turned at the sound of his boots on the flagstones. He saw red-rimmed eyes but also a stubborn, uptilted chin. "Did the matron of the sanitarium know who the members of the Demons Club are?"

That stunned him. He'd thought she would be lost to shock and grief. "The only one she could identify was Sherringham, because one of the other men used his name."

"She didn't see any of them?" Jane pressed.

Tell her and she'll embark on a search.

At his pause, she frowned. "I knew you wouldn't give me the names of Del's lovers, but I've got them anyway—"

"Christ, did you ask *Del*?"

"No, *she* came to *me*. I asked about Petersborough and she told me, to protect you. She couldn't face telling you."

Hell, he couldn't have faced it, either. "Who did she say?"

She grimaced, wrinkling her freckled nose. "Petersborough, Salaberry, Lord Pelcham. And one of Mrs. Brougham's prostitutes, a charming young man, Del said. His name is Rory Douglas."

They matched Brougham's list. He didn't know whether to be reassured by that or more saddened. "I know. I spoke to all those men."

"We must find out where they were last night," Jane continued, her voice firm and resolute. "Petersborough and Pelcham both have dark hair, and Pelcham is broad-shouldered and trim, exactly like you. We must find out who the members of the Demons Club are. Treyworth might have been blackmailing the other members—"

"No." Christ Jesus. "It is bad enough that you tried to lie to a Bow Street Runner for me."

She frowned. "I didn't lie. As far as I knew, you were in bed with me."

For a heartbeat, Christian was taken back in time, to

their many arguments on the terrace of his family's Hartfordshire estate.

Eyes wide and earnest, Jane faced him. "I have to do this, and it isn't just for you. I want to stop the members of the Demons Club. I want to do it for the women that my husband killed."

God.

"I'm sorry, Jane—sorry I kept it a secret from you. I planned to tell you. I should have told you. As you now know, I was with Radcliffe when the matron of the mad-house told her story. But what I said was the truth—we don't know for certain that Sherringham was a murderer."

"I can believe it, though, Christian. I know what he was, how vicious he was when enraged. He was the sort of man who liked to take his anger out on a woman. With me, he always stopped himself. But with a woman who had no protection at all? He was capable of it."

He drew her into his arms. When she didn't resist, he cradled her tightly. "If Sherringham was guilty, it has nothing to do with you, Jane. I'll ensure it doesn't become public."

"You can't do that, Christian. There will be a scandal. But I don't care—those women deserve justice." She pulled free of his arms. "Since Sherringham died, I've been at a loss. I didn't have a penny to my name. I've survived by being my aunt's companion. Before Del went missing, I had even started to go out in society again. At balls and routs, I would sit at the side and watch the world whirl past."

"Jane—"

"I want to *do* something, Christian. Something meaningful! Not just for the women who were killed, but to save those who might have been ruined by these men in the future. Helping these women is something I *can* do. And first, we need to find Mrs. Brougham. She will know who the members of the Demons Club are."

He would humor her—but he was not about to let her go investigating the Demons Club. "Brougham has probably fled England."

"Yes, I suppose she has." She gave him a suspicious glare. "Do you *know* who the members are?"

The sun cast its last warm embrace around her, limning her in gold. Her squared shoulders revealed a deeply wrought strength. Then he saw a slight tremble. A hint of the vulnerability behind the courage.

"You aren't going to tell me, are you?" she complained.

"Just to prove you wrong, angel," he said, as he would have done in the past, "I will. The matron could give only vague descriptions of the members of the Demons Club. They generally wore masks, but she saw glimpses of their bare faces through a keyhole. She saw six men. Two had dark hair, one was a handsome blond, the fourth was balding with a beaked nose, and the fifth had brown hair streaked with gray."

"And my late husband?"

"Just over a year ago, she saw a silver-haired man she believed was called Sherringham."

Jane stood in silence, her expression so blank, it unnerved him. Then she looked to him. "I gave you an alibi because I believe you're innocent, Christian. But you seemed determined to make yourself sound guilty. I want to understand why."

"Sweeting, lying only makes matters worse. Everyone believes I'm capable of murder. I've accepted that."

"No, actually I don't believe you have. I believe it hurts you deeply to think that." Her intelligent gaze pierced him. "I am beginning to wonder if everything you told me in the past was a lie, to make me think the worst of you."

"Not everything," he answered. But he realized what she said was the truth.

"I remember I called you heartless once, because you were telling me that you went from one lady's bed to the next." She blushed lightly. "But you were never heartless at all, were you? Everything I believed about you was wrong. I've come to see that."

Stunned, Christian realized in that moment as he stood in the dying sunlight in his garden, with Jane peering up at him and seeing far too much of him, that *she* was the real reason he had left England. She had always insisted he should be something other than a wicked rake. *Isn't that a rather empty way to be?*

Now he saw it was her condemnation that had made him strive to be more than just a bitter scoundrel, angry because he was a bastard and because both his father and mother hated him for it. He had walked away, but it had been her words—nagging in the back of his head—that had spurred him to try to become a better man. The gentleman his father had claimed he could never be.

When she'd asked him if he still played bondage games with women, he hadn't told her the entire truth. He hadn't had a mistress for a year before he'd left India to return to England. He'd had both English and Indian lovers up to that point, had gambled deep, and had been cavalier with his own life. It had taken him time to embrace that better man, but he doubted he would have tried if it hadn't been for Jane's words. And for that, he owed her more than he could ever express.

The problem was, he couldn't even begin to say that to her, without having to tell her the truth about him.

"Tomorrow, I'll question Salaberry," he said instead. "And investigate the other names on the list Brougham gave me. I intend to get into Treyworth House and search for other letters."

"Tomorrow, I am going to call on my friend Charlotte."

Hell. "No, you are not. There's a murderer on the loose. You are staying in this house, where I know you will be safe."

"I will be perfectly safe. Charlotte is my *friend.* I must tell her what has happened—"

"Charlotte is also Dartmore's wife. No."

"I will take servants."

"Christ, Jane. Sometimes I think the only way to stop you is to tie you to your bed."

He saw her eyes widen in shock. He cursed himself. What a warning to give a vulnerable woman. "Stay here. Stay with Del. For me, Jane."

Before Jane could protest, he closed his mouth over hers and kissed her as the evening breezes showered them with rose petals. And even after his clumsy words, she lifted up on her toes and passionately kissed him back—she devoured him with a hunger he didn't deserve.

Christian sloshed brandy into a tumbler. In India, he would smoke the hookah to relax. But nothing would ease the knot in his neck, the binding tightness of his shoulders.

A clock chimed the hour. One in the morning.

He'd been sitting here for hours, studying the book he'd stolen from Mrs. Brougham's bedroom, hoping to determine if any had been members of the Demons Club. He'd hunted for any kind of clue to their identity. But he had nothing.

And he kept thinking of Jane's kiss.

Candlelight glinted on a pair of spectacles as Huntley looked in the doorway. "You are still awake, my lord?"

Huntley had been in earlier to update him on the various threads of his investigations—reports from the men he'd assigned to watch the club and the now empty Blackheath house, and reports from those watching the docks for Mrs. Brougham, in case she had waited to run. Today, he had sent a servant to keep watch on Salaberry's house, since it seemed likely the marquis was involved in the Demons Club.

Christian had to admire Huntley for his ability to administrate so many things. Hiring Huntley had been the one decision of his father's he admired.

He gestured to the chair opposite his desk. "Have a brandy, Huntley."

The secretary gaped at him. Christian shoved the bottle across the table. "Take a drink. I've been mulling something around in my head for the last few hours and I need to talk it out."

Huntley sat but did not take the bottle.

Christian got to the point. "Treyworth was blackmailing Lord Sherringham. Sherringham had already handed over twenty thousand pounds and I suspect that if he hadn't died, Treyworth would have demanded more."

"Indeed," replied Huntley with conviction. "Blackmailers are rarely satisfied."

"Let's say a man has committed murder and is being drained of his wealth by a blackmailer. Many peers have escaped England for less. Bad debts drove Brummell away. I heard Byron had to flee rumors of sodomy and the scandal over his affair with his half-sister."

"True, my lord."

"What do you know of the fire that killed Lord Sherringham?"

Huntley blinked. "I know the gossip of the time, my lord."

"Thought you might. You're a fount of gossip, Huntley."

Huntley took off his spectacles. "Your father found it useful, my lord. As to the other...two badly burned bodies were found. And since there were witnesses who claimed Lord Sherringham had visited the woman that night, the assumption was the two bodies were theirs. I believe several personal items were found, which gave proof of his death and allowed his cousin to inherit. The bodies themselves could not be identified."

"You know quite a bit about it."

"For weeks, everyone else spoke about little else. I am sure it was a hardship for Lady Sherringham."

Despite the warm brandy in him, Christian's blood ran cold. Yes, it must have been. "So a charred body was found and buried and everyone believed Sherringham was dead. Which lets a man get away with murder."

"I beg your pardon, my lord?"

"Sherringham. He could have faked his death. If he'd remained in England and been found guilty of murder, he could have been hanged. And if Treyworth continued to bleed him to keep the secret, he would have ended up impoverished. Leaving the country would have let him escape prosecution, but he would have known he could never return. Would he burn down a house, kill his mistress, make it appear that he died, and walk away from everything?"

His secretary considered. "I believe the estate was heavily in debt, my lord. Large mortgages and loans had been taken out. Lady Sherringham was left destitute."

Christian scrubbed his jaw. Jane had faced scandal and poverty, but had survived. She truly was a remarkable woman. As for the money... he'd known men in India who kept a cache of portable wealth, usually in jewels. "Sherringham could have cleaned out as much as he could and took it with him," he mused aloud. "He loses the title and his estates—which he leaves bankrupt—but he can live like a king wherever he chooses. Unlike many peers who fled the country and have had to live in genteel poverty."

"Do you wish for me to make further inquiries, my lord? For if Lord Sherringham is still alive—"

"Find out everything you can about the house fire, Huntley. I need to prove to myself that he's dead." Because if Sherringham was still alive, hiding somewhere in the world, Jane was still his wife. And if that were so, he couldn't marry Jane to give his child a name, if that eventuality arose—if she even agreed to it. He'd be making her a bigamist.

Christian drained his brandy.

But in the eyes of the world, Sherringham was dead. And Jane Beaumont was free. He would be the only one who would suspect otherwise.

For the first time, he realized how intensely he wanted

her. But he couldn't have her. And she was determined not to marry him.

Jane alighted from the carriage at Lady Petersborough's town home on Berkeley Square. Del had insisted Lord P. would not have killed Treyworth for her, but she had to make sure.

Christian would be furious that she had left the house, but she had two footmen and the coachman with her. It was, after all, broad daylight. The squeals of children rose from the park in the center of the square, along with the squeak of perambulator wheels. Many carriages rattled along the streets.

There was nothing to fear. She doubted Lord Petersborough would be at home. At this time of day, most gentlemen sought refuge at their clubs.

Within moments, Jane was led to a drawing room and announced to Lady Petersborough. She stood transfixed on the threshold. Elspeth was not alone. Georgiana, Lady Carlyle, reclined on a chaise like a sleek cat. Her blond hair was a tower of perfect curls, and ivory and violet silk clung to her voluptuous form.

Elspeth, dressed today in a respectable gown of muted bronze, rose, and Jane found herself embraced in a false hug. "Poor, dear Lady Treyworth," Elspeth declared dramatically. "I cannot believe Lord Treyworth has been murdered. And Lady Treyworth locked up against her will in a madhouse. It's all so terribly shocking."

Rolling her eyes in the background, Lady Carlyle sat up and gracefully poured tea. "I do hope Lady Treyworth is recovering." She held out the cup—it rattled on the saucer. "And C—Lord Wickham? I heard there was to be duel between Wickham and Treyworth."

Aware of Georgiana's eyes boring into her, Jane took a seat and the proffered cup. "The duel did not take place."

"So it is true that Treyworth was murdered in the night," Elspeth breathed. "And that is why he did not go to the duel. I heard that from Charlotte, who of course learned it from Dartmore. He stood as a second. And it has been so good of you, Jane, to remain in Wickham's house and care for poor Delphina." A malicious gleam showed in the sharp, dark eyes. No doubt tongues had been wagging about her and Wickham, too.

"Yes," Jane said slowly. "She is in a great shock at the loss of her husband. And I believe the club is now closed and Mrs. Brougham has disappeared."

There was a silence. Jane looked innocently from Lady P. to Lady Carlyle.

Elspeth gave a theatrical shudder. "It is said that Mrs. Brougham was acquiring innocent girls from the country. How appalling!"

"It is a shame it has closed, though," Georgiana added. "I have had to attend balls on the last two nights. Lady Matchford's and the Duchess of Fellingham."

Lady Petersborough nodded. "As did we. Along with the come-out for the Earl of Coyne's twins. Three balls in two nights. Terribly dull affairs. I miss the . . . diversion of the club."

Both women had taken care to tell her where they had been last night.

"Did your husbands accompany you?" Jane asked, with a careless wave of her hand, as though the question held no import. "My husband used to merely put in an appearance and then leave."

"The club has ignited a spark in my husband." Elspeth gave a conspiratorial wink. "He has been unable to leave my side. We had the most exhausting nights in my bedroom. I knew where he was every minute of each night—whether I wished to or not."

Elspeth was making it clear she would swear her husband had been with her and could not have murdered Treyworth. Was it the truth?

Lady Carlyle gave a rueful smile. "I attended alone. My husband has traveled to his estate." Her eyes spoke of the pain of a woman who hated going back to her life as it was.

"I wonder," Lady Petersborough mused, "if a new club will be created?"

Jane frowned. Did they truly miss the carnal games they'd played at Mrs. Brougham's club? She knew how hellish it was to be married to a man one desperately didn't want to bed. Now she couldn't imagine ever wanting to make love to any man other than Christian.

Elspeth tapped Jane's knee. "I've heard Lord Wicked has a harem of orphaned girls in his house. Is it true?"

"It is not a harem," Jane protested. "They are decent girls."

"Do they not have family?" Georgiana asked.

"Wickham wrote to their families but all refused to have the girls sent to them. They have abandoned the poor girls."

"They are ruined, dear," said Elspeth. "What can you expect?"

"Some simple human compassion?" Jane asked angrily. She set down her cup and stood. "I am sorry, I must go." She could not stand to stay any longer. Even if she stayed for hours, she doubted she'd learn anything more. And she was in danger of throwing cooled tea at someone if she did.

She now knew where Elspeth claimed her husband had been. The next step would be to find out if it was the truth.

Georgiana also stood and gave a feline stretch. "I must return home as well."

In a stretch of the hallway far from servants' ears, Jane waited for Georgiana. "Bow Street suspects Christian is the murderer, partly because of the duel with your husband."

Georgiana's sultry green eyes widened. "I feared that." Then she frowned. "*You* were the one beneath the black veil, the one who played the saucy tart."

Jane ignored that. "Christian claims he did not intend to kill your husband. If you know that to be the truth, you could—"

"Oh yes, I know that to be the truth. But since I was Christian's lover at the time, I doubt my word would be believed."

"You are a marchioness."

"Yes. They would listen to me at Bow Street. They would be polite, deferential, and discreet. But I fear my word—the word of a woman in love—would have no sway. I was not there at the duel. I know only what Christian told me, and what I knew in my heart."

"If there were a trial, your word could help."

"A trial?" Georgiana staggered back and pressed her gloved palm to the wall. Color leached from her cheeks, and she looked as horrified and fearful as Jane felt. "I would say anything to protect him. Do you know what Christian did after the duel? He barged into my drawing room and dropped to one knee before me. I knew it meant Harrington was dead. While I was still taking that in, Christian apologized profusely, then offered me marriage because he'd left me a widow. He told me he'd wait until after my mourning, that he would wait forever if he had to. And I refused him."

"You must have been in shock—"

"The truth is," Georgiana said bitterly, "I was in love with the Marquis of Carlyle by then. I could not see Christian for the strong, wonderful, noble man he truly is. I was dazzled by Carlyle's handsome face, his wealth, his obsession with me. So that morning, I refused Christian and I had the servants drag him out. I had to be rid of him to have Carlyle. And all I could think was that Christian had left me free to pursue the man I truly loved. What a fool I was."

Jane blinked. Georgiana had rejected him, just as she had done. Was that why he'd really left England? Not over the duel, but because of a broken heart?

"I've regretted it since the moment I realized that I truly loved Christian and not Carlyle." Georgiana sighed, and harsh lines bracketed her mouth, revealing strain and regret. "Do you know why Christian fought the duel?"

"Yes. Because your husband had hit you."

Georgiana recoiled in surprise. "So he told you... Harrington had hit me, had bloodied my nose and blackened my eyes. It was anger over me that led Christian to duel. And I realize now that Carlyle would never do such a thing for me. I never understood how

passionately Christian could love until it was too late."
Bright with unshed tears, the marchioness' eyes became
pleading. "Now there is something I must ask you, Lady
Sherringham."

"What?"

"Late that same night, Christian came to see me
again. He'd been drinking heavily. He looked ravaged.
Haunted. He told me he had been wrong to ask me to
marry him. That he could not marry, and that he could
offer me nothing. I told him then that I intended to
marry Carlyle. I assumed his father had forbidden the
match, but when I said that, Christian laughed harshly.
He told me he could *never* marry. That he'd never punish
a woman that way."

"But why?" Jane demanded.

"He would not tell me the reason. For all these years,
I've wondered what it was. You knew him when he was
young. But you do not know why he believed he
couldn't marry?"

Jane shook her head. She was stunned.

Christian had asked her to marry him. Only because
of possible pregnancy, but he had made an offer. He had
not told her there was a reason he could not ever marry.

Was it still true? Why then, had he asked her? What
would he have done if she'd said yes?

Chapter Twenty-One

*M*Y LADY, A MISSIVE HAS RETURNED in response to your query."

Peeling off her gloves, Jane handed them to the maid, and turned to Mr. Huntley, knowing raw hope must be written on her face.

Before she could unfold the letter, he nodded. "It is a reply in the affirmative, my lady." The gray head nodded and admiration showed plainly in the gray eyes behind the spectacles. "I took the liberty of reviewing it. Shall I tell his lordship?"

"No, Mr. Huntley. I will."

"Lady Treyworth is in the morning room, my lady. She has asked for you."

Jane went at once to Del and found her seated on a windowsill, an ignored copy of *La Belle Assemblée* spread on her lap. "Mourning dresses," Del said, as she glanced away from the sunlit window. Her eyes were darkly shadowed. "But I don't feel yet prepared to mourn Treyworth."

Jane sat at Del's side. "The truth is, I never really mourned Sherringham. I did feel sorry that our lives together had been so terrible."

"Did you feel sorry you couldn't make him happy?"

"I felt sorry that he did not want to be happy with me."

Del's gentle blue eyes met hers. "I mourned my parents while being angry with both of them. I was angry with my father for pushing me into marriage and pushing Christian away. And I was angry at my mother for doing nothing to stop him."

Jane laid her hand on Del's knee. Years ago, they would sit like this, side by side on a window seat, and speak of favorite stories, trade gossip, or even talk about their dreams. Right now, she felt as close to Del as she had before, and she breathed a small sigh of relief.

"Have you forgotten the bad parts of your marriage?" Del asked. "Did you put the painful memories behind you?"

The nightmares about Sherringham had not gone away, but Christian had shown her she could make love and delight in it. He had given her new memories to hold dear—the thrilling experience on the piano, the exotic dance in front of his mirror, the scandalous delight of pleasuring him with her mouth.

"The memories are losing their power to hurt me," she said. "With time there is less pain."

"And perhaps more hope?" Del asked.

"I had not thought of it that way, but it's true." Then Jane caught her breath. Large, dark, foreboding, Christian stood in the doorway. He smiled gently at Del, then glowered at her.

It was now time to deal with an irate man.

She was not afraid. She realized that. With Christian, she knew she did not have to be afraid.

She stood and held out the folded paper. "I believe I have found Sapphire Brougham. I thought she might try to help her mother and it appears she has. Brougham has been trying to take her mother out of Bedlam, and is supposed to be returning tomorrow to collect her."

"You cannot come with me, Christian. I can just imagine Charlotte's reaction if you begin to question her." In the foyer, Jane gathered her reticule and gloves from the maid, and turned to face Christian as he slid his arms into his greatcoat.

"Given there is a murderer on the loose," he growled, "I am not letting you go alone."

She swept her gaze from the top of his fashionable hat, down over broad shoulders and his powerful build. "Your very presence will intimidate her, Christian."

"Jane, I need to keep you safe. Will you let me do that?"

His question stunned her. He was not dictating to her. He had asked her permission to protect her. He was giving her control—though she did wonder what he would do if she said no.

She would feel safer with Christian. "But I fear Charlotte will never open up to you."

"Then I will stay in the background and let you take charge of asking her questions. But I want to be at your side. And I intend to watch you at all times." His tone might be cool but the way he looked at her as he spoke heated her from head to toe.

How could she refuse that? "All right," she said softly.

And a quarter of an hour later, they were in his carriage, clattering to a stop on the drive of Charlotte's home. "You are brilliant, you know," Christian said, startling her.

"Yes, of course I know that," she teased, for it helped ease her nerves.

"Brilliant for recognizing that Brougham loved her mother too much to desert her. I never thought of sending a man to question the staff of Bedlam." Christian's grin dazzled. Then he gave a low whistle and Jane looked out the window. A dainty blue carriage drawn by four white horses had drawn up behind theirs.

"Charlotte's carriage," she told him. "A birthday gift from Dartmore."

"A beautiful gift."

She narrowed her eyes. "Don't be fooled into thinking that shows affection. He lavishes gifts on her to make up for his indiscretions."

"So you don't believe lovely gifts reveal what is in a man's heart?"

"Of course not."

"Then what does, Jane?" he asked softly.

"I've never seen a man in love. I have no idea." What had possessed her to delve into this conversation? Speaking of love with Christian was like dousing oneself in brandy and standing too close to a flame. She'd very likely wound herself. And she wanted—but didn't dare—to ask what had happened between him and Georgiana.

Instead, she jumped up from the seat, then hurried down the carriage steps to the drive. A plume of deep blue preceded Charlotte out of her carriage. Then Charlotte saw her and paused.

Jane's heart gave another poignant tug—this one for friendship. Only days ago, she had realized she could no longer trust Charlotte. And now she was here to try to obtain the truth from her former friend, in any way she could. She felt wretched, but she had no choice. "Charlotte—"

To Jane's surprise, Charlotte hurried over with her arms outstretched. "I'm so sorry, Jane. I've heard that Treyworth was murdered. Del must be devastated."

Jane found herself caught in an embrace, smelling the familiar vanilla of her friend's perfume. She hugged Charlotte back. "She's suffered a great shock, but at least she is safe now."

"Thank heaven for that!" Charlotte's eyes widened as Christian stepped out of the carriage. "W-why is he here? Why did he come with you?"

She couldn't say *because he would not let me out of the house unless he did.*

But in truth, he had treated her like a partner. Though at first, he had threatened to have the heads of the servants who had taken her to Lady Petersborough's home. She had refused to let him punish his staff for her decision. Then, to her complete surprise, he'd relented.

Jane grasped Charlotte's hands. "He came because we need the truth. Will you help us?"

While Charlotte nibbled a biscuit for her roiling tummy, Jane carefully told her friend about Del's ordeal in the madhouse, the innocents, and the Demons Club. They were in an exquisitely decorated drawing room, and Christian sat discreetly in the corner.

Jane feared she was causing Charlotte distress in her delicate condition, but she forged on. She had no choice. Finally she asked gently, "Charlotte, was Dartmore a member of that club? Is that why you have been so frightened?"

Charlotte swallowed hard. "What do you mean? What has that to do with Treyworth's murder?"

"Treyworth was blackmailing other members of the Demons Club, including my late husband."

"Over . . ." The soft voice died away. "Over the virgins?"

Jane blinked. Charlotte knew. "So Dartmore *is* a mem—"

"No!" The biscuit in Charlotte's hand broke and sprayed crumbs. "Del and I had guessed there was a darker side to Mrs. Brougham's club, and we both suspected Treyworth was involved in it. But I didn't know about the secret club until Randolph told me he had been invited to become a member. He did not accept, Jane. He *refused*."

Jane had forgotten Randolph was Dartmore's given name. She could barely remember Sherringham's— Martin.

"He told me they used very young courtesans and kept the girls in dungeons," Charlotte whispered. "He said he was not interested in their games. Randolph never pursued the . . . darker activities at the club. He just . . . likes to make love in groups." Charlotte flushed.

Jane felt her cheeks heat, too. But was Dartmore's tale the truth? "Did he tell you who else was involved in the Demons Club?"

"Treyworth and Sherringham, but I don't know of any others."

"Did you know of a gentleman in the club who uses a silver-headed walking stick? The handle is in the shape of a stallion's head, with rubies for eyes."

Charlotte frowned while thinking. "I am not certain, but I believe Lord Pelcham owns such a thing. He brought it to the club. I remember him tracing the silver head along Lady Pelcham's curves."

Pelcham. One of Del's lovers, and a man with a very young wife.

Charlotte gave a look of anguish. "Please believe me, Jane. I had no idea Treyworth had locked Del away in a madhouse. Three weeks ago, Del confided to me that she'd learned dangerous things about Treyworth. She mentioned the Demons Club, but only by name. When I asked her to tell me more, for I feared that my husband might be in trouble, she refused. And then she was gone. I wanted to believe that Del had really run away, that she had found a man to protect her, and that she was safe."

Charlotte tore the biscuit between her fingers to shreds. "I wish I'd had the courage to tell you more, Jane. But I was afraid Treyworth knew that Del had confided in me. He had begun to watch me at the club. He looked at me with dark, bitter hatred. I think he feared that Del had revealed his secrets to me."

"Did he ever threaten you?"

"No. But he frightened me." She buried her face in her hands. "And I was wrong—Del wasn't safe at all. Perhaps I could have helped her, if only I'd had the strength to speak to you or Lord Wickham."

Christian rose from his seat in the corner. "It was only natural you would be fearful, Lady Dartmore. You had to put your own health and safety first."

And just like that, Charlotte lifted her face and her tears dried. It was as though Christian's deep voice and forgiving tone could weave magic. His lined forehead revealed nothing but concern for Charlotte—a depth of caring that touched Jane's heart.

"Th-thank you, Wickham," Charlotte whispered. "And I must thank you for sparing my husband's life."

"Both Dartmore and I realized that shooting each other would serve no purpose. And he did mention he is enthusiastically awaiting an heir."

Charlotte blushed. "I was afraid, Jane, you would rush in and make accusations, endangering yourself and me. You always were such a crusading sort of person."

Jane frowned. Both Charlotte and Christian seemed to think she blundered in, taking too many risks. She dreaded asking Charlotte, both pregnant and upset, the next question. But she looked to Christian—whose freedom might depend on it. She took a deep breath. "Charlotte, do you know where Dartmore was on the night before the duel?"

"Early in the night he visited his mistress. And then, at midnight, he came home to me."

Jane flinched at the cool, collected way Charlotte spoke of her husband's fancy piece. And saw Christian retreat again to give them privacy. Then Jane almost tumbled off the edge of her seat as Charlotte asked, "Did my husband try to entice you to the club?"

At her shocked, embarrassed hesitation, there came a heavy sigh. "I thought so. He's desired you for years, did you not know? Even more than he wanted Del. Years ago, he approached your parents for your hand, but you had already accepted Sherringham. My husband has had to content himself with auburn-haired mistresses ever since."

Jane was stunned. "I—I'm sorry." How useless that sounded. "I didn't know."

"I knew you didn't, Jane."

"All these years, you have been such a good friend. You must have hated me."

"No. I couldn't hate you, for you were such a good friend to me. It wasn't your fault. And I have finally realized I will never be the woman Randolph wants."

"And he is not the man you deserve."

Charlotte gave a tremulous smile. "But I love him, Jane. I know you've always believed I should stop loving him because he has not treated me well, but I cannot."

"No, I do finally understand how enduring love can be."

"It doesn't matter, because now I'll have the baby. You used to insist that we should escape our husbands, Jane, but I don't want to run away. I want to make the best of my marriage. I may never capture my husband's heart but I will love him and his child. And that will be enough for me."

"Will it?" When she had insisted they should leave their husbands, Jane had only thought of survival and freedom.

But now she wondered—shouldn't there be more to their lives than simply survival? "I want you to be happy," she told Charlotte. "I want you to have the love you deserve."

"Always determined to save us all, Jane."

"Yes," she said firmly. "And I will."

"Dartmore denies being a member, and Lord Pelcham, the poet, owns a silver-headed walking stick."

Typical Jane, Christian thought as his carriage lurched off. She got immediately to the point. "I found Salaberry in Onslow's, the newest hell near St. James's Street," he said. "Since I purchased and forgave his vowels, which freed his credit, he's been gambling heavily again."

Jane rolled her expressive eyes. "Gentlemen can be such fools. I supposed he denied belonging to the Demons Club?"

"He said that, along with Dartmore, he was invited to be a member, but did not accept. Onslow, two prostitutes, and his partner at whist, Carlyle, claimed he remained at one table, playing from ten o'clock to past dawn." He paused. With Jane, whose opinion mattered to him, he couldn't share the entire conversation...

In the gloom, Salaberry had tugged savagely at his cravat. The shutters of Onslow's gaming hell had been closed to keep out the early morning light. "Lost ten bloody thousand tonight," Salaberry had muttered, his breath reeking of alcohol.

"What about the Demons Club?"

"Wasn't a member," Salaberry slurred. "Treyworth invited me to join. I refused."

Christian had let his disbelief show. "A witness claims one of the members was a handsome fair-haired gentleman."

"The compliment's appreciated, but it wasn't me. Seducing unwilling innocents is not my pleasure. I enjoy rutting with wives in full view of their husbands. Nothing quite like poaching on another man's preserve, and making a lady scream her ecstasy for the first time in her life."

Christian struggled again with his temper. "You like to prove your superiority."

A jaded laugh. Bleary, drunken eyes met his. "*You*

must understand, Wickham. I've heard married ladies were all you pursued in your youth. Heard you liked to make them holler. Liked to prove you could give them what their husbands couldn't."

He'd stared at Salaberry, sucking in stale smoke, watching daylight struggle into the dark games room— the sort of place where he'd spent most of his youth. Back then, making a married lady shriek in ecstasy had let him live up—or down—to his father's expectations. *You were born wicked and you'll always be wicked.*

It was the reason he'd bedded some of his friends' wives when he'd been in India. He'd wanted to scandalize his father, and making love to a friend's wife was a way of doing it. But he'd made love only to women who approached him and tried to seduce him. The ones who were clumsy at it—the women who hurt deep inside because they were lonely and neglected and their husbands had mistresses—those were the ones he bedded.

He'd realized then that he couldn't imagine making love to anyone but Jane. Jane—who had been the only person to tell him he should aspire to more.

A fierce shaking of his right arm brought him back to the present—to the interior of his carriage, and Jane's wide brown eyes. "Did you say Lord Carlyle? Lady Carlyle, who I encountered at Lady Petersborough's house, said her husband was in the country."

Christian knew little of the Marquis of Carlyle, only that he had captured Georgie's heart, had married her, had given her a title and security. In doing so, the man had cleaned up Christian's mess. Carlyle was both blond and handsome. "I'll hunt down Carlyle."

"Good." Jane crossed her arms resolutely over her full breasts. "Because I am determined you will not be hanged."

A curl dangled by her cheek. Christian twined it around his finger and tugged—something he would have done to irritate her eight years ago, but that he now did because he needed to touch her. "I was thinking of what you said to Lady Dartmore."

"I worry about Charlotte. She is hopelessly in love with her husband. That kind of love is terribly dangerous."

She looked so serious he pulled her onto his lap. Lush and full, her bottom settled on his thighs. Desire ignited and his cock tried to stand proud in his trousers. He struggled to tamp down lust. "You look so very serious, sweeting. Have you loved hopelessly?"

Her gaze met his for one breathless moment. A guilty flush, the pink of cherry blossoms, flooded her face down to her pointed chin.

Did it mean—? Could it? He'd saved children from flood-ravaged villages, pulled soldiers out of swollen rivers, but his vaunted fearlessness was failing him as he waited for Jane to speak.

His heart thundered out of control. In his gloves, his hands were hot and sweat pooled on his palms. His neck burned, but the rest of his body felt ice cold.

The stone pillars of the gates of his home flashed by the windows. In a heartbeat the carriage would stop, the door would open, and this moment would be gone.

But if Jane told him she loved him, what could he say in return? What would he say if she revealed she loved someone else?

"I've never been in love," she said softly.

It was the safest answer he could have received, but he

didn't want to believe it. Her cool, matter-of-fact tone twisted his heart. "You deserve to have love, Jane."

And you deserve more, he thought. *You deserve a man worthy of your love.*

"But I don't want it," she said firmly. She twisted on his lap to face him. "My mother spent her life hopelessly loving my handsome, self-absorbed libertine of a father. I saw her descent. She became bitter, obsessed, and finally mad. She was so delighted when Sherringham offered for me, for I didn't love him and she believed he loved me. She told me it would be the perfect marriage, as I would always have the upper hand."

The upper hand. Stunned, Christian stared down into Jane's haunted eyes. Had that been why his father had agreed to marry his mother, even while she carried another man's child? Had his father believed her sin would always give him power and control? His father had been a physically weak and sickly man who buried himself in books, his mother a ravishing, charming beauty with an enormous dowry. A woman who turned every man's head.

With a featherlight caress, Christian stroked Jane's lovely, smooth cheek. She had, without knowing it, clarified his past for him. She'd made the reasons for his father's cold anger and his mother's subservience brutally clear.

"My mother was completely wrong," she said. "If Sherringham loved me—and I don't believe he did, for I don't believe a truly loving man could hurt his wife—it was a worse situation than hers. But she always said love is a dangerous and frightening emotion."

"Do you believe that?"

"No, I don't. My Aunt Regina had a happy and

devoted marriage for forty years. She tells me that love is enriching and uplifting. But I think it must be shared. Both parties to the marriage must love each other. Otherwise, it brings only grief."

He knew that to be true. "Hades," he muttered, "I don't even know what love is."

The carriage halted, the door swung open, and Jane nimbly moved from his lap. Before he could stop her, she left him.

But I don't want it, she had said. And it wasn't true. If she had stayed in the carriage, on Christian's lap, for one more second, she would have revealed that she did want love—to a man who'd told her he had no idea what love was.

Which certainly meant he didn't love her. He would know what it was if he did. He would know his heart could feel both swollen with joy and tight with sorrow at the exact same instant. He would understand why he couldn't stop thinking of her, just as she couldn't stop thinking of him. He'd know he felt *something*.

Jane darted across the gravel drive toward the front steps of Christian's house...

Crack!

Gravel leapt up at her feet, splattered her skirt. She stared down at it, surprised—

Another explosion lanced her ears.

Powerful arms wrapped around her waist. She fell to the side, tumbling as she had in Hyde Park. Her breath left on a whoosh. This time, she let her body go limp, she let herself fall, and once again she slammed on top of

Christian. His strong, hard body protected her from the sharp gravel.

"Find the blackguard!" Christian bellowed to his servants. Then he rolled, so his body shielded her and his arms enveloped her, pinning her to his chest.

His hat had flown off. His servants raced around, shouting commands. Their voices sounded muffled, indistinct, as though she had treacle in her ears. Jane spied his black beaver hat, lying neatly on its brim a yard away on the drive. Someone's boots passed perilously close, almost squashing it. Sunlight glowed through the center of the hat, making a small bright circle. A *hole*.

Her shocked brain still couldn't understand until Christian's voice whispered by her ear, "Do not move, Jane."

She had squirmed in his arms, desperate to get up. To see. "But what is it?"

"Rifle shots."

Chapter Twenty-Two

Lord Pelcham, the romantic poet. Port, potatoes, and pride for his young wife—this sums up the true man. He might be romantic on paper, but he is self-centered and vain in reality. He is a man obsessed with youth. One of my triumphs.

Jane squinted to decipher Sapphire Brougham's large, decorative handwriting. Behind her a cheery fire crackled, filling the somber library with warmth. Two lamps flanked her on the table. Row upon row of shelves towered over her, each one packed tight with books.

Christian had not told her he had stolen this book from Brougham's office. He had never even mentioned it. But just as when he'd accompanied her to Charlotte's, he had obviously realized they should work together— he had instructed Mr. Huntley to let her search it for clues, while he was out seeking Carlyle and Pelcham.

"His lordship did not find any answers in its pages, my lady," Huntley had told her. "But he believed you may have better luck. Perhaps due to the intuitive sense of ladies, especially ladies of great fortitude—?" Surprisingly, the secretary had cracked an admiring smile.

She had taken the book, opening it on the spot in her eagerness.

"I would suggest the library, my lady," Huntley had said, "as there are two fireplaces in that room and several lamps. His lordship does not ever go into the library, but it was the pride of the late earl—which I fear might be why the present earl refuses to cross its threshold."

He had all but pushed her to the room. Now, seated at the end of the long table, Jane tapped the end of a quill pen to her lips.

Triumphs. Surely, that word had been used in another entry. . . . There. *Lord Carlyle. A dashing man brought to heel by my understanding of his deepest and most forbidden desires. How delicious to triumph over this angelically handsome marquis.*

And it was used in the description of Lord Treyworth's dark perversions.

Within minutes, she had scratched a list of five names. The only entries to contain the word *triumph*. Treyworth. Pelcham—the dark-haired poet. Lord Carlyle, with his fair hair. Sir Rodney Halcourt, an MP—balding with a beaked nose. Sherringham had not been included in the book. And the fifth was another black-haired gentleman—

"What are you doing in here, Jane? It is one o'clock in the morning."

Flushed with excitement, she looked up to find Christian leaning against the door frame. He had discarded his tailcoat, rolled up his shirtsleeves. In that pose, with his black hair tousled, he took her breath away.

He frowned and his gaze riveted on the red rococo binding of the book. "Where did you get that?"

"From Mr. Huntley, of course." She leapt up from her chair. "And I think I have deciphered Mrs. Brougham's code. I believe I've found the names of the men of the Demons Club!"

Why in hell had Huntley given Brougham's book to Jane, when he had not instructed the servant to do so? Christian wanted to tear a strip off the man for encouraging Jane. He wanted her out of this. He wanted her safe.

But if she'd found something—

As he looked down on her, his gut tightened again with primal fear. *He could have lost her today.* He'd never responded to danger like this—it normally spurred him to act. But fear for Jane froze his blood; it left his limbs stiff, his heart in pain, and his head reeling.

Jane pointed to the entry on Carlyle, then flipped through the pages to find Pelcham. "Mrs. Brougham uses the word *triumph* for each of these men. She only uses it for five. I wondered if it was because she knew the power she had over the Demons Club, because of the dangerous secrets she kept for them."

The only name that surprised him was the fifth. The Duke of Fellingham. The war hero.

Christian scrubbed a hand over his jaw. "I found Petersborough, Carlyle, and Pelcham tonight. As you discovered, Petersborough spent the night going to balls with his wife, then slept in her bed."

Jane tucked a curl behind her ear, looking astonishingly calm and not like a woman who had been shot at hours before. Her bravery set off an emotional war inside him—it humbled him, and heightened his need to shield and protect her. "What of Lord Carlyle, since he lied about being in the country?" she asked.

"He did spend the night at Onslow's, gambling as Salaberry's partner. I don't know why he lied to Georgie. Our noble poet, Pelcham, got drunk and enjoyed the services of young prostitutes at an East End flashhouse. It appears he slept there until noon."

"So we must find out about Sir Rodney Halcourt, and the last man. After all, he has dark hair—"

"Stop. No more talk of murder and the Demons Club and danger." He bent to kiss her, needed to surround himself with her scent, her passion, and vitality.

But she avoided his questing mouth. "You looked displeased when you saw me with the book, yet Mr. Huntley told me you asked him to give it to me. That wasn't true, was it?" Her auburn brow lifted. "And he all but insisted I come into this room, after telling me you would not."

Blast Huntley. And Jane was astute and clever and far too perceptive for his good. He did not want to answer but she impulsively said, "Don't try to protect me from knowing about you. I want to so much. And you did come in."

"I avoid this room because my father used to punish me in it when I was a young boy."

Her slender hand went to her mouth in shock.

"I wouldn't have come in if you hadn't been here. But I think I see old Huntley's intent. Being in this room lets me prove I can put the past behind me." He almost laughed. He wouldn't have thought Huntley cared.

"Come with me," Christian said. "I want to show you where the worst of it happened."

But Jane wrapped her fingers around Christian's wrist and tried to hold him back at her side. "I do not need to see it."

"I do. But I need you with me." She watched him pick up one of the lamps. Then he led her to a small door set in the shelves, in the corner of the room farthest from the warming fireplace.

"I would be locked in this closet in the dark."

The lamp he held threw only a little light in the yawning darkness before them. But quickly her eyes adjusted and Jane saw a tiny space—one that would be constricting even for a small child. And terribly frightening. "Why?"

"I had a hard time learning to read. I only did so years after I was expected to. My father believed a gentleman should be well read and well educated."

"You were put in a closet because you could not read?" Jane heard her voice shake. In shock. Horror. Outrage.

"My father wanted to believe I refused to read to spite him. He thought I'd learn if he punished me enough. He believed I was wicked and willful and I needed to be frightened until I learned to toe his line. My mother feared I was just . . . weak in the head."

"You are hardly stupid," she protested.

There was a silence. She realized he had gone to stand near a large, masterfully crafted wooden floor globe with six enormous feet and the world displayed in fading color. "I did come in here sometimes when my father was out, to look at the globe. I couldn't read any of the names of the countries then, but I could see where they were and I dreamed about traveling to them."

"And you did."

"In part because of you, Jane. I realize that now. You nagged me, goaded me, and insulted my behavior until I knew that I did want to be the better man you expected me to be."

She stared at him, captured by his direct, honest gaze.

"It didn't matter in India that I had been slow to learn to read as a boy. There, I quickly learned to survive, to speak dialects, to communicate."

"Your father was a complete idiot." She set the lamp on a shelf and moved to him. "And I think I was a complete idiot, too."

Boyishly adorable, his smile sent heat coursing through her. "Never, Jane. You are brilliant, my love."

She pushed him back and caught him off guard. His derriere bumped against the large ring that surrounded the globe. "Later I want you to show me everywhere in the world you have been," she murmured huskily, "but now I only want to explore you. Are the backs of *your* knees as susceptible as mine?"

She heard him suck in a sharp breath.

"Every inch of me is susceptible to you, Jane."

She stretched up to kiss his scarred jaw, to trace with her tongue up to the rim of his ear, avoiding the healing wound on his cheek. She played with him—letting her breath blow gently, then suckling the lobe, and she treasured his hungry moan.

"Jane, God. I need this. I need you."

She had to pull at his cravat, then fight his collar, and he reached up to help. She was certain he'd done damage to his shirt, but his neck was bare. She tasted the hollow of his throat. His pulse beat beneath her tongue, rapid and strong. All the while, his hands caressed, stroking

her cheek, her shoulder. Then her skirts were going up.
She looked down. He held fistfuls of the muslin, pulling
them up to bare her legs. She wasn't wearing drawers.
"No, you do your trousers."

He opened the buttons fast and pulled aside the
placket. She liked the haste, though he murmured, "I
should be making this erotic torture for you."

"It already is. I'm wet and slick and I don't want to
wait."

"When you talk that way—" He lifted her hips and
pulled her to him. By some miracle, his erection seated
itself against her nether lips, and she was so wet he began
to slide inside.

The globe slid back and they almost toppled. "Blast,"
he muttered.

His strong hands settled again on her hips, then
cupped her bottom. He lifted her onto him and she
cried out as he filled her, stretched her. But it felt right.
He filled the emptiness she'd never truly understood she
felt. "It's good," she whispered, so he knew.

He tried to walk that way. "Christian!"

"To the table."

She caught hold of the waistband of his trousers, and
then his neck, and finally her breath for the steps it took
him to reach the long worktable in the center of the room.
"Sit me on my bottom," she suggested. "Like the pianoforte."

"I'd like you to be comfortable."

"I'd like you to make me climax."

Her rump landed gently on the polished surface. She
locked her legs around his lean hips, but his arms were
already braced on the table, and his muscles strained as

he began to thrust inside her in a slow, loving, unbearably wonderful rhythm.

Bang! A pile of books fell from the table.

She held him close, savoring the intense intimacy. She drove up to him, sobbing with pleasure. Each thrust wound her tighter. Each pounding surge of his cock made her fingernails drive harder against his shoulders. She had been so ready, so aroused, so richly aware of Christian that she reached the brink in minutes. She gave herself in complete trust, clinging to him, thrusting on him, this man she loved—

Crash! More books hit the floor.

Sheer ecstasy hit Jane. She burst. Her wits scattered, her body surrendered, and mind-melting bliss claimed her. Christian held her tightly as she came around him. Dimly, she heard his guttural cry and knew he'd climaxed too.

Christian caught Jane's mouth in a languorous kiss. He tweaked her nipples to make her squeal in both indignation and delight. Even when they had teased and battled years ago, they had belonged together.

He saw that now. And he had not used a sheath again. He'd been so caught up in the moment with Jane, he'd forgotten. But he knew he couldn't propose a duty marriage over a child again. She would never agree. She might club him with one of his father's tomes.

So he lifted her hand to his lips and bestowed a gentle kiss to her fingers. "Jane, would you come to India with Del and me?"

The question stunned her.

"We can hand over the names of the Demons Club

members to Radcliffe," Christian continued, with her hand at his lips. "Let him find the truth."

Jane stared at him. Stickiness tickled her inner thighs, and she smelled of him—his rich and earthy scent. "W—why?"

"We were shot at today. Christ, Jane, you could have been—" He broke off. Kissed her hand again. His lashes lowered, a lush, black shield for his eyes. "It's too dangerous to stay."

A halo of light beaming through the hole in his tall hat. That was all she could think of. The shooter had aimed at Christian's head and missed by mere inches. He was the one at risk. She wanted him to go to India, where he would be safe. But for her—

His hoarse voice cut through her thoughts. "While I was hunting for those men through the clubs and brothels tonight, Jane, I was treated to a lot of spurious gossip about my sister. People suspect she killed Treyworth—at the very least they are talking about her lovers, about her imprisonment in the madhouse. People are saying she deserved to be there. I have to take Del away to protect her from scandal."

Then she understood. "Y-you mean you want me to come as a companion to Del?"

"No, angel. I am asking you to come for me."

"As your mistress?" Of course he was not proposing again. She had thrown his proposal in his face. She had insisted she would never marry.

"I've realized I can't let you go. I want you at my side, I want to show you the world." He laid his hands on her hips and guided her in a slow, sensual dance there, in the middle of the library he despised. "I want you, Jane."

But she did not understand *exactly* what he wanted

from her. All along she had known she would have to let him go. Now she knew she didn't want to. But to be his mistress? Men acquired and discarded mistresses all the time. Christian had had dozens of lovers in his youth.

His lips coasted along her neck. "India is filled with challenges. The heat can be blistering. Summer brings monsoons, with the sky filled with lightning. Fierce floods. But it is beautiful, too. Almost as beautiful as you."

When she didn't answer, he traced the outline of her lips with his thumb, making them tingle. "I would like to pluck a ripe mango for you. They are succulent and the fruit is a luscious orange. I would love to see you with the juice of a mango dribbling from your lips."

He was trying to seduce her with the allure of an exotic, exciting, sensual world. Jane closed her eyes and pictured Christian holding a fruit for her to bite—though she could not even begin to imagine what a mango might look like.

Familiar and cold, like a draft in an old cottage, fear crept over her. She would be in a foreign land. An exotic land she could barely picture. She would be at the mercy of Christian's whims. What if she ended up abandoned there? She had no money, no means of supporting herself, or even of buying her passage home.

He was offering his passion—and himself. And risk.

But he was also offering her more to her life than just survival.

"No," she said through her tight throat, aware of how small her voice sounded in the enormous, book-lined room. "I could not. It's too far away. I—I wouldn't want to leave England. And my aunt . . . I owe her so much for taking me in. I shouldn't leave her."

He was silent for a moment. Then he drew back, but

let his hands rest gently on her shoulders. "I understand. I will think of you when I next see a nautch dancer or bite into a mango. India for me, now, will be filled with memories of you."

She couldn't breathe. This was worse than fear. Her aunt had been correct—she was going to have her heart broken. But it wasn't his fault. It was hers.

Christian stroked her cheek. "I won't leave you, Jane, until I know you are safe."

A half-dozen tough-looking men stood in a circle on the black and white tiles in the foyer of Wickham House. Jane leaned over the banister to search for Christian. She found him in the center of the group, issuing commands.

As though he sensed her, he looked up. Pushing his way between two burly men, he raced to the stairs, and took the steps two at a time. A triumphant grin lit up his face. "Your plan worked, Jane. Sapphire Brougham visited her mother at Bedlam. She did not take her mother away, but my men followed her, and found where she's hiding."

Of course, Christian intended to go himself to fetch the madam. "Do take care," she begged.

He gave her his most wickedly rakish smile, flashing dimples, and kissed her cheek. Just that quick buss sent pleasure shimmering down her spine. "Of course, my love," he assured, all confidence.

She knew he would be careful; she knew she should not feel this fear that made her throat so tight. Christian had matured from the wild careless rake he'd once been. He was a sensible, intelligent, heroic man. She trusted him with her life. Surely she could trust him with his own.

She watched him leave, his veritable army following at his heels. She had refused to go to India because she was afraid of risk. Yet she realized she didn't want to stay at home and be safe now.

Where she wanted to be was at Christian's side.

Christian pressed his bare fingertips to the woman's neck. His own heartbeat thudded in his throat. Jane's clever idea and understanding of Sapphire Brougham had led him here, to the madam's hideaway, a small, rough-looking townhome on the fringe of London's stews, but was he too late?

Brougham lay in a heap on the floor of a tiny drawing room, her arms flung out at her sides. The henna hair was a snarled halo around her bruised face. One eye was blackened. Bruises ringed her throat, along with ugly red marks the size of a man's fingers.

She'd been strangled.

Had he felt something? He waited. There . . . her pulse beat against his fingers, stronger than he expected.

Younger burst back into the room, flanked by two other men. "The rest of the house is deserted, my lord. No sign of her killer."

"She's not dead." Christian scooped her limp body into his arms. "Bring the carriage, Younger. I've got to get her to a physician."

"You don't need to be the one to do this. I can have a maid tend to her."

Christian paced, watching Jane sit at Sapphire Brougham's bedside and spoon thin soup to the wretched woman's lips. He folded his arms across his chest, his senses alert. A loaded pistol rested in the waistband of his trousers.

Jane shook her head. "I despise her for what she has done, but I am determined to make her well. So she can pay for her crimes. And you have been watching over us every minute. Along with them." She glanced toward the four footmen who stood along the wall opposite the foot of the bed.

For hours, since he had brought Sapphire Brougham to his house from the physician's, Christian had stood vigil as Jane tended to the madam. He had brought the woman to this bedroom in a long-unused wing of the house to keep her away from Del. After maids—under his footmen's guard—had stripped Brougham to her shift and helped her into the bed, Jane had bathed the blood off the woman's beaten face, had applied cold cloths to her throat, had held a cup to the woman's lips and gently coaxed her to take the tea. In short, Jane had been an angel.

Sapphire turned plaintive eyes to Jane and her trembling hand reached out. "M-more." She motioned to the soup.

Jane complied. As she bent her head to scoop a spoonful, a gleam of power showed in Sapphire's eyes. The spark faded and the madam bestowed a thin, grateful smile to Jane. Christian stiffened. The canny witch was trying to play Jane.

But Jane cocked a brow. "This is of necessity, Mrs. Brougham," she said coolly. "Do not believe I feel any sympathy for a woman who sold innocent girls to brutal men."

Bravo, Jane, he thought. Christian paced toward the head of the bed, to confront Sapphire Brougham. To think his father had called him wicked. His father had no idea of wickedness. Perhaps Jane was right. His father *had* been a complete idiot.

"The physician told me you were not as close to death as you made it appear," he said, watching fear flash in Sapphire's eyes in response. "What really happened? Who attacked you?"

The madam limply put her hand to her throat. "I *was* close to death—a hairsbreadth away. The man wore a black mask. He burst into my bedchamber, wrapped his hands around my neck. I fell to the ground. I tried to make it appear I was dead. He heard a sound—it was you, my lord. You and your men arriving. *You* saved my life," she said huskily. "And the sentry you had left to watch my house, was he—?"

"Conked on the head, but all right. We know everything, Sapphire. About the Demons Club and the innocents you procured for them and kept imprisoned in your madhouse. We know about the murders."

Sapphire reached out, imploring him. "I've done nothing wrong," she croaked. "I knew nothing of this. I did not know who my matron admitted to the house. As for deaths—women die every day. By disease inflicted on them by men. In childbirth or by a man's fists. The women in my sanitarium died of these things. The medical schools could use the bodies. In a court of law, I can argue I was completely blameless—"

"We know who belongs to the Demons Club," he broke in. "I've already handed the list over to Bow Street."

"How—? You could not know the names."

In her shock, she had revealed her denial to be a lie. And her eyes widened in terror as he repeated each one. Her reaction was proof they were correct.

"And there is the matter of Lord Treyworth's death—"

"I had no hand in that!" Sapphire cried. "But I know who did. It was the same person who did this—" She clasped her throat. "I can hand you the murderer on a silver platter, Lord Wickham, if you make a bargain with me."

Christian waited.

At his disinterest, Sapphire sat up in bed, obviously stronger than she appeared, and she sneered at him. "Perhaps this will persuade you, then. I know a secret about Lord Sherringham. One that would destroy Lady Sherringham if it was revealed."

"You are too late," Jane said softly. "I know what my deceased husband did. And I am willing to endure the scandal of the truth to ensure justice is found for those dead girls—and the ones who were ruined."

Resolve showed in the lift of Jane's chin. Christian could see her reaction startled Sapphire Brougham. Then the madam's face flushed red and her eyes blazed. For some reason, Jane's strength enraged her.

"You stupid fool," Sapphire shouted at Jane. "I dragged the mask off my attacker as I fought with him. I was looking into the face of a ghost. It was Lord Sherringham. Your husband."

Chapter Twenty-Three

*A*LIVE. SHERRINGHAM WAS STILL ALIVE. IT was impossible.

Jane stared helplessly into Sapphire Brougham's hard, desperate blue eyes. Around her the bedchamber shimmered, the walls spun, and sound roared.

Suddenly Christian's broad-shouldered frame loomed over her. Strong arms wrapped around her, and he massaged her wrists. "Jane, love, can you hear me? Put your head between your legs."

"I—I am not going to faint." Her shaky voice belied the words. But she couldn't swoon. She had to face this. Fiercely, she blinked away the spots bursting before her eyes.

Christian spoke—or rather barked—at the madam. "What proof do we have that you are telling the truth? This could be a lie to frighten Lady Sherringham."

"The proof of your own eyes," Brougham snarled.

Jane looked up at Christian. There was so much she wanted to ask. But one look at his face stilled her questions. Haunted eyes. The downward tug at his mouth. The hard set of his jaw. This was the expression he had worn when he'd approached her at the rose bower two days before, after Radcliffe had questioned them all.

Sapphire's claim had not been a shock to him. He... he'd *known*.

"Why?"

Both Christian and the madam jerked around to look at her. Jane hadn't realized she'd spoken. She rushed on. "Why did he attack you? Why would he pretend to be *dead*?"

"As you know, he murdered several women," Sapphire Brougham said coolly. "Two women who worked for me, and four of the girls in my sanitarium. He was rough in his carnal games—he would lose control. It excited him to wrap his hands around a woman's throat and cut off her air as he pounded into her."

Sapphire paused to sip tea, and Jane's stomach churned. "Sometimes, in his excitement," Sapphire continued, "he would press too hard and crush a woman's windpipe—"

"How could you!" Jane was standing—she must have jumped out of the chair. A bang made her heart jump. The chair had toppled to the carpet. "How could you bring him young girls and hold them captive for him, knowing—knowing that?"

Christian drew her to his side, curving his body around her protectively. "Jane, you do not have to listen to this."

"But I do. I *must* learn about my husband's crimes."

She heard his harsh breath.

Sapphire gave her a sorrowful look that belonged on a Drury Lane stage, it was so exaggerated. "I was afraid of him, my lady. He threatened my life if I did not help him. But he grew more fearful of his own safety, more terrified that the truth would come out. Perhaps he was more violent with you. Perhaps, if you reflect, you will remember how he changed."

Jane shuddered. She didn't want to remember.

"Already Lord Treyworth was blackmailing him, and he knew he had to escape. He convinced me to help him fake his death so he could run away to Italy. He had to leave his title behind, but he was able to take his fortune."

Christian's arm tightened around her. Her legs were weakening, and it was his powerful grip that kept her from slumping to the floor. "Then why has he come back?" Christian demanded. "Why did he attack you, Sapphire?"

"I don't know why he returned. But he has, and he is determined to murder the only witnesses to his crime—Lord Treyworth and me." Hope, desperation, and grasping need all poured out of Brougham's eyes. "I know where he is, my lord. I can lead you to him. Spare me from arrest, allow me to leave England, and I will give you Lord Sherringham. He would be hanged for his crimes." She leveled her hardened gaze at Jane. "And his wife would be free."

Jane lifted her left arm and pinched the inside of her forearm as hard as she could.

"Jane?" Christian spoke cautiously. Perhaps he feared this shock might drive her into madness—into the same hopeless mental state her mother had fallen into over *her* husband.

She was alone with him in an unused parlor a few doors away from Sapphire Brougham's bedchamber. Holland covers draped all the furniture, making the room appear filled with ghosts.

"I wanted to see if this was another nightmare," she said. "But it isn't. It's real."

She was still married. By the law, she still belonged to Sherringham and he had the power to do whatever he wished to her—

Stop, Jane, she cried in her head. Sherringham had committed murders. He would swing for those crimes if he were caught. She had to remember he had no power over her at all. She would not let him suck her back into the nightmare of her married life all over again.

"Talk to me, Jane," Christian urged. "Don't keep this inside you. Let it out."

"You knew, didn't you? None of this was a surprise to you. Did you not tell me in order to protect me, as with my husband's murders?"

"Sherringham is not your husband," he said harshly. "Jane, he should still be dead to you."

"Legally—"

Christian dragged her into a kiss, a fierce one that lifted her to her toes and banished the icy cold creeping through her veins. But she pulled free. "I don't want you to think you have to rescue me because I'm wounded and weak. I want you to give me the truth."

"And I will." He raked back his hair with a swift pass of his long fingers. "If I'd known for certain he was still alive, I would have told you."

But she saw the quick flick of his gaze away from her. No, he would not have done so.

"When I learned he was being blackmailed over the

murders, I began to put the pieces together. You had told me about the fire, the fact the estate was almost bankrupt. Having left England myself, I saw how it could have leapt into his head as a solution. Huntley confirmed the body was . . . badly destroyed, and I realized a body could have been bought from the resurrectionists. So I had Huntley make inquiries. But I had nothing concrete, I swear to you, Jane. And I didn't want to frighten you with speculation."

She couldn't fault him on that. But she felt there was a distance between them—far more than the few inches that separated their bodies. It was her marriage and Sherringham. He was between them like a wall.

"As for protecting you, I will never stop doing that, Jane. No matter what happens, Sherringham will never touch you again. If it means never letting you out of my sight, I will keep you safe."

It would be so easy to nod her head and accept his pledge. She wanted to so much. But what if Sherringham wasn't hanged? He was a peer—he might be imprisoned or transported. What if he fled from England again? Could she even obtain a divorce in such circumstances? If not, she would never be free.

She stepped back from Christian, away from his strong, powerful body and the promise of protection she sorely yearned to take.

"No, Christian. I vowed I wouldn't marry again because I feared being trapped. I won't trap you at my side, protecting me from a ghost that might never materialize. You deserve to find love and happiness. I will not tie you to me when I have nothing to offer you."

He tipped up her chin. "Jane, I am going to go after Sherringham and catch him."

"With Sapphire Brougham? You aren't going to agree to her terms and give her freedom in return for Sherringham. You can't."

But from his silence, she knew he was. After bringing her to this parlor and leaving her under the guard of two footmen, he had returned to talk more to Sapphire Brougham. Whatever they'd spoken of had obviously made him believe Sapphire could lead them to Jane's husband.

"I hate the woman," he said. "I wondered why they had kept Del a prisoner for so long, when her knowledge was a threat to the Demons Club and Sapphire Brougham. When I talked again to Sapphire, she let it slip that Treyworth really hoped to eventually let Del out of the madhouse and bring her home. Her eyes were cold as stone as she told me that—then she quickly looked away and wouldn't meet my gaze. Her hands had clenched into fists. I couldn't make Brougham admit it, but I suspect, from her reaction, that it was her plan to eventually get rid of Del and tell Treyworth she'd died. Probably she intended to tell him Del had died by illness or accident."

"Then you cannot make a bargain with her."

"I've had to make bargains with the devil before."

He was willing to let the woman who had planned to kill his sister escape in return for her freedom. "She could be lying. She could lead you into a trap."

"I'm aware of the risk, love—"

"And it's too great!"

But he shook his head. His grin dazzled her, and his dimples were deeper than she'd ever seen them. Wild excitement poured off him, but behind that she sensed a dark resolve. Major Arbuthnot from India had called him a madman. He was going to charge in like a madman to rescue her, because he believed her frightened and vulnerable.

"I won't let you do this."

"You couldn't stop me, Jane. Let me protect you."

Her mother had been correct about one thing—love could be a frightening emotion. It brought the most glorious joy, but the deepest fear also.

Jane forced a smile to her lips as Del clasped her hand and gave a comforting squeeze. *I am so sorry, Del,* she whispered in her head. *So sorry Christian is throwing himself in danger for me.*

She couldn't say it aloud. They were both trying to act as though nothing was amiss. Obviously Del was trying to keep her calm and strong, just as she wanted to do for Del.

They had sat together in the music room for the hour since Christian had left with Mrs. Brougham, Younger, and four of his other men. By their door, two footmen stood on guard, and other men patrolled the grounds. Jane had been deeply grateful to learn Christian had sent some of his hired men to watch over Aunt Regina's house.

A clock began to chime and Del jumped in her seat. "S-sorry," she whispered. She turned to Jane. "It's foolish to pretend all is well, isn't it? I know how frightened you must be. But Christian will be safe. He's survived many dangers. And I am sure he will be determined to return safe and sound for you."

"And you," Jane added. "I am sorry he is risking his life to rescue me—"

"Stop. There was no other option, Jane. I see the glow in his eyes when he looks at you. In fact, when we were young, each time his gaze alighted on you, there was *always* a special gleam in his eye—"

"Because he was planning to tease me."

"Oh, it was more than that, I think. I think he's always cared very deeply for you. He simply had no understanding of what it was to love someone. I know I would not, if not for you and Charlotte, my dear friends. When Christian returns, I intend to help him understand exactly what he feels for you."

"No, Del, please . . . you could be wrong." Jane's cheeks warmed with a blush. She had turned down his offer of marriage, then told him she would not go to India with him. She had seen how much he loved India when he spoke about it. He would want to return—she could not stand in his way.

She'd refused him twice. Surely that had destroyed any feeling he might have for her.

Del stood and held out her arm. "You must be exhausted. Come, let's take you to bed."

Jane peeped through a narrow opening in the door and waited until Del went into her bedroom. Then she slipped out into the quiet, gloomy, hallway.

There were so many questions. Had Sherringham been the one to shoot at them, because he feared they might find the truth? He could not have pushed her in front of a carriage in Hyde Park. She would have seen him—or at least sensed him—if he had been that close to her. That incident must have been an accident.

Why had Treyworth's servant seen a dark-haired man

running away from the house? Sherringham had possessed a head of thick silver hair.

Was Sapphire Brougham truly afraid of Sherringham, or had the money been the reason she had procured girls for him? When he'd tried to kill her, she must have been furious as well as terrified. Sapphire must have thought she had power over him, only to discover how vulnerable she truly was—

"Why won't you leave? You cannot have Wickham; you are still *married.*"

Jane spun around. Illuminated by a wall sconce, Mary glared indignantly at her. Her golden hair hung loose around her shoulders, and an ivory satin nightgown accentuated every curve of her shapely figure.

The venom took Jane aback. "I am staying because Lord Wickham wished me to and because Lady Treyworth is my friend."

"You hope he'll fall in love with you!" Mary cried. "You hypocrite! You told me to wish to be more than a courtesan. You filled the other girls with mad hopes, while you became his lordship's lover."

"They are not mad hopes," Jane began, but she stopped as movement caught her attention. A maid wearing a dark brown wool dress materialized out of the shadows in the hallway ahead. She bobbed a curtsy. "Lady Sherringham? One of the young ladies is asking for you."

"Which one?" Mary asked. "I will go and see to her."

But the maid fervently shook her head. "No, miss. The young lady asked for her ladyship."

Sullenly, Mary stepped aside, and Jane realized the girl felt even more hurt. She would have to resolve this issue with Mary, but how could she make a young girl fall out of love? She hadn't been able to do it herself.

She hurried after the maid, who moved swiftly, but they were heading in the opposite direction to the girls' bedrooms. "Is the young lady not in her bed?"

"No, my lady. She went downstairs. She is in a terrible state. I found her sobbing and screaming."

A nightmare? Walking in her sleep? The girls were fearful for Christian's safety, too.

The maid pushed through the door of Christian's study. Jane saw his desk where the dueling pistols were locked. It seemed as though weeks, not days, had passed since he had proposed marriage in this room, and she'd refused him.

"Where is she?" Jane glanced around. Only moonlight illuminated the room, but she could see no one else was in it.

"Out here." The woman rushed to the large windows. Jane realized, for the first time, they were actually glass doors that led to the terrace.

She shivered as she stepped outside and the cool evening air rushed around her. "Why did you not bring her in?"

The terrace was empty.

Jane was suddenly pulled backward, and she stumbled. A hand clamped over her mouth. Her scream swelled up, but the instant her lips parted, a sickly-smelling rag jammed between them.

"Shut it," the maid snarled behind her, "or I'll shoot you." The woman's left arm clamped around Jane's chest—she was tall and astonishingly strong—and the cold barrel of a pistol banged hard against Jane's left temple.

"I knew we could not trust that witch," the maid spat. The deferential servant's tones had vanished and pure malevolence spilled out. "If you make a sound, I'll happily blow your head off. You escaped that carriage and the rifle shots, but you'd never escape a ball drilled into your skull at such close range."

Jane fought to breathe through the rag at her mouth. This *maid* had pushed her in Hyde Park and had shot at her and Christian? Why?

"I have another pistol and several blades," the woman warned. "I am willing to kill anyone who gets in my way. And I know there are several young girls in this house."

Jane managed to shove the cloth away, and she gasped, "W-who are you?"

With a curse, the maid thrust the rag in once more. "You have no idea, do you? Don't you remember? I was buried in a pauper's grave while you had your darling husband placed in his family's mausoleum."

She didn't understand. And each breath sucked through the cloth now made her woozy.

"Blast. I don't think this stuff will knock you out. Well, having you able to walk will help. Saves me from having to drag you. As for who I am, I am the woman your husband truly loves, my dear. I am Fleur des Jardins."

Fleur? Jane's brain focused on the most impossible possibility—

"Have you figured it out finally, *my lady*?" Fleur sneered. "I am your husband's mistress, the one you believe died at his side when my house burned to the ground."

The pistol jabbed against Jane's head. A dull pain shot through her skull.

Ahead was the rose bower where she had vowed to

find justice for Sherringham's victims. Jane stared beyond it, toward the walls that ringed the grounds of Wickham House. She could not see the guards—but they must be there, hidden in the shadow.

"Looking for saviors?" Fleur's husky laugh mocked her. "The foolish men who thought me only a maid? They are watching for your husband—for a *man*. The guard at the gate was easy enough to dispatch. And now that I have you, they can't stop me."

Dispatch? Fear and sickness combined with the sickly aroma filling her nose. She tried to marshal her thoughts, but her head felt stuffed with muslin.

Fleur shoved her ahead. "Don't think to scream, even if you are willing to sacrifice yourself. I didn't come alone. There's another woman in the house disguised as a maid. She could very easily get to those young whores of Lord Wicked's. If you scream—or if I shout a warning—she'll slice their throats. If you want to see Wicked again—one last time—you'll keep your mouth shut and come with me."

The crumpled body lay in the shadows near the rear gate. Jane's heart thudded in her chest as she glimpsed the man's face, ashen even in the faint light. Clouds had scuttled across the moon, and Fleur had waited for that moment to cross the lawns. Jane worked her lips around the gag Fleur had tied in place, but she couldn't loosen it. Nor could she slacken the cloth that bound her hands, though she tried in vain to wriggle her wrists. Fleur had flung a black cloak over her, covering her hair and her gown, and had donned one herself.

Fleur dragged her around the body.

Was he dead? Dear God, had someone died for her?

What had happened to Christian? Had Fleur meant that she had already captured him? And even if he were dead, she would still be able to see him one last time—

"Halt! Stop there or I'll shoot!"

At the fierce masculine shout, Jane's heart soared. She tried to jerk against Fleur's grip to run toward the man. But Fleur shoved her against the wooden gate. She hit it, and it swung wide. Jane's breath flew from her chest at the impact, and she fell forward into space.

Behind them a shot exploded. Pain burst through her head.

Then came the shattering of wood. Debris and splinters showered her. She had fallen to her knees in the dirt of the lane behind the garden. She wasn't shot—the pain had been Fleur's pistol cracking against her head. The ball fired by Christian's guard had slammed into the garden gate.

"Get up," Fleur snarled. "Hurry. Or the next shot will be the one through your skull."

A dark shape stood ahead, filling the narrow lane. A carriage—a black one. Before Jane's eyes, the door opened. A man leaned out, and she fell back in horror. He had no face. There was nothing but a black hole where his face should be—

"Make haste," the man roared. "They're in pursuit."

"I know," Fleur shouted.

The pistol jammed into Jane's ribs. Fleur grabbed her shoulder and dragged her toward the carriage. She was thrown forward and the man caught hold of her cloak. Moonlight slanted down and hit his face. He wore a black mask.

He hauled her up and Jane fell to the floor of the carriage. He dropped back to the seat, shaking and drawing in harsh breaths. She could hear them rasp through the hole at the mouth of the mask.

Fleur leapt up, a faint crack sounded, along with the coachman's shout, and the carriage lurched into motion. Jane rolled on the floor, thrown by the sudden jerk. The horses were being flayed into a mad dash and the carriage rocked as the wheels banged through ruts. Two more explosions roared behind them.

But the carriage swung abruptly to the left and the wheels sent up a frantic clatter—they had reached the street. They were charging down it, swerving wildly.

Jane cried out as Fleur pulled her up off the floor and flung her onto the seat. The masked man sat opposite them, facing the direction of their careening travel. Jane gulped as she stared at the pistol he held leveled at her heart.

"Jane."

She knew the cultured bass voice. She knew it enraged and bellowing. She knew how it sounded when laced with cold, deliberate anger.

She screamed fruitlessly into her gag. *Do not swoon.*

The man tore off his mask. "You have not changed a bit," he said and a smile lit up his face. "If anything, you are lovelier than I remembered."

His mistress, who still held her pistol, gave an angry gasp.

"Hold her," Sherringham said to Fleur. "I want to kiss my lovely wife. We have been parted for much too long."

"I don't like this, milord. It screams of a trap."

Hearing the tension in Younger's warning, Christian

stared out his carriage window at the swinging sign of the Elephant and Rook Inn. A young woman in a tawdry gown stepped out to accost every gentleman who passed. Plenty of tall beaver hats threaded through the crowd, while grubby children followed, waiting for the opportune moment to cut a man's purse.

Christian had to admit he agreed. Though there would have been places less public for Brougham to lure them, if she really planned to have them walk into a trap.

At his side, Brougham leaned into him. Deliberately, she rubbed against him.

She believed she could manipulate him. No doubt she'd done it with men so long, she knew of no other way. He thought of Jane, who had been through hell at a man's hands but wanted to rescue others, not use them.

"It is not a trap, my lord," Sapphire insisted.

She had revealed to Christian that she had known Sherringham wanted to return to England. She'd agreed to help Sherringham, for a price, only to discover that he intended all along to murder her. Sherringham had believed he could kill Treyworth and Brougham and reclaim his title, his estates. Reclaim his old life.

Doubtfully, Christian studied the seedy inn. "Why would he come here?"

"He had to be sure he wouldn't be recognized," Sapphire said. "His plan was to commit the murders, then leave for France. In a few weeks, he could return, pretending he was on the Continent the entire time. Who would suspect a man who was not even in the country? If he thinks I am not dead, he will be preparing to sail—he might flee and never return."

She was certainly free with her information. Desperate to avoid the noose? Or playing him?

"I'm leaving you with Roydon, Sapphire." Christian nodded to the man who sat at her side. "He has instructions to take you to Bow Street if there's trouble."

"Hell," Younger added, rubbing at a scar on his tanned cheek. "I've told him to wring your bloody neck if I end up scragged for you, you witch."

"There's no trap," she croaked. "I want Sherringham to hang."

Christian leapt down from the carriage to the dirty cobbled street, its length illuminated only by the odd lamp and a few small fires. The smell of horse dung and human waste assailed him. He had two pistols in his pocket, a blade in his boot, and one slipped up his sleeve again.

With Younger and two more armed men at his heels, he burst into the inn. Drunken howls and merry laughter poured out from the taproom, and the proprietor, a bulky man with three chins, rushed to the desk.

Christian laid a few sovereigns. "I am Lord Wickham."

The man jumped to attention, and Christian gave a description of Sherringham, as he looked now, thirteen months after his "death."

"You must mean Mr. Neville, my lord. He is in room seven," the innkeeper said. "But he has gone out tonight."

"Where did he go? Did he take his belongings with him?"

"No, my lord. The lady took care of that this morning. She said they were traveling and had a trunk brought down."

"The lady?" Could he mean Sapphire Brougham? "What did this lady look like?"

"She is Mrs. Neville, my lord, the gentleman's wife. A kind, dark-haired lady."

Who then, was she? "Where were they traveling?"

Wide-eyed, the burly man shook his head. "I don't know, my lord."

Christian's shoulders sagged. Was he too late? Had Sherringham already returned to the Continent? Would it be possible to find him if he had? If Sherringham knew he hadn't killed Sapphire Brougham, he might never return—and Jane would never believe she was free.

Christian left the desk and the surprised proprietor, and took the sagging stairs two at a time, in search of room seven. In case the innkeeper was wrong—or had lied—he had one pistol drawn. The door proved locked so he slammed his booted foot into it. Wood splintered as it crashed in. Down the hallway, a woman screamed.

With the barrel of his gun leading the way, Christian stepped into the room. It was empty. There was nothing to show it had been occupied—only mussed sheets on the bed. The doors of an empty wardrobe stood open.

Then he saw it, barely visible against the white of the pillow. As Younger pushed his way into the room, Christian snatched up the square of folded paper. A note, written in a woman's handwriting, but not Brougham's flowing script.

W. Know that I have something you desire. You can find it at the theater.

Jane. She was something—or rather, someone—he desired with every beat of his heart. But Sherringham could not have Jane. He'd left his house heavily guarded, and Jane's husband could not have breached the guard. Could he?

Was he being tricked and lured? Or was Jane truly in danger?

"The theater," he muttered aloud. Drury Lane? It made no sense. If he was being drawn into a trap, why send him to a crowded theater with no instruction?

He should return home and ensure Jane was safe.

The *theater*. Could it mean the theater in Sapphire Brougham's club?

Chapter Twenty-Four

THANK HEAVEN FLEUR HAD NOT OBEYED Sherringham's command. His mistress had not grabbed her and held her to receive his kiss.

Jane stared bleakly at her husband from the corner of the carriage. Wedged between the wall and the seat, her hands bound behind her, she was thrown back and forth with each jostle.

He was a stranger to her, this apparition who sat across from her. Thirteen months had brought a stoop to his shoulders, a rasp in his voice. He seemed to have collapsed in on himself. The once silver hair was now thin. Slicked down with sweat, it was the color of a London sky on a dismally wet day.

She'd lived eight years with this man. She had thought she could read his moods. She'd known when he lied. Had known by the tread of his footstep whether he was enraged. But in truth, she had known nothing about him at all. And that frightened her now.

He turned angry eyes to Fleur. "She is my wife."

She realized he was not Lord Sherringham anymore—his cousin had the title—but she could not think of him in any other way.

"What do you expect?" his mistress snapped back. "That I'll drag up her skirts so you can have your husbandly rights?"

Jane shrank back as Fleur angrily jerked the pistol at her with a shaking hand. Would she end up shot by accident before it was supposed to happen by design? And what would the other woman at Wickham House do?

"She's Wickham's whore now," Fleur spat. "I have watched them. I've seen her in his arms."

Jane had learned not to say a word to her husband when he was furious. To survive, to limit the damage he inflicted on her, she had behaved like a silent, timid mouse. Strange to realize she could barely remember that woman. Just these few days with Christian had reminded her of the stronger woman she had once been. "I am not a whore," she stated. "In the eyes of the world, you are dead, and I am not your wife."

Fleur slapped her, not Sherringham, and her head snapped with it. Stunned, she blinked back tears of shock.

"You are my wife," Sherringham roared. "I am not dead and you, Jane, are still mine." Dangerous fury licked at his words. "And you've been in Wickham's bed."

With two pistols trained on her and her arms tied, she had no chance to escape. She should be terrified and she was astonished at how controlled she felt. She would very likely die if she lost her head, but Sherringham expected her to be frightened. He'd worked for eight years to make her a whimpering coward, but she tipped up her chin. "I thought I was a widow."

"You know everything, don't you?" Sherringham

spoke in an oddly conversational tone. "About Molly and Kitty, and those other whores of Sapphire Brougham's."

Not whores. Tears brimmed in Jane's eyes.

Fleur angrily said, "Of course she knows. Both she and Wickham know."

Jane forced her eyes up to meet her husband's. "Why don't you leave England again, now? You could escape."

Sherringham's gaze raked over her slowly. The cloak had fallen open. Her hands were bound. There was an odd look in his eyes—

Fleur's fist smacked against her arm, jarring her against the carriage wall. "You've ruined everything. You and bloody Wicked. Why did you have to push your noses in?"

"It was Treyworth's fault," Sherringham muttered. "Locking up his damned mad wife instead of killing her."

Jane heard the familiar tones of his rage simmering. But then, he coughed and brought a handkerchief to his mouth. Blood spattered into the fine linen. Jane stared at the spots. Sherringham had consumption. He was sick—*dying*. "W-what are you going to do to me?"

"Silence, you bothersome bitch," Fleur snapped. "I saw Wickham bring Brougham into his house. You and he know the truth—and he has influence and power. If Wickham claps that bitch Brougham in Newgate, I've arranged for her to be done away with. So once you and he are dead, everyone will be gone . . ."

"We should leave England, Fleur," Sherringham argued. "It is too late."

Fleur reached over and patted his knee. She looked imploringly at him. "It isn't."

"It is," Jane said. She watched her husband. Did she

dare take this risk? "There are others who know the truth. Bow Street knows you are a murderer."

His cheeks turned mottled red. "Bow Street? Impossible."

Fleur gave a furious shriek. "It's not true." She turned the pistol to Sherringham. "She's lying to frighten you. You must not lose faith. You were always weak—you panicked over stupid Treyworth. It would have been so easy to have destroyed him a year ago!"

"I was not weak!" he roared.

He lurched forward, but Fleur aimed her pistol at him. "You will not strike me!"

The rage faded, leaving behind an aging man with pale, desperate eyes. He sank back to the seat. "It is too late. We should escape, Fleur... return to Italy... I'm dying anyway."

It stunned Jane to see Sherringham cowed by a woman. Then she realized he had been under Sapphire Brougham's control also. They had known how to defeat the bully in him and use him to their own ends. Could she, who had known him for eight years, figure it out?

Fleur threw a frantic look to him. "We do not need to escape. You can still reclaim your title and I can be your countess." The woman put her hand to her belly and waved the pistol at Jane. "She will be dead, and I will bear your heir. They're fools—she even believed I had an accomplice in the house. We'll destroy them easily, and then you won't die and be forgotten, Sherry, my love. Your son will continue your line. Your cousin will be stripped of his title—don't you remember how we laughed at that? What a grand joke that will be."

He said nothing and coughed again.

Jane felt a glimmer of relief—at least Fleur's tale of a woman in the house had been a lie.

Fleur's voice rose desperately over the rattle of the wheels. "I've devised this plan to return to you everything you deserve. And *I* deserve to be Countess of Sherringham. All we have to do is be patient—"

"I'll have returned to England to be arrested."

"And I'll be your legal wife by then, you fool. Then your son will be born and he will prevail." Fleur smiled evilly at Jane. "But if Bow Street knows, we have no use for *you*. It doesn't matter if we have you alive to lure Wickham." Fleur jabbed the pistol against Jane's temple, her finger touching the trigger.

Numbing fear cascaded over Jane like icy water. Both Fleur and Sherringham were mad—Fleur driven by the idea she could become a countess, he by the belief he could get away with murder. Fleur *had* to kill her. She couldn't marry a man whose wife still lived.

Jane had to fight for her life. And Christian's—for Fleur had revealed he was alive. "I bluffed about Bow Street," she gasped. "They don't know about the murders yet. But there *was* another witness. This witness was the person who revealed the truth to Lord Wickham."

Fleur's wild eyes stared steadily on her.

"Wickham would never give the name of the person to you," Jane continued, her heart beating a ferocious tattoo in her chest, "unless he thought he could save me . . ."

The carriage halted. Fleur sneered. "Then you may be of use to us after all, *my lady.*"

"Get on the bed."

Sherringham's curt command rang in Jane's ears.

With her hands still bound, she froze at edge of the bed as he closed the door. Two candelabra threw light upon the gold counterpane, but shadows loomed. Sapphire Brougham's empty club was as still as a tomb.

Jane would *not* get onto the bed willingly. If he wanted her there, he'd have to throw her. She would never obey Sherringham again.

The lock on the door clicked with finality.

Days ago, she had encountered Christian in the gallery above. He had pulled her into a kiss that had brought her fearful memories rushing forth. Now, her heart careened in her chest but she didn't feel that draining, weakening panic. And that was due to Christian. She felt stronger because he had protected her, championed her, and treated her like a partner.

"Get on it," Sherringham barked.

Once his sharp voice would have paralyzed her. He had freed her from the gag at least, allowing her to cry, "No!"

"Cow." Snarling, he pushed her onto the bed. She had thought him weakly and sick. How wrong she'd been. Even suffering consumption, he was far stronger than she.

By the final years of their marriage, she would have cowered there, afraid to speak. She was determined that woman would never return. "Please untie my arms. They hurt."

Jane doubted he would want to ease her pain so it surprised her when he tugged at the cord. Loosened, it dropped off her hands to the mattress. Tingling pain shot through her arms as she flexed her wrists. Sherringham perched on the bed beside her, the pistol pointing at her face, and she sucked back a sob. White flashed as he drew out his handkerchief and coughed.

Her hands were free, but even though his shoulders racked with the spasm, she knew she could not overpower her husband.

Light flared in the gallery above. Could it be Christian? Arching her neck, Jane strained to see. A candle cast a glow on Fleur's sharp features as she lit one wall sconce near the door, then crossed between the theater seats to the opposite wall. Drapes framed the edge of the balcony that overlooked the stage. Fleur lifted her pistol, then vanished behind the curtains.

Oh, God. Christian didn't know about Fleur. He would not know an armed woman was hiding. Fleur had lit one sconce—to give her the light to shoot Christian as soon as he stepped through her door. Horrorstruck, Jane saw she'd been brought as bait. She had to do something.

She turned pleading eyes to her husband. "You could spare us. At least spare Wickham."

"Wickham, your lover? Fleur saw how you embraced him. She saw the heat of your kisses. Yet in my bed, you lay beneath me like a corpse with your eyes shut."

"I was afraid of you—" Jane began. The need to tell him how he'd hurt her welled up, took control of her tongue. "I lay there because I feared that you would hit me. I lay like a board because you were never once gentle or loving—"

His hand arced back. But he didn't swing. "You loved another man all along—"

"There was *no one* else," she cried. "I was an innocent when I married you."

His palm slammed against her cheek. Her skin burned and her face throbbed.

"You are lying to me, wife. Who did you think of when I kissed you on our wedding day?"

Stunned by the blow, Jane tried to remember her first kiss with her husband. In their carriage, as they rumbled away from the church. She had felt...dazed. Then he'd grabbed her by the neck to hold her. His lips had slammed against hers. His kiss had been harsh and brusque. Shocked by the...the violence of it, she had wanted to pull back. It had been nothing like what she'd dreamed.

And she had thought of Christian...for some mad reason, even though he was far away, she'd thought of his sparkling blue eyes and his easy laughter and his wretched teasing—

Oh, dear God. Christian had always been there—in her soul.

Sherringham grabbed her foot and dragged her down toward him. Her skirts snagged on the counterpane and slid up her legs. She gasped in shock as his fist drove toward her face, but he moved slowly, and she twisted to the side. His punch plowed into the mattress.

"Damn you," he snarled. "You were nothing to me. Cold and unyielding in my bed. You couldn't give me a child. But I could not forget you, Jane, even in Italy. I dreamt of you at night and thought of you when I awoke."

His hands moved toward her throat.

Dizzy with fear, she gasped, "There was no one else. I promise." She wanted to placate him. But she wanted him to know the truth. "I went to our marriage willing to give you my heart." For she had.

"I'm dying, and you are going to die, too. You are my wife; you will come with me in death."

She swung up her knee, desperately aiming for his crotch. He fell on top of her. "Shut up. Can't have you crying the alarm to Wickham." His gloved hand pressed over her mouth and his weight crushed her to the bed. He gave a gloating smile as he gently stroked her breasts. For eight years she had endured his touch. She did not have to do it now.

"Wickam was the gentleman you loved when you married me, wasn't he? He was the one you imagined when you shut your eyes and spread your thighs for me."

He sounded so calm. Not blasting her, not releasing anger, but stoking it inside. "You made a fool out of me, pining for Wickham in your bed. Did you ensure you wouldn't give me a child?"

Spittle flecked at the corner of his mouth. But in all other ways, he looked so unconcerned, she was sick with fear. His hand clamped over her breast and roughly squeezed. Jane screamed into the palm of his hand, sucking in the smell of sweaty leather.

"Patience, my dear. Now we wait for Wickham."

God, he would not lose Jane.

With a pistol gripped in his right hand, Christian dragged Sapphire Brougham up the sweeping staircase of her dark and quiet club. His senses had kept him alive during battles, natural disasters, and rescues made in guarded seraglios. They were all he had to rely on now.

Below him, he heard the soft footsteps of two of his men as they took positions at the bottom of the stairs. The others surrounded the club outside. Above, on the next floor, he saw a glimmer of light.

As his foot landed on the last step, Sapphire clutched the banister and tried to stop. Ruthlessly, he pulled her up.

"Don't hand me over to Sherringham," she pleaded. "You can't."

"I don't intend to. I plan to get the three of us out alive."

Bringing her had been a gamble. Not for one minute did he think Sherringham would trade Jane's life for Sapphire Brougham, but it might buy him time to rescue Jane. He guessed the earl wanted the three of them dead—there was no other reason to use Jane as bait. Maybe Sherringham was mad enough to believe he could eliminate them and reclaim his title. For all Arbuthnot had called *him* a madman, Christian wasn't certain he could outthink a genuine one.

"I fear your lovely lady is probably dead, Wickham," she whispered. "We should run and save ourselves. This is madness."

He tightened his grip on her. "I could change my mind, sweetheart. Don't push me."

Sapphire matched his long strides as he ran down the hallway—just as he had on the night he'd met Jane here. He slowed as they reached the white and gilt door. It stood partly open.

"He could be waiting inside to shoot you," Sapphire whispered.

"I expect someone is. It's a risk I have to take." For Jane. He could send Sapphire in first, but he wasn't the kind of man to send a woman, even an evil one, to her death. "Play along, no matter what I say."

As he stepped inside the darkened gallery, he called out, "I'm here, Sherringham, and I've got Sapphire, very much alive. Let Jane go free and you can have the madam. This place is surrounded by my armed men. I can get you out of here alive, but you have to let Jane go."

It was a gamble. A dangerous one. He had to make Sherringham believe he needed to keep Jane alive. But if he overplayed his hand, he might make the lunatic desperate enough to kill.

Christian! Jane heard his deep, rich, beautiful voice and screamed against Sherringham's hand. Only a muffled squawk came out.

She had to warn him about Fleur. She fought to bite her husband's hand. Her teeth sank into the leather of his glove. He clamped his palm harder against her mouth.

A pistol roared and a brilliant flash lit up the gallery above.

An answering explosion made her scream into Sherringham's muffling hand.

Sherringham jerked off her, but he grabbed her arm and wrenched her off the bed. He pulled her against his body, the pistol at her temple.

"Hell and the devil, that witch is getting away!" Fleur's shriek echoed through the theater. To her horror, in the dim light of the gallery above, Jane saw Fleur lift a second pistol and aim at Christian, who had relentlessly paced forward and now stood in the middle of the aisle that ran between the rows of seats. She screamed and this time her cry swelled in the room.

But there was no roar of another shot. Instead Fleur's mocking tones rang out. "You've spent your weapon prematurely, my lord. Now, be a good boy and lift your hands above your head. I shall make this swift, but unfortunately not painless—"

"Don't shoot him," Sherringham barked. "The pleasure is to be mine."

Jane's heart thudded in her throat. He wanted revenge because he believed Christian had always been in her heart.

She must act. No one was paying attention to her—Fleur's pistol was trained on Christian, and Sherringham was focused on the man he perversely thought was a rival. Her husband's grip on her had loosened; his pistol now pointed up toward Wickham, not at her head. In Sherringham's eyes, she was not a threat. She was his frightened little wife.

Instead of trying to pull away, she slammed her body back as hard as she could. Sherringham cried out as he stumbled and she lurched ahead. She raced toward the narrow stairs that led from the stage up to the gallery. The other door was locked. And by crossing the stage, she prayed she'd draw Fleur's attention.

Sherringham grabbed her before she reached the stair. And above, the pistol fired.

Jane felt as though her heart had stopped beating. Tears rushed to her eyes. She'd failed. It had been a desperate gamble and Fleur had shot Christian—

"I have your partner here, Sherringham, with a knife at her throat."

He was alive!

"I'll stand by what I said before," Christian shouted. "Let Jane go and I'll ensure you get out of this club. I'll ensure you get safely out of England."

"Don't believe him," Fleur cried.

"You can use me as your leverage, Sherringham," Christian called down. "The other option is to die here."

He was offering to become Sherringham's prisoner to save her. She could not let that happen.

Her heart sank as she spied the glinting arc of a blade.

It clattered to the plank floor of the stage. For her, he had left himself disarmed and vulnerable.

"I'll bring her up there," Sherringham shouted by her ear. The pistol at her breast did not waver and he kept her close to his body. His chin hovered above her. He smelled foul—of sweat, stale cologne, bad breath. "You're mine, Jane," he muttered. "I will not let you go."

As she and Sherringham reached the gallery, she saw anguish on Christian's face. Fleur held a blade pointed at his stomach, but he seemed oblivious to it. "Jane, are you all right?" he shouted. "Did he hurt you?" Christian tried to move toward her but Fleur stilled him with a threatening jab of her arm.

"I—"

Sherringham shoved the pistol harder against her. "Shut up. Speak to him and I'll kill you." He chuckled evilly behind her, then caressed her breast through her gown with the nose of his weapon. Her body went stiff with fear.

"I'd like your ballocks on a silver platter, Wickham," Sherringham mockingly shouted. "For Jane's life, would you be willing to cut them off yourself?"

"For Jane's life, I'd be willing to do anything, Sherringham."

How could Christian speak so calmly? That cool control frightened her in Sherringham, but when Christian displayed it, her alarm eased. Still, her wits whirled. She couldn't let Christian do *anything* her husband would demand to save her life. She felt Sherringham's arousal pressing against her skirts and bile churned in her belly.

"I will go with you, Sherringham," she said softly—it was no struggle to sound meek and terrified. "I will leave

England with you, if you want me. I am your wife. I still belong to you."

"God, no, Jane." Christian took a step forward. He was so fixated on her, he gave Fleur the chance to race around behind him, and press the blade to his throat.

"Not another step," the mistress warned.

"I would ensure your safe passage out of England," Jane continued. She saw wild fear in Christian's eyes for her. But this was her battle. "I would be as good a hostage as Wickham. Better, if you leave him alive. He would never let me be hurt. But it is my duty to be at your side, Sherringham."

"You belong to me, Jane." He kissed her cheek with a harsh press of his lips, and she fought not to show revulsion. "You always will."

Jealousy, control, power—those were the emotions that had ruled Sherringham's life. She had to play on them now. "Do you still desire me?" she asked, trying to sound alluring.

"He never desired you!" Fleur screamed.

"There is no gentleman who could not fall in love with Lady Sherringham," Christian said. "She is a true lady—pure of heart, graceful in manner, refined, lovely, and noble."

"A true lady!" Fleur's sharp features flushed red. "She was a mouse. She has no charm. She does not know how to please a man."

Christian laughed and the blade bounced with the movement of his throat. "Ah, but she does. It's not just the tarts who know how to entice. And when a gentleman wants a wife, he takes a perfect lady. Like Jane."

Jane saw the brilliant gleam in Christian's eyes. He kept his gaze on her. He'd understood, she realized. He had immediately grasped her plan. And instead of trying to stop her, he was working with her. He truly was her partner.

Christian's words had left Fleur white-faced and shaking. "You don't love her," she shouted at Sherringham. "You never did."

"I couldn't forget her, Fleur," he said. "When we first married, she was exquisite. Beautiful and possessing such verve, such intense spirit—"

The spirit he had crushed in her. His words left Jane reeling.

"I adored her when I married her," Sherringham continued. "Now, I realize I will love her always." He moved the pistol away from her breast.

"No!" Fleur rushed forward. She flew at Sherringham and in that mad, panicked moment, Jane felt herself be snatched free of his grasp. Startled, she looked into Christian's fierce eyes as he dragged her away.

"Stop!" With a swing of his arm, Sherringham stuck Fleur and sent her tumbling to the floor. Then he jerked around and trained the pistol on Wickham's chest. "Get up," he snarled to his mistress. His finger lightly touched the trigger—

"Fleur," Jane cried desperately. "It was my husband's plan to return to Italy all along. He told me that while we were alone on the stage—on the *bed*. He came back for me and used you to do it. It was always for me. He doesn't even care about the child." It was all a lie, but it worked.

"Blackguard! I did everything for you. I killed Treyworth for you—"

Sherringham jerked his attention to his mistress, who swung her knife at him in a wild rage. "It's a lie," he shouted, but Fleur's blade slashed at him, tearing his black cloak.

Jane clutched Christian's arm and moved to retreat, but Sherringham fired. At that instant, Christian crashed into her and she fell to the side. She landed hard, sprawled over one of the theater seats.

The ache in her ribs was wonderful. She could not believe she was alive. It was a miracle neither she nor Christian had been hit—his instant reaction had saved them both.

"You bastard!" With a roar, Sherringham leapt at Christian. He had a blade in his hand and he sliced at Christian's face.

Jane struggled to sit up, but her skirts were caught on the seat's arms.

Blood. Dear heaven, blood spurted from Christian's cheek.

In a flurry of hatred, Sherringham slashed at Christian, who had to shield himself with his arm. Then silver glinted in his hand and Sherringham backed away. Christian must have had another knife. And now, in the narrow area between the seats and the gallery railing, the two men slowly circled each other.

Behind Jane, a shrill, bitter laugh turned her blood to ice. Fleur was rushing between the seats toward her, her blade raised. Jane had only an instant to act and she tried to wrench her skirts free—

Sherringham's mistress gave a gloating smile.

Jane grabbed the chair beside her and shoved it back. Fleur had not expected the seat to move and as the back slammed against her leg, she stumbled, waved her arms wildly, then toppled over the seat on her other side.

Rrrip. Jane's skirts came loose. She scrambled to her

feet and rushed to the end of the row, away from Fleur. Christian. She had to get to him.

She skidded to a halt.

Sherringham had driven Christian back against the gallery railing. Blood streamed from the cut on his face and welled at a slice in his neck. His waistcoat was soaked with red splotches. Sherringham bore wounds too, but he seemed to be untouched by pain, driven by madness.

"I'll kill you, Wickham," he bellowed. "You were the one she always loved and you will die for it." He launched forward with all his weight behind him.

Trapped in horror, Jane saw the blade arc toward Christian's stomach.

Christian jumped to the side.

Sherringham slammed against the railing. His shoulders continued forward but he dropped the knife, caught the rail, and held tight. He looked back, saw Christian lunge to capture him. Like a trapped animal, Sherringham glanced to the stage below. He vaulted over the railing—

"Stop!" Jane shouted uselessly.

He wasn't going to fight. Just as before, he was going to flee.

His scream flew up. A sickening thud shook the floor. Fleur screamed and streaked to the edge of the railing, then rushed toward the stairs.

Jane heard shaky breaths and realized they were hers. A mournful keening wail came from below, and suddenly Christian's arms were around her.

"Are you all right?" He cradled her to him. "Christ, of course you aren't."

Jane reached up and touched his face, and her heart

lurched as he winced. Blood dripped down his cheek and leaked from his nose. She touched his arm and saw red ooze out of his coat sleeve. "Christian, you are the one who is not all right. I am fine." She tried to move to the edge of the gallery, but he held her tight. "Fleur was the one to push me in Hyde Park. And she shot at me—not you. It must have been her dark hair that Treyworth's butler saw. He mistakenly assumed she was a man."

Footsteps thundered into the room. Younger and several men stormed in. "We caught the madam trying to escape. Had to chase her—" Younger broke off as he fully took in Christian's wounds. "Christ Jesus, my lord."

Christian pointed to the stage below. "Get the woman down there, and take her to Bow Street along with the madam. I gave Brougham a promise—I'll see she's not hanged. But I'm not letting her go free."

As the men ran to the stair, Jane whispered. "I have to see, Christian. I have to know."

She was certain he would refuse, but he took her to the edge of the railing, held her as she looked down. She saw Fleur on her knees, sobbing. She saw a motionless face and staring eyes.

Sherringham's body lay crumpled on the floor of the theater below.

Chapter Twenty-Five

CHRISTIAN TIPPED HIS HEAD BACK, CLOSED his eyes, and savored Jane's soothing touch as she eased his coat off his shoulders. Pain shot through his arm, but it was Jane he worried about. She had insisted on staying at his side. She'd held him as though he were an invalid and led him up to his bedchamber.

"You shouldn't be doing this, love," he murmured. But a selfish part of him was glad she was. "Huntley has sent for a physician. I should be the one tending to you."

With care, she drew the coat down his arms. "You were the one wounded. The worst I endured was a slap from Fleur."

Not the worst. Christian knew there were far deeper wounds than physical ones. The horror of what might have been—losing Jane forever—hit him cold, bringing a pain to his heart much more brutal than the sting of his wounds. On their way home, she had told him everything that had happened in the carriage with Fleur and

Sherringham. And once again, he'd been awed by her bravery.

He turned to Jane and kissed her—he couldn't embrace her since his shirt was soaked with blood at his arms and his chest. But he could have kissed her forever. He would have happily given up eating and sleeping to stand here with his lips locked to hers until the end of time.

Jane pulled back. "I mustn't. You're *injured*."

"Not everywhere, love." He managed a grin. He yearned to clamp her to him and never let her out of his sight, but they both needed to be tended to first. And in truth, he was still dazed from Sherringham's punches and the loss of blood. Keeping his voice light, he assured, "I've had worse wounds." He saw her worried gaze linger on his old scars. "And I've survived them all."

The corner of her mouth twitched upward at his smile—a highly reassuring sight.

"As for you, crusading Lady Jane," he continued, "I am taking you to your room and sending a dozen maids to wait on you hand and—"

She blanched. Too late he remembered that Fleur had infiltrated his house disguised as a maid. Mary had told him the tale—she had followed the maid and Jane, had spied upon them, and had seen the pistol. Thanks to Mary, he had walked into the theater aware that he was facing both Fleur and Sherringham.

Surprise had leapt into Jane's bewitching brown eyes when he'd revealed Mary had helped. But Mary had taken one look at his face when he returned in search of Jane, had seen the fear and pain etched in his features, and had whispered, "You truly love her." That seemed to snap her out of jealousy.

Jane's insistence that Mary aspire to be more than a courtesan had deeply touched the girl's heart. Jane had made her believe in herself. With a tug at *his* heart, Christian gazed at Jane, seeing the most beautiful woman he'd ever laid eyes on. Disheveled curls of red-gold dangled by her determined mouth, as she rolled up her sleeves, prepared to take care of him. In that moment, he understood what love was. He couldn't describe it, but he knew what it was.

And what could he do with this new, exhilarating knowledge?

Claim Jane. Make her yours.

But she'd vowed never to marry, and she'd told him she was not willing to leave England with him. The enormity of what he had to do hit Christian cold. If he wanted Jane, he owed her the truth. He couldn't lie to her. And not telling her who he really was—what he was—was tantamount to doing that. He had to tell her about his parentage.

Hades, he could not do that. He could not look into her eyes and watch them fill with disappointment. Not this time.

He had done that in his youth. He could not do it now.

"That is quite enough, my lady." Huntley strode into the bedchamber, followed by a footman carrying a basin of steaming water. He frowned down his long nose at Jane. "You, my lady, should be looking after yourself."

Jane stood firm. "I wish to help."

"Go, Jane. For me," Christian murmured, but Huntley bustled between Jane and him. "You will help his lordship by letting me get to business, my lady." Huntley motioned to the door and Del appeared, clad in a rose silk robe, with soft pink color in her cheeks. Del looked prepared to take Jane in hand, but also so much like the gentle, lovely young woman Christian remembered.

Jane glared mulishly at first, but faced with Del, Huntley, and himself, she relented. And let Del guide her out the door.

From the hallway, he heard Jane speak softly. "We've been through so many nightmares. But it's over now. Finally, it is over."

"Yes." Del answered. "We can both wake up now."

Jane's shaky sigh almost broke his heart. Out of his sight, she obviously wasn't as strong as she'd appeared to be. "But I don't know what to do, Del. Do I mourn Sherringham again? Am I supposed to? Do I wear black again for a man who wanted me dead?"

Christian jerked and Huntley, trying to cut his shirt-sleeve, cried, "Have a care, my lord. I do not want to slice your arm."

Hades, he was too stunned to care if Huntley took off his arm along with the sleeve. Jane would have to mourn Sherringham again. He hadn't even thought of that.

"Hush now," his sister said firmly, from the hallway. "I've ordered a bath, and then you will have tea with brandy until it does the trick."

"What trick is that?"

"It lets you sleep."

Skirts rustled as Del took Jane away. Christian closed his eyes. Bow Street had Sapphire Brougham and Fleur, Treyworth's killer, which meant he was free of suspicion. Sherringham was dead. Del was safe. Jane was safe. He had thought it was over.

But it wasn't.

"Where are your thoughts, Wickham?" Huntley

demanded. "I've been swabbing the cut in your arm with hot water and you have not leapt through the ceiling yet."

Christian glanced to the side. Huntley had cut the sleeve away. A dull, stinging sensation rippled through his biceps. "I hadn't noticed," he admitted. Now he did and he gritted his teeth. But a deeper pain had settled in his heart. "How do I begin to help them heal?"

He didn't expect an answer. But Huntley cleared his throat. "I am no expert on family matters, my lord, but I believe you help them heal with love. You give them time, you take care of them, and you love them."

Then the door opened and the physician walked in.

"Good heavens, my dear. You should have summoned me before now!"

In a flurry of trunks, lavender, and hugs, Aunt Regina swept into the foyer of Wickham House. Jane found herself pulled into a fierce embrace while the plumes of her aunt's turban tickled her nose.

"Your husband returned from the dead and utterly mad. Kidnapping you! Completely unforgivable. But that is now in the past. It is time for you to move forward."

Jane sputtered in the hug. Only her practical aunt could sum up a night of terror as "unforgivable" and move so swiftly to thoughts of the future. And dear heaven, she imagined what they included. She was not entirely certain if she was ready to cope with voluble Aunt Regina. Christian had not wanted her to return home yet—instead he had brought her aunt to her. His heart had been in the right place. And he was here in the foyer, standing at her side to face Regina. That was a gesture that only made her love him more.

Christian led Regina toward the drawing room, but her aunt paused at the door to the music room, where the girls were playing.

Seated at the pianoforte, Philomena spread her small fingers as wide as she could and lightly pressed the keys. Jane smiled at the halting music, the tentative notes. Philly shyly returned the smile as Mary applauded.

"There, Philly," called Lucinda. "You'll be the most accomplished musician of us yet."

Without a word, Aunt Regina swept onward. She waited until she sat on the settee in the drawing room, sherry in hand, before thumping her cane on the floor. "Well, Lord Wickham, I demand an explanation. Jane was under your care, yet ended up in grave danger—"

"Aunt, it was not Christian's fault," Jane protested.

"Ah, Christian, is it?" Her aunt's brow went up at the familiarity. She wagged her finger. "Then give me the entire story, Jane. Do not leave anything out. I'll know if you have. I can see at once when you are lying."

If she had the courage to face Sherringham, she could do this. But Christian stepped in and began, so she joined him, and between them they told the whole tale. The search for Del. The truth of the Demons Club. Treyworth's blackmail. Sherringham's crimes and Fleur's attempts on Jane's life.

Aunt Regina drained her sherry. "Unconscionable!" she exclaimed. "I told your foolish mother not to push you into a loveless marriage. I would have had my Richard help with a loan to your father. But your mother thought, in her way, she was doing the best for you, and protecting you from a broken heart."

Jane had not cried in the theater, nor had she cried after Sherringham had died, or even in relief when she and Christian had returned home safe. But now, tears sprang to her eyes and she couldn't stop them. If only her parents had not been so unhappy—

Well, she was determined not to be. She was not going to be as foolish as her mother. That helped her stop the waterworks and wipe away the few tears on her cheeks.

Regina tapped her on the knee. "I feared I would find you extremely distraught, yet here you are, a tower of strength. I always knew you were a woman of great fortitude, even though you did not see that yourself." Regina gave a long, considering look at Christian. "Or is this also your doing, Lord Wickham? I see you are not quite the rogue I believed you were."

"Aunt Regina!" After he had saved her life and suffered injury to do it, Jane could not have him called a rogue.

"Well, he has endeavored to build his own black reputation, has he not?"

Christian grinned sheepishly. "Yes, I have."

"Some members of the ton have been spinning decidedly risqué stories about those girls of yours. However, they look like ordinary English girls to me."

Jane stared at her aunt, mystified. Before, Regina had used the girls as proof of Christian's poor character.

In a delectably handsome way, Christian inclined his head. "They are still shadowed by their experiences. But I have decided to make them officially my wards." Jane felt his gaze land on her and as she looked to him, Christian said the most astonishing thing. "If you approve, Jane."

"I—of course, I do. I think it is a wonderful and kind idea."

He grinned, showing his devastating dimples. "They've enriched my life. My motives aren't entirely noble. The girls make me smile, and I'm tired of living life alone."

"That is all well and good," Regina said, "But you will need help establishing them in society."

Jane seized on Regina's words. "Would you help, Aunt? A few days ago—it seems a lifetime ago, now—I promised the girls they could have futures, but I had no idea what to do. How could they be governesses or companions or wives? But I refuse to stand by and let them become mistresses because society won't let them do anything else. I—"

Regina held up her hand. "Of course I will help, Jane." She turned to Christian. "My dear niece championed your sister when she needed rescue. I see I must follow her example. I will be happy to use whatever influence I have in bringing out your wards."

There was a moment's silence. Christian stared at her aunt, taken aback. "Thank you."

Jane was equally as stunned. She hadn't actually thought Regina would agree. "Thank you. The girls deserve a chance—"

"Of course, my dear." Regina fixed her gaze on Christian. "It appears you have rescued many women from terrible situations. Those orphans, your sister, and now Jane. I am the one who must thank you, Wickham. I could not have borne to lose Jane. And now, due to your bravery, I can arrange for her to have what she truly deserves."

Oh, dear. She did *not* want to talk of husbands now. By

society's rules, she should mourn a man she despised—a man who had been vicious and cruel. She loved Christian but did not even dare breathe the word to him. She could not tie Christian to her while she wore her black and weathered scandal. "Aunt Regina—" she began, in warning.

"I mean happiness, my dear."

"Lord and Lady Pelcham have left for the Continent, my lord. Sir Rodney Halcourt has retired from his seat. And the Duke of Fellingham, who admitted he was paying blackmail to Lord Treyworth, has left his wife behind and sailed for Boston."

Christian nodded to Huntley. A week had passed since Sherringham's death. The girls who had been prisoners in Brougham's madhouse had been reunited with their families. Christian had taken on the task of finding the families of the murdered girls and breaking the sad news.

He'd kept his word to Sapphire Brougham and had asked for leniency. She was a ruthless woman, but she'd brought him to Jane in time to rescue her, and he owed her an enormous debt for that.

Huntley paused before retreating. "Should I book passage to India, my lord?"

Before he could answer, Lady Regina Gardiner rapped on the door and marched in. With a wry grin, Christian dismissed his secretary. A week in the lady's company had taught him to head at once to his brandy decanter, but she waved the glass aside.

"I have waited a week, Wickham, and now it is time for me to speak." She rapped the floor with her cane. "Jane deserves to have love and marriage. And children.

You must see her with my granddaughters. She glows as she holds the children, yet I also see the poignant regret in her eyes. Jane insists on denying her heart's desire—a husband and a brood of little ones. And you, my dear fellow, have a nursery to be filled."

Christian blushed, and realized he hadn't done that for over twenty years.

"What exactly are you proposing, Lady Gardiner?" He was stalling, because he knew. "Jane believes she must mourn Sherringham again."

"Bah. She has wasted far too much of her life on that evil blackguard. She mourned him once. I will not stand for her mourning him again. It was always my plan that Jane would remarry—to a gentle, quiet, devoted man. A man who would never raise a hand to her. Who would bring peace into her life."

A gentle, quiet man. He had never been that. But he would never raise a hand to Jane. All he yearned to do was to go through his life with her at his side. "Lady Gardiner, I—"

The cane thumped. "Do let me finish, Wickham."

He had to smother a smile. Would Jane be like this in many years? He would imagine so. And the thought was incredibly endearing.

Jane would make his life hell if she grew into her sharp-tongued aunt, walking stick and all. And what could he want more than to be the gray-haired gentleman who made her thump her cane?

Lady Gardiner barreled onward. "I did not want her to marry a gentleman who would break her heart. No rakes. No gamblers like her father. And no men who seduced their friends' wives. I had in mind a man who would be the exact opposite of you, Wickham. In fact, on the night Jane admitted she'd encountered you, I warned her not to fall in love with you."

"You are telling me I don't deserve Jane because of the man I was."

"I am telling you I made a mistake. It happens very rarely, but I am not too proud to admit it, with Jane's happiness at stake." Her shrewd brown eyes speared him. "I thought I knew what type of man Jane should marry. Now I see I was entirely wrong. She deserves a man who loves her passionately, Lord Wickham. And a man she will love as intensely in return."

The lady took a breath and kept going. "If Jane were to leave England, she would be far from gossip. No one would see whether she wore her black or not. I believe you have already asked her to accompany you to India— without marriage."

"Only because she told me she didn't—" He stopped. He'd never explained himself to anyone before. Except Jane. "How can I ask her to marry me after what she's been through?"

And, he thought, bloody coward that he was, *how can I ask her without giving her the truth?*

Lady Gardiner rolled her eyes heavenward. "To start, you acquire a ring. And I suggest you drop down on one knee. Prepares the woman for the event. No lady wishes to be taken by surprise. And I assure you the gentleman also does not want to do so. It increases the possibility of receiving a 'no.'"

Christian stared in astonishment.

"I must warn you that she might refuse you, Wickham. Jane is confused at the moment. If so, you must ask her again. And again, if necessary. I had Richard ask me three times. One refusal was to ensure his proposal was not merely a gentleman's quest for victory over his peers. The second was to make certain he was not asking out of wounded pride. And the third time I said yes, because I knew any man who attempted a third proposal was most definitely in love."

Her next words almost knocked his legs out from under him. "The love Jane feels for you surrounds her like a glow. So you may be assured she will eventually say yes. I would not think of setting you on an impossible task. I will work on her, too. Together we will give Jane the future she deserves."

It was more than that to him. It was the future he didn't believe he could dream of.

He understood. He had to tell Jane he loved her and brace himself to have his heart broken if she rejected him. He might not be the man to give her the future she should have, but he intended to give her the proposal of marriage she deserved.

Lady Gardiner, however, bestowed a dazzling smile on him. "I shall take that brandy now."

Before he attempted the pivotal third proposal, he had one thing to do.

Christian found Del in her bedchamber, seated at her vanity while deft hands styled her hair. With a smile, his sister dismissed the maid, then waited patiently for him to speak.

He rubbed the back of his neck. "In a way, I've come to ask your permission."

Her brows jerked up in surprise. "I've never been asked such a thing before. But first, I must tell you something, Christian. I fear you felt guilt over my marriage and that you believe you should not have left. But there was nothing you could have done."

The old pain and guilt roared up. But he crouched down and clasped Del's hands. "You need to know the truth, Del." He told her the entire story of his parentage. Every detail his father had revealed to him.

No denying the tale shocked her—not when her eyes grew large, her brows shot up, and she clapped her hand to her lips. He flinched, waiting to see her recoil from him. Instead, she hugged him. Into her neck, he mumbled, "It's why Father pushed you into that marriage. You were his true daughter and he wanted you to be a marchioness."

"Christian, I am sorry you had to suffer so. It was not fair. I am sorry you had to almost fight a duel for me. You and Jane took so many risks for me—"

"Stop. You are my beloved sister and I'd fight to the end of time for you. And I suspect the remarkable Lady Jane Beaumont would do so, too."

"She would. And you grew into the wonderful gentleman I always knew you would be."

He had to laugh. "You and Jane were the only ones with such faith. God, how I love you, Del. I came to tell you I want to propose marriage to Jane, but I will wait if you want. I fear that it's not the time yet—"

"Now you must stop!" Del pulled back. And when he freed her, Christian was stunned to see tears on her cheeks. She impatiently brushed them away.

"I've always thought you two had to be in love. I saw it in the way you argued and fought with each other. It was not mean-spirited, not like the way our parents hurt each other. You two could not stop thinking of each other. Please ask Jane, Christian. I want very much for my best friend to become my sister."

But as he left Del, Christian realized his clothes were utterly wrong for a proposal—he should change to more formal dress. He was retying his cravat in front of his cheval mirror when Jane slipped in. She carefully shut the door behind her and turned the key.

One look at the nervous play of her tongue on her lips and he was lost to need and desire.

"Am I wrong to want this?" Jane whispered. "I've realized I don't want to wait. I want to feel alive. I want you."

In answer, Christian tore off the clothes he had just put on, stripping naked in the blink of an eye.

"It's not so easy for me to remove my clothes," Jane protested as Christian drew back the covers and climbed into his bed.

Then Jane saw his long, bare legs slide under the sheets and she couldn't draw breath. White fabric surrounded him like a downy cloud. With his bare chest, he looked like a god emerging from some heavenly plane.

"Come here," he urged, and she did.

She trembled with anticipation as he opened her dress and dealt with her corset laces. All she wanted was to climb into bed with him and a reluctant knot had her growling, "Oh, do hurry, please." He chuckled, but took the time to unpin her hair, and she tapped her foot in anguish.

His black hair tumbled rakishly across his forehead and he winked. "Now you are free. Naked. And all mine. But only if you want me."

"You know I do. You know exactly how devastating

you look—with your hair like that and your eyes smoldering and your dimples tempting me into sin." This was sparring of a different sort. She had put on an indignant voice, but a teasing one.

Laughing, he held the sheets up. "Sweeting, I could not begin to look as devastating as you."

It was like living a fantasy to join him and he drew her into his embrace. Even though they'd made love before, this felt magical. Special. His skin was hot against hers as their legs entwined. She stroked the length of his calf with her foot. Savoring all that long, lean muscle.

"I want you," she whispered again, frankly. She was enraptured by the sheer wanton delight of this. Afternoon sunlight washed over his bed. Servants were passing up and down the hall beyond the locked door. Here she was, beneath the covers with Christian in the afternoon.

"Decadent, isn't it?" he asked.

As though he had read her thoughts. And she realized it had always been that way. In their youth, he'd known how to tease her because he'd guessed exactly what she'd been thinking.

It was a startling thought.

"For me, this is an adventure," she whispered.

"For me, too." He eased her onto her back. He nudged his erection inside her, without using his hands, and she gasped in surprise. She was so creamy and molten and ready for him. Slowly, Christian thrust into her and she felt suspended in time, warm and safe, watching his eyes as he filled her.

He moved lazily, his gaze locked on her in a sizzling connection as she took him within. The hilt of his erection kissed her sensitive nub, and she wrapped her arms and legs around him. "Somehow," she breathed, "this feels like a sultry summer's day. I can't explain it. It's so hot and wet and luxurious."

His laugh was strained, then he half rolled, so he was lying along her, still pumping his thick erection deep within her, but his hand was free to tease her nipples and stroke her aching clitoris. She moaned, fighting hard not to be loud, not to alert the entire household to their scandalous behavior.

His thumb teased a spot that almost made her swoon. "Christian!"

He continued his delicious torture. She closed her eyes and sunlight painted patterns of gold on her lids. This was heaven. Sheer heaven.

Into the sun-drenched room, she cried, "Oh, yes!" and lost control. Her climax sent her nails digging into his shoulders. And as she floated back to earth, he thrust and teased more. She came again and the orgasm rushed over her like a summer's breeze. It lasted forever, and he laughed down into her eyes the entire time, and she knew—with the last bit of her mind that could think— he was enjoying her pleasure almost as much as she.

It amazed Jane that he could hold back. She couldn't. His touch, his thrusts, his wonderful delicious knowledge of what made her melt sent her hurtling into ecstasy again.

"You can lose your control with me," she gasped, "if you want."

"I lost my control with you long ago."

He plunged in and she slapped his buttocks to urge him deeper. Now she understood what he had meant about fingernail scratches. The need to pull him into her made her spank him rather fiercely.

He obeyed her. He drove to the hilt and she squealed in delight. His strokes sped up, his urgency arousing her, and she clasped her legs around his waist and moaned hungrily in his ear. To be pounded into by Christian was exhilarating, fervently erotic, and wonderfully naughty. A droplet of his sweat hit her lower lip, and she swept it up with her tongue, savoring the salty tang. He groaned at the gesture and plunged deep, then he uttered a hoarse groan that made her fear he might be in pain. His powerful body tensed, then suddenly jerked. His mouth was strained. His eyes shut tight and he dropped his head forward, so vulnerable and beautiful and endearing, she wrapped her arms about his neck.

"Jane, wonderful, exquisite Jane." He bucked wildly into her. She held him tightly, sharing his ecstasy with love.

He fell at her side and stroked her hair. Jane rubbed against him, purring and content. Then he said something entirely surprising.

"I had a spot in the garden selected. A lovely spot with a stone bench surrounded by roses."

Jane slapped her hand to Christian's chest. "For making love? A spot in the garden? In the *afternoon*?"

A laugh rumbled up from Christian's soul. Shocked, Jane was adorable. He couldn't resist teasing her. "But here will do just as well." He levered up to his side and knew his face revealed the fear he now felt. "There's something I need to tell you, Jane. You know my parents did not love each other. Their marriage was an exchange—a large dowry for an old and venerated title. But . . . but the truth is, my mother came to the marriage already pregnant by another man."

He saw shock in her eyes. "Her plan was to hide it," he

continued, while he had courage, "Then present the child—me—to my father as his own. But she was horribly sick during the early months and one maid whispered to another, and finally a footman sold the information to my father."

"You weren't his natural son. But he still chose to marry her."

He felt his shoulder rise in a shrug. It was how he'd always tried, when he was young, to deal with this. To pretend it didn't hurt him. To pretend he was so damned wicked, he didn't care. "My father had little interest in sexual passion. Learning, punishment, denial, and austerity were his obsessions. My mother's sin gave him the perfect reason to ignore her in the bedroom."

"And Del—?"

"I believe she is our father's child. I talked to her earlier and told all this to her. She didn't know about me. I think my father pushed her into marriage with Treyworth because he wanted a child of his blood to have a higher title than me."

"It doesn't matter. He accepted you as his son."

"And made me pay for it. Hurting me also hurt our mother."

Jane had gone pale. She must be shocked to learn he was a bastard, but he had more to tell her. He closed his eyes, remembering his father's furious words after his duel with Georgiana's husband...

Your mother was a weak whore. She went to the bed of her sister's husband, after her sister had died of illness. The laws of consanguinity and the laws of the Church of England forbid such a relationship. She knew it was an immoral love but she could not resist. She tumbled willingly into his bed and got with his child. You. And she tricked

me—she only told me this long after you were born, when
you wouldn't read. I knew it must be punishment for her
sin. Your blood has been tainted by it—everything about
you has been.

Halting, Christian told the story to Jane, and he
couldn't look into her eyes as he did. "After I learned the
truth from my father, I went to my mother. I didn't want
to believe I was wicked just because of my birth, but my
father had made her believe it. She admitted the story
was true. When she became pregnant, her brother-in-
law had rejected her, enraged there would be evidence of
what they'd done. She was twisted up inside with guilt
and anger. She told me she wished she'd lost me in her
womb, then admitted she'd even tried to bring on a miscarriage. And she feared that the potions she'd taken to
do that, along with my sinful blood, had condemned me
for life."

He took a deep breath, to clear the tightness of his
chest. "I left England within hours. I suspect that my
mother either killed herself or fell from the ridge because
she was so distraught. I never should have revealed to her
that I knew. I should have guessed how fragile she must
have been. Foolishly, I hoped she would say she loved me
anyway. But she couldn't—I'd destroyed her life."

"*You* didn't." Jane sat up. "Your mother and father
made their own unhappiness. And your father seemed
determined to hurt everyone else."

"He told me I would never be normal because I was a
child of a such a relationship. I was conceived in wickedness, born in wickedness, and reminded of it every day
of my waking life."

"Lord Wicked," she said softly. "How that nickname
must have tormented you."

To Christian's amazement, Jane wrapped her arms around his neck. He couldn't believe she would want to touch him. "I should have told you this when I asked you to marry me," he said. "I was so angry with myself for potentially getting you with child without letting you know the truth. I had no right to do that."

"Well, I do not care who fathered you. I care about you. I was married to a truly evil man, so I know wickedness. And I know what you are, Christian. A true gentleman and the most noble and wonderful of men. You are strong and beautiful and perfect. I said it before, and I shall repeat it. Your father was an idiot."

He wanted to laugh. And because of Jane, he could open his heart and hope for joy. "I left England because I realized you believed I should become a better man. After the duel, I knew I had to try to find that man, or I would become the wicked blackguard my father said I was destined to be. But I traveled the world searching for something I could never find. Because only you could give it to me, Jane. Love and acceptance—things I feared I could never have."

It hadn't been frightening to reveal this secret to her. It made him feel free. As though his father's anger had been chains that had now dropped from his body.

"It is wrong that you were forced to think that," Jane cried, as wonderfully outraged as ever.

Christian lifted her hand and drew it to his lips. He traced his tongue over her palm until she sagged back against the bedpost. Then he gave her the naughty grin of his youth that he knew used to make her yearn to conk him over the head with her parasol. He slid out of bed and went to his coat.

When he returned, he dropped to one knee. "This

isn't how a gentleman is supposed to do this. Normally both the lady and the gentleman are not naked."

Jane gaped at him.

"I asked you once to marry me out of duty," he said. "I asked you to travel with me to India because I loved you, but was too much of a coward to say it. And this time, I'm asking you to marry me because I love you."

He flipped open the box, and the square-cut diamond within winked at them both.

"We're partners, Jane. And even years ago, when I was teasing you like a rogue, I realize now it was because you had already captured my heart. Will you marry me?"

"Now I understand why Aunt Regina told me that no woman should refuse a third proposal." Jane smiled. "It is so amazing how one simple word—partners—could make my heart to feel as though it might burst."

"Amazing," he agreed.

Her eyes sparkled more brilliantly than the ring. "You gave me the strength to put my past behind me. And to face Sherringham. And now, all the fears that held me back from love are gone." She took a deep breath.

"Yes, Christian," she cried. "Yes, because I love you. Yes, because I have always loved you and I can't imagine life without you. I want to travel with you. Grow old with you. To be with you would be more blessing than I could ever imagine."

Down on one knee, his lips were at the level of her stomach. He bestowed a kiss upon her ivory skin, just above her nether curls. "Yet another thing a gentleman is not supposed to do after a marriage proposal."

He tried for a rakish grin but his heart was so full of love, it was almost pain. His smile came out lopsided. "I am feeling very wicked right now." He nodded toward the bed. "And I cannot wait to make you my Lady Wicked."

It was his way of telling her how much her love meant to him—her love proved that he was not a hopelessly wicked man after all. Jane cradled his face. "*Lady* Wicked is feeling especially naughty and needs her partner, my lord."

He grasped her hands and kissed them both. Then rose to his feet, gathered her in his arms, and kissed her again. "My partner in love and life. In voyages around the world and a rich future at home," he whispered. "You are my true love. Forever."

Her soft laugh of pure delight was his reward.

Epilogue

Hartfordshire, December 1819

A BABY'S STRONG CRY ROSE FROM the bassinet at the foot of the bed.

"Oh, heavens." Jane sat up and put her hand to her breast. Her milk came, soaking her shift.

At her side, Christian rose sleepily. "Do you want me to fetch him and bring him to you in bed?"

"No." She giggled. "I'll go, sleepyhead."

They had tried to snatch a nap while baby Michael slept. In India, Jane had grown accustomed to spending the afternoon in bed with Christian while the heat raged outdoors. They would shut all the blinds and seek the coolness of the house.

A wry smile touched Jane's lips as she scurried out from under the covers. It had never quite worked—they had always gotten rather hot and sweaty in their bed. Though here at home, with snow blanketing their country estate, they snuggled in bed to delight in the warmth.

Jane leaned over the bassinet, her breasts full and aching. "Hush, angel. Your meal is on its way."

And he knew, of course. His fists waved and he cried just a little more fervently.

"I know what you are saying. 'Make haste, Mother, and pick me up.'" She scooped Michael into her arms. At once his mouth turned to her breasts, his little lips questing. Every inch the wee lord. Jane drew the neckline of her shift down and his mouth fastened to her nipple. Blessed relief flooded her.

"Lucky fellow." Propped on his elbow, sheets pooled around his hip, Christian grinned.

"Indeed." She cradled their son—a chubby little fellow of three and a half months—and walked to the window.

"It amazes me that you can do that so adeptly."

"Walk?" she asked. For they did that now—they teased each other over compliments. The sparring that they had once used to annoy each other had become something much sweeter, more enriching, and more devilishly fun.

"No, sweeting. Hold that hefty boy at your breast with one hand while you walk." He laughed—the sinful chuckle that sent shivers down her spine. That delicious sound was partly responsible for her current situation— one she had not yet explained to her husband.

He joined her at the window, slid his arm around her waist, and together they looked down upon the snow-covered world. On the frozen pond, two figures glided on ice skates.

"Mary and His Grace, the new Duke of Fellingham," Jane whispered. The older duke had passed away in America, and the new duke had astonished all by pursuing a love match with Mary. Jane knew Mary loved him deeply in return.

Christian lifted his hands to her shoulders and kissed the top of her head. "The passing months have brought many changes," he murmured.

She nodded. It was true.

"We have watched Lucinda and Bella get married," he mused.

"To military gentlemen who will end up looking like Major Arbuthnot. I did warn them."

"Ah, but they were head over heels," Christian teased. "And thank you for finding a way to let Philly pursue her dreams."

Both Bella and Lucinda had remained in India with their husbands, and Philly was to leave after Christmas. Philly had expressed a yearning to teach—and Jane had helped her find a country school run by an open-minded headmistress. "Mrs. Widdicombe is a sensible sort of woman who believes Philly deserves the chance to have her dream."

Even several of Sapphire Brougham's former prostitutes had carved out better futures. They had built a new club for risqué couples of the ton, one in which women were well treated.

"And there is Del—" Jane's heart warmed as she looked down upon the sloping lawns of Wickham House. In the very spot where she had once run out to stop Christian's carriage race, Del and Charlotte lobbed snowballs at each other, giggling like schoolgirls.

A year and a half had helped to wipe away shadows.

"Dartmore is building a snowman to entertain his son," Christian observed.

Jane smiled. During Charlotte's hard childbirth, Dartmore had recognized how intensely he did love his wife. He had, much to her astonishment, turned over a new leaf.

"I believe, Jane, that when you pointed out that Sherringham and Treyworth paid dearly for their cruelty, you made him realize he needed to become a better man."

"I think it was all Charlotte's doing. Not mine." As for herself, she never had nightmares now. The harsh memories of her marriage and of the night Sherringham had kidnapped her had faded to the recesses of her mind.

She had far too many wonderful memories instead. The sight of Christian standing beside her on the ship, holding her tight as they rose and fell with the large waves of the ocean. Her first ride upon an elephant. Her first bite into a succulent mango. And the most treasured—Christian's awed expression as he'd held his son and welcomed their wrinkly, beautiful baby into the world.

"Ouch!" Pain shot through her nipple and she abruptly pulled Michael from her breast.

"What's wrong, love?" Christian put Michael on his shoulder and rubbed the tiny back until a thunderous belch filled the room.

"He bit me."

Sharing her look of surprise, Christian cradled their son at his bare waist. They both stared down into Michael's mouth as he gave a fierce howl.

"There—" Christian gently laid his finger to their baby's lower lip. And Jane saw the small dot of white. "His first tooth."

She took Michael back and brought him cautiously to her breast. He suckled, then nipped her once more, smiling as he did. She suspected the little devil was teasing her. Like his father.

But soon, Michael's head, covered in soft black hair, drooped and his eyelids lowered. His lips worked, but Jane took him back to his bed.

"He's sleeping," she whispered. "I think we might have time to be wicked before dinner—"

Christian was already in bed. "If you insist, my lady." Winking, he lifted the sheets.

But Jane paused. "There is something I have to tell you. You see, I have defied conventional wisdom…"

He looked perplexed and she sighed. "Normally when a woman is feeding her baby, she doesn't quicken. But I did. I think I might be pregnant again. So…Merry Christmas."

Christian looked thunderstruck. Then he jumped out of bed and spun her around in his arms. "Thank you, Jane, for giving me the most precious gifts of all," he whispered. "Our beautiful boy, another miracle on the way, and your love—your amazing, wonderful love."

Hugging Christian's neck, Jane let him carry her to bed. Thank heaven they had both found the courage to open their hearts. For love was indeed the most marvelous miracle of all.